TAKING PA

'You have been caught red-handed, girl, and now you are to be red-bottomed.'

Whimpering softly, Lucy bent over the side of the bathtub, pressing her breasts into its rim. Thighs clamped tightly together, her bare bottom rose up to meet Captain Oxford's cruel gaze. The cheeks hung poised and rounded, like ripe peaches in the hot-house ready to be plucked and bitten.

'Where is your hairbrush, girl? I mean to chastise your bottom with it.'

'In my bedchamber, master,' she whispered, shivering at the sound of his dressing-gown being loosened.

'Then I shall have to spank you with my hand, girl. Bottom up, if you will.'

A NEXUS CLASSIC

TAKING PAINS TO PLEASE

Arabella Knight

This book is a work of fiction.
In real life, make sure you practise safe sex.

First published in 1999 by
Nexus
Thames Wharf Studios
Rainville Road
London W6 9HA

This Nexus Classic edition 2003

www.nexus-books.co.uk

ISBN 0 352 33785 0

Typeset by TW Typesetting, Plymouth, Devon
Printed and bound by
Clays Ltd, St Ives PLC

Contents

1	The Messenger	1
2	The Maid	21
3	The Secretary	40
4	The Nurse	53
5	The Astrologer's Apprentice	72
6	The Spanish Mistress	89
7	The Fitness Trainer	112
8	The Corsetière	137
9	The Novice	161
10	The Translator	180
11	The Actress	210
12	The Nanny	241

1

The Messenger

Charlie – she had refused to answer to Charlotte ever since being thrashed and then expelled from her boarding school six years ago – stepped out of the Hatton Garden workshop into a spectacular summer storm. The downpour raked her leathers as she scampered to her Suzuki, spangling the figure-hugging bike suit with translucent pearls.

The Clerkenwell junction at Gray's Inn Road, she knew, would be solid by now, so she kicked her Suzuki into life and roared off down into High Holborn. At the second set of lights, she drew up alongside a white Sherpa van. Three builders bunched up front peered down at the gleaming Suzuki, nudging and nodding appreciatively. Charlie swept her black helmet off and tossed her wild brunette curls, grinding her leather-sheathed buttocks provocatively into the saddle. The builders roared their approval. Charlie grinned, her red lips wet and shining as they split wide open.

Up in the dark sky, a silver lightning-fork flickered angrily. The traffic lights remained red. Charlie twisted her buttocks in the saddle as she bent her head down to inspect her right boot. She inched the Suzuki forward a few inches. Red and amber showed. Engines revved in response. As quick as the recent bolt of lightning, she unzipped her leathers down to her belly, revealing her naked breasts, then zipped up again. Green. The Suzuki snarled off in triumph, leaving the stalled Sherpa in a blitz of angry horns. Grinning, Charlie turned her powerful bike effortlessly into Shaftesbury Avenue.

Charlie loved the freedom her lusty bike gave her. It brought her obediently from Brixton to Bow, from Tottenham to Temple, submitting to the grip of her controlling leather gloves. The leather. Charlie felt the rasp of the supple hide at her nipples, crushing and squeezing her breasts and bunching them in bondage beneath the stretch of second skin. The one-piece bike suit moulded the contours of her body, hugging the breasts and buttocks tightly. Between her hips and thighs, it cupped the cheeks of her bottom with smooth hands of hide, and, in a seamless stretch across her pubic mound, it strained to kiss her labia devotedly. Yes. This was the way to be. Free – free from a desk, a mind-numbing word processor or a jangling phone. Free from the office uniform of a sensible blouse, restrictive brassière, sticky panties and irksome bronzed tights. For Charlie, dressing for work meant a sprinkle of talc palmed into her belly, breasts and across her heavy buttocks, then straight into her sensual leathers.

Pulling up behind an *Evening Standard* van, she straddled the bike, balancing her boots toes down into the wet asphalt. She relaxed her grip on the throttle and closed her eyes. The leathers. Every morning, the delicious ritual. The caress of the hide as it sheathed her thighs. The tightness of it hugging her buttocks and biting softly into her cleft. The unique thrill of zipping up the front to tame the swell of her bosom. The solid brass zip: Charlie shuddered, remembering the dark delight of dragging the zip up from her pubic nest, over her belly and breasts, to her white throat. Even on her days off, Charlie indulged in the private pleasure of donning her leathers – often coming violently as her nakedness surrendered to the leathers. After such orgasms, she would kneel, thighs apart, and finger the sticky warmth moistening the dark hide, plucking it slowly away from her hot slit. Delicious.

Green. She twisted the throttle, trailing the *Evening Standard* van on automatic pilot, judging her speed by its brake lights. Another red light. A taxi drew up beside her, the cabbie instantly burying his face in the racing page. In the back of the cab, through the rain-silvered window, Charlie saw the bowler-hatted pinstripe suit ogling her. Denying her pale-faced admirer eye contact, she raised her leather glove to her teeth. Nipping at the fingertips, she freed her hand, and plunged it down between her thighs and the saddle. With her fingers buried beneath her, she thumbed her leather-sheathed clitoris slowly, rhythmically. Red and amber. She was already getting wet. Green. Slipping her hand smoothly back into the gauntlet dangling from her teeth, she roared off single-handed, glimpsing in her mirror the whitened knuckles of her admirer gripping and twisting his umbrella handle in the back seat of the sluggish taxi.

The traffic had congealed at Cambridge Circus. Charlie closed her eyes behind her tinted, rain-speckled visor and summoned up the remembered pleasures of undressing. Getting out of her supple leathers was as exciting, as exquisitely erotic, as the act and art of donning them. The slow, deliberately slow, tugging-down of the heavy brass zip, allowing her confined breasts to burgeon and spill out. She would shiver at the sensation of her nipples rubbing against the hide in their bid for sudden freedom, often grazing against the teeth of the zipper and peaking in a flash of pleasurable pain.

Then, the struggle to peel her shoulders and arms free, followed by the sensual palming-down of the soft leather from her hips, bottom and thighs. The second skin always clung to her long legs lovingly, as if reluctant to release her limbs from its thrall. Squirming, her bare buttocks burning as they ground into the carpet, she would battle to kick herself free, the frenzied

3

cycling of her thighs leaving her hot and sticky. Naked, she would snatch up the leathers instantly and hug them to her breasts. Plunging her face down into the rubbery softness, she would sniff the intoxicating tang, the thrilling aroma of warm leather, and relish the blaze of images it kindled.

Burning images of other artefacts fashioned from sleek hide for the female appetite. Corsetières' creations that bound and squeezed; elbow-length gloves and thigh-high boots; smooth, oiled whips that licked bare buttocks with tongues of fire. Writhing in her nakedness, Charlie would rub a gathered fistful of the bike suit against her slit until, screaming softly as she pounded her buttocks into the carpet, she smeared the hide with her creaming climax.

A Daimler purred up alongside, the whisper of its fat tyres in the wet breaking into Charlie's reverie. The sole occupant in the back was a platinum blonde, sporting a black pill-box hat. The net veil across her face concealed her pale make-up, large dark eyes and pouting lips. Charlie studied the face in her mirror. Their eyes met in the silver square of rain-splashed glass. Poor little rich bitch in her gilded, four-litre cage, Charlie mused. Tamed and trapped in suffocating luxury.

Beneath the hammering rain, the Daimler's wipers swished. The rhythm of the rubber against the smooth glass was like that of an unseen but overheard punishment: of a bare female bottom being leisurely striped with a stinging leather belt. Swish, lash. Swish, lash. The suggestive sound of the wipers drew Charlie's labia apart in a welcoming smile. She rose up on the toes of her leather boots and planted her pubis down on the Suzuki's bulbous tank. Gripping the handlebars with outstretched hands, she balanced her pose, then swept her thighs down, crushing her slit into the polished metal of the petrol tank.

In her mirror, she glimpsed the net veil being removed

4

by a lavender-gloved hand, revealing a pair of sloe-black eyes wide with wonder. Charlie returned the gaze, locking the voyeur into full eye contact. Gripping her Suzuki savagely, she inched up on to her toes and offered her pubis to the top of the tank, then repeatedly dragged it down against the swell of polished metal. Each sweep of her leather-bound thighs was arrested as her taut buttocks bunched up against the saddle.

The engines in front revved as the traffic jam unglued into a trickle. Gazing steadily into the mirror, Charlie saw the spellbound blonde's red lips pressing against the Daimler's window. In response, Charlie flickered out her pink tongue tip, curled it up teasingly, then winked. Snorting warm breath that clouded the glass, the blonde flattened her tongue against the window. Straddling the Suzuki, Charlie tossed her head back as if in orgasm, clenching her buttocks and jerking her hips. The pink tongue at the Daimler's steamed window lapped hungrily. Charlie grinned, twisted the throttle open and sped away, weaving between a Fiesta and a silver Mondeo.

Down Shaftesbury Avenue and then into the Charing Cross Road, she nursed the Suzuki through the thick traffic until a sharp left brought her into Compton Street. Black plastic rubbish bags spilt off the pavements into the road. Threading through them, Charlie reached her destination.

The pert receptionist wore a flirty strawberry-print dress of see-through linen. Charlie had to look very hard to work out which were the ripe, red fruits and which were the riper, redder nipples.

'Package for Pleasure-me-please,' Charlie said, whipping off her helmet and tossing her tumbling curls.

'You're a bit late,' the receptionist warned. 'They've phoned down from the boardroom twice, already.'

'Traffic.' Charlie shrugged, signing in. 'Where to?' She

5

joined the receptionist behind her desk, bending down to study the building plan.

The receptionist's expertly varnished red nail tapped the laminated sheet. 'Take the lift. Fourth floor. Turn left, then left again.'

'Thanks.' Charlie's fingertip pressed down next to the red nail, touching it fleetingly. 'This the loo?'

'Yep. But I'd hurry.'

'Thanks.' After brushing her leather-ensnared breasts firmly against the strawberry print, Charlie strode off to the lift. As the silver door swished softly behind her, she heard the pretty receptionist announce her arrival into the phone.

On the fourth floor, Charlie scorned the women's loo and strode wilfully into the men's. It was, to her mild disappointment, empty. Charlie loved a scene as much as the freedom she enjoyed to frequently cause one. The washroom was clinical and spartan – a postmodernist exercise in onyx, beige tiling and minimalist aluminium. Not the soft pinks and powder blues she was usually condemned to endure.

Closing her eyes, she inhaled deeply, thrilling to the danger of entering this jealously guarded male lair. Her nostrils caught and savoured the musk of aftershave and the tang of sweat. Suddenly, her wide mouth crinkled into a knowing smile: somebody had been in here for a sly cigarette, risking the wrath of the politically correct pink-lunged brigade by avoiding the downpour outside.

In the cubicle, she wriggled out of her leathers and hung them up on the single hook. Her boots and helmet lay at her naked feet as she pressed her buttocks up against the cold beige tiles. Cupping her breasts, she squeezed and punished their warm weight. Recalling her bike ride across London, she captured each nipple between a pincer of finger and thumb. Behind her closed eyes, she glimpsed the blank faces in the Sherpa van suddenly seared with lust. She thumbed her nipples feverishly. Then her inner eye saw the whitened knuckles in the back of the black taxi gripping an erect umbrella in impotent fury. Her nipples were now aching under the ravishment of their stubby peaks. Charlie grunted as she recollected the Daimler in the rain. The parted red lips smudging the clouded glass, and the crushed pink tongue: the blonde mouthing silently but eloquently her arousal and desire.

Despite the images flickering behind her eyes, and despite the fingertips strumming her splayed labia, Charlie's orgasm proved elusive. A snarl of frustration escaped from her clenched teeth. What was it? she wondered. Why couldn't she come? She was wet and more than willing for her climax. Collapsing with a loud sigh back against the cold tiles, she thrust her soft buttocks into their polished sheen. Rolling her hips, she forced the heavy cheeks apart, dragging their swollen flesh rhythmically from side to side. The deep cleft yawned, its heat dulling the tiles.

Concentrate. She must be more disciplined – and concentrate. The images of her successful morning's teasing failed to fuel her orgasm. Frustrated, she tried to focus hard to fire her fantasies. A jet of water at the urinal outside her cubicle sounded strange and unfamiliar – then she remembered. She was in the men's room. An intruder in a forbidden place. Suddenly, she remembered an earlier escapade, a similarly forbidden thrill: when she had stolen on tiptoe into masculine territory and had unearthed dark, male secrets.

With her thumb stroking at her erect clitoris, Charlie arched her neck and ground her rump into the hard tiles. The tennis weekend at her aunt's house in the summer of her seventeenth birthday flooded back vividly. Her aunt's stepson, for whom Charlie had nursed turbulent passions, was away that weekend, at an Iron Age dig in the Mendips. The tennis had been indifferent, washed out by heavy rain. In the middle of the wet Sunday afternoon, with her aunt's gingerbread in the Aga filling the entire house with its spicy aroma, Charlie had stealthily entered the young man's bedroom to explore.

Thighs apart, fingers busy at her wet softness, Charlie felt her belly tighten in response to memories of her forbidden trespass. Memories of the tweed jackets smelling of earth and mothballs, the whiff of sweat from the rugby shirts, the linseed of an oiled cricket bat – and something else. Stale semen.

She had found the magazine buried deep down among abandoned Latin revision notes. It was a magazine from Germany devoted to the female bottom. Devoted to the worship and chastisement, the perusal and the punishment, of beautiful, bare buttocks.

In the silence of the bedroom, a silence broken only by the patter of the stubborn Sunday rain against the window, Charlie had slowly turned the pages, her nipples thickening and her mouth dry, gazing at the delicious female bottoms bared and displayed submissively before the devouring lens of the camera. Bottoms like peaches, peeled of their silk and satin second skins. Ripe, rounded cheeks, swollen and heavy in their utter nakedness. Creamy flesh-mounds, some freshly spanked, others striped pink by a bamboo cane: so lifelike, they seemed to tremble at Charlie's tentative touch.

Just as her thumbs came to the centrefold, the two pages refused to part. Curiosity forced Charlie to peel them open carefully, revealing big close-ups of two gorgeous bottoms. One, she remembered, belonged to a seductive Asian girl. It was plump and had been severely spanked. The chastised cheeks shimmered in their tingling pain above the dark bands of seamed black stockings. On the right-hand page, a pair of pert peach cheeks bore the cruel stripes of a whippy cane – arranged by the photographer to nestle up along her cleft between the buttocks it had just lashed. The pages had been stuck together by semen splashes. The faint tang of the young man's liquid spurt of release had stabbed at Charlie's nostrils. Thrilling to the punished bottoms, she had bent her face down, sniffing at the forbidden odour.

Yes. In her cubicle, naked and perspiring slightly, Charlie remembered her discovery of that wet Sunday afternoon. Relishing the perverted pleasure of stumbling across the erotic secrets of a virile young man, she had succumbed to playing with herself down on the carpet of the bedroom floor, using the rolled-up magazine between her thighs, almost collapsing as the image of the spanked Asian's cheeks skimmed against her slit. Then, as now, she juiced suddenly and came savagely. Then, as now, her belly imploded in violent ecstasy.

Panting, Charlie used a handful of tissue to dry herself, then struggled into her leathers. Outside the cubicle, after rinsing her fingers in a wash-basin, she used the hot air dryer, her face flushed and her heart still racing, allowing the rush of warm air to play across her breasts before she zipped herself up. Walking out of the men's room, she turned and paused at the door. Her climax had left a strong trace of female excitement in the air. That'll puzzle 'em, she smirked, picturing the expressions on the men's faces for the rest of the day – men haunted by the smell of a hot woman in their cool, exclusive domain.

Turn left, then left again. The boardroom was only a minute away. Charlie planned her entrance carefully. She would go in, unzipped and bosom bulging. Their eyes would rake her devastating cleavage. She would pause, running the tip of her straightened index finger down her inner thigh, then retrace the provocative gesture upward. Their eyes would devour the creased leather at her slit. Having delivered the package in silence, she would depart with a wiggling swagger. Their eyes would narrow as they drank in her buttocks, sculpted by the supple hide.

Charlie smothered her laughter, laughter at the thought of all those pale-faced men round the boardroom table inching their chairs inward to conceal their throbbing erections. Only last week, she had deliberately made an accountant come, her eyes smiling at the stain darkening his trousers beneath a hastily rearranged ledger. She really was a naughty little bitch.

Tapping twice on the boardroom door, then yanking her zip down an extra two inches for good measure, Charlie entered. She froze in the doorway.

'You're late, girl. What kept you? The receptionist announced your arrival at least twelve minutes ago.'

Blushing in her confusion, Charlie mumbled an apology.

'I'm afraid sorry is hardly good enough,' the blonde purred as she toyed with her chunky gold bracelet. 'Come in and close the door.'

Charlie, recovering from the shock of discovering five smart businesswomen seated around the boardroom table, obeyed.

'And zip yourself up, you little slut,' the dominant blonde snapped.

Charlie crimsoned, suddenly feeling awkward and vulnerable. Just as she had felt before being given a bare-bottomed caning in front of all the Upper Sixth girls assembled to witness her subsequent expulsion.

'The package,' the blonde demanded curtly, snapping her fingers.

Charlie passed the small oblong box she had collected from the Hatton Garden workshop. Ignoring the messenger, the blonde opened the package and extracted a black rubber dildo. It was nine inches in length, slightly curved towards the tapering tip – and studded with a cluster of smooth pearls at the thick snout. Charlie suppressed a gasp of wonder at the sight of the blackberry-like clump of pearls. What delicious thrills they would inflict when deep inside a warm, wet female.

The five members of the Pleasure-me-please management team concentrated on the phallic sex toy, fingering it delicately and weighing its passive potency as it was handed round the boardroom table. They ignored Charlie completely, allowing her the brief opportunity to study them surreptitiously. Their leader, the blonde, was snappily dressed in a severe Versace black suit, her chic jacket unbuttoned to reveal a silver blouse. Braless, the blonde's soft breasts rose and fell rhythmically beneath the stretched silk. Her hands were beautifully manicured, each nail winking under a coating of Chanel Nude varnish. Her lips were full and moist. Charlie, who held corporate glamour in contempt, suspected triple lip gloss.

Clockwise around the table, Charlie inspected the other four businesswomen: a second blonde, pertly petite, in a sinuous lime-green Valentino dress; a brunette in a figure-hugging Mondi pinstripe; a cruel-eyed, ash-grey beauty buttoned up in a Louis Feraud three-piece and – scratching her stockinged thigh lazily as Charlie glanced at her – a young redhead in a revealing, powder-blue Donna Karan. Their make-up was impeccable, their jewellery expensive. Hemlines were excitingly high, stockings sheer and glossy, cleavages generously on display.

In her damp leathers, and wearing the muted fragrance of hot oil and hotter sex, Charlie blushed self-consciously, like an unruly child gatecrashing its parents' dinner party. Scanning the chic women poring over the pearl-encrusted dildo, three images burned into her brain: the cruel eyes of the ash-grey beauty; the blood-red lips of the svelte brunette in the Mondi pinstripe, and the strong, slender hands of the boss.

The dildo completed its circuit of admiration and

11

rested back in the blonde's right hand. Charlie felt the pulse at her tightening throat quicken as she watched the perfectly manicured thumbtip caressing the pearled phallus slowly, deliberately.

'You have neither explained or excused your unpardonable lateness. You cannot simply walk in –'

'Heavy traffic,' Charlie blurted out, her tone a trifle sullen and defensive. 'The rain –' she shrugged '– snarls things up.'

'It takes one and a half minutes – two, at the very most – in the lift from the receptionist's desk to the boardroom door. You took twelve.'

Charlie sought refuge in silence as she worked on a convincing lie.

'We have,' the blonde continued imperiously, 'a valuable account with your firm, girl. One they would not wish to lose. I think we are entitled to a proper explanation.'

'I've got to go,' Charlie replied evenly, refusing to be cowed. 'I'm running late. Sorry I kept you.' She turned to go.

'One moment, girl. I am far from satisfied with both your behaviour and your attitude. Adding insolence to ineptitude will do little to help matters. Come here.'

Charlie hesitated at the boardroom door.

'At once,' thundered the blonde.

Reluctantly, Charlie approached the polished table.

'Do you enjoy your work, girl?'

Charlie nodded.

'Speak up.'

'Yes,' Charlie said distinctly. 'I love my job.'

'Then I am right in thinking that you would wish to remain in your present employment?'

Charlie agreed.

'And of course,' the blonde whispered softly, 'you would prefer to be punished for this morning's lapse rather than force me to have you sacked?'

Charlie dropped her gaze to the shining surface of the boardroom table. On it, her penitent eyes glimpsed the Chanel Nude varnished nails tightening round the dildo. She shivered.

'Well, girl?'

The sack: to lose her job; her beautiful bike; her freedom. Charlie felt her tongue thicken in her dry mouth.

'Yes.' She scarcely recognised her own voice.

'Yes?' queried the blonde. 'Yes, what?' she taunted, smiling around at her coterie of admiring colleagues.

'Punishment,' Charlie mumbled huskily.

'Strip,' came the dominant command. The blonde turned her face away – a gesture suggesting both her supreme authority and absolute control of the situation. 'Chloe, assist the bitch out of her leathers. Susie,' she added, 'lend a hand.'

The young redhead in the Donna Karan and the brunette in the severe three-piece pinstripe rose from the table. Their chrome chairs did not squeak – the carpet was at least two inches thick. Charlie struggled but capable hands unzipped and stripped her efficiently. The bike suit was peeled away, leaving her naked and ashamed before their collective gaze. Chloe returned to her chair as Charlie shielded her pubic snatch with one hand and flattened her other palm across her nipples. Susie remained at Charlie's side, her pinstriped trouser-leg pressing firmly against the nude's quivering thigh.

'Stand up straight, girl,' the blonde commanded, her eyes widening a fraction as they perused Charlie's nakedness.

Charlie straightened her shoulders but kept her protecting hands in place. The blonde nodded curtly. Susie spanked Charlie's left buttock with a sharp, ringing slap. Charlie gasped aloud – and gasped again as she felt her hands being dragged behind her and pinioned together at the wrists. Utterly exposed, she shrank from the piercing eyes that raked her breasts and dark pubic nest. Charlie wriggled, but Susie's grip was firm.

'Your delay was not only discourteous but a great nuisance to myself and my colleagues. Pleasure-me-please is a thrusting corporation, girl. Time, for us, means money. You have cost us this morning and I mean to know why. Show me her leathers.'

Flexing her knee, Susie guided her supple leg and jerked up the crumpled leathers from the carpet. With an adroit flick, she kicked them up on to the table. Charlie froze as she watched the manicured nails of the blonde prising her bike suit open for intimate inspection – exposing the smear of her orgasm to the neon light. Picking up the leathers, the blonde inverted them fully and bent down to sniff the damp patch of soiled hide. Charlie squirmed but remained helpless in Susie's pinioning grip.

'Playing with yourself in our time, hm? You deserve to be punished and I shall see to it that you are. And punished most severely. Bring her here.'

Charlie flinched as Susie propelled her roughly towards the stern blonde, who had jerked back her chair from the table. Sitting in it, the boss shrugged off her black jacket – Charlie saw the breasts bounce softly at the exertion – and drew her tight skirt up over her honey-coloured stockinged thighs.

'Bend over.'

Charlie, shivering and naked, eased herself down across the glossy nylons awaiting her, grazing her erect nipples against their rasping sheen, and settled herself, bare bottom upward, across the warm lap. She shivered as two controlling hands descended upon her nakedness: one at the nape of her exposed neck; the other palm down against the buttocks beneath the woman's heavy breasts. Charlie closed her eyes, hating yet thrilling to the touch of the manicured fingertips dipping down across the swell of her cheek into her sticky cleft.

The fingertips drummed, causing Charlie's labia to part and kiss the nyloned thigh beneath.

'Each of my colleagues is going to punish you, girl. And then,' the boss whispered menacingly, 'I will chastise you personally. Chloe,' she said briskly, 'you may open the account.'

Chloe approached.

'Be sure the bitch suffers.'

Chloe nodded. Kneeling down in front of the seated blonde, she slowly unbuttoned the cuff at the right sleeve of her Donna Karan. Charlie opened her eyes to glimpse her chastiser. She saw the redhead toss her head impatiently as she dealt with the cuff, and purse her lips as she removed a Mikimoto bracelet. The girl was preparing for the duties of discpline purposefully. Charlie knew that her bare buttocks were about to be blistered.

Seconds later, the blonde boss tightened her grip on Charlie's nape and swept her controlling palm down across her victim's buttocks to trap and tame the thighs. The spanking was severe, lasting a full three and a half minutes, and filled the boardroom with the staccato of flesh swiping harshly across flesh: of a firm palm savagely caressing two naked cheeks.

Spread across, and fiercely pinned down into, the warm glossy nylons, Charlie jerked and writhed as the stinging rain of pain scalded her defenceless buttocks. During the punishment, her loose breasts bounced, their weight jiggling against the blonde's outer thigh. Charlie squealed aloud as she felt the blonde relinquish the grip on her neck and slip her free hand down to cup, talon and squeeze the soft bosom.

Under the searing hand of the redhead, Charlie's bare bottom burned. A crimson fire spread its pink and reddening flames across the once-creamy flesh. Releasing her captive's breasts, the blonde returned her hand to Charlie's neck, pinning her absolutely. The other controlling hand, planted at the spot where Charlie's thighs swept up to her buttocks, prevented the possibility of any escape, rendering Charlie totally exposed to each and every stinging spank.

The final crack rang out. Charlie hissed.

'Thank you, Chloe,' the blonde murmured. 'Susie, please continue with the chastisement.'

Charlie sensed that Susie needed no second bidding. Kneeling down quickly at the blonde's feet – and Charlie's reddened buttocks – she immediately launched into a severe onslaught. The smacking was more urgent, more vicious, than Chloe's measured punishment. Charlie squealed as her bare bottom blazed.

The hand at Charlie's neck tightened its grip.

'Faster,' whispered the blonde. 'And harder.'

Susie responded, flattening each cheek beneath her burning palm. Charlie squeezed her eyes and her buttocks tightly as the pain seethed the swell of her bunched cheeks. Halfway through the second spanking, Charlie sensed her sphincter growing hot and sticky. To her alarm and shame, she felt the hot ooze of arousal moistening her cleft. Down against the delicious prickle of the nyloned thighs, her splayed labia kissed the sheen with wet lips.

The flurry of scalding spanks ceased abruptly. Catlike, Susie paused to lick her palm, flattening her pink tongue repeatedly into her hot hand. Glimpsing this, Charlie bubbled, dampening the dominant blonde's thighs. Charlie cringed as she felt the supporting limbs rise up a fraction to acknowledge the wet warmth.

'Excellent,' the boss told her kneeling colleague. 'And who would like to go next, hm?'

'Me,' squealed the young woman in the lime-green Valentino. Her voice was eager. Urgent.

Charlie caught the delicate fragrance of Elizabeth Arden 5th Avenue scent and felt the fluttering touch of the loose chiffon as the third punisher knelt down and addressed Charlie's helpless cheeks. Unlike her first two chastisers, the third placed a controlling palm down across the upturned buttocks, signalling her clear intention to spank the swell of the curved cheeks at the point where the buttocks melted into the fleshy upper thighs. Accepting this painful proposition, the boss moved her hand down three inches to accommodate this refinement. Charlie grunted, dreading the impending pain.

Despite her ultra-feminine choice of attire and perfume, the third Pleasure-me-please punisher proved a robust chastiser. The first eighteen spanks were meaty, the next twenty were cruel, and the concluding fourteen were memorable: all eliciting shrill squeals from the spanked nude – and causing Charlie to squirm and drum her heels in pathetic protest.

The fourth punisher, a sensual, cruel-eyed forty-something, did not lay a single finger upon her victim's proffered buttocks, but managed to make Charlie suffer sweetly. Kneeling, the mannishly dressed woman exuded an air of self-restraint that frightened Charlie. The measured dominance and stern malice of her new tormentress sent shivers of alarm down her spine. Slowly unbuttoning her sharply cut Louis Feraud jacket and waistcoat before removing them, the cruel-eyed beauty loosened a snow-white satin scarf at her throat and twisted it tightly into a taut skein. Threading the stretched satin between Charlie's quivering cheeks, she dragged one end down between the clamped thighs of her victim, gripping it in her right fist, and grasped the other end, winding it round her left fist.

Charlie moaned, seduced yet scared by the cool kiss of satin deep between her scalded buttocks. Slowly at first, then ruthlessly, the scarf was rasped back and

17

forth, biting into the softness of the cleft. Bucking and squealing in response, Charlie shrieked as her sticky flesh burned. Her suffering fuelled the determination of the kneeling dominatrix, causing the scarf to stretch more tightly and bite more deeply.

'Yes,' urged the blonde over whose knees Charlie was pinned. 'That will teach the bitch.'

Tensed and rigid across the soft thighs, Charlie suddenly slumped and surrendered, unequal to the struggle against the delicious pain. Passive across the glossy nylons that rasped her belly and breasts, she submitted her bottom to the scarf, accepting its dark delight with slightly parted thighs and raised bare buttocks. As the savage pleasure of the scarf increased, Charlie sensed the beginnings of a climax puckering the walls of her belly.

'Stop,' thundered the blonde. 'She's about to come.'

The scarf ceased its ruthless ravishment.

'I want that moment for myself,' the blonde continued, purring silkily as she fingered Charlie's spasming, reddened cheeks. 'Get the bitch across the table, face down. Quickly.'

Eager hands dragged Charlie up to her feet, then forced her, breasts and belly down, on to the polished wood.

'Hold her firmly.'

A fierce grip was applied to Charlie's wrists and ankles. Naked and immobile, she lay helpless in their thrall. Spreadeagled, her face pressed into the table, her mind was a riot of delicious dread as it imagined her impending doom. Strokes from a crisply slicing crop? Lashes from a sleek, whippy cane? Molten torment from a wickedly fashioned spanking paddle? Such instruments for discipline would be readily at hand, here in the offices of Pleasure-me-please.

Charlie writhed, crushing her breasts into the polished surface of the boardroom table. Her nipples dragged their hard peaks into the harder wood. At the base of the belly, the table's surface was wet from the smear of her slit.

'How opportune,' the boss remarked. 'We can test-drive our latest model and see how it performs.'

The dildo. Charlie thrashed in a frantic bid to escape the probe of the black rubber shaft, but her captors' grip was invincible. Pinning their victim down, they signalled to the boss that the moment was ripe.

The dominant blonde mounted the table and knelt, her face a mere seven inches from Charlie's freshly spanked bottom. Straddling Charlie's thighs and trapping them between her glossy nylons, the boss placed her hands upon the crimson cheeks before her. Charlie squealed in response to the gripping talons, and squealed again as her cheeks were spread painfully apart.

'Place the shaft between my teeth,' the boss instructed Susie.

Obediently, the willing hand swept the length of rubber up from the table and inserted the thick base between the blonde's parted teeth. Almost immediately, the blackberry of peals teased at Charlie's anal whorl as the dominant blonde guided the knout of the dildo between the splayed peach cheeks and into the seething sphincter.

Charlie groaned as the bulbous sphere stretched her muscled warmth – and slowly, deliberately, penetrated her. Half an inch. An inch. An inch and a half. A heartbeat at a time, the cruel blonde pleasure-punished Charlie with the shaft, her face getting closer and closer to the taloned cheeks as she plunged the dildo deeper and deeper. Jerking her head back, her neck straining and arched, the boss drew the shaft out – only to plunge it back, driving it deeper between the captive buttocks.

Charlie felt the tightly clustered pearls at the dildo's snout ravishing her inner flesh. Her groaning melted into a mewing moan as, once more, the length of stern rubber was inched back out of her anus in a supreme gesture of tantalising dominance. Mourning the shaft, yet dreading its return, Charlie begged aloud. Confused and incoherent, her squeals were laced with sweet obscenities.

Strictly denied the satisfaction she craved, Charlie lay tense and rigid, her shoulders glistening with sweat. Then the blonde struck: spearing the dildo deep into the cheeks until her lips pressed up against and kissed their swollen curves. Charlie screamed twice as she came, hammering her hips into the polished wood as the first of four orgasms shattered her naked helplessness.

Leathered and astride her Suzuki, thirty minutes later, Charlie roared down the Old Brompton Road towards her South Ken flat. Round the waist, she sensed the encircling arms of the pretty little receptionist squeezing tightly.

They slewed to a halt.

The receptionist peeled her arms from the warm leather and prised off her skid-lid. 'Just lunch.' She smiled, tugging fruitlessly at the hem of her strawberry-print dress riding high up her creamy thighs. 'You said a salad.'

Charlie knew that her fridge was empty – but that soon her bed would be full. Unzipping her leathers to reveal her ripe breasts, she tossed her hair free. The early-afternoon sunshine sparkled at the cluster of pearls encrusting a black rubber shaft nestling in her inviting cleavage – the dildo she had deftly purloined from under her tormentors' eyes.

'Well, OK, then,' the receptionist whispered, her eyes matching the sun's sparkle as they glimpsed the bejewelled phallus thrust between the swollen breasts. 'Perhaps just a little dessert.'

Charlie grinned.

2

The Maid

Lucy – nobody ever called her by her full name as, being merely the maid, nobody ever knew what it was – wished the hot tap filling her early-morning bath wouldn't make the boiler pipes behind the Aga gurgle so noisily. She had been warned by her mistress, Miss Oxford, that hot water was expensive and that a maid should be content with a luke-warm bath deep enough to cover her buttocks but not deep enough to bury her bosom.

'Your master will be very angry if I have to inform him of your profligacy, girl,' Miss Oxford had persisted. 'If he catches you being so wilfully disobedient, you will find yourself in very hot water indeed.'

Lucy wiped the steam from the cold bathroom window and, naked as she tiptoed up to the mullioned glass, peeped out at the bleak November dawn. A cruel frost glittered down in the orchard. Her nipples thickened and darkened as they peaked up stiffly in the chill air.

Outside, the Suffolk countryside was bracing itself for winter. The ploughs, dragged by teams of toiling horses, were scarring the rich loam fields as they buried the stubble of October's harvest. The men were all back from the war and the Kaiser had been beaten. Back from the trenches had come Captain Oxford, sullen and brooding after combat, to rule The Birches with a rod of iron.

21

Stepping gingerly into the deep, steaming bath, Lucy scorned the cracked block of yellow carbolic and luxuriated in a stolen tablet of Miss Oxford's scented soap. It creamed her breasts as she palmed them; caressed each nipple with teasing fingertips. Easing back into the forbidden depth of her hot bath, she surrendered to the warmth lapping at her shining bosom. Soon her hands were busy between her thighs, soaping her pouting flesh-folds.

Lolling back, her dampened curls tumbling down her white neck, Lucy gazed across at the scrubbed pine chair. Through the swirl of steam, she inspected her uniform intimately. Servants were hard to come by, since the war, and harder to train. A uniformed maid was a rarity in these rambling Suffolk mansions, where once liveried staff were plentiful. Go and seek work in a factory or obtain a position in a millinery shop, her friends and family would always insist when she saw them on her weekly half-day off. Why stay at The Birches and be forced to wear a uniform, for a miserable four shillings a week?

Lucy studied her silk stockings, starched boddice and cotton cami-knickers. Freshly laundered and crisply ironed, soon they would receive her nakedness to cup and squeeze her breasts, belly and rounded buttocks. Then she would wriggle into her pert black dress and complete the maid's outfit with a pretty little white apron and a saucy lace cap. Her uniform – the uniform of a maid, which she wore with pride.

Trained strictly by both the master and his sister, the stern Miss Oxford, Lucy had been schooled to serve her employers and was both willing and eager to please. Her friends and family would never come to understand how thrilled she was to be in service – and Lucy would never tell them the reasons why.

As she palmed the soap against her pubic nest, her eye caught sight of the bolt on the bathroom door. A burning flush crimsoned Lucy's cheeks. On the strict instruction of both her master and mistress, the bolt must never be drawn. The thought of either Captain or Miss Oxford intruding upon her intimate toilette angered her – almost as much as it excited her. At any moment, either one could stride into the bathroom, peruse her utter nakedness as she cowered in the bath, and punish her bare bottom for her flagrant misuse of so much expensive hot water.

Guiltily, Lucy scrunched her pink toes around the silver-beaded chain and inched up the rubber plug. The water swirled away, dragging the heel of her soft ankle down into the whirlpool at the plughole. She giggled and wiggled her buttocks into the dimpled rubber bath mat.

Lucy bit her lower lip pensively. Pity the hour was so late, she thought. How she would have adored using the loofah against her hot pussy, this morning. Standing up in the bath, thighs parted, with the length of hard golden sponge rasping upward and inward against her seething flesh. But, Lucy sighed, stretching for the towel, there was so much to be done before cock-crow: fires to set and light, kettles to fill and boil, eggs to be poached and the master's *Times* to be ironed. Her employers had very exacting needs, Lucy knew, and punctuality was a strict priority for them both. Tardiness meant punishment for a lazy maid.

The bathroom door creaked and yawned open. Lucy's dark eyes widened as they saw Captain Oxford, hair tousled and blue dressing-gown tightly fastened, enter.

'Have you been using the hot water, girl?' he barked.

'No, sir,' Lucy mumbled, gathering the soft towel belatedly to her bosom. 'Mistress said –'

'It is uncommonly warm in here,' her master interrupted curtly. 'The rumbling boiler woke me. Get out of that bathtub at once.'

Steadying herself, Lucy stepped out daintily, dropping her towel as she did so. It fell down to the cork mat and curled around her ankles, rendering her nakedness exposed to his lustful gaze.

Ignoring his naked maid, the master bent down over the side of the porcelain tub and pressed his palm into the dimpled rubber mat which had kissed Lucy's bottom only moments before. She winced as she saw his fingers and thumb pluck up one of her dark pubic coils.

'Hot. Just as I suspected.'

'No, sir, please, sir –'

'Silence, girl. Stop snivelling. You know the rules of this house. And,' he murmured, inspecting the coiled pubic hair, 'the tide mark shows it to have been a deep bath. Much deeper than is permitted. Bend over.'

'But, master, I –'

'Disobeyed two direct orders. You have been caught red-handed, girl, and now you are to be red-bottomed.'

Whimpering softly, Lucy bent over the side of the bathtub, pressing her breasts into its rim. Thighs clamped tightly together, her bare bottom rose up to meet Captain Oxford's cruel gaze. The cheeks hung poised and rounded, like ripe peaches in the hot-house ready to be plucked and bitten.

'Where is your hairbrush, girl? I mean to chastise your bottom with it.'

'In my bedchamber, master,' she whispered, shivering at the sound of his dressing-gown being loosened.

'Then I shall have to spank you with my hand, girl. Bottom up, if you will.'

Lucy, gripping the edge of the bathtub, inched her buttocks up until she knew that they met with her stern master's approval. After a flurry of brisk spanks, he suddenly paused in the act of punishing the bare bottom. Captain Oxford bent down, bringing his face an inch or so from the swollen curves of the cheeks he had just reddened. He sniffed.

'So, girl. Carbolic not good enough for you, what? You see fit to purloin perfumed soap from the boudoir of your mistress? Do you know what happens to scented whores, Lucy?'

'No, master.'

'Oh, come, girl. I rather think you do. What do the scriptures prescribe for the jade and the harlot?'

'Punishment,' Lucy whispered.

'They are whipped, girl, whipped. A spanked bottom,' he murmured, palming her quivering cheeks, 'is not, I fear, sufficient enough punishment. Be at my study door shortly after eleven. Bring the dog whip from the tackle room. Do you understand?'

'Yes, master.'

'Now put your stockings on. Quickly, girl.'

Lucy rose, blushing deeply, shielding her breasts and dark pubic nest from her master's piercing eyes. Raising her left knee up to her bosom, she guided her prinked foot into the sheer silk stocking. Stretching her leg out straight, toes pointing down into the cork mat, she slowly palmed the stocking up along her naked leg until the slightly darker band at the top strained at her plump thigh.

'And now the other one,' Captain Oxford grunted thickly, flinging apart his dressing-gown and grasping his erection.

Lucy, her eyes widening with delicious dread at the throbbing manhood imprisoned in the curled fist, struggled into her second stocking, the cleft between her buttocks parting invitingly as she raised her leg.

'Bend over,' the master ordered his stockinged maid.

Lucy obeyed, her eyes following Captain Oxford's impatient forefinger as it tapped the edge of the hand-basin. As she lowered her breasts into the cold sink, she shuddered as the porcelain kissed their warmth.

A firm hand alighted on the exposed nape of her neck,

pinioning her cruelly. She tensed, flinching slightly, as she sensed the dominant presence of her master against her quivering thigh. Pinned and helpless, she wondered what his pleasure – and her pain – would be. His grunts and heavy breathing filled the bathroom as, inches away from the curved cheeks of her naked buttocks, he punished his erection with a tightly clamped fist.

Out in the frost-fingered dawn, where the last of the late stars surrendered their pale light to the searing pink of the rising sun, ragged rooks wheeled and called high above the coppiced elms. Lucy held her breath as her pulse quickened at her throat. The master was moaning now, just as he always did, before the moment came. The moment when he would splash his hot seed over her bare bottom.

Panting loudly, he arched up. Lucy froze, stiffer in her tremulous expectation than the iced surface of the pond down in the paddock. Soon, she knew, his customary words would spill out, before the hot squirt of his release.

'Naughty maid. Naughty, bare-bottomed little maid. Must be punished, must be ravished –'

Intoning his tuneless song, his words rasping out in a gathering frenzy, Captain Oxford pumped with a renewed fury until, suddenly pulling the bare-bottomed maid up against his belly, he spilled his lust all over her quivering cheeks.

Out in the November dawn, high above the coppiced elms, the circling rooks scattered as a gamekeeper fired his shotgun into their midst. Gripping the edge of the hand-basin with whitened knuckles, Lucy fleetingly wondered what it must feel like to have tiny pellets of hot lead peppering into your flesh – not unlike the pitter-pat of the master's warm wetness splashing down upon your upturned buttocks, she supposed.

Drip. Drip. Drip. It was not the cold tap that filled her mind with the haunting sound but the ooze from her glistening cheeks dropping down slowly to her stockinged thighs.

Drip. Drip. Drip. The master had gone. Lucy rose up from the sink, pushing herself away from it with her elbows. As she stood, her cheeks tightened, squeezing out the sticky rivulet gathered in her cleft. It spilled down her inner thighs, staining her stockings' sheen. Staining and soiling her fresh silk stockings with Captain Oxford's fierce wet joy. Reaching down with her left hand, she fingered between her sticky buttocks and plucked away the tiny silver sixpence from her cleft.

The master always lodged a coin between the maid's cheeks after such encounters: a bright, brown penny after a spanking; sixpence after discharging himself over her bare buttocks; a shilling if he used her mouth; and – memorably – a florin piece in her hot hole after he had speared her there ruthlessly with his flesh-shaft.

Lucy palmed her sticky sixpence and smiled. Her friends and family pitied her, she knew. Pitied her being in servitude, at the endless beck and call of her demanding master and mistress. But little did they know of the dark pleasures a maid was forced to sweetly suffer – or of the tidy fortune a maid could quietly amass.

'Lucy, you wretched girl. Stop daydreaming and go and see to breakfast.'

Spank. The mistres spanked her maid's soft cheeks severely, then paused to examine her glistening palm.

'Lucy. Your bottom is unseemingly wet and –' she hesitated, frowning. Her tone sharpened. 'Has Captain Oxford been in here? Answer me directly, girl.'

Lucy caught the jealous, resentful note in the question.

'Did the master come in here?'

Lucy suppressed a grin; she had eavesdropped on the lewd talk down at the stables and recognised the other meaning of the naughty word. She fingered her sticky bottom where the master had come.

'Yes, miss,' she whispered, fearful of the spanking hand raised above her buttocks.

'And did he ...? Miss Oxford left the rest of her sentence unspoken.

'Yes, miss.' Lucy nodded, then lowered her head in a pretence of shame.

Spank. The hovering hand swept down across the naked bottom. 'Harlot,' the mistress spat, eyes flashing. 'I've spoken to you before on the subject of flaunting your wanton nakedness before my poor brother. He has returned to us from the war –' she hesitated, considering her words carefully '– damaged somewhat by the noise of the guns.'

'But please, miss, I didn't –'

'Give me the sixpence.'

Lucy surrendered her prize reluctantly.

'Wash it, girl,' the mistress snapped.

Blushing, Lucy rinsed the coin and dried it before placing it Miss Oxford's outstretched palm. Sighing, the maid consoled herself with the thought that her appointment in the study with the dog whip would earn her a striped bottom – and a whole shilling piece.

'Now go directly to my dressing room. I am going to punish you, girl. No –' she stemmed Lucy's squeak of protest abruptly '– there's no more to be said on the matter. Punished you shall be. You disobeyed me and now you must be made to suffer.'

Head bowed, Lucy scampered out of the bathroom, naked except for her stained stockings, and scurried down the draughty landing towards Miss Oxford's dressing room.

The maid knew her mistress well. Intimately well. She dressed the Edwardian rose from the skin out to the black bombazine gown every morning. She tamed Miss Oxford's rebellious ringlets with a firm brush every evening before the Captain's sister donned a cotton shift and slipped in between the cold sheets of her virginal

bed. Engaged to a dashing young subaltern in her
brother's regiment, Miss Oxford had been robbed of her
betrothed by the Somme. Now blossoming in the
summer of her thirtieth year, Miss Oxford resigned
herself to the devoted care of her younger brother.

'Get me my cane, girl.'

Lucy jumped, startled by the curt command breaking
into her silent reverie. Bending, she took the cane from
its hiding place beneath a sheepskin rug. Fourteen
inches long, it was a lady's cane – light, supple and
extremely whippy. Lucy handed the length of yellow
bamboo to her impatient mistress.

'Across the chair, girl.'

Lucy padded softly across to the ornate chair and
bent down over its sumptuous crimson cushion. The tip
of the cane grazed the seat half an inch from her belly,
dimpling the satin.

'The master must be excused. His condition causes
him a surfeit of –' she lowered her voice to an excited
whisper '– natural, vital juices. But, come the hard
frosts, and he will be able to ride out to hounds.
Exercise will no doubt abate his baser appetite. But you,
girl, must not –' the tip of the cane now tapped Lucy's
left buttock imperiously '– tempt him.'

The mistress pressed the cane down across her maid's
bare bottom, dominating the swell of both cheeks with
the cruel wood.

'And, I note, your stockings are soiled,' Miss Oxford
hissed, tracing her brother's sticky stains with the
whippy wand. 'More evidence testifying to your willing
harlotry.'

The cane swept up, hovered for a few agonising
seconds, then swept down, swiping the naked cheeks
with a vicious stroke. Lucy gasped aloud, jerking her
hips and crushing her heavy breasts into the crimson
cushion. The cane seared her upturned buttocks again,
and then again, striping her mercilessly. Lucy squealed.

The tip of the cane kissed her lips in a command for silence. Lucy whimpered, her wet tongue licking the yellow bamboo. Miss Oxford raised her arm up, and swept it down vigorously, four more times. Lucy writhed and squirmed beneath each searching stroke.

For a full three minutes, Miss Oxford plied her instrument of severe chastisement and punished her bare-bottomed maid ruthlessly, each crisp kiss of bamboo leaving a thin reddening line.

Dropping her cane, the mistress ran through the communicating door into her bedroom. Kneeling at the corner of her bed, she grasped her skirts and petticoat and dragged them up over her thighs to her belly, then feverishly thumbed her directoire knickers down to a tight, restricting band above her knees.

Across the red-cushioned chair, her bare buttocks blazing after the strict caning, Lucy peered up through her tears into a large cheval mirror. In the glass, she saw her mistress kneeling down at the corner of her mattress in the adjoining room. Lucy saw the rounded, tightened cheeks of the bare bottom spasming as Miss Oxford thrust her pubis into the mattress then rasped herself down on to and into it again and again. Shivering, the maid saw the neck of her kneeling mistress arch back; saw the supple spine and plump hips tense; saw the naked buttocks clench, rendering the cleft a severe flesh-crease. Moments, later, Miss Oxford choked softly on a sobbing moan as she shuddered, climaxing violently and hammering her hot flesh into the mattress with a fury somewhat unseemly in one of such genteel breeding.

Peeling her thickened nipples away from the crimson cushion across which she had been caned, Lucy crept out of the dressing room and stole away in silence.

Freshly stockinged, Lucy entered the kitchen down-stairs. The Birches was a large house, boasting over thirty rooms. A generation ago, eleven members of the Oxford family had lived here, tended to by some sixteen servants. Now the arrangements were more intimate, and the services offered by the maid strictly private and personal. The war had indeed changed everything, Lucy mused, filling a large kettle. Where once there had been aunts, uncles, cousins, pantrymen, cooks and a brace of footmen, now there was only the master, the mistress and their maid.

Lucy felt like a queen below stairs. It was her empire. And, like all shrewd monarchs, she made sure her empire paid her royally. Ordering three entrecôte steaks, she would guise the accounts book with the supposed payment for only two. Lucy lived well, dining handsomely. Better, more often than not, than those she served so assiduously. When Captain and Miss Oxford managed on haddock or trout, Lucy relished fresh salmon from the fishmonger's iced slab. To their bacon and eggs she would add mushrooms and a succulent pork sausage to her own breakfast plate and, when claret was decanted, Lucy made sure of her share of the expensive Bordeaux.

Breakfast. She commenced by opening a pint of champagne and drinking two glasses one after the other. Draining the fluted glass, her eyes sparkled as she licked her lips. For the master, there would be a deep, blue bowl of creamy porridge spiked with sweet dark rum. Then a couple of buttered kippers, toast and a silver pot of strong coffee. For the more fastidious mistress, pale Gunpowder tea, thin slices of buttered bread, lightly poached eggs and an apple. For herself, Lucy decided upon grilled rashers of Suffolk bacon, kidneys and tomatoes.

She was hungry, but deep inside a fiercer appetite clamoured to be sated. While the pots and pans on the Aga bubbled and seethed, Lucy checked the time by the walnut-encased clock. She had seven minutes. She resolved to attend to her urgent need – not the one in her empty belly, but the one burning below.

Up on the scrubbed kitchen table, Lucy lay back, spreading her stockinged legs apart. Inching the pert black skirt of her maid's uniform up over her hips and buttocks, she pawed blindly with her right hand for the wooden spoon. Her fingers found it and closed around the smooth handle. Guiding the curved back of the spoon to her seething slit, she tapped the wood against her wetness. Rhythmically, in time with the tick-ticking of the walnut-encased clock, Lucy pleasured herself with the spoon.

Closing her eyes, she summoned up the events of her busy morning. Her delicious hot bath, her soaped fingers at her nipples, then down between her thighs. The master's sudden entrance: spanking her, then pinning her down before spilling his liquid longing over her hot, punished bottom. Then, Lucy shuddered as she remembered, the dreadful delight of her stern mistress: inspecting her sticky stockings before caning her bare buttocks with such sweet savagery. The spoon at Lucy's slit outpaced the walnut clock as the memories of Miss Oxford flooded back. The memory of the mistress dashing into her bedroom to kneel down at her spinster's bed to perform acts of lewd wickedness upon her exposed maidenhood.

The wet wood of the spoon dragged against the wetter flesh. Lucy pumped the handle viciously at her erect thorn of joy. Rubbing the spoon frenziedly, she inched her buttocks up from the table, tensing herself for the imminent climax. Faster, faster – like the pistons that powered the express train screaming through Buddlestone Parva every afternoon at three: not stopping and unstoppable as it tore through the Suffolk countryside London bound.

Suddenly, the poached eggs in the saucepan rose up on the boil. The hiss of the seethe as it kissed the hot plate interrupted Lucy's love-play. Snarling, she tossed the stained spoon aside and slid down from the table, dragging her heavy buttocks against the smooth pine. Hobbled by her skirt still riding her hips, and by the stretch of her knickers just above her knees, she staggered to the Aga and rescued the eggs.

The heat between her thighs was unquenchable. Lucy snatched down a rolling pin from the second shelf above the stone sink, quickly smeared its surface with a dab of butter, then guided it down between her splayed thighs. Palming the pin, she rubbed her hands frantically, twisting the glistening shaft against her urgent heat. With a shrill scream, the perspiring maid buckled at the knees and orgasmed.

'Come in, girl. I won't eat you.'

Lucy grinned as she remembered the words of greeting at her first meeting with her future mistress.

Balancing the cooled poached eggs, one at a time, on the back of the stained wooden spoon, she levelled them between her thighs and, raising them gently, pressed them tenderly into her wet labia. Shuddering, she pretended each egg to be the Parson's mouth – the Parson being a handsome young devil who filled his evensong pews with all the parish belles – as she anointed them with her weeping joy.

'I won't eat you.'

Lucy giggled. Yes, you will, mistress. She smiled, arranging the eggs neatly on the Sèvres breakfast plate. Yes, you will.

'My breakfast eggs were a trifle salty, Lucy,' Miss Oxford observed as her maid removed the tray.

'Salty, miss?' Lucy murmured, her dark eyes sparkling wickedly.

'No matter. Breakfast was, as it always is, delicious. I think,' the mistress remarked, stepping into her bedroom and absent-mindedly patting the mattress at which she had earlier ravished herself, 'I had better do my prescribed exercises. Not the Swedish drill, this morning, but Doctor Nicholson's strict regimen. A punishing routine, to be sure, but in faith I must adhere to his instructions.'

Miss Oxford supposedly suffered from an incipient ligature. Whatever this was, nobody knew exactly. It remained a matter of confidence between the mistress and her Wimpole Street specialist, who came once a month to The Birches to attend to his private patient's needs.

'The ropes, miss?' Lucy whispered thickly.

'The ropes,' echoed Miss Oxford, her throat tightening with suppressed excitement.

Undressing her mistress, Lucy took careful pains to prolong the preparatory rites to this dark ritual of the ropes. Pretending to understand that this daily indulgence was a strictly medical matter, Lucy suspected her mistress of placating her carnal cravings – cravings which could only be satisfied by being stripped naked and solemnly bound, spreadeagled, to her brass bedstead.

'Stretching the arms, shoulders and spine is so efficacious for the correction of an incipient ligature.'

'Yes, miss,' Lucy agreed, palming the cami-knickers down from the ripe buttocks of her mistress.

'Tied and restrained so tightly,' Miss Oxford murmured, 'my body heals itself of inner distress.'

'Yes, miss.' Lucy fingered the dark lisle stocking-top at Miss Oxford's left thigh.

'Be quick about your business, Lucy.'

The maid gathered up the cami-knickers and stockings and shuddered as her palm grazed the wet patch at the cotton crotch. The wet patch caused by Miss Oxford's early-morning self-pleasuring against the edge of her mattress.

'Hurry, girl.'

'Yes, miss.'

Naked, and trembling with anticipation, the mistress stood before her maid.

'Will you take to your bed, please, miss?' Lucy whispered.

'Of course.' Miss Oxford, strictly for the advancement of medical science, submitted to Doctor Nicholson's strictures. She lay face down, squashing her bare bosom into the satin eiderdown. Lucy watched the upturned buttocks quiver as, buried into the soft satin, the nipples of her supine mistress darkened and thickened. Slowly, luxuriously, Miss Oxford spreadeagled her naked limbs.

Lucy, happy to collude with the whims of her mistress, pressed her thigh into the side of the bed and bent over the waiting nude. In her left hand, she held the gathered coils of several waxed ropes.

'Feet, please, miss.' Lucy deliberately dangled the ropes across the upturned buttocks as she spoke. The bare bottom jerked in response as Miss Oxford stretched her feet wide apart, pointing them into the corners of her bed. Lucy addressed the left ankle, taking it and binding it tightly to the brass bedstead with a two-foot length of cord. Almost immediately, she turned to the other foot, leaving it, moments later, similarly bound. Between the splayed thighs, Lucy saw the dark fig of her mistress ooze and glisten.

'Tighter,' Miss Oxford hissed, unable to conceal a note of pleading. 'Doctor Nicholson is most insistent on that point,' she added hastily.

Playing with the waxed cordage, Lucy grinned. Bending down over each bound ankle, she tightened the knots until her mistress grunted her satisfaction.

'Doctor's orders –' Miss Oxford gasped.

'Must be obeyed, miss,' Lucy purred. The maid did not fully comprehend the dark delights her mistress derived from being stripped naked, then tightly trussed

35

and bound to her brass bedposts. As a maid, it was not her place to question – it was her duty to obey.

'The wrists. Quickly, girl. The wrists.'

'Yes, miss.'

Miss Oxford was twisting her outstretched hands into the satin in a ecstasy of impatience.

'Grasp the bed posts, if you please, miss.'

Lucy saw the knuckles whiten as, gripping each brass pole, her mistress obeyed. Dragging her maid's skirt up over her hips, Lucy climbed on to the bed and mounted her mistress, straddling the naked buttocks with her stockinged thighs. Perched upon the bare buttocks, she leant forward, crushing her breasts into Miss Oxford as she stretched to tie the wrists. Moments later, the maid had rendered her mistress bound and utterly helpless, roped to the gleaming brass. Lucy climbed down from the bed, steadying her descent by planting her left hand across the swollen buttocks. One day, next week – next month, perhaps – she knew that her mistress would beseech Lucy to lightly whip that bare bottom. Lucy bubbled at the thought, and plucked her wet knickers away from her pubis.

'Perhaps,' Miss Oxford's lips whispered into the satin, 'an extra pillow under my hips. As Doctor Nicholson recommends.'

Lucy obliged, managing to brush her fingertips against the pubic coils of her mistress as she inserted the extra pillow.

'A little further down, I think.'

Lucy, smiling, obliged again. Her efforts were rewarded by a soft moan as the calico pillow-slip rasped at Miss Oxford's pouting labia.

'You may leave me now, girl. Return on the hour. The treatment should have worked by then.'

'I have been reading, miss,' Lucy ventured gently.

'Reading?' Miss Oxford echoed faintly.

'From a book in the Boots penny library, miss. It was all about ligaments, miss,' Lucy lied easily.

'Ligaments? Well? Go on, girl.' Miss Oxford nestled herself into the pillow at the base of her belly. Her soft buttocks dimpled.

'In the chapter on ligaments, a German doctor,' Lucy embroidered inventively, 'recommends the vigorous exercise of the hips, miss.' Lucy casually swept her palm across the swell of the upturned cheeks. 'He also writes that contortions here –' her fingertips drummed lightly across the fleshy cheeks '– almost certainly help to assuage the condition.'

A silence fell between the mistress and her maid. Emboldened, Lucy fingered the left buttock delicately. It spasmed at her touch.

'Exercise?' Miss Oxford mumbled into the satin.

'Vigorous contortions. Violent muscular contractions, miss,' Lucy corrected. 'I took the liberty of preparing a paste recommended for that very purpose, miss. Raw ginger to four parts mustard powder,' Lucy purred, picking up a small saucer and teaspoon. 'Applied to a certain place. A place that is, of course, medically approved.'

'A German doctor?'

'Yes, miss.'

'Very well,' Miss Oxford sighed, feigning indifference. 'Apply the tincture.'

'It is most fearsome on application, miss. In order to stem your cries I will bind your mouth with this lint.'

Before Miss Oxford could consent – or protest – the maid had gagged her mistress.

'Now I'll apply the tincture, miss.'

Lucy stood at the bedside, the hem of her black skirt skimming the naked cheeks of the upturned buttocks. Gazing down at their swollen flesh, she saw the creamy mounds flinch and spasm with excited anticipation, then clench with a sudden frisson of fear. Palming the saucer, she took up the silver teaspoon – heavily anointed with the fiery paste – and placed the saucer down. Bending closer, she prised the cheeks apart with the finger and thumb of her left hand, exposing the pink anal whorl. The helpless mistress, bound, gagged and naked, twisted in her strict bondage. Lucy guided the spoon down to the cleft and dragged it between the parted cheeks, deftly working the paste into the rosebud sphincter.

Despite the lint gag, Miss Oxford's squeal was quite audible. Burying her face into the pillow, she writhed and screamed again. Thrashing, her spine twisting and her fingers splayed at the bed posts, the nude jerked in exquisite torment as the paste burned deep within her.

Disregarding the moans just discernible through the gag, Lucy tapped the left buttock with the teaspoon.

'The treatment is a success, miss,' the maid whispered huskily. 'See how your hips are being so vigorously exercised.'

Hammering herself into the strategically placed pillow, Miss Oxford groaned.

'I shall return presently and apply fresh paste to your person, miss. Perhaps it would be wiser to continue with this efficacious treatment until noon. By then,' Lucy murmured, fingering the pillow which would, she knew, already be wet and stickily stained, 'your body should have some relief from its present anguish.'

Smiling, Lucy left the bedroom and skipped down the polished stairs towards the tackle room. She was expected at her master's door, dog whip in hand, in eight minutes. She dared not keep Captain Oxford waiting. Besides, there would be a shilling for her pains.

'Where is the whip I distinctly remember ordering you to bring?'

'The mistress is most anxious that you do not over-exert yourself, sir.'

'To blazes with my interfering sister and her infernal ministrations. Where is she?'

'The mistress is abed till noon, master.'

'Capital. Then I'll have some sport this morning, maid. Come here,' he thundered, jabbing down at the floor with a stiff finger.

Lucy approached her master, who was seated, legs planted wide apart, in his studded leather chair.

'Kneel, my little penitent. Kneel before your master.'

Lucy's knees kissed the carpet. She rested her hands lightly down on his thighs to steady herself.

'Closer,' came the curt command.

She shuffled in between his scissoring thighs. They closed, squeezing and pinning her helplessly. Would it be her breasts? Or – her heart skipped a beat – her mouth? The maid eyed her master's tumultuous shaft, straining in its concealment.

'Be gentle to a poor girl,' Lucy whispered coquettishly as fierce hands cupped and squeezed her breasts, pleasure-punishing their tender, swollen flesh. It was, she realised, to be her bosom for his sport and satisfaction. Soon, her bustier would be peeled away from her proud, rounded globes – then the spear at the base of his hot belly would be dragged out and thrust into her cushioning warmth. Cruel thumbs would ravish her peaked nipples as, buried between her ripeness, the throbbing shaft would spill the master's wet seed.

'Open your mouth, wanton,' he grunted thickly, his hands still brutal at her bosom.

Lucy realised her mistake and, sensing her imminent doom, gasped.

'Wider, my little wench. Wider. The master is at his full measure and means to have his maid.'

39

3

The Secretary

Closing her grey eyes tightly, Imogen kissed the seat of the black leather chair twice. The thrill of the hide at her lips caused her to shiver pleasurably. She sank her face down into its supple warmth. This was the seat of power, and Imogen knelt down before it in a private act of submission. Her pulse throbbed as she licked the leather, dragging her tongue across the smooth surface and relishing the tang. Moaning, the secretary nuzzled the exact spot where The Boss sat – the sleek stretch of hide which dimpled beneath her employer's buttocks.

Imogen opened her eyes and glanced at her watch. Twenty to nine. Rising, she palmed her skirt down over her thighs and patted her hair. Surveying the office, she checked that everything was in order. Imogen was an efficient secretary, and imposed strict organisation on the busy chaos of each working day. On the desk before her, letters to be signed were arrayed neatly. Good. The morning post – opened and arranged in order of priority – lay waiting for inspection. Imogen adjusted the date on the desk-calendar and straightened the pens. Touching the surface of the polished desk, at which The Boss sat every day, brought a bubble of desire between the secretary's labia. Patting her fingertips down at her pubic plum in a brief dabble, she pricked the warm bubble and shuddered as her white cotton panties grew moist.

It was a cold, overcast morning. A bleak sun struggled through the clouds. Imogen turned up the thermostat and pulled down the blinds. Returning to the desk, she stretched out her finger and clicked on the lamp. Perfect. Everything had to be perfect for The Boss. Ten to nine. Just the coffee to make.

Back in the outer office, Imogen paused at her own desk. Her eyes narrowed as they saw the bunch of yellow tea roses over on Susie's desk. Susie was the latest in a long line of pretty, young temps. Yesterday, The Boss had presented the roses with a flourish to Susie and, later, Imogen had watched them head off towards the lift together. Had they parted in the car park? Or had they gone on for a drink? Imogen's knuckles whitened as she kneaded her desk angrily. Her breasts felt swollen and heavy, her face hot. Suddenly, she strode across towards Susie's desk and snatched a fistful of petals from the roses, her jealous hand quivering with rage.

The lift door opened. Panicked out of her trance, the secretary scampered back to her desk, tossing the petals into her waste bin. By the time the door opened to admit Susie, Imogen was buried in her work.

'Can't do a thing till I've fixed my slap,' Susie giggled, fishing out her compact and plying a candy-pink lipstick.

Imogen merely nodded, furtively appraising the lusciously curved temp. Appraising – and strongly disapproving of – the temp's suede mini, red tights, scuffed trainers and tight lambswool sweater stretched across braless breasts. Breasts which were firm, rounded and which bounced at the least provocation. Imogen saw the nipples peeping with bold impudence through the taut lambswool. Returning her gaze down to the document on her desk, Imogen compared and contrasted her own appearance with that of the pert temp as Susie, oblivious to any scrutiny, deftly applied her lipstick, pressing the glistening pink shaft up against her mouth.

A secretary must be sober and sensible, and Imogen was exactly that: adhering strictly to the office dress code of a dark pleated skirt, crisp white blouse and cashmere cardigan. She always wore light bronze stockings and inspected the seams every morning to ensure that they were uniformly straight. Her only concession to feminine indulgence was her underwear – the tasteful Lejaby bra with half cups, the waspie suspender with matching white panties cut high at the thigh. Sober and sensible. Even when the secretary's thighs brushed together beneath her desk, the whisper of her nylon stockings was barely audible.

Imogen watched the lipstick retract into its gold sheath then disappear into the temp's spangled purse. She secretly preened, certain the The Boss would soon tire of the easy allure of the brash young temp. Imogen was supremely confident that her understated style – provocatively demure – would outshine Susie's babe-chic.

The lift doors hissed. Imogen's heart fluttered. The Boss was coming. Susie was doing her eyes. Good. Imogen unfurled a complicated spreadsheet and bowed down over it. It rustled beneath her trembling fingertips. The door opened and The Boss entered. She was dressed in an impeccable black Chanel outfit. Imogen immediately approved. The Boss always achieved that severe City look. The secretary also approved of the Aigner leather satchel, expensive shoes and the discreet perfume – Givenchy's Organza. The Boss, Imogen noted, was wearing Fogal tights. So soft, so sooty black. Imogen's mouth felt dry; her tongue thickened. She flushed and wrestled with the spreadsheet as she struggled to ignore the heat between her prickling thighs. The heat fuelled by the cool competence and exquisite elegance exuded by The Boss. The heat which threatened to dampen her tight panties with her ooze of arousal.

42

'Susie,' The Boss murmured, approaching the temp's desk. 'Too much mascara. Makes you look like a panda.'

Susie giggled. Imogen squirmed.

'Get the Meadowhouse file and come straight in. I need you.'

Imogen's eyes darkened to a shade of steel. Her lipstick-free mouth compressed into a tight line as she watched the mini-skirted hips sway insolently, as Susie followed The Boss into the inner office. The jealous secretary splayed her fingers and then clenched them up into a fist of fury – almost breaking a nail that dug into her soft palm.

Forty minutes later. Susie was still behind the closed door with The Boss. Blinking away the tears gathering in her grey eyes, Imogen failed to wipe away the images tormenting her inner eye. With it, she pictured The Boss pacing the carpet in the office next door, treading the soft pile silently as she stalked behind the temp. Susie would no doubt be sitting in the big leather chair, casually swinging her legs. The eyes of The Boss would be watching the scuffed trainers, then sweep up the curved lines of the young temp's legs and pause at the spot where the suede mini teasingly concealed the swell of the thighs. Susie would swivel round, sucking on a pencil, her pink lips sucking hard as she frowned. As she swivelled, her breasts would joggle under the lambswool sweater, the swollen spheres of firm flesh straining at the taut stretch across the nipples. The Boss would be gazing at the moist lips – lips full and glossy with candy-pink lipstick. Lips as wet and succulent as those between the temp's thighs, tormentingly concealed by the pert mini.

Why was it so quiet? In the loud silence, Imogen suddenly surrendered to panic. They were not talking in there. But in her feverish imaginings, she was convinced that The Boss would be busy with her tongue. Busy at the temp's neck, then at each soft breast. Or was Susie already bent across the desk, thighs wide, her tights dragged down? Was The Boss probing Susie's succulent fig – flickering her tongue and flattening it against the sticky labia? Or plunging it repeatedly into the warmth of their welcoming smile? Licking, sucking and lapping.

A sweat blinded the secretary's eyes, eyes screwed up in impotent fury. Yes. She could hear the faint liquid sounds. A soft, haunting lapping. Imogen opened her eyes – and saw the coffee percolator. Plop. Plop. Plop. A soft, liquid sound. She breathed out loudly. Her breasts felt heavy and tight. Panting slightly, she dried her wet palms against the swell of her hips, but the images returned to torment her. In her jealous rage, she now imagined The Boss inching up her Chanel skirt to straddle the plump buttocks across the desk. The Fogal tights would be peeled down, then the panties, so that The Boss could dominate and enjoy the upturned cheeks with her pubis, sweeping her slit down across the passive bottom again and again.

Imogen snatched a tissue from the box on her desk and strode across to the water-cooler. Wetting the tissue, she patted it against her flushed cheeks and then pressed it against her forehead. The throbbing in her head ceased, but her aching heart was still hammering. She turned and scanned Susie's desk, wincing once again at the yellow tea roses in their vase. On the desk, she spotted two neatly typed sheets, both signed by The Boss and waiting to be faxed. Small square post-it notes, each bearing a scribbled fax number, were attached to the typewritten sheets. Imogen recognised the paperwork, each sheet representing two weeks' hard work. Part of an important two-way deal The Boss was setting up. Any mistake at this stage of negotiations would be fatal. Imogen tiptoed across to Susie's desk. Any mistake, she whispered softly, smiling with feline malice. It was the work of a ruthless moment to swap over the two post-it notes.

The rest of the morning slipped by quickly. Imogen had held her breath as Susie – back at her desk after a full hour with The Boss – sent off the two faxes. At twelve, the secretary told the temp that she was taking an early lunch.

Lunch for Imogen was usually a hurried tuna and sweetcorn roll, followed by a leisurely interlude in the lingerie section of a nearby department store. As a woman among women, Imogen could pass unchallenged in the intimate atmosphere of the changing cubicles. Clutching a suspender belt or an underwired brassière and wearing the harassed frown of the busy lunchtime shopper, Imogen could draw back the cubicle curtains and – smiling an apology – withdraw: after drinking her fill of the near-naked bodies swathed in silk and satin confections.

Once, only two weeks ago, Imogen had drawn back the beige curtain to discover a dark-eyed Italian, a raven-haired beauty in her early forties, stripped down to a pair of navy tights. The shapely matron was gazing into the mirror indecisively, hesitating between a cotton sports bra and a sensuous lace bustier. Imogen had shrugged her well-rehearsed apology but the Italian detained her with red, pouting lips. What did Imogen think? The cotton or the frothy lace? Stepping into the cubicle, and drawing together the heavy curtains behind her, Imogen had been willing to oblige. Turning to face Imogen, the Italian planted her feet slightly apart and filled the cotton sports bra with her swollen olive-hued breasts. Thumbing the straps at her shoulders, she had offered her freshly bondaged bosom up to Imogen's steady gaze for approval. Nodding appreciatively, Imogen had indicated the lace bustier. Crushing her buttocks, bulging within the sheen of the navy tights, back into the full-length mirror, the Italian had peeled off the clinging sports bra. Bending, so that her heavy breasts tumbled deliciously, she had plucked up the bustier and sheathed her bosom in its delicate lace.

Imogen licked her fingertips and dabbed at her lips with a paper tissue. The tuna and sweetcorn roll had been delicious. Imogen always prepared her lunch herself, adding dill and chives to the mayo. She always had tuna and sweetcorn on a Tuesday. She rose from her park bench and headed towards a huge weeping willow tree. She was not going to the lingerie department today. Today was Tuesday. Imogen lived her life to a precisely planned schedule: a life driven by order and discipline. On Tuesdays, Imogen had a regular appointment under the weeping willow.

Eleven minutes past one. In the distance, at the edge of the park, the hum of busy traffic seemed to fade. Nearby, in a holly bush, a linnet sang sweetly. Shrouded by the cascade of tapering branches of the weeping willow, Imogen was invisible. She rested against the slender trunk, bathed in the green light of the canopy, listening intently. Thirteen minutes past. Imogen frowned, irritated by any lack of punctuality. No, wait. She sighed as she heard the approach of horse's hooves clip-clopping along the asphalt pathway.

The jingle of harness and the soft neigh of a horse stretching down to graze caused Imogen's heart to thump excitedly. The curtain of foliage parted and a svelte brunette, attired impeccably for the saddle, strode into the seclusion beneath the weeping willow. Imogen's eyes watched with excited fascination as the polished boots trod the mossy grass firmly. The rider pushed Imogen down on to her knees, then settled her shoulders and jodhpured buttocks against the tree trunk before tossing her black velvet riding hat down on to the sedge. Imogen shivered expectantly and raised her eyes up, gazing at the tangle of brunette curls being shaken free.

Imogen lowered her eyes, taking in the yellow-gloved fingers slowly unbuttoning the black fitted jacket. As Imogen knelt in silence, her eyes wide with wonder, the yellow-gloved fingers inched the taut jodhpurs down.

The rider (her name unknown – Imogen had retrieved and returned a dropped crop, several Tuesdays ago) wriggled her pantied buttocks into the trunk of the willow, riding the wood with splayed cheeks so that her hot cleft kissed the silvery bark. Imogen responded, her hand instantly down at her pubis, but the tip of the riding crop swept the kneeling woman's fingers away from her prickling heat.

The jodhpurs bound the brunette at her knees. Imogen moaned and tongued the roof of her mouth as her eyes feasted on the dark nest of pubic curls beneath the stretch of white panties. In continuing silence, the rider applied the tip of her crop to her pubis, guiding it down against her belly and into the panties. Imogen shuffled, closer, but the crop – now wet at the tip from the labia it tormented – stayed her progress.

All Imogen was allowed was the little wet leather loop. She was allowed to sniff it, kiss it, suck it and bite into it softly. Still kneeling, alone beneath the willow, Imogen heard the retreating clip-clop of the horse – and a nearby church clock strike two.

All hell seemed to have broken out by the time she returned, flushed, from lunch. Stepping out of the lift, she heard The Boss shouting. Entering the outer office, she saw that Susie was in tears. Imogen threaded her way diplomatically between them and resumed her seat at her desk. As she had planned, the rogue faxes had found their way to the wrong destinations – potentially destroying any chance The Boss had of pulling off her deal. Susie, Imogen gathered, was in very hot water. The Boss was seething.

'Get into my office, girl.'

'But I only –'

'At once.'

'I didn't –'

Imogen relished the bewildered protests from the tearful temp.

'At once,' The Boss barked. 'I'll teach you –' but the slammed door cut off the flow of anger in the middle of its spate.

As soon as the echo of the slammed door had faded, Imogen darted across to it and knelt down. There was no keyhole for her to peep through but, with her ear pressed against the wood, she could hear.

Voices – one in anger, one in penitence – from behind the closed door brought a sleek smile of satisfaction to the secretary's lips. A silence followed. Then a barely audible rustling. Decoding the sound, Imogen knew that a bottom was being bared and prepared for punishment. Muffled whimpers confirmed this, as did the first sharp slap: the unmistakeable sound of a firm palm spanking soft cheeks. Imogen clenched her fists in delight. At her slit, the hot wet arousal generated by her lunch-hour fantasy rekindled and blazed with an unquenchable flame. A second spank was swiftly followed by the searing crack of a third. A grunt of satisfaction from The Boss was drowned by Susie's wail. Four more crisp spanks came in rapid, merciless succession. Imogen hugged her breasts as she relished every second of the temp's chastisement.

As The Boss punished Susie, the secretary knelt at the door. Dragging her skirt up over her hips and bottom, Imogen splayed her thighs – burning her nyloned knees briefly as she swept them into the carpet – and sought out her juicy plum-flesh with first two, then three fingers firmly welded together. After a brief pause, during which Imogen pictured The Boss palming the temp's reddening buttocks as more harsh words were spoken, the spanking recommenced behind the closed office door. Imogen masturbated urgently, determined to come to the sound of Susie's suffering. Insinuating her fingers beneath her panties she worked them busily at her clitoris. Beyond the door, the temp squealed beneath a renewed staccato of stinging spanks. Tossing her head back, Imogen snarled with frustration. Easing her buttocks up from her heels, she thumbed down her white panties and speared her fingers into her hot slit. Pumping ruthlessly, she sensed her climax welling. Her nipples peaked painfully into the captive silk of her Lejaby bra. Her belly spasmed. Spank. Spank. Susie screamed softly, the sharp cry of anguish spilling Imogen into orgasm.

As if the door had suddenly opened, Imogen could clearly see the punishment inside in perfect detail behind her closed eyes: the pinioning hand of The Boss at Susie's neck; the temp bent firmly across the Chanel skirt; the mini riding the writhing thighs; the red tights peeled down below the soft hollow of each knee; the sweep of the clamped thighs up to the poised peach-cheeks. Poised, plump peach-cheeks: already red-ripe from the hot hand that bruised them.

Tumbling head-first down into the carpet, Imogen rasped her open wetness into its roughness. Smothering her scream of ecstasy just in time, Imogen came again, her orgasm redoubled by the final flurry of spanks as The Boss vented her fury on the bare-bottomed temp.

The door to the inner office opened and Susie skittled out, sobbing. She darted out towards the loo. Feigning an indifference to the drama, Imogen kept her head bowed down over her desk. The perfect secretary, and the very picture of sobriety, diligence and efficiency. The Boss stormed out of her office, marched across to Susie's desk and cleared it with one imperious sweep of her arm. The yellow tea roses crashed down, spilling petals into the sudden puddle below. The Boss withdrew to her lair in angry silence.

49

Susie returned, twelve minutes later, peering cautiously into the office. Still snuffling and rubbing her sore bottom, she stooped down at the edge of her desk and retrieved her possessions: a bottle of purple nail varnish, a KitKat and several small plastic toy animals. Rising, she wiped a stray tear from her cheek, sniffled, then turned to go.

'One moment,' Imogen whispered.

Susie paused.

'Your money,' the secretary continued in a soft tone, approaching the temp and handing over the small envelope.

Head bowed, Susie stretched out her hand.

'Just one more matter to attend to,' Imogen murmured.

'What?' Susie replied sulkily.

Ignoring the retort, Imogen steered the temp backwards towards the photocopier. Pinning her prey against it, the secretary yanked up the suede mini and jerked down the tights, then the panties, of the startled temp. Susie's reddened cheeks squashed up against the xerox.

'Up,' Imogen commanded curtly.

Struggling, Susie obeyed, splaying her punished cheeks down on to the cold glass.

'Sit still,' Imogen snarled, pinning the squirming temp down. Deftly jabbing her forefinger, Imogen blinked as the bright greenish light exploded beneath the scarlet buttocks. By the time the copier had disgorged the A3-size haunting image of the spanked bottom, Susie had scampered out through the door.

Six minutes past six. Imogen secreted the xerox of Susie's suffering she had been scrutinising intently into the bottom of her trophy drawer. It nestled down on to a pile of similar images of similarly ousted temps.

Six fourteen. The hectic day was almost done. The

Boss emerged from her inner sanctum, discovering her assiduous secretary still networking on the phone.

'I think I've got everything under control. Back to how they should be,' Imogen purred, putting the phone down. 'We're back to square one.'

'Start again as if nothing ever happened,' The Boss countered suavely.

'Exactly,' Imogen rejoined primly, adding, 'I'll see to it that you get what you want.'

'You always do.' Bending down, The Boss kissed Imogen full on the lips. The secretary grasped the sides of her chair as she felt the muscled tongue probe her mouth. Beneath her desk, she squeezed her nyloned thighs tightly together, as if to contain her arousal. Withdrawing her tongue, slowly, then her lips – even more slowly – from Imogen's mouth, The Boss stood up straight and, gazing down, studied the enigmatic mask of servile obedience below.

'You always do,' she whispered.

Imogen shivered with pleasure.

Suggesting that they might have a coffee before going, The Boss returned to her office and closed the door.

Milk. Imogen – the perfect organiser and strategic planner – had not calculated for this, but she knew that a half pint could be bought from the late-night Asian shop opposite reception downstairs.

On her return, the carton of milk clutched triumphantly in her hand, Imogen saw at a glance that her trophy drawer – like the door to the inner office – was open. The voice of The Boss called out sternly, summoning the secretary. Imogen obeyed. Inside, she saw The Boss waiting, a cane gripped in one hand, the xerox of Susie's chastised cheeks in the other.

The Boss tapped the seat of the leather chair with the tip of her whippy cane. Imogen's eyes widened a fraction as the yellow bamboo dimpled the dark hide.

'Bend over. You may be indispensable, but that does

51

not preclude my rewarding you for your unique brand of loyalty.'

Imogen, flushing at the mocking irony, approached the leather chair in a daze of delicious dread. This morning, she had kissed it with her lips. This evening, she kissed it with her breasts, then her belly, as she eased herself down across the chair for punishment.

'And tomorrow,' The Boss whispered softly as she arranged the secretary's pleated skirt, adjusting it up over the thighs and hips in preparation for the impending caning, 'I will interview and appoint another temp.'

Imogen raised her hips up as The Boss thumbed down her panties, baring the buttocks for the bamboo.

'We must make sure that she has the right qualifications, of course.'

The cane traced a dominant line up along the quivering seam of Imogen's stockinged left leg. It hesitated briefly at the swell of the cheek above the darker band of nylon, teasing the button of the suspender strap that bit into the stretched stocking-top. Imogen clenched her naked buttocks tightly. Expectantly.

'She must be pretty,' The Boss hissed.

Swish. The cane swept down, cutting into the proffered buttocks.

'She must be pert.'

Swish. The second slicing stroke drew a moan of dark pleasure from the lips of the whipped secretary.

'And, before her departure in disgrace, see to it that I have good cause to punish her.'

Burying her hot face in the leather chair, Imogen inched her seared cheeks up: up for the next delicious stroke.

4

The Nurse

A cow elephant trumpeted faintly in the distance. Her call was answered by a squeal from her calf. Anna smiled. From her window at the rear of the Regent's Park private clinic, she could hear but not see the nearby zoo.

Lunchtime. The elephants would be tucking in. Anna curled her tongue along the edge of the stolen blini and captured the elusive pearl of caviar. It slipped down to her chin. Lapping it up, she grinned. Eating caviar was just like kissing a wet slit. Shivering with pleasure, she relished the slightly salty tang.

The patients enjoyed a *de luxe* range of menus at the exclusive clinic – and so did the nurses, if they were quick-witted and light-fingered.

It was hot. Stripped to her bra and panties, Anna stretched out on her bed – she wasn't on duty for another hour – and slowly enjoyed a third caviar-laden blini.

Footsteps. The measured tread of Matron's brogues. Anna scrambled from her bed and dashed to the window. The footsteps stopped outside her bedroom door. She tossed the two remaining blinis out and frantically wiped her palms against her pantied buttocks. The sharp double tap at her door caused her heart to quicken. Had she locked her door? She usually took that precaution when scoffing luxurious titbits

53

stolen from the patients. A second double tap, then the handle was tried briskly. Anna held her breath. The door remained closed. Swallowing silently, Anna tiptoed to the door and bent down to listen, her breasts bulging as she stooped. She heard Matron's predatory footsteps retreating. Sighing, Anna rose and rested her back against the wall, crushing her soft buttocks into its cool surface.

Closing her eyes, she shuddered as memories from her time at the strict training school haunted her. Pupil nurses were punished for the slightest misdemeanour, and Anna had on numerous occasions found herself across the stern Sister's knee for a blistering, bare-bottomed spanking. And there was a particularly cruel blonde staff nurse, Anna remembered, who had – during a brief but memorable reign of terror – almost come to regard Anna's buttocks as personal property to be reddened and chastised at the slightest sadistic whim.

Grinding her soft cheeks against the wall as if to erase the memory of those painful punishments, Anna shivered as one particular episode flooded back – the evening when she had been caught soaping and fingering another pupil nurse in their shared shower. After forcng Anna to stand naked under a cold jet of water for several agonising minutes, the blonde staff nurse had taken Anna by the hand across to a bathtub and forced her down by the nape of the neck – still shivering and slippery from her shower – over the white porcelain rim.

Staff had slowly taken off her broad blue belt and the whipping of Anna's naked cheeks had continued for eight searing minutes, leaving the chastised pupil nurse sniffling in her burning shame and pain. Yes, Anna smiled ruefully. She had certainly graduated from training school a thoroughly well-disciplined nurse.

Suppressing a giggle at the distant memories – memories which had managed to moisten the cotton panties kissing her pubis – Anna cautiously unlocked her door and inched it open a fraction. Her eyes widened as they met Matron's penetrating gaze. Anna saw the pair of brogues clutched in Matron's left hand. Unshod, the stern Director of Nurses had returned, unsuspected, to Anna's door on nylon-stockinged tiptoe.

'Major Spens has complained about the loss of several of his luncheon caviar canapés,' Matron snapped, pushing the door – and Anna – aside and entering the room. 'You were the last member of staff in the vicinity. Did you take them?'

Anna denied the charge, secure in her knowledge that any incriminating evidence had been destroyed.

'Hands,' Matron commanded.

Timidly, Anna surrendered her hands, palms up, for Matron's inspection. Grasping each wrist, Matron drew the trembling fingertips up to her nostrils. The nostrils flared as she sniffed suspiciously.

'Been playing with yourself, nurse?'

Anna, blushing, shook her head. 'No, Matron.'

'Then it must be the smell of stolen caviar.'

Anna shook her head more vigorously, but sensed her doom.

A breeze ruffled the curtain. Dropping the captive hands, Matron paced across to the window. Scanning the outer sill, she suddenly stretched down her forefinger and dabbed at a single caviar pearl. Anna felt her belly flutter with fear as Matron turned around, her admonishing finger aloft.

'Kneel. Face down across the bed.'

'But –'

'Arms outstretched,' Matron purred. She sucked her fingertip, noisily consuming the caviar.

Anna obeyed – to refuse would mean instant dismissal and exile, without references, from the pampered existence of the private clinic.

Face-down across the bed, her buttocks poised for punishment, Anna heard Matron busy at the wardrobe.

'There's no more,' Anna murmured, her words muffled by the satin duvet at her lips.

'I'm not looking for stolen titbits, nurse,' Matron replied ominously. She rummaged about at the bottom of the wardrobe; then Anna heard the grunt of satisfaction.

'Ah, perfect.' The wardrobe door clicked shut.

Risking a peep, Anna glanced over her shoulder. She saw Matron meditatively fingering the ribbed sole of a white tennis pump. Anna buried her face down into the duvet, the fleeting image of Matron flexing the supple pump burning behind her tightly shut eyes.

'Petty pilfering must and most certainly will be punished, nurse. I propose to beat you. And if I ever catch you stealing from any of our patients –' Matron swished the pump down across her open palm, making her meaning painfully clear. 'Major Spens must be compensated,' she continued, bending down to finger Anna's panties. 'An apology, then a little treat to make up for his loss. I will think of something.'

Nuzzling her duvet, Anna flinched and pressed her thighs together. Matron's words seared her brain just as fiercely as the pump would soon be blistering her bare bottom. A little treat. Anna shuddered, knowing that by nightfall her plastic-gloved hand would have pleasured and brought relief to the Major – a relief which he would spurt all over her uniformed bosom.

'Bottom up, nurse,' Matron rasped, tapping the cheeks quivering before her with the pump. 'Knees together. Come along, nurse. You know perfectly well how I want you,' she added, dropping her voice to a tone of whispered venom.

Anna felt the capable touch of competent hands at her bottom and thighs as Matron positioned the kneeling nurse and prepared her for her pain.

Would Matron kneel alongside? Pressing her stockinged thighs into Anna's naked flesh? Or would Matron remain standing, feet planted slightly apart, to administer the pump across her victim's rump? Tormented by these thoughts, Anna shivered.

A soft rustling sound broke the silence. Anna flinched as the white pump, tossed down on to the duvet, landed an inch from her face, a stray curl of lace tickling her nose. Matron, her skirt up over her hips, straddled the kneeling nurse, instantly pinioning Anna's pantied buttocks between a firm pincer of nylon-stockinged thighs. Anna squirmed beneath the sudden weight of Matron. It was a futile gesture. With her heavy buttocks pinning Anna down, Matron remained dominantly in control of the bottom she was about to beat.

Anna whimpered softly as she felt her cotton panties being peeled down across the swell of her upthrust cheeks, and whimpered again as the tight band of fabric welded her thighs together three inches above her knees: bunching her buttocks superbly for the ravishes of the impending pump. The hands that had bared her bottom and rolled the panties down into a cunning band of bondage returned to the naked cheeks. Palms down, they rested lightly across the curved flesh. Anna gasped as the controlling hands across her bottom slowly taloned and squeezed. As her dark cleft yawned painfully, Anna made a last-ditch bid to escape, wriggling frantically beneath Matron's plump bottom. Matron grunted softly, squeezed her thighs tightly and ravaged the captive cheeks severely to quell the token defiance beneath her. Anna writhed, grinding her brassièred breasts into the duvet, and squealed. In their tight cups, her breasts bulged, the nipples inflamed into thickened peaks of anguish.

The moment she squealed, Anna was crisply spanked into silence. Satisfied that her little thief was utterly subdued, Matron swept her right hand back, knuckles dimpling the duvet, to retrieve the white pump. Anna saw the pawing hand move crablike across the silk until it found, and grasped, the rubber-soled shoe. The inquisitive hand withdrew, clutching its prize. Anna gulped – and clenched her buttocks in a reflex of dread.

'No,' Matron chided, tapping each buttock dominantly with the toe of the pump. 'Relax your bottom.'

Anna obeyed, digging her toes into the carpet as the rubber pump kissed her soft flesh.

'Thighs together.'

That was the signal. Anna knew that her punishment was about to commence. She buried her face in the smooth silk, biting into it to smother her squeals of suffering.

Swiping the pump down savagely, Matron administered three cruel strokes to the unblemished right cheek. It darkened quickly from cream to crimson. Four more strokes followed, the punishment delivered at a slower, more searching, pace: two across each cheek. Anna bucked and writhed as the rubber burnt her rump, but remained utterly helpless beneath Matron's weight and between the fierce grip of the imprisoning stockinged thighs at her cheeks.

The menacing pump paused in mid-air above the reddening buttocks. Anna felt her punisher inching backwards, so now it was Matron's knees pincering her trapped bottom – pincering and squeezing the ravished cheeks. Anna moaned as her hot buttocks bulged.

'And don't think that I have forgotten that you must make full reparation to Major Spens,' Matron said, levelling the sole of the pump across Anna's bottom. 'Full reparation.'

The pump spoke loudly again, barking out a staccato of pain across the hot cheeks five more times. Tossing the white pump aside, Matron massaged Anna's scorched flesh slowly and rhythmically. 'Do you understand?'

'Yes, Matron.' A tear silvered the duvet beneath the penitent's face. A thumbtip traced the outline of her left cheek. Anna wriggled.

'And now you know the penalty for pilfering, nurse?'

'Yes, Matron.'

'Now get dressed and be about your duties.'

'Yes, Matron.' Anna held her breath in her tightening throat as she sensed the thumbtip sweep across the crown of her buttock and dip down fleetingly into the sticky heat at her cleft.

As the door closed behind Matron, Anna struggled up from the bed and dragged her panties to her bottom. She shuddered as the tight cotton cupped her scalded buttocks and gasped aloud as the fabric bit into her cleft. Fingering her panties to loosen them, she snatched up the white tennis pump and tapped its toe against her tingling slit. Parting her thighs and scrunching her toes into the carpet, she guided the rubber toe to her clitoris and gently stroked. Beneath the stretch of wet cotton, the pink thorn stiffened. Worrying the rubber into herself, Anna hissed as she felt her juices bubble. The bubble burst into a warm dribble, and her clitoris rose up in response.

No. She was on duty soon. There was not enough time to achieve the release she ached for. Tossing the pump down, Anna reached out and snatched up a fresh pair of panties. Black. The cool silk slithered in her palm. Stepping out of her soiled cotton pair – which she used to wipe her puffy labia dry – she moaned softly as she relished the crisp feel of her fresh panties. She changed her bra to match, gently easing her swollen breasts into the cool cups and gasping as her stubby inflamed nipples rasped into the waiting silk.

A black waspie suspender belt encircled her waist, hugging her soft flesh deliciously. Hurrying now – fearful of Matron's remarkable capacity for vigilance and vengeance – Anna did not linger over the customary sensual pleasures of donning her black seamed stockings. She quickly palmed them up to her thighs, smoothed and then snapped them into place. Her candy pink-and-white-striped uniform followed, fitting her figure like an amorous glove. The addition of a wide belt at her waist, an inverted watch at her bosom and a pert little lace cap completed her attire.

Better check. Several patients were known to report untidy or unkempt nurses to Matron – and known to eavesdrop on the chastisement that quickly followed. Anna swivelled and checked her seams in the mirror. She pulled a face as she saw that her left stocking was slightly awry. Clutching the hem of her tight skirt, she wriggled and struggled as she pulled her uniform up over her bottom.

Her eyes caught the reflection in the glass. She paused, transfixed, seduced by the image of her own bottom. Her own bottom, recently punished, framed by the black suspenders. She blinked and, bending, attended to her task. Stretching down, Anna palmed the errant stocking into position. The seam arrowed obediently up towards the buttock above. Excellent. Anna paused once more. In the glass, she saw her reddened cheek bulging out from the tight silk of her panties. Her throat tightened. Arousal maddened her prickling slit. No. I mustn't. Not now. But the crimson flesh against the black silk juiced her, flooding her brain with the dark pleasures of her recent pain, and her hot labia with fresh pulses of arousal.

But fear of Matron's lash was stronger than her longing to finger herself and come. Besides, she could grab a quick shower just before tea. Her bottom would still be pink from punishment – pink enough to excite her and fuel her fingers at her slit.

In Cassandra Wing, Anna found her patient lying naked, face-down, waiting for her pubic shave. The well-known actress was flicking through *Vogue*, the 'nil by mouth' sign above the pillows keeping the lid firmly down on a huge box of exquisite Belgian chocolates. Anna teased the ribbon aside, prised the lid up and pinched a praline. The slight movement – and slighter sound – arrested the next page of *Vogue*. The lizard eyes flickered up, blinked, and returned to peruse the La Perla underwear ad.

'May I prepare you?' Anna murmured deferentially.

Ignoring Anna, the celebrity (in for a lipo job on her heavy buttocks) gazed down intently at the bra ad.

'Theatre's waiting,' Anna cajoled pleasantly, smothering the urge to spank the bare bottom before her.

Allowing *Vogue* to slither to the floor, the star of stage and screen sighed petulantly and rolled over, her eyes closed, her ripe bosoms jiggling. She was not, Anna spotted, a natural blonde.

'Proceed.' The vowels were languid. The tone was 'box office' bored.

Bending down to the bed, Anna slipped a draw sheet under the raised hips and generous buttocks of the naked actress and arranged the silver dish, shaving foam, tissues and tiny razor on the bed.

Spread 'em, bitch, Anna wanted to say, but meekly suggested that the household name should inch her thighs apart a fraction. The household name obliged, presenting her dark bush that belied the tumbling golden curls on her pillow.

'Relax; you won't feel a thing,' Anna murmured reassuringly as she squirted and then fingered foam over the tempting pubis.

'You remind me of my latest leading man,' the star drawled.

The razor rasped against the quivering foam, leaving half-inch-wide bands of pink flesh in its wake. From the pillow came a soft sigh, then a carnal grunt. The blonde cupped her breasts and squashed them. Anna plied the blade deftly. Two minutes later, she was almost done. Stray wisps had eluded her efforts. Pinching the rubbery lips of the labia together, she dealt with them. Spreading the flesh-lips apart with the finger and thumb of her plastic-gloved left hand, she dealt with the few remaining. The succulent plum was now bald, pink and gleaming. Anna longed to tongue the freshly shaven skin. Tongue, lick and lap the stretched satin of the delta.

'There,' Anna whispered, dabbing with a tissue. 'A little sprinkle of medicated talc, hm?'

A snarl from the blonde – now squeezing her breasts with vicious tenderness – caused Anna to glance up anxiously.

'Talc? No. Just pleasure me.' The nude rolled over, wriggled down into the sheet and inched her buttocks up. Parting her thighs, she presented her wet fig for Anna's inspection – and attention.

'I'm not –' Anna said, huskily. It was purely a preliminary precaution. Residents all got what they demanded and desired in this exclusive clinic.

'It's there on top of the cabinet,' the blonde snapped, jabbing her forefinger impatiently.

Following the flash of the varnished nail, Anna spotted the two twenties folded tightly under the stem of an empty champagne flute. 'Yes, miss,' she whispered, her voice softer than the rustle of the crisp notes sliding into her stocking-top.

Anna snapped on a fresh pair of plastic gloves, then adroitly annointed the index fingertip of her right hand with lubricant jelly and, to the waiting blonde's delight, plunged it firmly into the rosebud sphincter between the swollen cheeks.

'Yes,' the blonde hissed – then bit her pillow as Anna teased, then twisted her finger, in the tight warmth.

'Harder, faster –'

Anna pumped rhythmically, ruthlessly. The bare buttocks arched up in supplication. Anna inched her finger out slowly and worried the puckered anal whorl

– the blonde mewed – then rammed it savagely into the hot hole. The blonde screamed her loud delight. The first orgasm was sudden and shrill. Anna worked busily at the bottom until a second climax exploded, announced by a husky moan.

'No,' Anna said sternly, planting her splayed fingers across the wide bottom and pinning the cheeks down. 'I'm not finished with you, yet.'

Writhing in delicious expectation, the actress begged for more. Anna peeled away her soiled gloves and replaced them. Gathering the blonde's wrists together above the bare bottom – and pinioning the nude fiercely – she bent down to locate the fleshy hood that hid the clitoris.

'Please –' the nude squealed.

A sharp spank both reddened her bottom and silenced her lips. Anna fingertipped the clitoris and teased it out. It rose into a tiny stiff salute. Anna nipped it gently between a pincer of fingertip and thumb. The blonde jerked her hips. Her soft, fleshy cheeks, bearing the single red spank impression, wobbled. Anna tugged and tweaked the captive pleasure-thorn.

'Yes,' gasped the blonde, pounding her breast and belly into the bed. 'Yes.'

Anna quelled the excited nude with two crisp spanks. In her controlling left hand, the two helpless wrists writhed. In a reflex of pain, the blonde's hands tightened into clenched fists.

Fists. Anna scrunched her plastic-gloved hand up into a shining fist and gently knuckled the wet fig. The actress spread her thighs wide. Anna felt the heat of the exposed flesh through the plastic gloves. The knuckles skimmed the sticky labia, then fleetingly grazed the inner softness. The thighs were now painfully widened to receive and relish this exquisite torment.

'Ride me, girl,' the blonde groaned. 'There's a strap-on in the second drawer. Please,' she half-commanded, half-implored. 'Chick-dick me till I'm raw.'

Anna paused, slowly dragging her knuckles up to, then against, the pink clitoris. She inched her thighs away from the edge of the bed. The moment was coming. Her moment of erotic ennoblement. The moment when she would be transformed from being a mere menial to becoming the dominant mistress of the nude stretched out on the bed before her. Face down, naked and helpless before her. In her absolute thrall.

Anna savoured the moment as she palmed the crown of each fleshy cheek slowly and rhythmically. As a basic-grade nurse in this exclusive clinic, Anna was for the most part treated little more than a paid slave. She had to learn to obey very quickly and strive to satisfy the whims of each and every patient. But on such occasions as these, she became the queen of the moment: totally in control and in command of the quivering flesh she ruled.

'Ride you?' she echoed faintly. 'Yes, miss.' Despite the pretence of submissive obedience, Anna's voice thrilled with assured dominance.

A surge of savage joy blazed within her as Anna snatched up the hem of her uniform skirt and, mounting the bed – and the blonde – straddled the proffered buttocks.

'And just what particular treatment do you call this?' the voice of Matron rasped from the doorway.

Frozen in the very act of guiding her wet slit down on to the submissive bottom, Anna gasped aloud and then sank back slowly on to her heels, dragging her sticky lips down across the swell of the naked cheeks. The blonde squealed her delight. Anna shivered in terror.

'Well?' thundered Matron, closing the door behind her and striding towards the bed.

'I –' Anna stammered.

Matron stepped up to the bed, severely spanked

Anna's bare bottom twice and snatched the two twenties from the exposed stocking top.

'Disgraceful,' she spluttered. Immediately, in a silent mime, Matron nodded to the blonde's hands. Hold them tightly together, she both mouthed silently and pantomimed, pinning her own starched cuffs together.

Taking her cue, Anna nodded.

'Absolutely disgraceful,' Matron apologised, pocketing one of the twenties and returning the other to Anna's thigh with a wink. Producing a large dildo from her side pocket, Matron inserted it in between Anna's teeth – then stormed out in a pretence of outrage.

Lowering her head so that the tip of the bulbous shaft nuzzled the pink of the nude's wet plum, Anna grabbed the actress by each wrist and pinned her to the bed. The blonde grunted softly. Closing her eyes, Anna drove the dildo home. The blonde grunted again.

'We set very high standards here, nurse. Very high. Do you understand?'

'Yes, Matron.'

'Did you prepare our celeb for her liposuction?'

Anna, who had finished the blonde off with her tongue and her teeth, nodded. 'Yes, Matron.'

'To her utter satisfaction, I trust?'

'Oh, yes.' Anna nodded vigorously. While sucking and softly biting the pungent flesh, the blonde had climaxed three times.

'But there still remains the not insignificant matter of the stolen caviar. Be at the door of Major Spens by 7.30.'

Anna lowered her gaze and blushed. 'Yes, Matron.'

Major Spens, a dashing young blade who had taken a bad knock to the knee during his regimental tennis tournament, gripped the silver frame of his wheelchair as Matron entered, with a bamboo cane in her right hand and a prettily uniformed nurse in tow.

'Very boring for a fit young stag like you,' Matron commiserated. 'Thought I'd lay on a little diversion. Something of a treat, to speed recuperation.'

The hands dropped down to the rubber wheels, clutched them and reversed the chair to clear a space.

'This wretched young nurse was caught red-handed, earlier today,' Matron purred as she tapped Anna's bottom with the tip of her cane. 'I will not burden you with the sordid details of her misdemeanour, but I can assure you that she thoroughly deserves the stripes I am shortly to bestow across her bare bottom.'

Underneath the silk dressing-gown of Major Spens, something stirred. Rising like this anticipation, his shaft thickened expectantly.

Matron continued, studying the gleam of her cane beneath the lightbulb. 'She will take off her uniform, very slowly, for your perusal. Allowing you to inspect and appreciate the buttocks I propose to punish with this bamboo. Commence.'

Blushing, and bowing her head in shame, Anna parted her thighs slightly as she drew her trembling hands up to the buttons of her striped uniform.

'Shoes first, I think,' Matron barked.

Anna stumbled slightly as she struggled to kick off her shoes.

'Cap, collar, then cuffs,' Matron commanded. 'Then we'll have that uniform off and your bottom bare.'

Matron retreated to a chair. Sitting down, she ignored Anna and studied the sparkling yellow cane across her dark-stockinged knees.

Divested of her pink-and-white-striped uniform, Anna stood before the wheelchair-bound major in her delicious underwear. His eyes widened as they devoured the swell of her bosom in its satin bondage, and narrowed into fierce slits as they raked her body down to the pubic snatch behind the panties' sheen.

Matron rose from her chair and paced across the

carpet, coming to rest behind the near-naked nurse. Anna shivered.

'Stockings,' Matron murmured, tracing the seam of the left leg with the cane tip. 'No,' she cautioned, as Anna hurried towards utter nudity. 'Slowly.'

Anna's fingers unsnapped each suspender in turn. The darker bands of her stocking-tops shrivelled instantly down her thighs. Raising her leg slightly – and bending to crush her breasts into her knee – she palmed the nylon down until it gathered like a dark shadow at her scrunched toes.

'The major will oblige,' Matron whispered.

Anna, crimsoning at the indignity, offered her raised foot unsteadily up to his mouth. He tore the nylon stocking away with his teeth and returned his lips and tongue to the tiny white toes. Sucking at them savagely, his erection sprang up and stood firm, twitching as his lips worked busily above.

'And now the other foot,' Matron whispered, swishing the cane crisply across Anna's bunched cheek.

Anna squeaked, withdrew her foot and palmed down the other stocking. The major's wet lips dealt with it – and the exposed toes – ruthlessly.

'Continue to undress. I want you naked for the cane.'

Obediently, Anna took four paces back, then reached behind to unclasp her brassière. As the cups spilled down beneath the weight of the unbound bosom, she attempted to cover herself with crossed arms. Within her modest embrace, her squashed breasts bulged. The cane whistled down, slicing into her pantied buttocks viciously. Anna's hands flew down to soothe her punished cheeks, revealing the ripe splendour of her bare bosom to the major's burning gaze.

'Give them to him,' Matron snarled, tapping the peaked nipples with the shining bamboo shaft.

Offering each breast in turn, Anna surrendered her nipples to the cruel mouth. Six minutes later, she

stepped back away from the wheelchair, both nipples –
wet from his devouring adoration – thickened little
peaks of pain.

'Turn,' Matron instructed. 'And bare your bottom for
the cane.'

Anna whimpered as she fingered the elastic of her
panties. The major's angry red-tipped shaft pulsed
excitedly.

'We're waiting, girl.' Matron's tone was curt.

The suspender belt was removed sensuously and, inch
by inch, the panties peeled down. Anna, her soft bottom
joggling invitingly, trod down then stepped out of them.
She was now utterly naked. Naked before their cruel
gaze.

'Touch your toes.'

Tremulously, Anna obeyed. As her cheeks bulged and
her cleft yawned, she heard the major rattle in his
wheelchair, jerking in mounting agitation.

Matron swept the thin cane down across the bare
upturned bottom four times, each stroke bequeathing a
red line across the swollen cheeks. As the cane kissed her
helpless flesh, Anna squealed, and the major grunted
appreciatively.

'No, Major. I do not recommend any exertion on
your part,' Matron cautioned, turning briskly away
from Anna's whipped buttocks to admonishingly tap
the knuckled fist encircling the hot shaft. 'Hand down,
please.'

Anna heard the wheelchair rattling in a spasm of
frustration.

'After all,' Matron's voice continued silkily, 'we pride
ourselves here on the quality of our nursing care.
Kneel.'

Anna dropped down to her knees, dreading the
impending strokes that would sear her with each swipe.

'No, turn and face the major. I want you to ease his
discomfort.'

Burning her knees on the carpet as she turned, Anna – naked and ashamed – faced the wheelchair, her breasts level with the angry erection thrusting up from the parted silk dressing-gown. The tip of Matron's cane alighted against the buttocks it had just blistered. Propelled by the tap-tap of the bamboo against her bottom, Anna shuffled forward until her nipples kissed the major's knees.

'Down,' Matron commanded, using her cane now to force Anna's head face down into the lap before her. Anna took the hot, firm flesh into her mouth, shrinking at its salty tang.

Four more times, but with a long pause between each stroke, the cane lashed Anna's buttocks. As the whippy wood sliced her proffered cheeks, Anna's mouth worked busily, and the major's knuckles whitened as they gripped the rubber wheels.

'Up.'

Releasing the hot flesh slowly, Anna staggered to her feet. As she swayed unsteadily, blinking away hot tears of shame, she saw Matron's cane tame the throbbing erection, then teasingly tap the glistening knout. Anna shuddered as the spurt of liquid silver splashed her breasts, the warm, sticky semen dripping down her belly to shine on her thighs.

Groaning in an anguish of ecstasy as he spasmed and came, the major thrashed in his wheelchair.

'Excellent,' Matron murmured. 'Now, girl. Turn, bend over and let Major Spens examine your naughty bottom.'

With her breasts still sticky and her belly smeared with his spent seed, Anna turned and presented her caned bottom for his intimate inspection.

'You may enjoy her for no more than thirty-five minutes, Major. No longer, mind. Too much excitement may set back the splendid progress you have been making. Understand?'

Major Spens nodded, impatiently waving Matron away. Shouldering her cane, she briefly examined her handiwork, finger-tracing each red line of pain across the cheeks she had punished. Nodding appreciatively, Matron departed, closing the door softly behind her.

Anna surreptitiously thumbed her left nipple dry, flinching suddenly as she heard the wheelchair creak, and flinching more violently as she felt the cold metal of the two footrests against her heels. The Major's face was, she realised, a few mere inches from her bare, striped bottom. It was his entirely, to examine leisurely and inspect intimately. Matron had disciplined her staff rigorously – and Anna was the most disciplined nurse on that staff – to obey one simple rule: the patient must always come first.

Behind closed eyes, Anna formed a mental picture of the sumptuous room. She remembered the delicious chocolates on the octagonal table. Yes. She would smuggle out a pocketful. And he wouldn't miss a couple of packets of those Balkan cigarettes. And – dare she? – pinch a bottle of vodka from the glass and chrome trolley groaning with abundance.

Yes. She'd leave this room with plenty of spoils, beside her reddening stripes. But before that moment of triumph there would be thirty-five minutes of humiliating servitude. Thirty-five long minutes, during which the virile young officer – *hors de combat* for the past three weeks – would feast his eyes, then his hands and mouth, upon her nakedness: upon her chastised cheeks.

Wet or dry? Anna shuddered as she struggled to ignore the question which burned as fiercely as her caned bottom. Would she leave this room with a wet or a dry bottom? Would the major obey Matron's strict injunction? Or would he once more squirt his hot delight over the naked nurse bending before him?

The silk dressing-gown rustled softly. Anna tensed, her nipples tight peaks of fire. She knew, instinctively, that before the allotted time had passed, a sudden splash would leave the cheeks and cleft dripping with the major's liquid lust.

5

The Astrologer's Apprentice

Sulima hid behind the onyx pillar, crushing her breasts into its cool surface, and risked a forbidden glimpse. Down in the high-walled courtyard, in a sunken marble bath, Princess Alizam sang as she splashed.

Six white turtle doves fluttered as the naked bather clapped her hands. Sulima slunk back behind the pillar, her tongue thickened with desire. On the single clap of royal command, two slave girls skipped on silent feet to the edge of the bath. Princess Alizam rose, her body glistening. Sulima, peeping around the pillar, glimpsed her mistress in utter nakedness – longing to touch the slender legs sweeping up to thighs the colour of precious amber; yearning to kiss the streaming black hair; burning to bite the beautiful bottom. The softly swollen, superbly rounded buttocks. Sulima swallowed silently as she worshipped from afar.

The obedient slave girls, now kneeling down at the feet of their princess, stretched up to dry her nakedness. Sulima watched as a towel of combed Egyptian cotton dabbed between the slightly parted thighs then visited the swell of the shining buttocks. She saw each curved cheek wobbling beneath the caress of the towel. At the royal breasts, another towel was applied with a timid touch. Sulima grunted as she saw the white cotton sweep down devotedly across the belly to the dark delta below.

Sulima closed her eyes, shivering slightly as she heard the princess squeal with delight. No doubt a squeal in response to the touch of a towel between the royal thighs, Sulima thought, knowing that the rasp of cotton at the secret flesh-lips had thrilled the naked princess with its amorous impudence. And would the slave girl be whipped? Sulima held her breath. She opened her eyes. Princess Alizam had parted her thighs wide. Taloning the hair of the kneeling girl, she was guiding her terrified, upturned face into her ripe fig. Sulima's throat tightened at the sight of the slave's tongue protruding. Sulima thumbed her own fig as the slave buried her face between the royal thighs. Closing her eyes, Sulima shuddered as she heard the royal scream shatter the silence of the sun-drenched courtyard.

Later, Princess Alizam clapped her hands again. The slave girls scampered away. Sulima withdrew her thumbtip from her wetness as she watched a more matronly figure emerge from the shadows. It was the royal dresser, whose heavy breasts bulged within her purple robe of office.

Seated on a small silver stool, the attendant bowed her sleek head down deferentially before motioning the naked princess to sit on her lap. Sulima smothered a gasp when she saw the cleft between the royal buttocks widen as Princess Alizam squashed her soft cheeks into the firm thighs. The matron sprinkled her mistress with rose water, palming it gently into the bosom, belly and thighs, then lovingly took an onyx comb to the long, wet hair, taming it with two hundred firm strokes.

The six white turtle doves were scattered by a sudden brilliance as the princess, pampered and perfumed, allowed her beauty to be embraced by a gown of spun gold. Sulima loved that particular attire, for it did not deny her hungry gaze the delights beneath its sparkling sheen. The cloth of gold contrived to reveal rather than conceal the mulberry nipples, the pubic plum and the ripe buttocks of the princess it adorned. Sheathed in her spangling robe, Princess Alizam retired, the matron following several respectful paces behind.

The turtle doves returned to the marbled surface of the courtyard, slipping drunkenly as they trod its polished gleam. On tiptoe, Sulima scuttled down the steps from her hiding place to the edge of the sunken bath. Peeling off her simple tunic, she sat down and dappled her feet in the scented waters. The bath was as warm as honey oozing from the hive. Moments later, emboldened yet shivering at her own audacity, Sulima felt the water lapping at her thighs and tonguing her bottom as she lowered herself into the bath vacated by the royal mistress. Settling her buttocks on to the smooth marble beneath, she sank breast-deep into her bliss.

Sulima's people lived beyond the Blue Mountains. Just as the Phoenicians knew how to fathom the oceans, her kinsfolk could read the heavens and divine their starry secrets. As she sank back into the bath, Sulima's face darkened with a fleeting sorrow as the memory of her days in slavery revisited her.

The harsh crack and searing lash of a Bedouin whip. The harsher treatment in the midnight tent as, splayed across a goatskin rug, she had been forced to submit to the lustful desires and dire demands of her cruel master. Then, the long journey south. A bid for freedom. A severe whipping. The slave market, where her recently striped buttocks had caught the eye of a passing princess, leisurely perusing the naked throng for a suitable Nubian girl. A few words had been exchanged – Sulima remembered the dominant caress of the royal hand across her punished cheeks – and then the sale. Hard silver coins had been exchanged for her soft golden flesh.

To the delight of her royal mistress, Sulima's lore and

ability to divine the night sky's portents had been discovered, and quickly deployed. Rising from the rank of slave to become the astrologer's apprentice, Sulima enjoyed the protection and stern affection of the princess. Princess Alizam, a priestess of Venus, was appointed by her father to scan the night sky for omens, and to advise the King when to wage war and when it was more auspicious to parley for peace. As astrologer royal, she was the most powerful – and most feared – woman in the realm. Spurning all men, she lived apart, surrounded by love-slaves like Sappho before her.

In her forbidden bath, Sulima opened her eyes and smiled. Cupping her breasts and squeezing them, she dimpled the milky surface of the pool as she quivered in pleasurable pain. Remembering her good fortune, she marvelled at the journey her life had taken her along, from the servitude of a Bedouin tent to this marble palace. From the kiss of the whip to serving the astrologer royal, the beautiful, stern mistress whom she adored.

Gliding beneath the surface, Sulima parted her lips and swallowed a mouthful of the sweet water that had, moments before, held the naked princess in its invisible embrace.

Nightfall. The turtle doves slept, undisturbed by the distant bark of foxes or the hooting of a nearby owl. Against the dark sky, silver stars and golden planets glistened.

Sulima ascended the stone steps, following her mistress up to the top of the tower, a black basalt minaret built by the King for his daughter. Raising her eyes up from their downcast gaze, Sulima perused the buttocks swaying before her as the princess mounted the stone steps, swaying sinuously like a date palm in the wind. The royal thighs were sleek and smooth beneath a tight silk robe. Mesmerised, Sulima felt her nipples pucker and tighten. She blushed in the darkness, struggling to drown her dangerous desires. An incautious word, or look, could merit harsh chastisement. Sulima lowered her gaze and followed her royal mistress up into the waiting night above.

Three Chinese merchants had brought news of a comet along with their satchels of jade. Princess Alizam was determined to capture the image of this omen in her glass and, plotting its course with Sulima's help, interpret its meaning for her father's kingdom.

There were two telescopes on the roof of the dark tower. One, a small, hand-held glass, had been seized from Levant pirates captured plundering a coastal city. The other, more highly prized, had been traded for ten bales of raw silk – and a submissive, dark-eyed girl chosen from the seraglio. Made in Genoa, it was mounted on a cradle of sandalwood. Through its blind eye, tonight, Princess Alizam would scour the horizon for a glimpse of the comet and, at her side, bending over her charts, Sulima would be making notes and plotting the movements of the heavenly spheres.

It was a hot night. The desert wind was as fierce as the breath of a sultan at the breasts of his favourite. The astrologer and her apprentice stripped, relishing the kiss of the milky air on their nakedness. Sulima glanced up, her eyes widening at what they saw: as the princess bent to peer through the telescope, her breasts bulged and spilled down – ripely rounded, like melons aching for their harvest. Returning to her scrolls and parchment charts, Sulima scratched her raven's quill, etching the orbit of a polar star. The perfume of rose water, splashed on to the royal body after the bath, maddened the night air. Sulima breathed in deeply, scenting the feral whiff from the sticky plum between the royal thighs. Her fist tightened, making the dark quill quiver in her thrall.

* * *

After several hours dedicated to the night sky and its astral secrets, the astrologer princess sighed and yawned softly, stepping back from her glass and stretching. Gazing up at the splayed legs, Sulima saw the buttocks of her mistress become firm globes as the tired muscles tightened. Moving across to the damask divan, the princess sprawled out, belly down, to drink sweet wine. Sulima saw the dark cleft between the peach cheeks yawn as a tired leg slipped from the couch. After nibbling some wheat-and-honey cakes, and drawing her leg back up alongside its partner, the naked princess nestled her bosom into the dark silk beneath, sighed, and fell asleep.

Sulima stole across the moonlit basalt and finished the wine and cakes in surreptitious silence, wiping her chin with the palm of her hand and chasing away stray golden crumbs from her breasts with her wrist. Curling up sleepily at the feet of her mistress, she crossed her arms over her bosom and closed her eyes.

But sleep did not come when bidden. Thoughts – not dreams – filled her mind. Over the parapet, down below in the royal city, night was cloaking the adventures, the pleasures and the pains of men and women free from the royal yoke. Like her mistress, Sulima was forbidden the companionship of men and, in her enforced abstinence, her curiosity ran wild, tormenting her each night with a frenzy of erotic fancies. Even the gross encounters with her former Bedouin master had not been, she would now admit, devoid of dark, secret delights.

Sulima rose up on one elbow and studied the body of the sleeping princess in the moonlight. The regal face, the face of one born to command and to be obeyed, was of such stern beauty. The full mouth, sensual and cruel, completed the mask of proud sovereignty. The neck was slender, the shoulders gently sloping like those of a rare white deer. Her eyes flickered then steadied on the royal bosom, upon the heavy breasts. Sulima's heart quickened as her eyes feasted on the swollen splendour of the naked bosom. Breasts to bury one's face into, she thought, breasts to kiss devotedly before sucking submissively.

A hot wet prickle glistened the flesh-lips opening between Sulima's thighs. Terrified – she could be whipped from dawn to dusk, beheaded even, for harbouring such thoughts towards the royal personage – she fell back on to her cushions and, trembling slightly, gradually sank into sleep.

Dawn broke, its pink fingers probing the dark belly of the eastern sky. Sulima was woken by the yapping of foxes scavenging for bones in the Place of the Dead beyond the temple. It was chilly but not cold. Hugging her breasts, she shivered slightly, then rose up in silence and wandered across to the parapet. Up above, the black night was retreating before the lemon-gold rays of the rising sun. At the parapet, Sulima sighed as the cold sheen of the basalt received the warm weight of her naked bosom.

Tiny points of light from oil lamps glinted in the darkness of the city below. Stretching up on tiptoe to peer down, Sulima grazed her nipples against the stone. The sudden stab of pleasurable pain caused her fig to peel apart. Soon her inner thighs glistened with the wet ooze of her arousal. Her boredom grew heavy and became discontentment and, as her secret flesh-folds ached, her discontentment became a carnal yearning.

Down in the city, men were tumbling women in the pleasures of the bed – and, more furtively, women rode the nakednes of women in a frenzy of delight. Delights and pleasures forbidden to Sulima, the astrologer's apprentice.

Steadying herself against the parapet, Sulima spread out her arms, crushing her nipples into the hard stone.

The fingertips of her left hand shrank back as they felt a sudden cold presence. Sulima feared it was a lizard. Snatching her hand away instantly, she glanced down and sighed with relief on seeing the cold brass length of the hand-held telescope. The barrel seemed to point out like a finger into the dawn sky: at the end, the thick lens gazed unblinkingly over the rooftops. The rooftops, beneath which naked bodies coupled, sweated and writhed.

A wanton thought stole across Sulima's mind. She picked up the telescope and raised it to her eye, almost immediately snatching it away and crushing its weight against her breasts. No. It was forbidden. She must not succumb to temptation, the temptation to spy upon the inhabitants down in the city at their nocturnal sports. She wished the sun would grow strong and bright, and that her mistress would wake. Then she would be safe, and there would be no more dangerous temptation. But the sun hung like a lemon, pale and cool, on the horizon; and, on her damask couch, the naked princess sighed in her undisturbed sleep.

Sulima denied her burning desire to use the glass in a manner strictly forbidden. To do so, she knew, would merit severe punishment. The princess would summon the purple-robed matron up to the top of the tower and Sulima's buttocks would receive many lashes from the cruel camel whip. The camel whip kept coiled in a cedarwood box for the chastisement of maids, slaves and wrongdoers in the royal household. Sulima feared the little whip, feared its soft whisper and harsh slice.

But, Sulima reasoned desperately, the princess need never know. Yes. Sulima glanced over her shoulder at her sleeping mistress. She was in no danger. She could spy upon the erotic games being played as dawn broke and her bottom would be safe from the sharp kiss of the camel hide.

With trembling fingers, Sulima positioned the brass at

her eye. Elevating it up, her elbow at an angle, her breasts proud and free, she focused on the pale morning star – the jewel of Aphrodite – and frowned. An annoying blur spoiled her view. Pulling her head away, Sulima gently thumbed the eyepiece, wiping the lens. Back at her eye, through the clear glass, she saw the star twinkling. Sulima smiled, and dipped the spy glass down to the horizon.

Three leagues away, a camel train emerged from between towering dunes heading towards the royal city. The sun, now climbing above the distant hills, caused long shadows to stalk each beast, matching the camels stride for stride. So powerful was the glass, Sulima glimpsed the tiny clouds of dust puff up from the desert sands beneath the leading camel's measured tread.

One league away, behind the temple guarding the Place of the Dead, Sulima caught sight of two vixens in their very act of sacrilege. She felt a wave of disgust sweep over her as she saw them through her glass, licking at an unearthed skull.

Should she? Dare she? So far, she had not disobeyed the strict rules of her apprenticeship. So far, she reasoned, her heart hammering and her fig prickling stickily, she had done nothing to merit the whip. So far.

The brass inched down slowly until the barrel rested on the basalt stone of the parapet. Sulima trained it on a point of light she knew to be an oil lamp. A bedroom lamp. As her eye became accustomed to the shadows, her throat tightened, as did her fingers around the smooth barrel. It was a small room filled by a huge white bed. A bridal bed. Even as Sulima gazed, several more lamps were lit by a naked bronze-skinned man. He strode around the bed, his manhood proud and eagerly erect, arranging the lamps. On the bed – a bed strewn with pink rose petals, in accordance with nuptual rites – the young bride lay, legs apart, patting the silken sheets impatiently.

Sulima, spellbound, gazed steadily at the bride and groom. He threw himself upon her as the wolf leaps upon the lamb, his mouth at her throat. Soon, Sulima saw, his lips and teeth were upon her naked bosom. She raked the glass feverishly across the image, just in time to glimpse the groom burying his face between his bride's parted thighs: her wide, welcoming thighs. The bride taloned the silken sheets with fists clawed in ecstasy, then clutched and tossed handfuls of pink petals in her delight. Beneath the fluttering petals, the groom's mouth was busy, sucking deeply at the exposed sweetness. Suddenly, the bronzed buttocks clenched and Sulima shuddered as she watched the naked man spasm, his spine as straight as a broadsword, then curved like a scimitar. Sulima knew that he had just spilt his hot seed. She gripped the brass barrel tightly. Through it, she saw the wetness at the bride's bosom. Saw the naked breasts glistening with his fierce wet joy.

Playfully – Sulima glimpsed the silent laugh – the naked bride wiped her breasts, squashing them with flattened palms, then mockingly reproached her ardent lover, cupping his upturned face between her sticky hands. She laughed a silent laugh once more and buried the groom's face in her soft bosom. Maddened into an erotic frenzy, the groom struggled free, knelt up and grabbed his prize with both hands. Sulima saw his erect shaft spear her hip and soft thigh as he turned her over and pinned her, belly and breasts down, into the bed.

Sulima felt her belly tighten as she watched the frenzied groom grasp his naked bride's hips and draw her rounded buttocks up against his belly. Twisting her face on the pillow to allow Sulima a sight of her silent scream, the bride struggled but succumbed, surrendering to her lover's fierce will. Sulima sensed her fig spilling its warm ooze as she gazed down upon the groom taking his newly-wed from the rear, as the desert lion ravishes his dusty lioness.

Standing, stiff-nippled and wet between her thighs, Sulima remembered. Remembered her nights in the Bedouin tent. Remembered her face pressed into the rank goatskin. Hot from the wine in his belly, hotter from the lust in his loins, her master would use her thus. The memories swept over her naked body as she leant against the parapet. Her body responded. Sweat prickled her temples and the salt of it stung her parted lips. Her bosom grew heavy and swollen, heaving gently and aching pleasantly. Between the soft peaches of her buttocks, where the Bedouin had enjoyed her ruthlessly, her tiny rosebud unfurled and grew sticky.

Sulima pressed the brass barrel against her lips, as if kissing it with gratitude. For several silent moments she continued to kiss it, clouding the bright sheen with the warmth of her breath. Soon, she was licking it feverishly, shrinking slightly from the metallic tang, then pressing the flattened surface of her tongue into it devotedly. Panting slightly, she palmed the barrel down to her nipples, rolling it slowly back and forth across their inflamed peaks. Shuddering, she crushed the telescope into her breasts viciously – and came.

Vultures winged silently in from the south. Sulima, wiping the beads of sweat from her brow – and the droplets of honey weeping down below – trained the glass on them to track their predatory progress. Over the Place of the Dead, they wheeled slowly and descended, their ragged wings beating the milky air. On the ground, frightened by the swirling shadows, the two vixens broke away from their bones, circling them skittishly twice, then scampered off, tails down, back into the desert. Sulima watched the vultures settle to feed.

Between her thighs, her wet flesh was hot. Placing the cold brass barrel beneath her belly, she rubbed her secret parts, arching up on tiptoed delight as the cool metal eased her heat. Rotating a little more firmly, so that the barrel dragged open her sticky lips, she teased and tormented herself deliciously. Dare she risk another glimpse? Another furtive peep of dawn being greeted in by the rites of lascivious Eros?

With her eager eye back at the lens, Sulima swept the glass over to the sunrise, guiding it to a point just beyond the communal fountain. Yes. There, in the household of the King's aunt, two maids were about their early morning duties. They were baking the day's bread. Leavened loaves, some spiced with cinnamon, others heavy with the flesh of ripe dates. So clear was her view, Sulima could see the blaze of black thornwood twigs as they crackled in the belly of the oven. She could also see the nutmeg-brown hands of the naked maids grow white as they fisted the floury dough into shape, and grow dark-skinned once more when rinsed with water. No. Nothing there for her to feast upon, she sighed. Sulima, pouting, shrugged. Perhaps . . . no, wait. A squabble was breaking out. The two maids edged closer, their mouths ugly with unheard, but understood, curses. They collided, bosom to bosom, and grappled. Tumbling, they fell entwined on to the rush-strewn floor.

Sulima tensed, gripping the spy glass firmly. Down in the kitchens of the King's aunt, ignoring the bread blackening in the fierce oven, the two naked girls wrestled. A red-robed woman, one breast bared, ran into the kitchens, a short whip raised. Sulima swallowed, training her glass on the bare bottoms she knew were about to be striped.

A soft sound from the royal divan almost caused Sulima to drop the telescope. Glancing anxiously, Sulima saw the princess twist and turn over on her crimson couch. It was, the frightened girl realised, only her mistress in a troubled dream. But what did a beautiful young princess dream of? Her mistress turned back on to her belly, nestling her bosom into the couch. The royal thighs parted slightly. Sulima saw the naked buttocks of her mistress spasm and tighten, then watched in covert fascination as the belly and the pubis ground rhythmically into the crimson silk. A secret, knowing smile spread across Sulima's mouth. Royals shared the same deliciously troubled dreams as those they ruled. Sulima, aiming her glass back down into the kitchens below, knew that the damask divan would have a wet smear upon it when the sleeping princess awoke.

Blue smoked filled the kitchens. The bread had burned to ashes. The red-robed woman, both breasts now bared, was whipping the upturned bottoms of the two kneeling maids. Thigh to thigh, punished cheek pressed against punished cheek, the two naked girls suffered the stinging lashes: moments before, divided by jealous rivalry, now united in pain. As the whip was raised and lashed down yet again – striping both bottoms with a searing slice – Sulima guided the fingers of her free hand around to her left buttock, taloning and squeezing the ripe flesh in time to the whipping below.

In the upper chamber of the House of Topaz, the city's seraglio, a Persian onyx merchant sat, robes parted, his manhood in his hand, watching a Nubian cane a melon-buttocked nude. The oiled Nubian, naked except for the topaz at each dark nipple, plied the yellow cane across the upturned cheeks slowly, striping the rounded cheeks of the luscious rump twice within each slow minute. Sulima tongued the roof of her mouth as she espied the delicious debauchery: the breasts of the Nubian swinging as each slicing stroke was delivered; the feverishly pumping fist of the merchant; the jerked hips of the punished nude as her buttocks received – and resented – the searing whippy wood.

Sulima wondered when the frenzied merchant would achieve his release. How many more withering slices would bite into the bare buttocks of the bending nude before his quicksilver would spurt? Four? Seven? Her answer came three strokes later. As the glinting cane swept down, the Persian lurched forward, buckling at the knees. The oiled Nubian stepped back – continuing to tame the bottom she had been whipping with the tip of her cane – as the merchant squirted his hot seed across the punished cheeks.

Sulima, squeezing her thighs together, choked softly on her delight. Closing her eyes, and lowering the spy glass, she shuddered as she imagined the sticky warmth splashing against her own whipped buttocks: shuddered and moaned.

Her mistress murmured in her sleep, the sound muffled by the crimson cushion at the royal lips. Sulima froze, the pulse at her throat quickening with fear as she strained to listen. Princess Alizam grunted and rolled over on to her back, crushing her buttocks into the silk. Sulima remained motionless. Had the danger passed? Was her mistress still sleeping? She dared not turn round. Glancing up, Sulima blinked as her gaze met the rising sun. Cranes flapped lazily, high above the city, their huge wings white against the pink and gold of the dawn sky. Stretching out her trembling fingers, the astrologer's apprentice pushed the telescope away and then stepped back from the parapet. She squealed as she felt the imperial hand of her mistress clutch and talon her hair. Shivering, Sulima sank obediently to her knees.

Princess Alizam silenced her bleating apprentice with a single harsh command. Sulima bowed her head, shivering with dread. Her heart pounded as she watched her mistress reaching out for the telescope and examining the eye piece. Sulima suddenly remembered the annoying blur and the small coil of pubic hair she had removed from the smooth glass. It had been a trap. She shivered as she watched her mistress thumbing the glass for the missing hair. Raising the brass tube to her nostrils, the royal astrologer sniffed the smear where Sulima's juices had dulled its sheen – sniffed, and nodded decisively. Lowering the telescope and turning, the princess pointed to the crimson couch, ordering her slave to prostrate herself face down upon it.

Sulima flinched as her breasts bunched into the cool silk and shuddered as her belly kissed the dark wet stain from the weeping fig of her mistress. Moments later, grasping an Egyptian fly whisk fashioned from a score of knotted strands, the princess approached the couch and played the dancing tips across the upturned cheeks. Snapping the whisk down harshly – six, seven, eight times in rapid succession – the royal mistress latticed the naked bottom with a crimson patchwork of pain. Sulima squealed as the knotted cords danced across the swell of her bare buttocks, mercilessly stinging her defenceless flesh.

The princess paused, tossed the fly whisk down and knelt alongside the couch. Taking each hot buttock in her taloned hands, she spread the punished cheeks apart until the cleft within yawned painfully to reveal the pink rosebud of the sphincter. Thumbing the anal whorl ruthlessly, the mistress severely admonished her maid for such wilful disobedience and flagrant transgression.

Salt tears glistened on Sulima's face as she whimpered her contrition into the crimson couch. Ordered by her stern mistress to reach back and hold her cheeks apart, Sulima obeyed, dreading the pain to come.

Princess Alizam had a supple, strong wrist. It effortlessly flicked the fly whisk two dozen times, lashing the sensitive flesh between the exposed cheeks with the knotted cords. Soon the muscled dimple of the anus grew red and angry, swelling up to pout in crimson rage. Sulima's shrill squeals subsided into a sobbing whimper as the fire in her sphincter spread its fierce flame deep into her belly.

The punishment ceased. The princess drank thirstily from a wine flagon, then tipped the purple stream of wine over her breasts to cool their heated flesh. Sulima clenched her buttocks as droplets of wine dropped down from the swaying nipples above into her whipped cleft. Harshly, the princess instructed Sulima to turn over, and expose her breasts to the whisk. Demanding to be told – sparing no detail – of all that her slave had seen through the spy glass, the princess raised the cruel little whip and cracked it down. Sulima, writhing as her breasts were scourged, rapidly confessed to all that she had witnessed. As her detailed account unfolded, she found that the knotted cords visited her nipples more frequently and more fervently. Mistress and slave girl gazed into each other's eyes as the princess splayed her legs apart and applied the whisk to her pubis. Snapping the cords across Sulima's bosom, and then down between her own parted thighs, the princess demanded more details.

Sulima faltered, suddenly gasping as a climax overwhelmed her. Pounding her buttocks into the satin couch, she squirmed and moaned incoherently. The princess was impatient and plied the lash across her slave's belly and thighs. Trembling, Sulima rallied and launched into a detailed account of the Persian merchant, the oiled Nubian and the caned nude. Princess Alizam buried the whisk between her thighs and tormented her wet flesh with it frenziedly – then, grunting, swiftly straddled the couch. Sinking her buttocks down on to Sulima's upturned face, she rode the helpless slave, raking her secret parts across her captive's mouth.

Buried beneath the heavy buttocks, Sulima's muffled words became a piteous whimper, a whimper soon silenced by the hot trickle from the oozing fig grinding down upon her own open mouth.

* * *

Nightime. The yapping in the darkness betrayed the return of the vixens to their unholy feast of bones. Pressed against the parapet, with the telescope at her eye, Sulima anxiously scanned the city below. All was darkness. It was a moonless night, with even the stars hiding their faint light behind high, rolling banks of cloud.

From her crimson couch, drawn up close to the parapet, the princess asked her slave for details. Naked, Princess Alizam sprawled her oiled limbs on the divan, the fly whisk in her hand. Sulima panicked, fearful of the stinging whip across her bare buttocks. In a tone of increasing impatience, the princess demanded to know what the telescope had espied. Unable to see anything in the darkness, Sulima stammered a halting reply. The fly whisk flickered, the knotted cords whipped the slave girl's soft cheeks. Words spilled from Sulima's mouth – inventions and imaginings of severe pleasures and cruel delights down in the darkness below. Again the fly whisk lashed her scalded buttocks, prompting Sulima to supply details that grew more lubricious.

A double lash of the whip was followed by silence from the crimson couch, a silence broken only by Sulima's delicious lies. Then a soft liquid sound filled the night air. Sulima closed her eyes, dropping the telescope down to her left thigh, knowing that her royal mistress was now fingering herself feverishly, perhaps probing her sticky wetness with the thick stock of the whisk.

'Tell me,' Princess Alizam grunted, her words a pleading command.

Fearing the lash, the slave obeyed, fuelling her royal mistress with fresh pictures formed behind tightly closed eyes.

6

The Spanish Mistress

'Strap or cane? I'm never quite sure which instrument I prefer to use for punishment.'

'Oh, my dear, always the cane. The cane every time. So satisfactory, is it not, to stripe the bare bottom of a naughty schoolgirl?'

'Then keep your bamboo supple.'

'Supple?'

'Elements within the Upper Sixth are getting completely out of control. I fear our Dean of Studies is becoming somewhat lax.'

'I am inclined to agree. Somewhat lax. We must not lose the upper hand.'

The two middle-aged teachers, crisply bloused and sensibly brogued, paused to sip their morning coffee in the sunlit corner of the Senior Common Room that, through time-honoured usage, had become their own haven of mid-morning peace. Between them, they had taught at Dreadnoughts for almost half a century, serving the exclusive private academy for wayward young women with loyalty and vigour.

'And to keep the upper hand, one must have a cane grasped firmly in it.'

They exchanged smiles, then, like cats lapping at cream, they sipped their coffee contentedly.

'What price the Iberian appointment?' purred Miss Edritch, putting her cup and saucer down on the polished mahogany table and dabbing at her pursed lips with a starched cambric.

'Senorita Garcia? Sheer folly,' her colleague replied waspishly. 'I do think our Dean of Studies should have given the post to a more mature candidate.'

'Yes. The Upper Sixth need sterner stuff than our dark-eyed little senorita.'

'Do you think we should write a letter to the governors?'

'A vote of no confidence in our Dean? Would that not be disloyal?'

'To the Dean, possibly, but not to Dreadnoughts. We must maintain strict discpline.'

'Absolutely. It is, after all, what the poor parents of these priviliged brats pay so dearly for, is it not?'

The china cups chinked delicately as the cats returned to their cream.

Across the quad, in the changing rooms adjoining the hockey field, the Dean of Studies paced through the noisy throng of eighteen-year-olds. Freshly showered, the half-naked girls struggled into their uniforms: green pleated skirts, white blouses, green and gold ties, white ankle socks and black pumps. Nylon stockings and tights were not allowed at Dreadnoughts – and only the Upper Sixth girls were permitted the luxury of a cotton brassière to support their rapidly ripening breasts. The girls were all excited, their eyes sparkling and their slender thighs mottled after the brisk March morning on the hockey field.

Under the stern gaze of the Dean of Studies, the girls hurried, scampering to retrieve abandoned pumps and to borrow hair-brushes to deal with their tousled manes. Distributing crisp spanks to pantied bottoms – and harsher double smacks across the bare-bottomed slowcoaches – the Dean approached the cubicle at the far end of the changing room. It was the only curtained cubicle and was designated for staff.

'Senorita Garcia,' the Dean growled, wrenching the curtain aside. 'You are supposed to be in charge of this rabble.'

The new Spanish mistress, having just towelled and talcumed her breasts, was filling her sports bra with their warm weight. The Dean paused, her eyes narrowing then widening, as she savoured the sight of the cups receiving the delicious bosom.

'Senorita Garcia,' the Dean continued, her tone a little gentler, 'you must keep a closer eye on these girls. The Upper Sixth need a particularly firm hand, as I thought I had made plain at your appointment. Hockey finished twenty minutes ago and there are still at least two girls in the showers. They are due in Latin translation in three minutes.'

The young Spanish mistress looked up guiltily and blushed.

'I do hope you are not going to give me cause to regret my decision to appoint you.'

'No, Dean.'

'Dreadnoughts only takes young ladies other public schools refuse to accept. Fees are high precisely because we promise a regime that it tightly structured and firmly disciplined. Do you understand?'

'Yes, Dean,' Senorita Garcia murmured, avoiding the other's stern gaze.

'Hurry up and get dressed. I will see to these wretched girls for now, but in future –' the Dean paused, unbuckling the leather belt from her svelte waist '– I expect you to take control.'

The new Spanish mistress turned and buttoned her blouse up to her throat with trembling fingers. Gazing into the steam-clouded mirror before her, she caught sight of the two naked girls being summoned out of the shower. Her fingers froze at the top button as she saw the two girls, pink and shining in their wet nakedness, being ordered to bend over, side by side, soft bare buttock to soft bare buttock. The Dean stood directly behind the bare-bottomed girls, the leather belt raised aloft.

Senorita Garcia cupped her left breast and squeezed it slowly, cruelly, as the strap lashed down twice, kissing the naked upturned cheeks with its burning hide. Her nipple thickened and peaked into the cotton cup of her bra. Words from her own language flooded her brain as the strap was brought down again with a severe double crack across the writhing bottoms. *Severo*. Yes, the Dean was *muy severo*. Harsh. Strict. Stern. The leather left another red line across the naked cheeks. The naked cheeks of the *travieso*, the naughty, mischievous girls. *Apenar*: to cause pain and bring sorrow. *Zurrar*: to spank or whip the bare bottom. The two naked bottoms crushed into each other as, buttock to buttock, thigh to thigh, the girls bent for and suffered their chastisement.

Gripping both breasts firmly as she arched up on stockinged tiptoe, Senorita Garcia risked thrusting her hips forward to grind her pantied pubis into the cold glass. Gasping slightly, she glanced up – to meet the steady gaze of the Dean meeting her own dark eyes in the mirror. Blushing furiously, the Spanish mistress zipped up her skirt. From the sound of the almost empty changing room, there came the muffled sniffles of two punished girls. *Sollozar*, Senorita Garcia shivered, as she murmured the Spanish word for sobbing.

True, the nuns in Ciudad Real had been harsh, but there had been nothing like this. She had been at Dreadnoughts only a week, but already the new Spanish mistress was wondering if she had made a terrible mistake. Perhaps her family had been right, after all. Ignoring their advice had been an even bigger mistake. She couldn't go back now. Not after that terrible row. She was fiercely proud and would not admit to any mistake. No. She had to stay. Stay here at Dreadnoughts. Stay and try to please the Dean, the *muy severo* Dean of Studies.

The night was windy and wet. At the windows of the Upper Sixth dorm, the wisteria danced against the rattling panes. Inside, the flickering light from four candle-stubs wedged into grease-encrusted wine bottles caused shadows to dance along the spartan whitewashed walls. Most of the dorm were in bed, obediently observing the strict lights-out and silence rules – but five girls remained defiant, sitting on the floor in their vests and panties, swigging from a bottle of sherry and sharing a forbidden cigarette.

These meagre midnight luxuries were enjoyed in giggling whispers. At home, these girls were accustomed to champagne cocktails, thinking nothing of sending a maid or footman down to the pantry for smoked salmon or caviar canapés. Here, in the strict privations of Dreadnoughts, a sly cigarette or sip of sherry was a delicious treat: even though the shadow of punishment and pain hovered darkly over their midnight pleasures.

Suddenly the door opened and the new Spanish mistress strode in. The fragile candle-flames spluttered and died in the cold draught. In the darkness, the girls scrambled to their beds and quickly burrowed down between icy sheets, shivering as they feigned sleep.

Senorita Garcia's fingers fumbled for, then found, the brass light switch and clicked it down. In the blaze of five bright bulbs, her dark eyes widened as she saw the glint of the sherry bottle. Her nostrils flared angrily as they caught the tell-tale trace of the hastily crushed cigarette.

'Who has been out of bed?' she demanded, her voice rising. 'Which of you was it?'

Suppressed giggles greeted her sharp questions – giggles from faces pressed into pillows. Stung by this insolence, the proud Spanish mistress dashed from bed to bed, dragging down coverlets and sheets to expose squirming girls to the cold night air. Those who had been asleep resented her intrusion and protested loudly. The guilty few taunted her with renewed mocking laughter.

'Smoking. Drinking. It is forbidden. I demand to know who has been doing these forbidden things.'

'I know nothing. I'm from Barcelona. I know nothing,' a voice piped up, echoing Manuel from *Fawlty Towers*.

Senorita Garcia turned towards the bed the derisive voice had come from, only to find the occupant feigning deep sleep. Loud laughter rang through the dorm. Stung by her humiliation – and the hot tears in her eyes – the new Spanish mistress retreated in confusion.

The Dean of Studies palmed the slipper she had just swiped eight times across the bare-bottomed girl and launched into an equally stinging homily on the importance of the past pluperfect.

'And so, in future, when you are set a piece of prep, be sure you do the task thoroughly,' she admonished, bringing the sole of the slipper against the punished cheeks and tapping their reddened curves admonishingly. 'Now be off with you, naughty girl.'

Rubbing her bottom before pulling up her white knickers, the chastised girl thank the Dean and withdrew, sniffling loudly. Tossing the slipper down on to her desk, the Dean strode across her study to the open window and gazed down pensively into the rose garden. The winter had been harsh. The rose trees looked frail. Perhaps the autumn pruning had been a little too severe. Adjusting her spectacles, she blinked as the bright sunshine flashed against the lens.

Voices drifted up from the gravel path below her window. The Dean, frowning at what she overheard, withdrew to eavesdrop.

'More trouble in the dorm last night, I believe.'

'Yes,' Miss Edritch replied. 'I fear the Upper Sixth were quite impossible this morning.'

'Another sherry party. Senorita Garcia failed abysmally.'

'So I understand. I would have had them all up and across their beds. Thrash the entire dorm. It's the only way to flush out the guilty party.'

'Quite hopeless, I'm afraid.'

'That letter you proposed to write to the governors about the increase in laxity at Dreadnoughts. I have been giving it some further consideration. I happen to be a friend of Lady Northburgh and I thought perhaps . . .'

The voices faded out of earshot as the speakers reached a set of stone steps and descended into the rhododendrons to dead-head late frost-damaged blooms. Returning to the open window, the Dean fingered her spectacles against the bridge of her nose. Once more, the sun flashed ominously on their lens. 'You, yes, you, girl,' she called out imperiously.

A coltish fourth-former who had been feeding crumbs of cake to a robin on the lawn looked up, guiltily.

'Go at once and find Senorita Garcia and inform her that I wish to speak with her in my study.'

The girl showered the robin with crumbs and scampered away.

The Dean sat at her desk, waiting for the tap at her study door. Moments later, there was a respectful knock.

'Come.'

Senorita Garcia was ushered in by the fourth-former, who beat an instant retreat.

'You wished to see me?'

'Just a little chat,' the Dean purred, motioning the Spanish mistress to approach the desk – but not inviting her to be seated. 'How was your morning?'

The new mistress gave a gushing account of an entirely successful morning's teaching.

'And dorm duties last night? I understand you got to grips with some nonsense in the Upper Sixth dorm. Sherry party, was it?'

Senorita Garcia blushed slightly, but assured the Dean that she had dealt with the matter effectively.

'You see, my dear, Dreadnoughts promises the parents of these pampered delinquents that they will be strictly supervised and sternly disciplined at all times.'

The young mistress, who had been *en route* to a netball match, palmed her yellow sports shirt nervously as she listened.

'And so congratulations are in order,' the Dean continued, her gaze unflinching.

'Congratulations?'

'Last night.'

'Last night?' the mistress echoed, blushing.

'In the dorm. You disciplined the miscreants.'

Senorita Garcia nodded. 'Yes,' she conceded, twiddling with the hem of her navy-blue pleated gym skirt.

The Dean rose from behind her desk and approached a large polished rosewood table. Smoothly pulling out a deep drawer, she started to extract various instruments of punishment and arrange them carefully upon the gleaming surface.

'And what was it you used to quell the naughty Upper Sixth, hm? Was it a cane?' The Dean placed an eighteen-inch length of yellow bamboo down on the rosewood table. The highly polished wood reflected every inch of the supple cane's potent malice. 'Or was it with a leather strap?' The Dean lovingly uncurled two feet of dark leather, arranging the cruel hide lengthways alongside the whippy cane.

Senorita Garcia, wide-eyed and shivering slightly, merely gulped and swallowed, before shrugging nervously. 'I'm not sure,' she whispered.

'Then perhaps it was a paddle? So very satisfying, the sound of a paddle across the plump little cheeks of a naughty sixth-former.' The Dean palmed the pearwood paddle reverently before placing it down between the cane and the strap. 'Well? Just how did you punish the girls last night? Tell me exactly how it was you established control over the dorm. Was it by using one of these?' The Dean's hand pointed to the strap, the paddle and the cane. 'Or did you simply put each of the miscreants across your knee and give them a sound spanking?'

Dragging her white pump across the carpet, the Spanish mistress cast her gaze down. 'I'm not sure,' she said softly.

'Not sure? But such an occasion – indeed, an event – as a full dorm discipline must be a memorable one, must it not? I can vividly remember my first experience of silencing a rowdy dorm. It was with a slipper. My goodness, how they squealed.'

'The cane,' Senorita blurted out suddenly. 'I used the cane.'

'And so if I were to telephone Miss Ackroyd, the music mistress, and instruct her to examine the bare bottoms of the Upper Sixth, she would discover striped cheeks beneath their blue serge knickers, would she not? Hm?'

Silence greeted this question. Squirming slightly, the reddening mistress ground the toes of her left white pump into the carpet below.

'Wouldn't she?' the Dean repeated, her tone firmly insistent.

'I think I spanked some –' the younger woman faltered.

'Oh, I see. You think you spanked some of them. The Upper Sixth are presently at their singing class. Miss Ackroyd is, I believe, introducing them to Thomas Tallis. I personally have a marked weakness for

Schumann's *Frauenliebe und Leben Lieder*, but I'm sure Tallis will stretch their technique. And you now inform me that some of those girls have striped bottoms and others sport spanked cheeks.'

The Spanish mistress gazed down miserably at the carpet, her hands entwined, fingers twisting, at her pubis.

'Do you know the school motto, Senorita Garcia? You are familiar with it?'

The other nodded. Screwing up her eyes, she quoted the Latin words.

'*Dicere verum,*' the Dean repeated suavely. 'Tell the truth. It is similar in the Spanish, is it not?'

'It is very similar,' the young mistress replied, thinking her moment of danger had past. 'It is so with many words for me –'

The Dean cut in briskly. 'We place a very high priority here at Dreadnoughts on the truth. I expect all the pupils, given their pedigree of privilege, to misbehave. That is normal in high-spirited young ladies. But –' the Dean paused, fingering the bamboo cane gently '– I always insist on the truth.'

Averting her gaze from the cane, the Spanish mistress flushed deeply.

'From the girls, and from my staff. And you have lied to me this morning, haven't you?'

'No. I mean –'

'Do not heap falsehood upon wicked falsehood. You have lied to me and rewarded my trust in you with blatant dishonesty and deception.'

'I'm sorry –'

'Easy words, my girl, easy words. I find myself forced to reconsider your position here –'

'No, please.'

'You show no capacity for discipline whatsoever. Absolutely no ability to control the naughty Upper Sixth. To make matters worse,' the Dean continued in a grave tone, 'you attempt to conceal your shortcomings. Dreadnoughts cannot have weak links in the chain of command. All my staff must be willing and able to take a firm line. A very firm line.'

'I will learn. I want to learn.'

'And why should I believe that? Have you not lied to me already?'

'No, please. Do not send me away. Teach me to be strict and stern.'

'Very well, Senorita Garcia. So be it. Across the desk –'

'But –'

'At once,' the Dean barked.

Crushing her bosom into the leather-topped desk, Senorita Garcia stretched out across its hard surface.

'Legs apart. More,' the Dean insisted, approaching the bending mistress and flicking the hem of the pleated skirt over the rounded buttocks. 'Bottom up, please.'

The beautifully buttocked Spaniard obeyed reluctantly, shuffling her white pumps as she spread her honey-gold thighs wide and surrendered her pantied cheeks submissively.

'See how easy that was? In all aspects of discipline, it is important to establish absolute control over the subject. You give an order: the subject obeys. No quibbling.'

'Yes,' whispered the lips kissing the desktop, dimming its polished gleam with warm breath. 'I see.'

'Once you have dominated your subject into submission, you may commence to administer the discipline. Remember, assert your authority and establish control before chastisement. Understand?'

'Yes.'

'I am going to cane you, my girl –'

The Dean's words were drowned in a squeal of protest.

'Ten strokes,' the stern voice from the rosewood table

continued imperturbably. 'Five for lying, and a further five purely to demonstrate exactly how a bare bottom should be punished. Understood?'

The bending girl gripped the far edge of the desk with clenched hands, her knuckles whitening.

'Ten strokes of the cane. Do you understand?'

'Yes,' came the whimpered response.

'How many strokes?' the Dean purred, scooping up the whippy bamboo from the rosewood table and thrumming the air with it vehemently.

Clenching her tightly pantied cheeks, the young mistress closed her eyes and shivered. 'Ten,' she said huskily, her bottom spasming with dread at the promise of approaching pain. 'Five for lying, and five so that I may learn how to punish the naughty pupils.'

'Excellent. You make an apt pupil yourself, my girl. Now, in a moment,' the Dean announced briskly, 'I'll have those panties down. No – leave them alone, please. Hands back upon the desk. I will attend to your bottom when the moment is ripe.' The Dean tapped the left buttock admonishingly with the tip of the yellow cane. 'You see, girl? I remain in control throughout every stage of the punishment. It is I who dictate terms. You bend over only when I say so – and when I do say so, you obey immediately. You present your bottom up to me, offering it up to my cane upon my instruction and to my complete satisfaction. When I deem it appropriate, you will suffer your stripes. Remember all of this, Senorita Garcia,' the Dean murmured, tapping the Spaniard's soft cheeks firmly – and briefly tracing the tip of the cane down along the valley of the cleft between them – before levelling its thin length against their luscious swell. 'Remember all that you learn for the dorm, tonight.'

'Yes, I will remember,' came the whispered response.

'When baring the bottom,' the Dean continued in a businesslike tone, 'always use the thumb of the right hand, inverted so, into the elastic. Press the thumbtip into the cleft between the upper cheeks – and so.'

With one smooth yank, the panties were swept over the bulging cheeks and brought down into a tight restricting band around the upper thighs.

'Never, I repeat never, allow the penitent to remove the panties prior to punishment. That would be a mistake, and lose absolute control. Understand? And arrange them around the upper thighs. It acts to restrict wriggling, keeps the upturned cheeks poised and positioned for their pain.'

The girl across the desk strained her thighs and felt the stricture of the taut panties. She murmured her acceptance of this minor, but important, detail.

'You may allow the penitent you propose to punish to count out the strokes. Many prefer this practice. I do not. I prefer silence, though I do not object to their squealing under the strokes.'

The bare bottom tightened apprehensively.

'Ten strokes, we agreed, did we not?'

Swish. The cane swiped down, cutting into the rounded cheeks savagely. It was a vicious cut – the supple whippy wood biting into the rubbery flesh mounds and searing them with a thin line of crimson. Senorita Garcia choked on a sobbing gasp of surprise, anguish and suffering, drumming the carpet with the toes of her white pumps.

'And be careful to pace the strokes. Pace is important in punishment. Do not rush the chastisement. Allow the dread of the impending stroke to build up in the sufferer's imagination. Let them endure the sweet agony of anticipation as well as –'

The yellow bamboo glinted as it sliced down once more.

'– the sharp delight of experience.'

Jerking her striped bottom, the Spanish mistress suppressed her squeals. The tight panties at her clamped

101

thighs rendered her helpless and immobile – and utterly at the Dean's mercy.

'Do you now appreciate my pre-punishment preparations?'

'Yes,' hissed her victim, writhing.

'You are in my control. Your bottom is mine.'

The cane whistled softly as it whipped down twice in rapid succession, swiping the bunched cheeks with savage affection.

The Dean paused, tapping the open palm of her left hand with the wand of woe. 'How many strokes have I administered?' she demanded suddenly.

Senorita Garcia blinked, squeezing a tear down on to the leather surface of the desk below. 'I – I don't know –' she stammered. 'I forget –'

'One, two, three, four,' the Dean counted aloud, tapping each reddening weal with the tip of her quivering cane. 'You can demand to know at any moment during the punishment. And if the miserable wretch has lost count, you can begin again at one.'

The Spaniard shuddered, crushing her bosom beneath her as she moaned softly into the leather at her lips.

'Five,' barked the punisher, swiftly delivering the fifth stroke.

The whipped girl grunted, gripping the far edge of the desk in anguish.

'Those five were punishment, pure and simple. The following five strokes are intended to teach you something of the art of discipline. It is a lesson you would do well to remember, girl. Up.'

The Spanish mistress peeled her breasts and belly – tightly sheathed in the yellow sports shirt – away from the desk, and stood, head bowed, tugging at the hem of her stretchy top to shield her pubic mound from the Dean's hungry gaze. Hobbled by her panties stretched below her striped buttocks, she stumbled awkwardly in her shame and pain.

'Leave that alone.' The Dean brushed aside the younger woman's protective gesture, tapping the tugging fingers with the cane. 'Hands up on your head.'

Blushing furiously, Senorita Garcia reluctantly obeyed the strict command, instantly revealing her slightly moist pussy-lips beneath the nest of coiled pubic fuzz.

'And now we'll have those panties off completely,' the Dean murmured, using the cane tip to depress their taut stretch.

Breasts bulging as she bent down, the mistress palmed her panties off, steadying herself against the desk as she kicked them free. The tip of the questing cane rose up between the parted thighs and tapped the labia lightly. The Dean withdrew the cane and drew it up to examine the sparkling wet tip. Senorita Garcia gasped and shuddered.

'Top off. I want you completely naked.'

Slowly, crossing her arms over her tummy, the caned girl grasped at the hem of her yellow sports shirt and, elbows angled, peeled it up over her bosom and head. The Dean's grip on her cane tightened as she saw the heavy, swollen breasts bounce gently within the tight cotton bondage of the sports bra; the cane flickered up to salute the rounded bosom spilling free as trembling fingers unhooked and removed the bra.

'Splendid,' the Dean whispered, tracing the tip of the cane up from the dark pubic snatch to the inviting cleavage above. 'You make an excellent pupil, my girl. I'll make a Dreadnoughts mistress of you yet. Hands back up upon your head, if you please.'

Clamping her thighs together, the naked girl obeyed. The Dean stilled the slight wobble of the bare bosom with her outstretched palm, then strode behind the punished girl to inspect the striped bottom. Senorita Garcia mewed softly as she felt the Dean's knuckles brush against the swell of her caned cheeks.

'Four paces forward.'

The Spaniard took four timorous steps and paused.

'Bend over, touching your toes.'

Whimpering softly, the naked girl presented her beautiful bottom up to the cane. Two strokes were instantly delivered, bequeathing twin crimson lines of pain across the perfect peach cheeks. The punished girl's toes scrunched the carpet, attesting to the vicious accuracy and venom of the bamboo.

'A traditional posture favoured by seasoned disciplinarians,' the Dean remarked, continuing suavely, 'but variety is important. One hopes to develop one's repertoire. Kneel. No, girl, on all fours. That's better. Now give me your bottom.'

Before slicing down to swipe the proffered rump, the cane tapped the outer curve of the left cheek twice – a double touch of dominance. Then the cruel wood spoke; as the second stroke bit into her upturned buttocks, the kneeling girl sobbed aloud.

'Fifth and final stroke,' the Dean announced briskly. 'I do hope you are learning your lesson. For the fifth, I think we'll have you right across the seat of this chair. Over you go.'

Stumbling as she rose, first on to one knee, then on both feet, Senorita Garcia wiped away her tears as she approached the chair.

'Right across. No,' the Dean directed curtly, 'get your tummy further over the seat. No, a little more. Let your breasts spill over the edge of the chair.'

Wriggling, the red-bottomed nude strove to obey, easing her squashed breasts and thickened nipples across the smooth hide until her bosom hung and swung in heavy splendour over the seat. Kneeling down on the carpet to address her victim, the Dean flicked the cane upward, tormenting the peaked nipples with the supple bamboo. The young mistress squealed and ground her pubis into the leather seat, kissing the hide with her sticky labia.

The Dean addressed the exposed breasts with her cane, bunching them up meancingly. 'Stop that.' She spanked the caned cheeks sharply with her left hand, stilling their writhing. 'You are here to learn about punishment, not pleasure. Understand?'

The Spaniard froze and bowed her head in silence.

'Understand?' Taking a pincered flesh-fold of the nearest buttock and twisting it ruthlessly, the Dean demanded a response.

'Yes, yes, I understand,' the punished girl gasped.

'Good. Though,' the Dean continued in a silky whisper as she gently palmed and soothed the ravaged rump, 'I perceive that you have an appetite for the darker delights of discipline.'

Swish. Whipping the cane smartly down as she uttered the words, the Dean sliced the upthrust cheeks with a cruel stroke of unerring exactitude. The Spaniard hissed and hammered her slit into the leather beneath.

'Stop that, my girl. Stay exactly where you are,' the Dean warned, rising and taking a half-pace back from the chair. Raising her brown-brogued left foot, she guided it down upon the crown of the upturned cheeks, then trod the caned bottom dominantly, her studded sole dimpling the firm flesh.

'So, Senorita Garcia. Have you learnt anything? Have I taught you the rudiments of how to be an effective disciplinarian?'

The question was greeted with silence. The brogue trod firmly, splaying the rubbery cheeks so that the sticky cleft yawned wide.

'Yes, Dean,' the punished mistress whispered.

'And do you feel equal to the task of working here at Dreadnoughts?'

'You have taught me much.'

'Enough to cope with the Upper Sixth dorm tonight? I truly hope so.'

* * *

105

The bell, an eighteenth-century casting to replace the bell Cromwellian troops had destroyed in an orgy of Puritanism, tolled out four times from the ivy-clad tower across the school quad. Teatime. The Dean put her pen down after the task of completing the daily entry into her own, very private, punishment book. In it, she had faithfully recorded the chastisement of her Spanish mistress, together with details of those unfortunate schoolgirls she had occasion to spank or slipper that day.

Teatime. Soon the refectory would be teeming with smartly uniformed girls, and echoing to their squeals and laughter as they jostled for scones, raspberry jam and that dark, strong fluid every boarding school serves up as tea. The Dean smiled as she pondered upon a universal truth: the more exclusive the private education, the more undrinkable became the tea.

She chose not to join her staff that afternoon in the universal scrimmage for scones and jam, electing instead to have a glass of sherry in the tranquillity of her study. And, yes, perhaps a piece of fruit. Having secured a glass of amontillado, she approached the silver fruit dish and allowed her fingers to stray over a pear, explore the firmness of a peach and caress a softly scented apple. Her dappling fingertips alighted upon an orange. With a deep sigh, she taloned the fruit's weight as she would the breast of a sixth-former across her knee for a searching spanking.

Sipping briefly from her sherry, she closed her eyes and squeezed the orange, remembering Senorita Garcia's ripely rounded buttocks which she had caned earlier that day. Raising the orange to her lips, she licked, then softly bit, the fruit of Seville. As her white teeth pierced the peel, a spurt from the sharp zest lanced her mouth. The Dean shuddered, imagining the sweet, feral juice weeping from her young mistress after a bare-bottomed punishment.

Punishment. And there would be many more punishments. The Dean's pungent slit pulsed and oozed a warm trickle. Weighing the heavy sphere once more, she squeezed it hard. From her pouting labia, wet and stretched, the trickle became a wet bubble against her silk knickers. She trembled as the bubble popped silently and juiced her upper thighs. Dragging the orange down across her blouse to the waist of her herringbone skirt, she trapped and palmed it, guiding it down across her plucking pubis. Rolling the fruit expertly across her erect clitoris, she clenched her buttocks as she placed the glass of sherry down.

From the ivy-clad tower, the bell tolled the single knell of the quarter-hour, scattering rooks from the elms up into the darkening evening sky. Before the wheeling birds had returned to their roost, the Dean, inflamed by her memories of the young Spaniard's whipped cheeks and by the orange rasping her wet heat, grunted and came with a soft curse.

A little after midnight. The Upper Sixth were out of bed and the dorm was on the brink of chaos. A raunchy pillow fight was underway, the two combatants – braless – perched upon a bed, surrounded by cheering onlookers. Breasts bounced deliciously as the soft pillows collided. Further down the half-lit dorm, leggy girls in scanties exchanged lipsticks and gossip in one corner. In another, an almost naked girl tried out a forbidden underwired confection, gazing into the looking glass with pride at the coveted cleavage. By the radiator, a threesome played cards, guzzling chocolates between sticky-fingered hands. Two radios, tuned to different stations, filled the dorm with thumping funk.

Unselfconsciously naked and at play, the Upper Sixth knew that Senorita Garcia was on dorm patrol that night (after last night's fiasco, they deemed her a poor little Iberian cousin who really hadn't got a ghost of a clue) and presumed their bottoms to be safe from any painful reprisals.

A pillow landed across one of the kneeling girls, tipping her on to her back. She rolled over, her legs splayed inelegantly. Nobody heard the door open or noticed the young Spanish mistress entering, cane purposefully in hand. She slammed the door shut behind her. They all looked, catching the anger in her dark eyes and the imperious swish of her sleek ponytail. Flicking her cane across the bare-bottomed girl busy at the glass with her bra, the young tutor on dorm patrol called for silence.

'Now get to your beds. I want you all standing by your beds. At once,' she snarled.

Startled, but not unduly alarmed, the languorous Upper Sixth sauntered impudently and unhurriedly from their sport to their narrow beds.

'Every girl will bend over her bed to receive two strokes –'

A chorus of jeering drowned the angry young Spaniard's command. Stung by the response, Senorita Garcia raised her cane and stamped her foot. The catcalls ceased and the Upper Sixth, fourteen delightful specimens of late girlhood, stood uncertainly around the dorm.

'Not the cane, my dear,' the voice of the Dean said in a crisp, clear tone from the doorway. 'Too tiring. For a group punishment, I rather think you will need this.'

A murmur of dismay rippled through the dorm as the Dean stepped inside, brandishing the polished pear-wood paddle.

'You heard Senorita Garcia, girls. To your beds with you, this instant.'

Scattering like midnight mice before the kitchen cat, the chastened Upper Sixth scampered to their respective beds.

'Undress completely, all of you. After your punish-

108

ment, you will all sleep – without sheets, blankets only – in the raw.'

All moaned at this dire, prickly punishment, but peeled off bras and panties. The Dean, palming the paddle as bare bottoms loomed, nodded approvingly at the alacrity with which the naughty girls bent over, surrendering the peaches for punishment.

'Excellent, my dear,' the Dean murmured, approaching her young mistress and exchanging the cane for the pearwood paddle. 'You were doing splendidly, quite splendidly. I merely thought I would come and observe.'

Basking in the Dean's praise, Senorita Garcia smiled as she thumbed the smooth surface of the wooden spanking paddle. Gazing down at the delicately patterned grain of the pearwood with sparkling eyes, she thought it politic to seek advice.

'How many strokes –'

'As many as you see fit, my dear. But make your mark; be sure to make your mark. They must both fear and obey you, from now on. This is your moment. This is your dorm. These are your girls. Tonight, their bottoms belong to you. Punish them as you please.'

'Thank you, Dean,' the young mistress whispered.

Bed by bed, the ponytailed Spaniard punished the peach-cheeked, bending miscreants, administering five harsh paddle swipes to every shivering nude. Her progress down the dorm was brisk and accomplished, leaving in her wake bed after bed filled with crimson-buttocked, snivelling girls.

At the ninth bed, Senorita Garcia encountered the first show of sullen resentment. A full-bottomed daughter of the Shires, heavily annotated in *Debretts*, refused to be beaten. The young mistress faltered slightly, then deftly grappled the naked sixth-former across the bed, crushing and pinning the disobedient girl breasts and face down into the duvet. The paddle cracked down harshly seven, eight, nine times, eliciting shrill squeals of protest and then smothered sobs from the struggling girl.

A twittering of concerned voices heralded by bobbing torch beams approached and entered the dorm. Senorita Garcia, contemplating the plump rump she had just ravaged with the pearwood paddle, looked up to see Miss Edritch and her poisonous companion marching towards the bed.

'We heard the row and came to see if you were coping,' Miss Edritch gushed, struggling to overcome her mixture of disappointment in – and admiration for – the young Spaniard's undoubted prowess with the paddle.

The poisonous companion agreed vigorously.

'Capital,' they crowed in unison, their eyes raking the reddened bottom across the bed. Turning as one, they congratulated the Dean on an excellent appointment. 'And of course,' they simpered, 'you always had our full confidence. But really, this surpasses every expectation.'

The Dean, busy at a bare bottom with her cane, paused, turned and bowed, graciously accepting their tribute.

'Dreadnoughts, like this naughty girl's bottom, is in capable hands,' Miss Edritch opined, bending to fleetingly finger the curve of the left buttock.

The Dean, guiding her young mistress by the shoulder, propelled the girl towards the staff quarters. She was most fulsome in her praise.

'I believe I can teach you all you need to know, my dear,' the Dean purred, 'and I feel sure you are willing to learn.'

It was more of a statement than a question. Senorita Garcia nodded meekly, anxious not to displease the dominant Dean.

'That paddle, for example. There are a few points I propose to demonstrate,' the Dean continued, slipping her hand down from the young Spaniard's shoulder to her bottom below. 'But first, a nice hot drink. Here is my bedroom. That's right, go straight on in.'

Biting her lower lip apprehensively – and shivering at the thought of the paddle across her honey-gold cheeks – the young tutor entered.

'I believe you say *con leche*?'

'With milk. Yes.' Senorita Garcia nodded, slightly puzzled. 'That is how we take our coffee,' she agreed. 'But coffee at night – so late – keeps me awake.'

'Good gracious me, girl, not coffee *con leche* at this hour. No, we shall have chocolate. I was merely wondering how you liked your coffee when you wake up in bed in the morning,' the Dean of Dreadnoughts murmured, closing the bedroom door firmly behind her.

7

The Fitness Trainer

Roberta took a deep breath. It was now or never. The session was almost over – her client was relaxing on the leather couch, plucking the clinging leotard out of her hot cleft – and then the moment would be gone. The moment to establish intimacy. The moment to suggest extra-special services. The moment, Roberta thought, to notch up a few more precious points.

'I'll just take your pulse,' the fitness trainer murmured, pressing her thighs into the side of the leather couch.

Her client, a shapely ash-blonde, gazed up, blowing up at her fringe and blinking the beads of sweat from her wide blue eyes. She held out her wrist.

'There's a better way,' Roberta murmured, replacing the hand across the thrusting bosom below. 'Here,' she said softly, sliding the tips of two fingers down between the warmth of the clamped thighs.

On the couch, the ash-blonde wriggled, her blue eyes widening as she parted her thighs to receive the probing fingers. Consulting her watch with a professional air, Roberta firmly pressed her fingertips into the warm flesh where the pubic plum nestled between the upper thighs.

'I'm picking up a good aortic echo,' Roberta remarked crisply, absently strumming the sticky labial folds with her index finger.

The ash-blonde tensed, shivered slightly and moaned – but offered no resistance.

'A good workout. You did a half-circuit, but no weights. Your pulse is perfect. How do you feel?'

Their eyes met, the brown of Roberta's focusing searchingly upon the ash-blonde's sparkling blue.

'Great.' The girl on the couch grinned. 'How did I do? Any suggestions?'

Roberta stroked the labial lips more emphatically, then withdrew her fingers. As she did so, she sensed the thighs tighten together to trap and retain them. She scrutinised the line of lycra biting into the soft flesh around the thighs. 'Just your bikini line. Needs a wax.'

The ash-blonde pouted as she struggled up on one elbow to peer over her ripe breasts at her pubis below.

'See?' Roberta whispered, gently fingering a stray coil and tucking it away beneath the stretchy fabric. 'The Greeks and Romans used to body-shave for the gym. I can do that for you now.'

Their eyes met once more across the heaving bosom. The blue eyes of the ash-blonde blinked as she smiled uncertainly.

'Could you?'

Roberta nodded, turned to draw the opaque plastic curtain around the leather couch and, speaking casually over her shoulder, instructed her client to strip off the leotard. A few moments of soft rustling, followed by the whisper of flesh upon leather, told her that her client was now naked. Turning back to the couch, a steel dish in one hand, a soft linen cloth in the other, she fleetingly examined the nude. All that the taut leotard had struggled to conceal now lay bare beneath her brown eyes – the exquisitely rounded, slightly heavy breasts, the flat, firm tummy and the perfect pubic plum below.

'Pussy has her winter coat on,' she remarked, placing the linen cloth down on the client's belly and pinching a plucked wisp of pubic fuzz. 'Too warm, especially when working out. I'll make you feel sleek and spartan.'

The ash-blonde looked up – a shadow of

apprehension clouding her blue eyes for a fraction of a second – then nodded. 'Please,' she whispered huskily.

Deliberately nudging the thickening nipple of the exposed left breast with the cold edge of her dish, Roberta trapped and crushed the berry-brown peak down before placing the tray upon the linen cloth. The left breast wobbled gently; the nipple darkened and peaked painfully. As she traced a dominant forefinger down into the lacelike pubic fuzz, Roberta heard the ash-blonde gasp aloud.

'We'll get pussy shaved and then tidy up elsewhere,' she announced crisply, picking up the small electric razor and switching it on with her thumbtip. The soft snarl – like a wasp trapped in a jam-jar – precluded further speech. Bending down to her delicate task, Roberta guided the tiny razor over the contours and along the creases of the pubic mound, denuding the delta of its wispy fuzz.

The ash-blonde lay rigid at first, her breasts quivering imperceptibly as she clenched her fists and buttocks. Slowly, she relaxed, her body easing into submission. To the fierce buzz of the razor, and to Roberta's tender touch, the client surrendered her pussy – thrilling to the tickle of the skimming blades that shaved so closely.

'That's right, relax,' the fitness trainer encouraged, stretching the pubis between her finger and thumb.

The squirming nude sighed and snuggled her bottom down into the warm leather, squashing her heavy buttocks into the polished hide. Splaying her thighs wide, she proffered her pubis up to the razor as it skimmed and trimmed, licking her most private flesh with its tiny tongue of honed steel and leaving the flesh between each thigh crease and labia bare.

The buzzing stopped as abruptly as it had commenced. 'I'll wax you now,' Roberta murmured, bending down to blow away a stray wisp. 'And trim you,' she added, thumbing the glistening labia. They

114

spread in a smile of greeting at both her suggestion and her probing thumbtip.

The client clamped her thighs together at the ominous threat of the waxing. By her left buttock, her hand became a fist of anxiety clenched against the impending pain.

'It won't hurt. Think of it as a sweet torment,' she whispered. Smiling, she stroked the fist back into an outstretched hand. 'I'm very good,' she soothed. 'Then I'll do elsewhere.'

'Elsewhere?' the ash-blonde echoed faintly.

'We'll take a peek at your bottom.'

Snapping on a pair of plastic gloves, Roberta opened a packet of waxing strips and applied them firmly to the bikini line. The nude grunted softly as each strip was deftly peeled away, leaving the glistening flesh pink and shining.

'Just the outer lips,' Roberta warned. 'Keep absolutely still.'

The nude whimpered. A wax strip was applied along the slightly juiced flesh of each labial lip. Roberta heard her client mewing anxiously.

'I said, absolutely still,' Roberta repeated, stretching out her left hand to grasp the left breast. Taloning the warm mound, she squeezed. The hard nipple rose up into her plastic-sheathed palm.

'Look at my hand,' Roberta commanded. 'Look at it holding your breast.' Squeezing the ripe flesh, she released her grasp and palmed the captive flesh dominantly, rhythmically. The client wriggled, grinding her swollen cheeks into the leather below.

'P–please be careful,' she whimpered.

'Trust me,' Roberta whispered, bending to pluck at the end of a wax strip. The labial flesh, so soft, so sensitive, rose up with the strip.

'N–no –' pleaded the nude, her eyes wide with fear.

'Shush,' Roberta soothed.

115

There was a soft, snatching sound. The ash-blonde squealed.

'All over now,' Roberta said.

It always worked. Tweak the nipple viciously and you diverted their attention from the brief but blistering agony below.

'How does pussy look now?'

'She's lovely,' the ash-blonde purred, massaging her sore nipple as she gazed down proudly at her shaven delta.

'Just a little bit more,' Roberta said, her tone one of silky reassurance. She thumbed the clitoris up out from its satin flesh-fold and pinned it down with a waxing strip. The naked woman on the couch squirmed and begged her trainer with wide, imploring eyes not to hurt. Roberta noted the two heels skidding as her client dug her ankles into the leather couch.

'Stay still while I attend to pussy's little pink tongue.'

'N–no, not that, p–please –'

Reaching out once more, this time the fitness trainer inserted two plastic-gloved fingers into her client's mouth. 'Suck on those for this bit. Just suck hard, don't bite.'

She felt the wet warmth of the mouth tighten round her straightened fingers, and instantly detected the tang of the nude's arousal as it oozed and glistened from the recently ravished labia.

'Suck,' Roberta ordered, inching up the end of the waxing strip back towards the belly.

As her clitoris seethed, the ash-blonde ground her bare bottom into the couch. Her tight cheeks squeaked audibly as they raked the gleaming hide.

'There,' Roberta exclaimed, ripping the wax strip away from the ultra-sensitive clitoris. 'All over. Brave girl. Look.'

Holding a small mirror down between the splayed thighs, the fitness trainer invited her client to inspect and admire the freshly plucked pussy.

'Thank you,' the ash-blonde whispered in a voice as thick as treacle.

'I'll oil you in a moment. Turn over. I want to see your bottom,' Roberta instructed, swiftly removing the cloth and the metal dish.

Her client obeyed, snuggling her thick-nippled bosom into the leather couch as she turned over, offering her heavily fleshed bottom up submissively. Roberta dabbed a swab of cotton wool with surgical spirit and deftly wiped it down along the cleft between the warm, soft cheeks. Her client squealed softly and jerked her joggling buttocks in response to the severe kiss of the astringent against her inner flesh.

'Spread your thighs wider apart,' Roberta instructed, 'and I'll need you to hold your cheeks open for me.'

The ash-blonde drew her hands to her bottom hesitantly.

'Just hold them apart,' Roberta murmured.

The nude's buttocks dimpled beneath the touch of her splayed fingertips. Gripping each cheek, she dragged them apart, revealing the deep, dark cleft.

'Tweezers, first,' Roberta observed, worrying the shrivelled anal whorl with a gloved thumbtip. 'Then, perhaps, a waxing strip.'

The pink sphincter seemed to pucker up into a tighter knot at these words, but the nude rubbed her breasts and pussy rhythmically into the leather, riding it eagerly.

'Naughty girl,' the fitness trainer whispered as her client smeared her slit against the hide. The tweezers glinted then dipped down into the cleft, busy at the sticky flesh for several minutes as single hairs were plucked. Rising to examine the results, Roberta tapped the rosebud sphincter twice with the tip of her tweezers. 'Just the one waxing strip, I think.'

Knuckling it down firmly into the cleft, the fitness trainer applied the white strip. Pausing for a moment, she drummed the crown of the right buttock's swell with her plastic-gloved fingertips.

'Do it,' the ash-blonde grunted, quivering with delicious dread.

A searing spank rang out, echoing off the white-tiled walls. Before the red imprint of her spanking hand had developed like a negative on the cream of the punished cheek, Roberta had whipped away the waxing strip – rocketing the nude into a renewed frenzy of masturbatory thrusts into the couch. Spank. Roberta's gloved hand swept down to sear the scalded cheek.

'Into the shower with you,' she whispered. 'I can see you can't wait any longer. Go and finger yourself properly there.'

Naked, flushed and trembling on the very brink of her climax, the ash-blonde stumbled through the opaque plastic curtain towards the shower.

'Come back to me when you have finished. I want to oil you,' Roberta called out, smiling as she peeled off her gloves.

I've notched up a couple of useful points there, she sighed, brushing a stray pubic hair from the surface of the couch before wiping away the gleaming slit-slick from the soiled hide.

Bodyworks was a hi-tech honey-trap for the gold-card-carrying City executives on the edge of the Square Mile. Just within the shadow of the NatWest tower, between a wine bar and a deli, it seduced busy corporate types in through its smoked-glass-and-steel doors with the promise of fitness and rejuvenation after a hard slog at the dealing desk – and kept them as loyal clients, once they had sampled the special services available.

Roberta was on a short-term, renewable contract. Renewable if she reached her monthly target of sixty points – points awarded by the manageress, according to the clients' comments. Special services usually notched up five points at least. The manageress, a shrewd forty-year-old brunette – twice Roberta's age – ran a very tight ship and used both rewards and punishments to motivate her crew. Now in her third month, Roberta had struggled but had managed to achieve her previous targets. This month – losing a week with the flu – she was a full twenty-one points off the mark. There were only four working days left.

Pamela Bronze applied her pale-pink lipstick sparingly, guiding the stubby shaft across the swell of her lower lip. In the mirror, she glimpsed the new fitness trainer – what was she called? Ah, yes, Roberta – bending over to straighten a rubber mat. In the mirror on her office wall, the steel-grey eyes of the watching manageress narrowed into a hungry gaze, as they feasted on the bulging buttocks of the bending girl. A pulse quickened in her tightening throat as Pamela Bronze paused, the lipstick pressed hard against her lower lip.

I'll have that bottom before the week is out, the manageress grinned triumphantly. She'll never make her sixty points now. There'll be no bonus for little Roberta. Just a sharp lesson in motivation. Flickering her grey eyes back into the mirror, Pamela Bronze frowned – then grinned again, as she saw the thin pink streak of lipstick on her jaw: exactly like the cane stripe across a punished cheek.

'And then?'
'After nanny and the nursery,' the merchant banker sighed, towelling himself dry after his post-workout shower, 'I went to board at prep and matron became my very special friend.'
'I see,' Roberta murmured, 'and was matron as strict as nanny?'
'Stricter.' The thirty-two-year-old schoolboy Sloane nodded vehemently, flushing pinkly as he remembered matron's strap. 'Much stricter.'

119

Roberta knew at once the line to take with her new client.

'You didn't do very well this afternoon, did you?' she demanded, her tone sharpening.

'Tried my best,' her client retorted sullenly.

'I think not. You were slacking and you know it. Weren't you?'

'No.' His frown was as sulky as his plummy vowels.

'Weren't you, you lazy little boy? And what did nanny do when her little chap was lazy, hm?'

'Spank me,' he replied in an excited whisper.

Roberta saw his erection rake up beneath the white towel.

'And would matron have approved of slacking, hm?'

'No.' The tent-pole beneath the white towel grew rigid at her waspish words.

'And what would matron have done to a lazy boy's bare bottom?'

'Used her strap,' he mumbled, his eyes tightly shut as he shivered with pleasure at the memories of matron's stinging leather across his defenceless cheeks.

'I shall punish you in a more appropriate manner,' Roberta pronounced firmly.

'Punish?' he echoed, hardly daring to believe his good fortune. Beneath the towel, his thick shaft twitched expectantly.

'Bodyworks,' Roberta continued primly, 'promises to put you in peak condition. It is therefore my duty to make sure that I work your body until you peak.'

The white towel slipped to the tiles below. His erection nodded and rose up to salute her stern gaze.

'Follow me.'

She led him firmly by the hand to a secluded corner of the hi-tech gym. He followed with docile steps, just as he had once been led by nanny's hand from his rocking horse to the bed, across which he would be spanked with nanny's delicious hair-brush.

'Face the wall bars,' she instructed, slapping his left buttock as she positioned him. 'No, don't turn round.'

She saw his chubby buttocks dimple as he clenched them in response to her strict command. Stretching out her foot, she steadied herself and guided the white-laced pump up between his parted legs. He shuffled, widening his thighs to receive the pump. Hands on hips, knee flexed then straightened, Roberta positioned the toe of her pump beneath his balls, tapping them dominantly.

'Hands on your head,' she barked.

He obeyed promptly.

'Thirty step-ups. Commence.'

She withdrew her pump and stabbed it down into the polished wooden floor of the gym as he diligently trod the lower wall bar.

'Faster, or I'll have to double your stripes.'

He faltered at the twenty-third – and was soundly spanked – and stumbled at the twenty-seventh. Scooping off her left pump, Roberta swiped it ruthlessly across his naked buttocks, instantly reddening the bunched cheeks with an angry weal. He grunted, dropping his hands to protect his bottom.

'Keep your hands up on your head,' Roberta snarled.

The hands resumed their former position, the fingers flexing anxiously in his tousled hair. Once – twice – three times more, the supple pump spoke, ravaging his defenceless rump with blistering swipes.

'Now I'll have ten press-ups, and no mistakes this time.'

He dropped down on to the prickly mat and stretched out face down, flinching and jerking his hips up in a recoil as his shaft speared into the harsh surface.

'Slowly,' she instructed, positioning herself alongside his nakedness so that she could tread his upturned cheeks with her bare foot. Scrunching her toes into his punished buttocks, she crushed him down firmly each time his elbows angled and his belly brushed into the

121

mat. He groaned as she propelled his thickening manhood into the fierce prickles, and strained to inch his rump up rebelliously – only to be trodden down imperiously.

'I'll cane you if you come, young man,' she whispered menacingly, sensing through her naked foot his squirming and writhing as a climax approached.

His bottom spasmed beneath her dominant tread.

'I've warned you. I will cane you.'

She knew his shaft must be gouging into the rough mat – and that he'd probably explode into it after the next press-up. She knelt, slipping her hand across his buttocks to palm and caress them with a touch of tenderness. She felt his body tense instantly, and saw the neck and shoulder muscles tighten ominously.

Deliberately continuing the smoothing touch at his bottom, she drove him to the edge with more whispered words of stern admonishment. 'Don't you dare splash your wicked stickiness, young man, or I'll take my little bamboo cane to your bare bottom and stripe you till you squeal.'

The words had their calculated effect. Beneath her flattened, dominant palm, she felt his buttocks shudder.

'Another four to go,' she murmured, thumbing his warm cleft.

He lowered himself down into the prescribed press-up, his nipples and belly kissing the prickles beneath. She fleetingly drew her fingertip down the length of his cleft, then probed his tight anus. His hips slammed into the mat, driving his moist glans into the bed of sweet torment.

'Naughty, naughty boy,' Roberta purred, twisting her index finger within his tight warmth as he came, screaming softly into the prickles at his parted lips.

'You've just splashed your sticky, haven't you?' she whispered in a tone of soft severity.

He shook his head, moaning. 'Didn't,' he lied.

She removed her finger from his sphincter, then tapped the crown of his left cheek with its sticky tip. 'Roll over. Let me see.'

He remained motionless, frozen in his shame – and dread of the painful retribution she had promised. She slipped two fingers down between his clamped thighs and tweaked his balls.

'Roll over.'

He shivered and obeyed, revealing a wet belly and glistening chest hairs that spoke with mute eloquence of his spurting orgasm. She briefly fingernailed an arabesque across his shining flesh, then, arrowing down across his sticky tummy, flicked his flaccid penis with supreme contempt.

'I promised you the cane, young man. Up.'

He staggered to his knees – then up, unsteadily, to his feet – and faced the wall bars. Roberta withdrew for a moment, returning with a wicked little bamboo cane. Standing close, deliciously close, to his naked body, she slowly counted the wall bars from the lowest up to the tenth – almost two metres high – with the tap-tapping tip of her bamboo.

'See that?' She paused, bringing her cane to rest high up above his head.

He looked and nodded.

'I promised to work your body until you peaked. Now that is exactly what you are going to do. I am going to cane your bare bottom very slowly and very severely –'

He whimpered a choking note – a note of desire drowning in its own dread.

'You will peak, when I permit it, and splash that bar. Understand?'

He looked at her swiftly, wide-eyed with wonder. She brought the tip of her cane directly to his chin and forced his face back towards the wall bars.

'Bodyworks promises perfection. You will peak, and

reach two metres. We refer to it affectionately here as the high jump. I feel sure you will not disappoint.'

He groaned.

'Feet apart, please,' she ordered, stroking his outer buttock with the cane.

As he shuffled them obediently, a cruel note cut the air with a whistling swish. The first of eight slow, severe strokes sliced across his naked cheeks. She paced the punishment, doling the discipline out with deliberately measured menace. After each cut of the cane across his cheeks, Roberta paused to teasingly tap his nipples, balls or twitching shaft with her glinting cane.

'Please –' he begged.

She cut him off with a sharp demand for silence. Seeing his toes whitening in an agony of ecstasy – and his veined erection straining for release after the brutally delicious seventh stroke – she warned him that he must hit the tenth wall bar with his splash or the exercise would have to be repeated all over again from the beginning.

'You may use your hands to cup and squeeze your balls, but do not touch it,' she warned, dragging the tip of her cane up along the length of his erection to emphasise her warning.

Gasping at the touch of the bamboo at his shaft, he cupped and knuckled his engorged sac, clenching his buttocks and panting loudly.

Swish. He screamed softly at the gravy stroke – jerking his head back to follow the silver stream squirting up the wall. Gobbets of his hot seed spattered the eleventh bar, dripping slowly down on to the tenth below.

'Excellent,' Roberta whispered. 'You peaked to perfection.'

He collapsed down on his knees and, turning, buried his ecstatic face in between her warm thighs. She cradled him tenderly, rocking his face across the swell of her pubis.

'You witch,' he sobbed happily, 'I adore you.'

'You may kiss me – just once.'

She felt his dry, swollen lips crushing into her own wet lips below. Then she felt his tongue tip probing through the cotton stretched across her pubis.

'No,' she warned, taloning his hair and jerking his head away. 'One kiss only.'

'Please –' he begged, straining to return to her heat.

'If you behave yourself, next time, perhaps. And I think, perhaps,' she continued suavely, 'we'll have you across the horse. Hm?'

'Oh, yes, please,' he gushed.

'Across the horse, bare-bottomed, with wrists and ankles firmly bound.'

He shuffled back into her, despite her cruel hand in his hair, to nuzzle her plum. She grinned as she felt his erection rake up along her inner thigh.

Seven points there, at least, Roberta thought. Might just make the target. She smiled, her large brown eyes flickering up to the spot where her happy slave had just made his.

Pamela Bronze took her frustration out on her corned beef and watercress bap, savaging it with her teeth like a panther at its prey. Damn that big kid of a merchant banker. Those unexpectedly high points earnt put little Roberta almost in range of her monthly target – and little Roberta's delicious bottom out of her covetous clutches for yet another month. How the hell did the minx do it? Still, the manageress mused, coping with a mouthful of her bap, there were nine points left between her firm hand and Roberta's bare bottom – nine points to earn and only two clients to be seen.

Two? The manageress drummed her fingers softly on the appointments book. Why should there be two more clients? Little Roberta's rump was, Pamela Bronze mused, merely a perk of the job, and the job of the manageress included the task of making – and altering – all the bookings.

'You're new.'

And so are you, Roberta thought as she turned her frowning face away from the altered rota and managed a wan smile. 'Yes, I am. This is only my third month at Bodyworks. Can I help you? Are you waiting for your fitness trainer?'

Avoiding the question, the slim, attractive brunette asked to be shown around. 'If it's no trouble.'

'No trouble at all,' Roberta replied, managing to conceal her dismay at discovering the loss of her two clients. 'Have you been here before?'

'What's that?' the visitor countered, indicating the pulleys and chains of the weights apparatus. 'Looks like torture to me.'

'The men work out on that,' Roberta giggled. 'Macho machines.'

'Toys for the boys?'

Roberta nodded. They giggled and exchanged grins.

The svelte brunette traced a gleaming alloy strut with a scarlet fingernail. 'And what toys do you have for the girls?'

Roberta paused – sensing a possible client – and absently drew the zip of her tracksuit top down over the bulge of her bosom. 'Won't you give it a try? Are you sure you can't be tempted?'

'I've a spare half-hour. Long enough for you to try to persuade me, do you think?'

'Oh, it won't take that long. Come.'

Roberta drew her visitor by the hand to a curtained cubicle. Inside, she slowly undressed the brunette – deliberately and maddeningly slowly, to build up the fever of anticipation. The near-naked brunette snarled softly, a curdling note of impatience, and brushed aside Roberta's attentive hands. Stooping, so that her bare

126

bosom bulged, she snatched away her panties and kicked them aside. Rising, slightly flushed, she presented herself naked to the younger woman.

'Put your panties back on, please,' Roberta said crisply.

'But –' the brunette stammered.

'I want to take them off myself,' the fitness trainer replied gently, stroking the woman's hip and thigh with a firm fingertip.

The brunette obeyed, snapping her satin briefs back over her ripe buttocks and fingering the smooth fabric as it hugged her proud pubis.

Dropping to her knees, Roberta raised her large brown eyes up. Her throat tightened as she saw the unbrassièred breasts heaving above, their swollen weight rising as the girl grew more excited. Roberta had never seen nipples so dark, so thick or so erect.

'Turn,' she commanded.

The tight stretch of satin across the brunette's buttocks swam into view. Framing and steadying the hips between controlling palms, Roberta inched her face closer, tugged at the waistband with her teeth and drew the panties down, raking her nose along the cleft between the plump cheeks. The brunette gasped and rose up on tiptoe. Roberta delayed the removal of the panties, pausing to tongue the inner thighs.

'Turn,' she ordered.

The brunette, utterly naked, did so. Roberta saw the spangle of wet arousal silvering the pubic wisps at the dark-pink labia.

'Now I'll undress you,' the naked woman whispered excitedly, the words half-instruction, half-entreaty.

Roberta rose. Naked beneath her tracksuit, she shivered as she sensed the fingers at the zip, and again as the soft material was peeled away from her skin. Moments later, they stood, nipple to nipple, belly to belly, in a tentative embrace. As the brunette cupped

127

and squeezed Roberta's bottom, their labial lips brushed in a teasing kiss of sticky flesh, then collided in a fierce embrace.

'Me, first,' the brunette snarled softly.

Roberta allowed herself to be twirled round, melting into happy submission at the maturer woman's sure and certain touch. With her bottom brushing the other's warm thighs, she felt the heat of the brunette's mouth upon the nape of her exposed neck and then the wet warmth of the brunette's tongue lapping between her shoulderblades. Slowly, the flickering tongue tip traced the dimpled spine down to the quivering cheeks below.

Inching her soft cheeks back as she surrendered her bottom completely, Roberta signalled her desire to be kissed.

The brunette obliged, kissing, licking and tonguing the firm young bottom before her. The tongue worked busily, brutally, against the curved flesh-mounds, moistening each swelling and each shadow of the perfect peaches – and, all the time, the brunette's thumbtip strummed at Roberta's parted labia, causing the young fitness trainer to drip her wet delight.

Murmuring endearments – and darker words of threat – into the bare buttocks as she mouthed them, the brunette suddenly began to bite. Roberta squealed softly as the precise teeth nipped her tender flesh. As if in response to the shrill squeal, the brunette's thumbtip flicked upward, expertly capturing and caressing the clitoris.

As the thick tongue probed her anus, Roberta felt the walls of her belly spasm. She came, sagging slightly at the knees and hammering her bottom before collapsing her soft cheeks fully into the kneeling brunette's upturned face.

'Now,' the mature woman murmured, 'let's see if you can recruit me. I am already half persuaded to join Bodyworks, but see if you can really make me want to come.'

Dabbing at her slit with a small towel, Roberta nodded above the brunette's head. 'Time for your workout. Grab hold of those.'

'Those?' the brunette echoed doubtfully, seeing the two hoops suspended from ropes.

Roberta threw the towel down and nodded firmly. Encircling the nude round her hips, she hoisted her up so that the brunette could thread her arms through the hoops and clutch the thick ropes above. Naked in her suspension, the brunette clamped her thighs together and gazed down anxiously.

'Don't punish me,' she whispered huskily, I don't –'

'No, there is no need for punishment, or punishment's sweet sorrow. Not today. Later, when I become your regular trainer, then we will explore discipline's dark delights together. You may come to worship the whip and crave the cane,' Roberta whispered, cupping and gently squeezing the heavy buttocks. 'Today, I am merely going to pleasure you thoroughly,' she continued, removing her hands from the bare bottom and placing them – palms inward – to crush the thick-nippled breasts.

She felt the suspended nude jerk in her bondage as she pincered and tweaked the captive nipples, and shivered with pleasure as the oozing plum between the brunette's thighs raked her own breasts as she returned her cupping hands to the heavy cheeks and spread them painfully apart. Rising up and stretching, she felt the pubis grinding against her nipples as she taloned the swollen cheeks mercilessly, and felt the wet heat bubble and explode against her own flesh as she thumbed the exposed sphincter.

Roberta withdrew and stepped back, then paced around to her suspended victim's buttocks.

'You really should sign up for a Bodyworks program,' she remarked, knuckling each cheek in turn. 'You have a beautiful bottom. Better to keep it firm and

129

in shape,' she sighed, pressing her face impulsively into the soft warmth. 'Such beauty must be cherished,' she muttered into the hot cleft. 'Cherished.' Her tongue rasped, the muscled tip seeking out and mastering the tight anal whorl.

Up above her gleaming brunette hair, the nude's knuckles whitened as they gripped the ropes. 'Eat me,' she urged, struggling to twist herself so that she could bring her pubis to Roberta's mouth.

Ignoring the pleading, and encircling the jerking hips and thighs to keep them firmly under control, Roberta busied herself at the bare bottom, biting its plumpness in between bouts of tonguing the hot cleft.

'Please –' the brunette begged, bucking her rump into Roberta's face as she swivelled and writhed in delicious anguish.

Remaining behind the suspended nude, the fitness trainer withdrew her face and guided her fist up between the lust-juiced thighs. Pressing her knuckles softly into the wet flesh above, she slowly jabbed, fisting and tormenting the squealing brunette into renewed paroxysms. Twisting and jerking to escape, the nude merely succeeded in impaling her wet velvet upon the determined fist – riding the now slippery knuckles – and shrieking as she approached her implacable climax.

Suddenly Roberta sensed her happy victim tense and stiffen. Looking up, she saw the brunette bow her head as she slumped in her strict suspension.

'Have mercy,' came the rasping plea. 'Finish me off. Let me come.'

'Have I persuaded you?' Roberta demanded.

'Yes.'

'Want to be my client at Bodyworks?'

'Yes, yes. Anything. Just let me come –'

'So it's a deal?'

'I'm yours. Just do it, do it –'

Roberta was almost clinically precise as she stepped

back and paced round to face the nude hanging from the hoops above. Spreading the glistening labia apart between her own sticky thumbtips, she inched closer and probed the pussy with her tongue. Using her nose with devilish cunning on the erect little clitoris – which made the brunette shriek with raw delight – she worked the wetness assiduously until the first, and then a second and a third, orgasm ravished the dangling nude, raking her helplessness with velvet violence.

Sobbing gently, the brunette extracted her arms from the hoops and, pressing her body into Roberta, slithered down. Grasping the sliding nude, Roberta shuddered as she felt the other's hot slit rasp against her breasts and belly.

'Persuaded?'

The brunette, broken and utterly spent after the succession of searing climaxes, merely nodded.

The next morning, the last day the month, Roberta was called into the office.

'Sign it,' Pamela Bronze instructed, tossing a pen down on to the contract.

Roberta picked up the pen and did so, managing to hide her smile of triumph.

'Don't bother to read it now. It's the same as the others. And here's your bonus,' the manageress almost snarled, skidding the fat role of notes across the desk top ungraciously. 'You made the target. Just.'

Roberta scooped up the bonus, trying to guess the weight of the twenties and convert it into a cash sum. Funny, she thought. How much does two hundred weigh? Heavier than a padded bra?

'Last-minute client, I gather?' the manageress queried, busying herself with next week's schedule. 'You seemed to have impressed her. Full workout, was it? Did she use the weights or was it a plyometric routine?'

Roberta played safe and mentioned tuck jumps,

springs and some squat thrusts. Thumbing her roll of notes, she lapsed into silence, hating being quizzed in such detail like this by the manageress – who always pressed for intimate accounts of the special services provided.

'Full of praise for you,' the manageress continued. 'Positively glowing after her session,' she added ambiguously. 'Special services, I presume?'

Squirming, Roberta nodded.

'Insists, absolutely insists, on seeing you again.'

Roberta accepted the tribute in silence.

'So what did you two get up to, then, hm?'

The young fitness trainer, glossing over the more vivid details, sketched out a hazy account of the brunette's time spent naked in the hoops.

Pamela Bronze feigned indifference, busying herself with the schedule, making minor adjustments with a red felt-tip pen. As Roberta's account came to a close, the manageress clicked the cap back on to the pen decisively.

'Bitch.'

Roberta looked up, her brown eyes widening with alarm.

'Little bitch,' the manageress hissed. 'I won't sack you. Can't. You're too damn good. But I'll make you pay –'

'Pay?'

There was a square, silver-framed photo face down on the desk by the phone. Pamela Bronze snatched it up and thrust it across the desk, inches from Roberta's startled eyes. Staring out from the silver frame was the face of the brunette she had stripped, suspended and so wickedly pleasured.

'My partner,' the manageress hissed, jabbing down at the pretty face in the frame with a forefinger. 'Came to pick me up to go shopping, but I was delayed. You entertained her, didn't you?'

Roberta crimsoned, her head suddenly pounding.

'Didn't you, you bitch? Don't deny it. I saw the rope marks on her wrists and got it all out of her, eventually. Sang like a little sparrow under the lash, last night. I dealt with her thoroughly, like I'm going to deal with you now.'

'But I didn't know –' Roberta wailed.

'Got your extra points but you've earnt yourself a little something extra,' Pamela Bronze snarled. 'You may have proved that I can't afford to let you go, but this is nothing to do with Bodyworks. Punishing you will be strictly pleasure.'

'No –'

'Across the desk.'

Roberta sprang up, knocking her chair over behind her. She backed away from the desk. 'You can't touch me,' she shouted. 'I am –'

'Perfectly free to go.' The manageress shrugged. 'Just don't expect to work as a fitness trainer ever again.'

Roberta knew the networks, and knew that every pair of smoked-glass-and-gold-plated doors would be closed against her from Brighton to Bath – never mind Wapping to Wandsworth – after a few phone calls from the manageress of Bodyworks.

Roberta hung her head down, signalling her reluctant acceptance of the inevitable. Like a schoolgirl about to be spanked, she kept her gaze down and rubbed her toe into the carpet. On the desk, the spotlight beamed down on the smiling face of the brunette. Roberta blinked in response to the blaze and bit her thumbtip.

'I said you are free to go,' Pamela Bronze whispered, then paused, before adding silkily, 'if you really want to wear a paper hat and serve up fries and cola.'

Roberta withdrew her thumb from her mouth and, dropping her hand down across her pubic mound, dried her damp palm on her tracksuit pants.

'Across the desk,' the manageress instructed, deciding

the issue firmly in a tone of one certain of her supremacy.

Slowly, uncertainly, Roberta planted her hands palms down on the desktop, dipping her tummy and offering her bottom up to the wrath to come. Strap or cane, she shuddered, dreading the impending pain. Closing her eyes tightly, she trod the carpet uneasily. Strap or cane? The harsh bark of the stinging leather or the cruel whistle of the whippy bamboo?

It was to be a riding crop. Opening her eyes, Roberta saw the manageress taking the evil specimen out of the desk drawer. Sixteen inches long, with cream stitching tightly sheathing the ox-blood-coloured leather along its cruel length, the crop seemed like a living thing as it flickered in Pamela Bronze's clenched fist. There was an inch of looped, soft leather at the quivering tip, and Roberta shivered as she guessed how that little loop would add an extra stinging bite across her whipped cheeks, as every withering slice cracked down across her naked buttocks.

'Tracksuit bottoms down to your knees,' the manageress instructed, approaching the bending girl. Rounding the corner of the desk, she stood alongside Roberta and gazed down upon the bottom as it was being bared. She tapped the proffered left cheek. 'Up,' she admonished.

Straining on her toes, the bare-bottomed young fitness trainer crushed her breasts into the desk and inched the swell of her cheeks up to kiss the crop levelled just above them.

'Higher,' Pamela Bronze insisted.

Grunting softly, Roberta managed to kiss the crop with her smooth cheeks. Standing directly behind the bending girl, the manageress guided the loop of leather at the crop's tip directly down between the cheeks, stroking the hide into the cleft repeatedly. Roberta mewed in response, rolling slightly across the desk so that her nipples grazed the polished surface.

'Tracksuit bottoms down another half-inch,' insisted the punisher, imposing her desire for meticulous detail upon the bare-bottomed girl.

Roberta struggled awkwardly to obey, conscious of how her cheeks spread and bulged submissively as she thumbed the elastic waist down as instructed. Resuming her position for punishment across the desk, Roberta ruefully conceded Pamela Bronze's prowess as a skilled disciplinarian: the tracksuit hugging her knees welded her thighs together, causing her peach cheeks to remain perfectly poised for the lash.

The soft touch of the leather loop continued at her cleft. Roberta spasmed, swivelling on her toes as she ground her breasts into the desk. The crop withdrew, only to revisit her labia with a dominant touch demanding her to remain still. Roberta moaned at the rub of the loop between her parted thighs, and gasped as the inquisitive hide parted her sticky lips – and withdrew, leaving them slightly splayed.

'Cunning little vixen, aren't you?' snapped the manageress, whipping away the crop with a flourish. 'Used waxing strips the other day to great effect, I understand. Waxing strips, eh? I'll teach you,' she chuckled darkly, placing the ox-blood-coloured crop down on the desk, three inches away from Roberta's anxious eyes.

Roberta's heart quickened its thumping beat. What was that terrible sound? Her mind pounced upon it, trying to decode the ripping tear – like silk between two angry fists. Then she felt it. The first cold kiss of a strip of Sellotape – an inch wide and five inches long – being thumbed down over the swell of her left cheek. She wriggled, and was instantly spanked into stillness. A second searing rasp announced the tearing off of another strip. Roberta understood, and dreaded the sound. She shuddered as the second strip and then five more pieces of the sticky adhesive tape were clinically measured and wrenched from the roll on the desk and applied firmly down over her bare bottom. Gingerly, she risked a quick squeeze and then a slight spread of her buttocks, and gasped as she felt the strip that had been pinned firmly down along the length of her sensitive cleft. Two inches longer than the others at either side, it had been patted firmly into place against her slit.

The crop was snatched up from the desk. Roberta closed her eyes, opening them almost immediately as something cold and alien was pressed roughly to her lips. It was the silver-framed photo of Pamela Bronze's brunette lover.

The crop lashed down, cutting savagely into the Sellotaped bottom. Across the desk, Roberta thrashed, the moist heat from her twisted lips clouding the glass and obscuring the brunette's ironic smile. The crop whistled down across her naked bottom again, leaving a second thin red line beneath the shining adhesive tape.

Roberta's throat tightened as the raw fear clutched her in its talons: the fear of the impending strokes; the dread of the subsequent slow peeling away of the tape from her whipped cheeks — and the horror of the moment when Pamela Bronze would toss aside the cruel crop and pluck away the final strip of Sellotape from the sticky slit.

8

The Corsetière

'New York?' Lady Kitty Gresham murmured, weighing a satin balconette brassière in her open palm. 'Again? And so soon? Really, my dear, at this rate, you will have to renounce your title and acquire American citizenship.'

Alice, sister of the Duchess of Erpingham, grimaced – both at her companion's suggestion and the price ticket on the silk stockings she had been inspecting. 'It's Charles and his precious League of Nations. Herr Hitler is becoming something of a nuisance. These stockings are wickedly overpriced. I could stable a hunter for a week at Belvoir for less. And Charles is so old-fashioned about money. Absolutely refused to reserve a state room for the voyage.'

'No,' Lady Kitty Gresham replied sympathetically, 'not really?'

'When it comes to money, Charles can become positively Mesozoic. Show me what you have in lisle, girl.'

Outside the Dover Street emporium, Lady Kitty Gresham's sedate Hispano-Suiza brought the late-morning traffic to a frenzied standstill. Inside the exclusive corsetière's establishment, Lady Kitty and her peevish companion withdrew into the privacy of a spacious fitting room, where the velvet drapes were so thick they silenced the angry car horns of the traffic jam.

Judith attended to her aristocratic clients assiduously. With her hair combed back into a bun, her plain black dress and the white tape measure falling down over the swell of each breast, the young corsetière exuded demure efficiency. Her quick dark eyes missed nothing – appraising the proud bosoms, narrow waists and plump buttocks of the women she served as, all the time, she scribbled busily in her little black book.

'The lisle, madam,' Judith murmured politely.

'Be quick, girl. I'm lunching at the Criterion in half an hour and the traffic is quite dreadful today.'

Lady Kitty nodded. 'Perfectly impossible, my dear. You should get Charles to raise the matter in the House.'

Judith knelt before Alice, sister of the Duchess of Erpingham, offering up for inspection the pair of stockings she had removed from the tissue wrapping in the flat white box.

'These are from Paris, madam.'

'Price?' the now naked woman demanded.

'Two guineas, madam.'

'Outrageous. I'll try them.'

Lady Kitty Gresham produced an eighteen-inch ebony cigarette holder and screwed in a Balkan Sobranie. Snapping the lid of her onyx lighter down, she blew a perfect smoke ring and watched as Judith, kneeling before her naked client, palmed the lisle stockings up along the shapely legs. Ignoring Judith, the two aristocrats continued to bemoan men, meanness and money.

Judith blushed slightly as she felt the fixed gulf between the privileged woman – naked except for her title – and her own, fully clothed, position of servitude. Gazing at the heavy buttocks above the darker bands of the stockings stretched at the thighs, Judith's throat tightened. To be so close, and so intimate, and yet so far from rank and privilege gave her a delicious pang of torment. One day, she reflected, she would have her own emporium. She would be a proprietoress, not a wage slave. Then she would command the respect her skills deserved from these arrogant society belles. They would come to her imploring to have their pampered flesh tightly bound in strict satin and sculpted in stern lace.

'Seams,' the nude snapped impatiently. 'Hurry up, girl.'

Judith guided her thumbtip slowly and firmly up the entire length of the quivering left leg, from the tiny ankle up over the plump calf to the warmth of the thigh above. The nude turned to inspect the result in a cheval glass behind her, spreading her legs wide as she twisted – and making the task of straightening the seams more difficult.

'Come along, girl.'

The aristocracy spoke to their spaniels more considerately. Judith flushed, resenting the stinging admonishment.

'Phoebe's youngest was caught *in flagrante* with the footman,' Lady Kitty remarked, flicking her ash casually on to the carpet.

'Bad bloodline,' Alice, sister of the Duchess of Erpingham, replied. 'All the girls are as hot as hornets.'

Knuckling the right buttock up as she pinched at the dark band of lisle around the thigh beneath, Judith shivered. To be so close to privilege. To actually touch aristocratic flesh – the smooth flesh all of her class and station grudgingly respected as much as they scorned.

Alice, sister of the Duchess of Erpingham, broke wind loudly.

Lady Kitty Gresham giggled and spilt more ash down around the spiked heels of her snakeskin shoes.

Tapping her left thigh impatiently, the nude demanded to see some silk stockings.

'Very good, madam.'

When Judith returned, moments later, she found Lady Kitty dragging the mouthpiece of her ebony cigarette holder down between the plump buttocks of her naked companion. Digging into the deep cleft between the swollen cheeks, Lady Kitty Gresham paused then probed the tight sphincter. Judith averted her gaze and kept her trembling hands busy with the tissue around the silk stockings.

The sister of the Duchess of Erpingham rose up on scrunched toes and screamed softly as four inches of the thin ebony shaft slid in between her clenched cheeks.

'Promise to get me a nice present in America?'

'Yes, you cat,' Alice moaned.

'Pearls?' Lady Kitty purred, giving the cigarette holder a ruthless twist.

'Pearls,' the nude whispered, riding the shaft with sinuously undulating hips.

Lady Kitty extracted the cigarette holder with a flourish and, returning the mouthpiece immediately between her lips, sucked hard.

Judith knelt and palmed down the lisle stockings, baring the legs before her in readiness for the softer kiss of silk.

'They'll have to be cultured,' the nude remarked, turning as she spoke. 'You know what Charles is like with my allowance.'

Judith's dark eyes widened. When Alice, sister of the Duchess of Erpingham, had turned round, she had presented the young corsetière with a glimpse of her labia – labial lips parted in a wet smile.

In her lunchbreak, Judith made a telephone call from a booth in a nearby hotel. Juggling with the four brown pennies, the candlestick stand, the earpiece and her little black book, she spoke rapidly, asking the exchange for the *Clarion* newspaper.

'Putting you through,' the operator replied primly.

Later, she walked on as far as Bond Street, scrutinising the plate-glass shop fronts and searching for an empty one. She did not find any unused premises. Eight years ago, in the shadow of the depression, leaseholds could be snapped up, she thought, walking back towards Dover Street. Now, despite the gathering storm clouds of the impending war and the appearance of anti-aircraft guns in Hyde Park, business was booming.

Passing the Criterion, she had to step into the road to pass the lazily parked Hispano-Suiza. Lady Kitty's selfishness once more causing chaos to the busy London traffic.

After her supper of grilled kippers, toast and coffee, Judith washed up her plates, cup and saucer then tidied her small West Kensington bedsit. It took only four minutes. Stretching, she unzipped her black dress and put it on a hanger. Slipping out of her bra and panties – having carefully removed her stockings and suspender belt – she rinsed them out in the sink and pegged the lingerie up above the bath to dry.

Feeding the gas meter with a shiny sixpence, she lay down on the red rug before the hissing fire. Naked, she stretched and enjoyed the fierce heat at her breasts and belly, thrusting her bosom close to the heat until the delicious pain in her dark nipples became unbearable.

Beside her, she had a biscuit tin and a copy of that evening's edition of the *Clarion*. She picked up the paper and made for the inside, thumbing the pages until she spotted 'Vanity Cases', the society gossip column.

She read, in the third paragraph:

Pity poor Alice, soon to be scuttling yet again across the Atlantic with her miserly husband, Sir Charles Belvoir. Denied a state room, presumably she will have to take pot luck in steerage . . .

Judith grinned as she read the final line, an ungallant allusion to pearls and swine, with the columnist impudently expressing concern for any pig planning a voyage to the States.

Judith sighed. Excellent. That paragraph, supplied from her little black book over the telephone at lunchtime, would earn her another crisp white fiver from the *Clarion*. Rolling over on to her side, offering her bare bottom to the gas fire, she struggled with the lid of her biscuit tin and opened it. Already four inches deep in paper notes, it was the key to her own shop and workrooms.

Deemed no more than a common maid by the rich clients patronising the Dover Street emporium, Judith was invisible to them as she measured their soft, naked bodies and strapped them up in sweet bondage. Perfect cover for eavesdropping on their little vices and lapses – and nobody suspected the contents of the little black notebook she was forever busy scribbling in. And 'Vanity Cases' paid well. Judith, as a trained corsetière, was accurate. When measuring and fashioning the cup of a satin brassière, she always ensured that there was provision for the nipple: an erect, peaked bud could chafe painfully if squeezed by a poorly cut cup. And when creating the crotch for silk cami-knickers, she always allowed for the swell of the pubis: so irksome when the crease of silk penetrated the sticky labia. Judith was very accurate. 'Vanity Cases' paid her promptly for every contribution.

Flinching from the heat upon her bottom, Judith squeezed her hot cheeks as she rolled back down upon the red rug. Grinding her buttocks pleasurably, she picked up the *Clarion* and reread the paragraph. Pearls before swine (a clever pun playing upon earls travelling cheaply on the Cunard line). Suddenly remembering the scene greeting her return with the silk stockings, she let the *Clarion* slip down on to her breasts. The image of Lady Kitty raking her companion's cleft with the cruel cigarette holder filled her mind. Judith's fingers strayed down to her thickening nipples. The *Clarion* crackled annoyingly as she tweaked and punished her pink buds. Tossing the newspaper aside, and squirming her hot bottom into the red rug, she palmed, then cupped and squeezed, her breasts. Cupping and squeezing rhythmically, she conjured up the image of Lady Kitty probing the fleshy cheeks, causing the buttocks to spasm and tighten. Judith clamped her thighs together as she imagined the ebony stem sliding in. Jerking her hips and pounding her bare bottom into the red rug, Judith remembered how Lady Kitty had twisted the cigarette holder and demanded a present of pearls.

Punishing her breasts furiously, Judith crushed their soft, pliant warmth. A wetness from her tingling slit oozed between her clamped thighs. Grunting softly, she stretched down across her belly to dapple the fingertips of her right hand below her dark pubic fringe. The nest tickled her palm; she closed her eyes tight and plucked up strands of the matted coils, blinking at the sweet suffering. Impatiently, she splayed her thighs wide and drove her fingers down into the wet heat, drumming them into the slippery flesh-folds.

The hissing of the gas fire grew louder in her brain. Like the hiss of pleasure-pain torn from Alice, sister of the Duchess of Erpingham, when the cruel shaft had been whipped away from her anus. Judith moaned softly as she remembered the cigarette holder being withdrawn, to be immediately inserted between Lady Kitty's sensually parted lips: Judith spasmed and cried aloud at the memory, haunted yet thrilled by the erotic decadence of the privileged at their pleasure.

Twisting her wrist, she plied her thumbtip against her erect clitoris, using her curled fingers to ravish the labia below. She could not blot out the searing image from behind her eyes: Lady Kitty's white teeth biting into the stem of the holder, and Lady Kitty's red lips sucking hard on the feral taste of the aristocratic bottom's warmth. Rolling over once more, her knees up against her bosom, Judith surrendered her bare buttocks to the blaze of the gas fire.

Working her nimble fingers as deftly as when she plied the tape over naked breasts and around joggling bottoms, Judith strummed and pinched her wetness until she sensed the first rippling contractions of her approaching climax.

The heat of the gas fire rendered her bare cheeks as hot and sore as if they had just been soundly spanked. Spanked. Judith jerked in her climax. Spanked – by the red-lipped Lady Kitty? Ignoring her delicious discomfort as the gas fire blazed, Judith savaged herself during her orgasm, slapping her wet flesh with an open palm just as Lady Kitty would have spanked her rounded bottom with that cruel, aristocratic dispassion and consummate skill. As her belly tightened before imploding in a paroxysm, Judith returned her fingertips deep inside her slit. Splashes of her hot joy prickled her. She was coming again. The heat at her buttocks was now unbearable, as if the spanking hand had been replaced by a thin whip, a whip that cracked down silently to kiss the helpless flesh with searing kisses of crimson pain.

Knees together, hips pumping, buttocks swollen and straining as they were spread apart, Judith surrendered to the next climax. The fire hissed, the orange flames burning with a tiny heart of violet. Judith squealed, desiring but denying the need to inch away from the painful heat at her bare bottom. Between her thighs her hand was wet. Wet. The image of Alice, stockinged and superb, returned. The open, shining slit of the titled nude. The glistening pussy of Alice, sister of the Duchess of Erpingham, displayed almost with contempt in front of the kneeling corsetière. Rolling face down into the red rug, Judith dragged her wet flesh against its prickling pile, then rubbed herself firmly until she had conjured up yet another orgasm of sweet ferocity.

* * *

144

Khaki was becoming more apparent in London. Judith saw a lot of it when travelling on the Tube, especially at Paddington. It was no surprise when three uniformed young subalterns sauntered self-consciously into the Dover Street emporium at teatime the following Thursday. A year ago, they would have sported tweeds.

Purchasing presents for their girls, Judith surmised, as the proprietoress steered the three young officers into the inner sanctum where Judith would tend to their needs. Off for a weekend country house party, no doubt. An occasion, it was generally agreed, for matching and pairing the offspring of the landed gentry – ensuring the consolidation of both capital and lineage.

Predictably, the swaggering young stags had no clue about feminine lingerie. They hid their ignorance behind crude jests and coarse remarks. Pressed by Judith, their spokesman, a dark-haired young buck, blurted out that they wanted to see something French and naughty. The other two giggled, then said what a bad show it was about young Captain Johnny Johnson of the Light Infantry.

'For the boudoir,' Judith enquired – listening carefully to the snippets of scandal being exchanged – 'or for the bed?'

'Prefer 'em naked in bed,' the dark-haired officer replied. 'Just show us a few of your fripperies, girl.'

Judith selected a delicious range of lingerie and spread the items out on a table for their inspection. Crowding around the table, the inspection quickly gravitated into horseplay, with the cups of brassières being worn as ear muffs and aquiline noses snuffing deeply into silk panties.

'Damned if I know what to choose,' the dark-haired officer shrugged, looking slightly helplessly at Judith.

His comrades agreed.

Judith, sensing money, intervened. 'Would it help sir, if I demonstrated some items for you?'

145

'Splendid. Good show.' They nodded vigorously in unison.

'Please be seated and make yourselves comfortable, gentlemen,' Judith replied, gesturing to the leather armchairs. 'I won't be a moment.'

To their amazement and unconcealed delight, Judith did not retreat behind a heavy curtain from their gaze but remained, her back turned towards them, and slowly undressed. With graceful but deliberate provocation, she donned a white suspender belt, sheer white stockings and then wrapped a fluffy white feather boa – eight feet long – strategically around her neck, breasts and below. Turning, she bowed, then strutted towards them, mincing coquettishly – and allowing the boa to slip from the swell of her breasts.

'Very popular, and very, very French,' she whispered, flicking the tip of the boa across their upturned faces.

They brought their large hands together in a staccato of spontaneous applause, then more eagerly reached out to grasp and snatch at the trailing feather boa. Removing it was but the work of a moment, revealing Judith in the splendour of her waspie suspender and sheer white stockings.

'The suspender,' she murmured huskily, presenting her bare bottom to them, 'accentuates the waist and defines the female posterior, allowing the voluptuous feminine ripeness full prominence.'

Angling her elbows, she cupped her heavy cheeks and bunched them together, splayed her fingers and parted them – revealing her dark cleft – then squashed them together again. Her audience roared its unanimous approval, one subaltern rising from his leather chair, falling to his knees and shuffling forward until his face was a mere six inches from her rounded buttocks. Judith gazed down over her shoulder at his upturned face, smiling indulgently into his imploring eyes.

'You may kiss my bottom, young soldier, but,' she

warned, wagging her forefinger at him in mock severity, 'briefly and only once. No tongue.'

He groaned and closed his eyes before shuffling closer to bury his handsome face deep into the soft warmth of her naked bottom. She felt his trim moustache tickle, and then his hot breath at her cleft. Thrusting her heavy cheeks down on to his face, she stifled his carnal grunt with the weight of her rump.

'Next,' she whispered, stepping away from the kneeling subaltern, 'I will demonstrate the wicked magic of the basque.'

Peeling off her white stockings – deliberately slow, so that her bare bottom was displayed to full effect – Judith unclasped and removed the white suspender belt. 'If your girl is naughty,' she instructed them archly, 'you may use this to whip her bottom.' She snapped the suspender down crisply across her own cheeks, leaving a thin red weal diagonally across their creamy mounds.

They shouted excitedly, baying for more.

'Shush,' Judith said softly, adding, 'you boys must learn a little patience.' Naked, she wriggled into the basque, a tightly fitting creation in dark bottle-green satin. Turning round, she offered her breasts to the dark-haired young officer.

'The basque displays the breasts to full effect, sir,' she murmured primly, twiddling with the ends of the black laces. 'The lacing at the front squeezes and supports their swell. See?'

He grunted thickly, his eyes devouring her avidly, as she tugged at the laces, instantly creating a magnificent cleavage at her bosom.

'May I?' he pleaded hoarsely.

'How bold you are, sir,' Judith taunted, offering the laces to his trembling fingertips.

'Delightful,' he whispered, pulling the laces tight, then loosening them, and appreciating the effect on her bosom, marvelling wide-eyed as the breasts rose and fell.

'Not too tight,' Judith gasped as he toyed with her experimentally. She felt his excitement rise and thicken inside his breeches, felt his hardness spring up in a most unmilitary salute to her beauty, and pierce her belly.

'And finally,' Judith said softly, dismissing him and mincing back to the display table, 'a simple boddice or vest. For the virginal, schoolgirl look. So perfect for bedtime.'

Stripped of her bottle-green basque – so patently wicked and fashioned for dark pleasures – she turned once more to face their adoring gaze, partially but not completely covered in a simple, ribbed-cotton sleeveless vest. Pale-blue periwinkles graced the peaks of her nipples. The hem skimmed the pubic fuzz at her delta. Turning, she briefly presented them with a glimpse of the lower curves of her delicious bottom.

'Now, boys –'

But Judith's faint protests proved too little, too late. Inflamed and engorged, they jumped up and pressed closely around her, stroking her slender shoulders, the swell of her breasts and her plump buttocks. Her neck arched as a firm palm swept down over the ribbed cotton stretched across her belly, and pressed dominantly at her pussy.

'This would seem to meet with your approval,' she teased, lightly tapping each of the bulges in their military breeches. 'Don't you want to show me your approval, boys?'

Unbuttoning in an ecstasy of fumbling, the three subalterns pulled out their thick shafts and pumped rhythmically. Sweating, grunting and cursing softly, they punished their proud erections.

'Take it easy, boys. This isn't a race. There's no prize for the one who comes first.'

They came, moments later, their spurts of sticky semen splattering and staining her ribbed-cotton vest at her bosom and belly and – from the dark-haired young

148

officer – her naked bottom. Dripping, Judith shrank back, plucking the wet vest away from her breasts.

'So glad you approve,' she murmured. 'I'll put together a selection of items for each of you and have them sent round to your club. You can settle now, though. In cash.'

They paid, unaware of the steep mark-up destined not for the till but for Judith's biscuit tin.

On Friday evening, Captain 'Johnny' Johnson made an appearance in 'Vanity Cases'. Lock up your spoons, the gossip columnist warned, changing Johnson's brigade from the Light Infantry to the Light-Fingered. Dud cheques at Eton and unpaid mess bills at Sandhurst were exhumed and deprecated. After reading the item with a proud smile, Judith added another crisp white fiver to the growing pile inside her biscuit tin.

Her work at the Dover Street emporium yielded little for Judith to pass on to the *Clarion* for several days. She dealt competently with the trickle of dowagers leading dull lives and ministered to the succession of blameless spinsters in search of sensible stockings – seamless and subdued.

Thursday delivered a Daimler to the door. It was with inquisitive speculation that Judith regarded the liveried chauffeur in his pale-blue jacket with gold frogging and smart black gauntlets. Standing erectly to attention, he opened the rear door and saluted as two middle-aged women, followed by a younger girl, emerged from the sumptuous interior. As swift as he was graceful, he beat them to the shop doors, to open them and usher his charges inside. Judith was impressed. The party reeked of money, and money had its secrets.

'Lady van Meister,' the proprietoress announced as she steered the new arrivals towards Judith. 'Recently from the Malay States. With such a change in climate, some additions to her daughter's wardrobe are essential.'

Lady van Meister's daughter, Celia, was a peach, and one – though perfectly ripe – as yet unplucked, Judith judged as she appraised the senior-prefect decorum of the young woman.

Judith nodded to the proprietoress and approached Celia, taking her gently by the elbow. They walked together into an inner sanctum of mirrors and drapes. The young corsetière patted her bun, drew the velvet curtains together for privacy and produced her measuring tape.

'Take all of your clothes off, please, miss,' she said softly, crushing down the note of anticipation in her voice.

Beyond the velvet curtains, the whispering voices were just audible. Judith strained to listen as she busied herself with the nude.

'Not a nibble, and there were at least three eligible men with both rank and money,' Lady van Meister sighed.

'Can there be anything wrong with the girl?' the other voice replied. 'Pretty little piece.'

'Struck up a ridiculous friendship with an impossible nanny in Sabah.'

'Chummy?'

'Quite inseparable,' Lady van Meister replied.

'You don't think –'

'Quite frankly, I despair of ever getting the girl off my hands.'

Behind the velvet curtain, Judith decoded the overheard conversation. A juicy little paragraph for the *Clarion* there, no doubt. Best make absolutely sure of the facts, she mused.

'Will you place your hands up on your head, please, miss?' she asked Celia.

The young woman obeyed, her breasts rising up

proudly as she did so. Judith slipped the measuring tape just below the naked girl's shoulders and drew it together tightly across the bosom, trapping the nipples.

'Thirty-four,' Judith murmured, inserting her finger inside the tape to check its tightness. Her knuckle skimmed the nipples. Celia's rosebud mouth opened slightly but her sigh was silent.

'Turn around, please,' Judith instructed gently.

The naked girl complied, her soft buttocks brushing against the corsetière's thighs. Judith stepped closer, forcing her pubic mound against the peach cheeks as she reached to cup and weigh Celia's breasts in her upturned palms. The nude mewed. Judith sensed the nipples thicken and peak.

'I insist on a perfect fit,' Judith whispered, squeezing the captive breasts. 'The breast must fit the brassiére cup like a glove. It must wear the stretched satin like a second skin.'

Celia nodded her understanding, and jerked her bare bottom back into the warmth behind her.

The corsetière whipped away the measuring tape. 'Now your hips,' she said, kneeling. 'No,' she continued, 'stay exactly as you are.'

She pressed her face close to – but not directly against – the swell of the naked young woman's left cheek. Slipping the tape around the slender hips, she drew it tightly across the heavy buttocks, drawing the nude towards her mouth so that she was forced to kiss the soft warm flesh.

Armed with the knowledge gained through her eavesdropping, Judith had little doubt of Celia's allegiance to Sappho, but, as her lips brushed the left buttock, the spasm of response confirmed the fact. The *Clarion* would receive a very choice little item for 'Vanity Cases.'

Celia sighed softly and rubbed her bottom sensually into the kneeling corsetière's face, grappling eagerly with her taloned hands to clutch and draw Judith more firmly into her flesh. Judith allowed herself to be forced to kiss, tongue, then teasingly bite the creamy cheeks, silvering their swell with hot saliva. Snarling softly, Celia turned abruptly, thrusting her wet delta into Judith's mouth.

'Kiss me. Kiss me there.'

Judith's tongue worked hungrily as it flickered lightly up along the labia before pausing to firmly probe, lick and lap at the sticky flesh-folds.

Yes, Judith decided, nipping at the tiny pink clitoris, then sucking hard upon the flesh-thorn trapped between her pinioning teeth, the *Clarion* will pay well for this little snippet.

Judith used the free time of her Saturday afternoon off carefully, determined not to waste a single minute. She had her tea at a Lyons Corner House, taking time over her poached eggs to scrutinise the 'nippies' as they darted between the busy tables. Judith's purpose was professional, if pleasurable. That pert little blonde minx with the tray of brown-sauce bottles – Judith determined that she needed an uplift, underwired brassière to tame and contain such superb breasts. And that willowy brunette. Such good legs, so lithe and shapely. Good legs spoilt by those school-teacher's woollen stockings. How fetching the girl would look in silk hosiery. Closing her mouth over a forkful of poached egg on toast, she imagined having both of the pretty 'nippies' as clients in her own establishment – stripping them slowly, plying the tape intimately, then fitting them with selected items. For the blonde minx, a Swedish brassière, cunningly cross-strapped for maximum support and uplift. Each cup heavy with the warm weight of the superb breasts. For the willowy brunette, a spell of tender dominance as each lithe leg was sheathed in whispering, seamed silk. Judith had some difficulty swallowing her warm mouthful – and when she rose from the table to leave the Lyons Corner House, she was dripping wet.

An open-topped bus took her to Fulham Broadway. Alighting, she walked through the busy Saturday-afternoon market along the length of the North End Road. Then she saw it. It was perfect. A millinery shop, the establishment now closed due to a family bereavement. The vacant premises, with a workshop at the rear and a small flat above, were to let. Judith opened her little black notebook and made a note of the agents. As she closed the book, her eye caught the entry scribbled down under the name Celia van Meister.

On Monday morning, just before noon, the proprietoress replaced the telephone and summoned Judith to her desk.

'A most extraordinary thing,' Judith was informed. 'Lady van Meister has just requested that you visit her daughter at their hotel. A second fitting, it seems, and the daughter insisted on you. Really, these colonials. Quite impossible. A car will be calling for you shortly.'

The Daimler, this time driven by a younger, more handsome liveried chauffeur, whisked Judith off towards Bayswater. The hotel was something of a disappointment – Judith had vaguely expected the Ritz. It was a four-storey red-brick edifice tucked away in a side street. Judith smelt mice in the corridors and traces of stale Brown Windsor soup.

The chauffeur tapped respectfully on the double doors and, curtly announcing Judith as 'the shop girl, madam', ushered her in.

Lady van Meister was perched on a horsehair sofa. Celia, in a simple black outfit, was at an occasional table, decanting pale sherry into a glass.

'So good of you to come, Miss –'

Judith supplied her name.

'I will not offer you sherry,' Lady van Meister continued suavely. 'There is work to be done. Thank you, Jenkins,' she said, taking the glass from the proffered tray.

Jenkins? Judith frowned. Surely the girl with the tray was Celia, Lady van Meister's daughter – not her maid.

'Interesting reading, the *Clarion*, though an utter rag,' Lady van Meister observed, picking up Saturday evening's edition and reading from the 'Vanity Cases' column. ' "We learn with interest that Celia, youngest daughter of Lady van Meister, spurns the attentions of ardent suitors, preferring, it would appear, the –" But I need not continue, need I? You know the rest perfectly well.'

Suddenly frightened, Judith turned towards the double doors. The chauffeur, arms folded insolently, blocked her retreat. Her throat tightened and her heart hammered as her dark eyes widened in alarm.

'Captain Johnson, would you assist the young woman with her clothing?'

Captain Johnson. Judith glanced over her shoulder. The chauffeur guarding the door had removed his liveried uniform and had assumed a crisper, more military bearing. He stroked his chin and studied Judith closely as he strode towards her.

'It will be a pleasure,' he chuckled.

'I want that black notebook,' Lady van Meister instructed, having refreshed her voice with a sip of sherry, 'and the girl, bare-bottomed, across that table.' The speaker jabbed urgently at a polished pearwood table-top.

Judith's brief attempt at flight was stalled by the fierce embrace of Captain Johnson.

'Got you at last, you little bitch,' he snarled, ripping down her dress from her shoulders, exposing her breasts.

'Gag her, Jenkins,' came the stern instruction from the maid's employer.

Jenkins obeyed, briskly gagging and silencing Judith's squeals of protest.

'Messy business, the courts. And there's been altogether too much scandal and sniggering at our expense. We've decided to settle this business privately. Privately and painfully.'

Judith, naked and trembling, stared wildly over at the horsehair sofa. Lady van Meister was flexing a riding crop.

'Take her to the table, Johnny.'

Moments later, spreadeagled face down across the circular pearwood table, Judith shuddered as she learnt her fate.

'My maid will whip you. She will do so vigorously and, I believe, with just cause. She is a normal girl with healthy appetites – as the milkman can quite readily confirm.'

Captain Johnson, pinning Judith down, brayed a harsh laugh.

'A whipping is no more than you deserve, girl. For many weeks we have all been wondering who was supplying the *Clarion* with gossip. The Copmanthorpes blamed their butler, Lady Kitty suspected her dentist – she is so peculiarly vulnerable under gas, I believe – and even a waiter at the Criterion came under suspicion. A simple process of elimination led us all to Dover Street – and you.'

The riding crop cracked down, striping Judith's upturned buttocks savagely. Her gasp of anguish was drowned in Lady van Meister's grunt of satisfaction. Judith writhed, flinching from Captain Johnson's firm hand pinioning her nakedness.

'You,' the punisher repeated, sweeping the crop down in emphasis. It was a stinging stroke, leaving a deep pink line of pain across the quivering cheeks.

'Baiting the trap with Jenkins was Captain Johnson's idea. He proposes to deal with you separately, when I am done.'

Judith's belly tightened. She struggled to protest, through her gag, but Jenkins had been thorough in her task. Collapsing back down – crushing her breasts into the polished pearwood – Judith shivered as Captain Johnson traced the two red weals across her punished cheeks with a firm forefinger.

'I have plans for you, my little corsetière, but first you must be whipped.'

'Commence,' Lady van Meister snapped, passing the supple crop to her maid.

Judith's buttocks spasmed as Jenkins gripped the crop in her right hand and raised it above the bare bottom.

'Twenty strokes,' barked Lady van Meister.

'Very good, ma'am,' the dutiful maid replied.

Judith made a last-ditch attempt to escape, wriggling and squirming frantically.

'Get her hands, Johnny.'

Judith groaned as her wrists were caught up in the strong young captain's fierce grip. He stretched at full length across the surface of the table and held her, face down, positioned for the punishing crop across her bottom.

'Wait,' Lady van Meister snarled. 'Pass me that cushion.'

Jenkins selected a small crimson cushion and handed it to her impatient mistress.

'Up,' the aristocrat ordered, spanking Judith's buttocks sharply.

Captain Johnson's grip was so tight, Judith barely managed to inch her hips clear from the polished pearwood.

'More. Higher, girl. Get your bottom up this instant.'

Fearful of the hovering hand above her defenceless cheeks, Judith raised her buttocks to Lady van Meister's satisfaction. The velvet cushion was slipped between Judith and the table. She sank into it, shuddering as the material tickled her splayed labia.

'That's much better.' Lady van Meister nodded, palming the proffered rump approvingly. 'Twenty strokes, Jenkins.'

Immobile, helpless and gagged, the naked corsetière closed her eyes and squeezed her cheeks together tightly. The maid, still smarting with resentment towards Judith after the charade she had been instructed to participate in as bait, plied the wicked crop viciously. The first seven slicing strokes whipped down to sear and stripe the naked cheeks in rapid succession. Judith squealed into her tight gag, jerking her bruised breasts and peaked nipples into the hard table at each cut. Jenkins paused, pressing the whippy cane down firmly into the yielding cheeks, dimpling their crimson crowns dominantly.

'Again,' Lady van Meister hissed, taloning Judith's hair and forcing her victim's face into its own reflection.

Jenkins cracked the leather-sheathed crop down three more times – slowly, deliberately and witheringly. At her mouth, the wet gag choked Judith's screams. Captain Johnson, taking both of her pinioned wrists in his left hand, stretched across and fingered her tear-stained face.

'There, there, my little beauty. No more tears. Soon the suffering will be over and our pleasure will begin.' With his free hand, he squeezed Judith's captive face, tilting it up so that Judith's tearful gaze met his lust-lit eyes.

'Not now, Johnny. You can have her to play with later. Give me that damn crop,' Lady van Meister snapped, 'I'll show you how to whip a bottom.'

Jenkins surrendered the supple cane.

'Hold her down. I'll administer the rest.'

Jenkins had been brutal in her revenge, and Lady van Meister proved no less savage in hers. Pinning Judith down between the shoulders with the tip of the crop, she roughly palmed the buttocks she was about to beat.

Pausing to thumb the cleft between the flesh-mounds – now crisscrossed with scarlet weals – she dropped her voice to a vehement whisper.

'We've got the measure of you, girl. Got you taped. You had a position of trust which you grossly abused. A judicious nod from Downing Street will silence the *Clarion* – but for you, my naughty little corsetière, more severe measures.'

Seven cruel slices followed. Each exploded with a crimson flash behind Judith's eyes, as crimson as the stripes across her seared cheeks. Between each stroke, Lady van Meister tapped the whipped rump dominantly.

'That one was from Alice,' she murmured, 'and that from Sir Charles.' Each searching swipe of leathered cane across quivering flesh was delivered with a sponsor's name – all victims of the scandalous reporting of 'Vanity Cases'.

Sobbing brokenly, Judith lost count. Lady van Meister had not. The concluding three strokes were particularly vicious. The punisher, perspiring and grunting with effort, relished the swish-crack of the crop, savoured the responsive jerks of the thrashed buttocks and hissed her pleasure as Judith squealed her pain. Tossing the crop down on to the carpet, Lady van Meister bent down close to peruse and inspect the seething cheeks. Judith flinched as she felt the hot breath of her excited chastiser.

'Excellent,' came the verdict, 'and so richly deserved.'

'Splendid,' Captain Johnson agreed huskily.

'We'll be off now, Johnny. She is all yours, as we agreed. Will you be needing this?' Lady van Meister asked solicitously as she scooped up the crop and placed it on the table two inches from Judith's tearfilled eyes.

'Leave the crop, Lady van Meister. I never mount without one.'

Judith groaned.

* * *

'Your position in Dover Street is no longer tenable,' he remarked, stroking Judith's hair gently, then allowing his hand to trace the dimple of her spine down to her reddened rump. 'You do see that, don't you?'

Judith, bucking her hips to rid her bottom of his hands now stroking it firmly, closed her eyes and jerked her head away. He spanked her sharply.

'Look at me. It is impossible for you to return to Dover Street. However,' he murmured, fingering the sticky warmth of her cleft – and chuckling as she squeezed her cheeks to deny him access to her hot sphincter – 'in the present climate, it would be a shame to ignore your talents.'

Judith stiffened.

'I'm going to see to it that your skills are put to very good use.'

Judith relaxed, easing her soft cheeks apart. His finger quivered with anticipation then probed her anus, sliding in with tender dominance.

'I'm in with a pretty rum crowd. We snoop and pry on all sorts of people. You'd be surprised, my dear. Need to know who'll be with us when the balloon goes up.'

Judith, still gagged, strained to nod – signalling her understanding.

'What a very pretty bottom you have, my little corsetière.' Bending down close to her bunched cheeks, he slipped his finger out from her sphincter and kissed the crown of each whipped cheek. Rising, he stretched over her naked body and loosened the gag.

'I'll set you up in Bird Cage Walk. You'll be able to eavesdrop on the Westminster wives. Nice to know which backbenchers we can count on. Interested?'

'Yes, of course. I will be your spy –'

He dropped his right hand to her wet pubis, knuckling it gently before taking the outer left labial lip in a cruel pincer of forefinger and thumbtip. Tweaking it, he gave the wet ribbon of flesh a sudden tug. Judith squealed, grinding her breasts into the pearwood and drumming her clenched fists into its polished smoothness.

'Eavesdropping, girl, not espionage. There'll be no medals in it for you. A pension, perhaps. We'll see. Yes, eavesdropping on the prattling wives – and mistresses – of our honourable members. I'll be your controller, of course.'

'Controller?'

'That's right,' Captain Johnson affirmed, unbuttoning himself and fingering out his erection. 'Are you game?'

She felt his hardness against her inner thigh as he adjusted the velvet cushion beneath her prickling pubis. She heard him snatch up the supple riding crop.

'Game?' he demanded, thrusting his hips forward and entering her, filling her completely with his hardness.

'Yes,' hissed Judith, spasming and clenching her inner muscles as she started to milk his length.

'Capital,' he roared, swishing the crop down across her bottom.

'Yes,' Judith moaned, 'I will do my duty. My duty to serve.'

The crop rose up, quivering above her cheeks, then lashed down with loving affection.

'To serve,' Judith whispered, tonguing the polished pearwood with increasing frenzy.

9

The Novice

The Crow, a spirited black gelding, two years old and sixteen hands high, was the most temperamental horse in the yard. Bred to sprint but built to stay, he had yet to find his distance – his best trip out being fifth in a bunch finish at Uttoxeter last month. Then he had gone lame. Debbie – who vowed to ride him first past the post one day soon – had worked hard, nursing then exercising The Crow to the vet's instructions. That morning, the vet had passed the gelding fit.

'Good boy,' Debbie murmured, tugging the horse's soft ears. Bending, her breasts bulging in her sports bra, she currycombed his forelegs.

The morning was hot. Up at six for tea and toast with the rest of the stable boys and girls, Debbie had already mucked out and stacked bales for two hours. The armpits of her white T-shirt were dark with perspiration. Grooming The Crow was a vigorous task, leaving her brow, neck and bosom glistening.

Debbie patted The Crow's neck affectionately, then went out of the dark stable into the blaze of the summer morning sun. Across the yard, a brass tap at a brick wall sparkled invitingly. The yard was deserted – all the horses were down at the gallops – except for the stable cat, stretched out asleep on the warm cobblestones.

Debbie risked it. She peeled her T-shirt up over her head, then hung it on a nail and turned on the tap.

161

Cupping her hands, she splashed the ice-cold water up into her face – and gasped aloud. It was such a delicious shock. Unfastening her sports bra, which strained to hold her heavy breasts in firm bondage, she added it to her T-shirt on the nail and bowed down once more to the brass tap. Cupping her hands to catch the cold stream, she dashed the contents to her neck and breasts. Her nipples peaked instantly in response, hardening and darkening as they dripped diamond droplets. She crushed her wet hands up to her shining breasts and squeezed, thumbing the sweet torment of her painfully prinked flesh.

'Hot?' a curt voice inquired.

Crossing her arms to shield her naked breasts, Debbie turned, blinking shyly in the strong sunlight. It was Captain Hinton, the yard trainer. An exceptional jockey, his career in the saddle had been finished by a spill up at Ayr, which had smashed his left hand, leaving it useless. It hung, lifeless, down at his thigh.

'Thought everyone was down at the gallops,' Debbie mumbled, relishing yet resenting his searching gaze, as she inched her hand desperately towards her bra on the nail.

Ignoring her remark – but enjoying her discomfort – Captain Hinton asked what the vet had said.

'The Crow's fine. Ready to race.' Debbie grinned.

'I'll be the judge of that.'

'But he is, and I want to ride him –'

A sharp horn sounded as a Range Rover swung into the yard. The sleeping cat shot across the cobbles and hid behind a straw bale. Sensing her chance – the Captain had turned, frowning – Debbie made a wild grab for her T-shirt. She was still struggling into it, braless, as the Range Rover squealed to a standstill. The engine revved then died as the electric window slid down. A blonde – early thirties, dark sunshades, pink lipstick – spoke brusquely.

'What did the vet say?'

'Your horse is fit, miss. He's fine,' the Captain told the owner.

'The Crow? Fit?' The blonde laughed harshly. 'I'll believe it when I bank some prize money.'

'He's a good horse, miss,' the trainer continued, dogged in The Crow's defence. 'He just needs the right distance. Uttoxeter was two furlongs too long –'

'And Brighton a furlong too short,' the owner interrupted sarcastically.

'The Crow's a winner,' Debbie chipped in loyally. She had managed to pull the T-shirt down over her wet breasts. Braless, their moist mounds clung to the thin fabric, revealing their proud swell.

The blonde ignored the stable girl, but snarled softly at the pert figure, the wet bosom and the explicitly peaked nipples beneath the stretch of taut white cotton.

'I'm going on down to the gallops,' she informed Captain Hinton curtly. 'I'll see you down there.' It was not an invitation but an instruction. She drove off.

'Best do as the boss says.' He shrugged, turning to Debbie.

She wanted to rescue her sports bra, but hesitated. She felt shy and awkward before the handsome, lean man. At night, in her narrow bed, she would close her eyes tight and conjure up images of him being tenderly brutal with her – and conjure up a wet heat between her splayed thighs with her scrabbling fingertips. In her bed, in the dark, she would make him do things that made her belly melt and her hips jerk in orgasm. Here, out in the fierce sunlight, she simply blushed and gazed across at the cat behind the straw bale.

Giving up her bra, she turned and walked away, hoping his eyes were drinking their fill of her tightly denimed cheeks and the inviting cleft deep between their rolling swell. In the safety of the cool tackle room, she tucked her T-shirt into her jeans and stretched up to unhook a martingale. Glancing out into the sunlight, she saw the yard was empty. Her bra. Skipping out silently over the cobblestones, she approached the brass tap. Beside it, the nail was empty. Her sports bra had gone.

A burning flush crimsoned her young face. He had taken it. Captain Hinton – lean, mean and desirable, the useless hand adding a dark menace to his erotic charge – had taken the bra. As a trophy? A keepsake? Probably just to keep the yard tidy, she thought, grinning. He was such a stickler and insisted on orderliness and neatness. It would be in his office, thrown away into the rubbish bin and already forgotten, Debbie decided.

She knew that the blonde owner had lustful designs on Captain Hinton. The sexual language between them was eloquent, if unspoken. Behind the dark sunshades, Debbie suspected that the blonde's hidden eyes were appraising his athletic build, his handsome face and – below the brass buckle of his leather belt – the pronounced bulge in his jeans. He would be down at the gallops now, following her like a lap dog. Debbie kicked sullenly at a loose cobblestone. Better go and retrieve her bra.

Just at the last moment, she hesitated. Lowering her hand from the door handle, she retreated from the entrance to his office and tiptoed to the side window. Lugging a loose bale of straw into place, she jumped up and pressed her face against the glass.

Inside, she saw Captain Hinton. His jeans were dragged down to his knees, his royal-blue briefs stretched just above in a tight band. Her eyes widened at the sight of his buttocks, pale and painfully clenched. Debbie nearly stumbled from her perch in surprise. Regaining her footing, she peered cautiously through the glass, her throat tightening and her tongue thickening in her dry mouth.

Bending over his desk and steadying himself with his good hand, he was holding up her brassière and kissing

164

the white cups. Debbie squeaked her shock and delight. Shock at the sight of her sports bra clenched in the fist of his smashed hand, delight at the sight of his lips, tongue and teeth busy at the cups. She clenched her thighs together. Beneath her, the straw bale wobbled. Gasping, Debbie spreadeagled herself against the brick wall. A soft moan escaped her lips as her nipples grazed the brickwork.

Inside the office, the trainer was using her bra against his erection, clutching it in his useless hand to masturbate. Between his parted thighs, she glimpsed his scrotum swinging gently as he rocked on his heels. A soft cotton cup capped his engorged knout. She swallowed and blinked as she watched the crippled hand punishing the cotton-sheathed shaft, saw his buttocks spasm as his hips jerked, saw the white cup trembling as it caught his hot spurt.

Panting so hard that her hot breath dimmed the window pane at her lips, Debbie pressed her breasts against the harsh wall. Deliberately dragging her nipples across the rough surface, she gulped and inched up on her toes to risk another peep. Inside, the trainer was holding the sports bra aloft. It spindled slowly in his grasp, dripping hot semen down to form opaque puddles on the polished desk top at the splayed fingertips of his steadying hand. Suddenly, he whirled the cotton bra then whipped it down, lashing the desk. Cracking it down with repeated ferocity, he called her name out harshly. Debbie. Debbie. Debbie.

Standing at the window's clouded glass, her legs turned to jelly so quickly she wobbled and tumbled from the straw bale. Debbie's brain burned as a dark desire flooded her mind, and her jeans, at the juncture where they bit softly into her pantied pubis.

In the cool of the evening, when all the other stable boys and girls had gone into Sudbury to the pub, Debbie took The Crow down to the gallops. After the heat of the summer day, the Suffolk night was perfumed with sorrel, wild violets and sweet sedge. She found the purple sky of the gathering dusk soothing after her inflaming discovery earlier, and, as she walked the gelding along, she gazed up to count the early stars. There was, she decided, just enough light to take The Crow safely along the six-furlong track. Reaching down to tighten the girth, she patted his neck reassuringly. The black two-year-old neighed and tossed his head. Debbie grinned and squeezed her thighs. She'd take him along at a canter, then turn on the throttle.

The rhythmic drumming of his hooves told her all she needed to know. He was back in his fluent stride and fit as a fiddle. Coming up to the two-furlong post beside the snaking white rail, she crouched in the saddle and shortened the rein. He flew, galloping down towards the mile-post as true as an arrow.

From beind an elm tree, Captain Hinton lowered his field glasses from the lark he was watching and, his ears catching the sound of a galloping horse, racked them along the track. Someone was taking a horse for an unscheduled run – at full stretch, too. Who could it be? He certainly hadn't given any orders for an evening ride. As his eyes picked out the crouching figure of Debbie, her pert bottom thrust up from the saddle, he nodded and grinned. Little devil, he chuckled, grudgingly admiring her use of a short rein.

Debbie hugged the sweating gelding before looping his reins over the white rail. Exhilarated by the ride, and by The Crow's return to form, she ducked under the rail and strode thigh-high through the nodding cow-parsley. The supple stems, swept aside as she proceeded, flicked back up to playfully whip her tightly jodhpured cheeks. The moon was out, casting a silvery light over the wooded Suffolk countryside. The heat at her slit was intense. Turning to retrace her tracks, she approached the white rail, yanked down her jodhpurs and spread her leather boots wide apart. Gripping her panties, she dragged them down over her thighs, shuddering as she sensed her sticky wetness stretched down from her labia to the soiled cotton between her knees. The spindle of spun sugar snapped and splashed against her inner thigh. Tossing her head back, she grasped the white rail with both hands. Pulling herself up slightly against the smooth rail, she kissed her pubis into the cool, white wood.

An owl screeched softly as it launched itself from a high branch in the moonlit elm. Down beneath, Captain Hinton ducked instinctively. Sometimes bats came out on summer nights and became entangled in one's hair. Annoyed at the interruption, the trainer brought the field glasses swiftly back up to his eyes and trained them on the mile-post. Got it. Now, a little to the left. Yes. There. Through his glasses, he could just discern the young girl, naked from her belly to her knees, bringing herself off against the white rail in the moonlight.

Debbie's cottage, a tiny one-bedroomed stone building set deep in a coppiced wood, had no gas or electricity. She went to bed, masturbated, slept, and rose early before dawn by candlelight.

With The Crow safely returned to his stable and bedded down, the young stable girl headed home for supper, hungry after her vigorous exertions. A small wood-burning Aga held a rich, meaty rabbit, onion and potato casserole in the warm belly of its oven. Without washing her slit-sticky fingers, she lit four candles, sliced two thick wedges of bread and brought the succulent casserole from the oven to the table. Salt and ketchup later, using her bread as a fork, she wolfed the delicious supper. She wiped her plate clean with a bread-crust, then rose and removed a bottle of beer from a jug of cold water in the stone sink. Unstoppered, the beer fizzled from the neck of the bottle as Debbie searched about for a glass.

The back door scraped open and Captain Hinton walked into the kitchen. Debbie greeted him with a shy smile and raised the bottle.

'Thirsty?'

'Not really,' he replied, 'but then, I haven't been out on the gallops.'

Debbie flushed and put the bottle down on the table. 'I –'

'Took him along beautifully. Didn't have my stopwatch, but saw everything,' he said softly, tapping the field glasses at his hip with his smashed hand.

Debbie fingered the froth oozing from the beer bottle.

'Everything,' he repeated.

Beer bubbled up and spilt down the side of the short, thick neck. She touched it again, bursting the tiny bubbles with her fingertip, just as she would burst the silver bubbles at her slit.

'She won't let you ride The Crow. You know that, don't you?' he continued, gazing at the girl.

Debbie shrugged and pursed her lower lip.

'Pretty old-fashioned, these new owners. Don't like trusting novices with a ride,' he explained.

'A girl's got to start sometime,' Debbie murmured, wiping her wet fingertip down along the taut thigh of her jodhpurs before taking two steps towards him. 'Do you think I'm ready for a ride?'

In the flickering candlelight, he gazed down at her and nodded emphatically.

'If you spoke to her, she might –'

'She might,' he whispered, taking a step closer.

Debbie reached down to stroke his damaged hand. Flinching, he withdrew it, his mouth suddenly twisting in anger. Her hand followed his and grasped it, drawing it gently against her pubic swell. He shuddered and closed his eyes. Up on tiptoe, her riding boots squeaking on the stone floor, she kissed him, crushing his damaged hand firmly into the warmth between her thighs. Kneeling down before him, she placed both his hands upon her head and unzipped him. He grunted softly, spreading his thighs apart as she fingered out his thickening length.

Out in the dark coppice, a jay disturbed a roost of sleeping rooks. They rose, flapping lazily and cawing harshly, then settled back down in the moonlit treetops. In the tiny cottage, the fire in the Aga perfumed the kitchen with the fragrance of apple logs. The single tap dripped slowly into the greasy casserole dish. A soft sucking, punctuated by moans and carnal grunts, filled the silence as Debbie kissed, licked then sucked at his hardness. She did not take him into her mouth, but plied her tongue and lips at the glistening knout. He came with a shout, blinding her as he pumped his hot seed. Grinning, she wiped her eyes and, leading him by the damaged hand, edged back towards the kitchen table. Easing herself down, she wriggled out of her jodhpurs and used the crushed knuckles against her sticky labia. Gripping his wrist, Debbie forced the clenched fist down the hot furrow of her wet slit, coming with a jerk that slammed her bare bottom down into the table so hard that the ketchup bottle rattled and keeled over.

In her small bedroom, in the darkness of the night, they made love. As his chest crushed down on to her soft bosom, the wiry hairs rasping her nipples, she cupped and squeezed his buttocks. Emboldened, he stroked her face with his twisted hand. Responding, she kissed it twice then licked it slowly, her tongue wet against his flesh, keeping time to the gentle thrusting of his hips as he slid his shaft into her welcoming warmth.

Being a novice, she was uncertain. Sensing this, he left little for her to do. Easing himself up slightly, he pumped, penetrating deeper, and brought his mouth down on to her parted lips. Their tongues flickered and fenced, but he easily mastered her quivering wet flesh, taming it before entering to occupy and possess her sweet mouth. She squealed as he thrust deeper, he attempted to withdraw slightly, but she hugged him fiercely to her breasts, to her belly and to the heat between her thighs. She cried out softly as she felt his body stiffen for release. He grunted, withdrew, and groaned in sweet torment as he emptied himself upon her breasts, the hot semen splashing down on her nipples like cream upon twin berries. She clasped her breasts and palmed them fiercely, wearing the wet trophy on her skin exultantly.

He seized her, grappling her soft nakedness more assuredly, with dominant confidence, and turned her over, face down into the bed. Kneeling astride her thighs, he fingered her cleft slowly, the firm strokes bringing small mews of pleasure from her lips. When the forefinger paused at the rosebud of her tight little sphincter, she tensed and spasmed. He spanked her twice; then, using both hands, spread her upturned cheeks painfully apart, revealing the tightening anal whorl.

His tongue-tip loosened the tiny muscled knot, leaving it moist and relaxed for his probing length. He pierced her, slowly filling her rectal warmth. She dug her fingers into the pillow, shrinking a little from his fierce masculinity and stern lust – then, as her belly imploded and her juices flowed, she submitted to him, surrendering her cheeks up to the flesh-spear thrusting between them.

He rode her ruthlessly, at full stretch. Back in the saddle after years of abstinence and exile, he straddled her, raising his thighs a fraction as if upon a spirited filly, using her hair as controlling reins. Squeezing her thighs between his knees, his hard belly at her buttock's soft swell, he lowered his mouth on to her right shoulder and bit. She screamed softly. He bit again, sinking his white teeth into her flesh as he climaxed.

She felt him loosen his controlling grip and ease himself up, peeling his wet skin away from hers. She wriggled her bottom and clenched her sphincter to contain him, urging him to recommence the vigorous ride. He slapped the left buttock hard.

'Yes,' she hissed into the pillow, 'spank Debbie, spank Debbie, spank Debbie.'

He did, leaving both cheeks red and shiny-sore. She tongued the pillow to smother her squeals.

'Now, my little novice,' she heard him whisper, 'I'm going to teach you the dark arts of the saddle. Milk me,' she heard him command, feeling his full length thicken within her.

Debbie, her hot bottom stinging sweetly, thrilled to the savage dominance. With his hardness deep inside her, she ground her breasts and belly into the bed and then concentrated vehemently as she contracted her anal muscles.

Spank. His good hand cracked down once more across her bare bottom. The creamy cheeks wobbled under the impact of the cruel caress.

'Milk me, girl. Come on,' he urged, making his words sound like an obscene prayer.

He was forcing her to do all the work. Suddenly she understood – understood how to contain his thickened length inside her and use her sinuous contractions to give him the delight he craved. Suddenly, she understood the true meaning of submission. The knowledge burned deep within her as fiercely as his swollen manhood. He was teaching her, the novice, how to really ride.

She closed her eyes. Two furlongs out. It was more

thrilling than a selling plate at Goodwood. She adored the rasp of his flesh against her nakedness as his belly kissed her upthrust bottom. The bed seemed to fall away beneath her, like the fleeting ground at a horse's pounding hooves. Her pulse raced, her heart galloped. One furlong out – and the finishing post rapidly approaching. She took in a lungful of air and closed her eyes, concentrating hard to discipline every muscle within her. She'd take him to the line.

He cried out, gasping, and stiffened. Rising up on his knees and toes a fraction, he slammed into her. They both paroxysmed. It was neck and neck. Quickly dragging his crushed hand round to her lips, she kissed it devotedly as they came together in a dead heat, rider and ridden, flashing past the finishing post in mutual ecstasy.

They lay still, entwined, for a long time. The stable clock chimed two. She stirred, kissed him and tried to slip away. He pulled her back and took her breast – the right one – greedily into his mouth. Prising herself free, she left the dark bedroom for the warmth of the kitchen. Field mice scampered away at the approach of her white feet. Smiling at their scuttling, she sprinked cake crumbs down at the back door for their return.

After spitting on the hot plate of the Aga, the kettle fell silent and then began to sing softly. Soon it began to whistle. She made milky, sugared coffee and heaped slices of cake upon a large plate. So hungry, she thought wonderingly. Just like after a couple of hours down at the gallops.

Balancing the impromptu feast, she returned to the bed.

'Hello, novice.' He grinned.

'Not any longer,' she said, teasing his lips with cherry cake.

He snapped at the cake, securing a huge mouthful. 'Still a lot to learn,' he said, his voice thick.

'I've got a great trainer,' she whispered, kissing his damaged hand.

Channel Four were there, but did not cover Debbie's race – going back to Wetherby for a selling plate while The Crow ran in the novice's cup for amateur riders. Going down to the start, Debbie, shivering with both excitement and the chill wind at her silk-sheathed thighs, heard the bookies shouting 5-1 against The Crow.

Flushed by the cold and her pride at seeing her name on the race card – and hearing it over the tannoy – she guided the gelding down to the start at a canter.

A lad from her own yard approached and held The Crow's head as she pulled up and steadied the horse for the stalls.

'Instructions from the owner,' he said, keeping his voice low.

'I've already had –'

'New instructions,' he said, tapping his mobile phone. 'Change of tactics. Don't ride him wide.'

'But –'

'Tuck him in off the pace and go for a gap in the last half furlong, got it?'

'No way,' Debbie bridled. 'The Crow always runs wide. Hates being boxed. I'll –'

'Do as you're bloody well told, lass. Tuck him in and don't use the stick. Orders from the owner.'

Debbie didn't remember much of the race. The five furlongs were eaten up in a couple of minutes by the cavalry charge. The Crow veered and ran wide, on the far side, alone. On the stand side, the favourite made good headway. Debbie hadn't time to settle – she just cannoned the black gelding along and gave her horse several crisp reminders within the last furlong, using her short whip judiciously. She didn't realise that she had won until she heard it over the echoing tannoy.

In the ring, she unsaddled and kissed The Crow. Captain Hinton hugged her. She trotted off, saddle cradled over her arms against her bosom, for the weigh-in.

The next morning, after a celebratory breakfast of bacon, eggs and mushrooms, she entered the yard and tackled the mucking out. There was no sign of Captain Hinton.

It was chilly – the weather had broken – and Debbie shivered as she shovelled.

'Cold?' the crisp voice of the blonde owner demanded.

Debbie turned round, startled by the sudden sound in the deserted yard. 'I didn't hear your Range Rover,' she countered.

'Captain Hinton's taken it. I sent him into Sudbury.'

Her words established the power the owner knew she possessed. She had sent her trainer off like a messenger boy. Debbie flushed angrily and was tempted to rudeness, but the blonde interrupted abruptly.

'I want a word with you, girl. Over in the tackle room. At once.'

Debbie jabbed her fork down resentfully, leaving it quivering in a heap of steaming horse dung. Following the owner across the cobblestones, she entered the dark warmth of the tackle room. Inside, the air was pungent with saddle soap and supple leather. Standing beside the door, the blonde reached out and snapped down two switches, flooding the interior with harsh light. Then, to Debbie's surprise, she closed the door, locking then bolting it firmly.

'I don't wish to be disturbed,' she purred, patting her pocket which now held the key.

Debbie frowned, but remained silent.

'Disturbed while we have our little talk. I will sit here,' the blonde remarked, tapping a straw bale with the tip of a riding crop she had removed from its hook on the whitewashed wall, 'and you shall undress –'

'What?' Debbie gasped.

'Undress,' the owner continued suavely, 'and position yourself for punishment.'

'P–punishment?' came the anxious echo.

'Just get undressed, girl,' the blonde snarled. 'I want you naked for your strokes.'

'Like hell –'

'Eight strokes, to be precise. I lost eight grand yesterday, because of you.'

'Lost? But we won. How could you lose?'

'You won. I lost. And you won,' the owner whispered vehemently, 'riding against instructions. You ran wide and used the whip.'

'Only a reminder –'

'Which is exactly what I am about to give you. I gave you clear instructions. You disobeyed. I am now going to teach you the meaning of obedience, girl. Strip.'

Debbie's fingers plucked uncertainly at the button at her bosom. Through the fog of fear clouding her brain, a light of understanding slowly brightened. The owner had bet against The Crow yesterday, putting the huge sum on the narrowly beaten favourite, and had tried to tip the odds in her favour by issuing riding instructions framed to scupper Debbie's ride.

'If you ever want to wear silks again, you'll do exactly as I say,' the woman with the supple whip suggested.

Head bowed, a scarlet flush across her cheeks, Debbie unbuttoned her shirt. It flapped open, revealing the swell of her bosom in the cupped bondage of a white bra. Slipping out of her shirt, she reached behind to unclasp the bra.

'Jeans next,' came the crisp command. 'Leave the brassière alone. I shall attend to it when I am good and ready.'

Debbie obeyed, reluctantly and resentfully, soon

175

standing before her seated tormentress, stripped down to her cotton scanties.

'Come here,' the blonde ordered.

Debbie, her toes scrunching on the red-brick floor, approached.

'Kneel.' The little leather loop at the tip of the whip tapped a spot directly in front of the straw bale.

Debbie knelt as instructed, grimacing as her knees kissed the hard brick surface. The blonde rose languidly from her bale and paced around the kneeling girl, who shivered in her bra and panties.

'In a moment, I am going to bend you across that bale of straw and whip your bottom. Whip your bottom very hard. Understand?'

Debbie hung her head in silence. The tip of the whip suddenly appeared underneath her chin, forcing her head up then tilting it back uncomfortably.

'Understand?'

'Yes,' Debbie whispered quickly, swallowing with discomfort at the arch of her neck.

'And why I am going to whip you, girl?'

'For disobeying your instructions.'

Nodding her triumphant satisfaction, the blonde placed the riding crop lengthways across the bale and, bending over her victim, undid the taut bra straps. Debbie's hands flew protectively to catch the cups and press them to her breasts.

'Hands on your head, bitch.'

The bra fluttered to the floor. Kneeling, her hands now positioned as instructed, Debbie's naked bosom was revealed in all its proud glory. The blonde's hands trembled, as if tempted by the delicious flesh mounds, above the breasts, but alighted upon the tight waistband of the white panties of the kneeling girl. Debbie hissed as she sensed the fingers digging into her flesh, and felt the panties being peeled down over her heavy cheeks, then yanked down savagely to her knees.

'Over the bale,' came the command from the blonde, who had just bared her victim.

'No, please, don't –' Debbie whimpered.

Placing the sole of her polished brogue just above the buttocks before her, the blonde propelled the nude belly down across the bale. Debbie squealed as the straw prickled her nipples. She drew her hands – elbows angled – to protect her ravaged nipples.

'Hands out in front across the bale,' the blonde snapped, stepping back and reaching up to the array of tackle and selecting a length of dark-brown leather. Flexing it for suppleness by whipping it down across Debbie's bare bottom, searing the creamy cheeks with a thin, scarlet stripe, the blonde straddled the kneeling girl.

'Straight out. Come on, stretch,' she commanded.

Debbie squealed her protest as the soft leather bit into her wrists and struggled as the blonde bound them together.

'Perfectly still or you'll suffer double, understand?'

Slumping down into the bale, Debbie surrendered her buttocks to the blonde.

'Perfect,' she heard the owner whisper excitedly – a tone of soft venom that brought a spider of alarm scurrying down Debbie's spine.

'I'm sorry –'

'You may squeal and shout during your whipping, bitch,' the blonde purred, picking up the whip and tapping the upturnd cheeks dominantly. 'I've made sure that we are entirely alone.'

With a soft swish, the first stroke sliced down, striping Debbie's poised rump and leaving a thin horizontal red line across the vertical weal bequeathed by the previous lash of leather. Debbie screamed softly, hissing her torment into the straw at her lips. The blonde laughed harshly. Swish, crack. Swish, crack. The next two strokes were delivered in swift succession, searing the bare buttocks brutally. Debbie, arms stretched out and bound, wanted to press her face into the straw to smother her suffering, but the harsh stubble forced her to inch her face away, leaving her straining in painful suspension.

Three more red lines quickly joined the scarlet weals already adorning the punished cheeks. Debbie writhed, rolling and crushing her inflamed nipples into the stubble, and squealed in anguish. As if seduced by the squirming rump, the cruel crop lashed down twice, planting stinging leather kisses deep into the helpless flesh. When the whipping ceased, the naked girl's bottom was criss-crossed with lines of living fire.

Debbie stumbled in her ungainly effort to rise.

'Get down, bitch. I've not finished with you yet. I want to know how you got the ride. Well?'

Debbie shivered with fear, not expecting this dangerous twist. She guessed the owner's designs on the trainer with the damaged hand. Bound, bare-bottomed and at the blonde's mercy, Debbie knew she must not boast about that night in the cottage, deep in the coppiced wood. That sweet night, when she had slept with the damaged hand wedged between her wet thighs. And had woken up to find it still there the next morning.

'I wonder,' the blonde taunted, tracing the whip around the outer swell of the naked cheeks. 'How did you manage to persuade Captain Hinton, hmm?'

'I work out with The Crow,' Debbie said quickly. 'I know him better than anyone –'

The tip of the whip silenced Debbie's lips.

'Ride for a ride, was it?'

Debbie, her eyes now wide with fear, bit her lip, shrinking from the tang of the leather-sheathed crop. The little leather loop fluttered, then disappeared as the whip was whisked away, instantly visiting her bottom with a searing lash.

'Was it?'

Debbie's silence told the angry blonde all she needed to know. Four harsh strokes followed, cracking down savagely across the naked rump.

'Bitch,' hissed the blonde, tossing the crop aside. 'Like to ride, do you? I'll show you.'

'No –' Debbie begged.

The blonde turned the bound nude over, so that the freshly whipped buttocks sank their soft flesh into the cruel stubble. With her harsh laughter drowning Debbie's squeals, the owner straddled her victim, planting herself down on Debbie's breasts. Squatting, and pulling down her jeans and panties, the blonde eased herself down, settling her wet sex upon the upturned bosom. Bending to scoop up the crop, she plied it accurately against the insides of Debbie's splayed thighs, each snapping stroke working the whip closer up to Debbie's helpless pubis.

Rubbing her hot slit across the bosom beneath, and grunting as Debbie's nipples raked her inner labia, the owner tapped the whip menacingly at Debbie's tightened flesh-lips.

'Keep away from the Captain, bitch. Owner's perks, get it? You're just a three-a-penny little wannabe novice looking for her next ride. Just make sure it's not him who gets to mount you.'

Debbie closed her eyes as she saw the whip sparkle as it arrowed directly down between her parted thighs.

10

The Translator

There were three long cricket bags on the tigerskin rug before the unlit fire. Constance gazed down at them, frowning slightly at their battered appearance. The brown canvas was stained, the stitched leather grip-handles worn with wear. When the handsome woman in the high-backed chair bent down and opened one of the bags, Constance saw that it was stuffed with sheaves of paper.

'Great-Uncle Otto was an avid collector,' the woman remarked, fishing out a specimen sheet.

'An academic?' Constance hazarded.

'Stockbroker by day, fanatical linguist by night. The Nordic tongue was his abiding passion.'

Constance studied the speaker, who was poring over the exhumed papers. Some ten years older than her own twenty-two, she wore her dark, gleaming hair combed up severely. Her lips were surprisingly thick and sensual, her neck slender, and her delicate hands fluttered restlessly. Heavily – indeed, beautifully – breasted, her bosom burgeoned boldly behind a crisp lace blouse. But it was the woman's eyes that held Constance's attention. The grand-niece of the late linguist had dark, sparkling eyes. Strangely virginal, yet disturbingly passionate, eyes.

'His estate has been disbursed according to the letters of administration. No great value was attached to these, which were bequeathed to me in their entirety,' the woman explained, giving the papers' provenance, 'but I am curious.'

Constance, sent by the translation agency for whom she freelanced, sensed little profit in the enterprise. Resigning herself to yet another disappointment, she accepted the paper and glanced at its contents.

'Swedish,' she pronounced.

'Swedish? It is remarkable that Otto made all his money, and such a fortune, south of the equator. Copper, diamonds, coffee even. Yet his true passion was for the language of the frozen North.'

Constance perked up, but concealed her interest. Sole heir, she suspected. A spinster, too. Lots of unspent inheritance.

'And the subject matter?' the woman asked, bending forward slightly.

Constance put aside her speculative train of thought and returned to the paper in her hand. 'Fines – no, penalties,' she murmured, raising her head and gazing directly into the dark, sparkling eyes. 'It's a paper describing a range of penalties –'

'Are you sure you have the exact translation? Could not the word mean "punishments"?'

Constance was taken slightly aback at the sudden note of eagerness. She hesitated. The document in her hand, after all, merely dealt with the range of fines, or penalties, imposed by Malmö magistrates on horse dealers who allowed their beasts to roam and cause a civic nuisance a century ago. 'Yes,' she conceded guardedly, 'in a sense, it is about punishments.'

'Punishments,' the woman whispered, pursing her sensual lips when echoing the word. Her tone became brisk, with a rising note of expectation. 'Read it out. Quickly. Translate it freely for now but read it out, please.'

Lowering her head down, Constance did so. Six

minutes later, after dutifully detailing the dull contents of the historical document, she looked up. The dark eyes had lost the sparkle and seemed dimmed with disappointment.

'How chilly it has become,' the woman observed, busying herself with matches and a spill.

She is disappointed, Constance thought, catching the flat tone. 'Allow me,' she murmured, reaching out and brushing her fingertips against the woman's hand as she took the matches and lit the spill. The little yellow flame grew almost instantly into a crackling blaze as the kindling spluttered beneath the neatly stacked coals. 'There,' Constance said softly. 'Now we will be warm.'

'A very interesting document,' the woman remarked.

Liar. The word flashed across Constance's mind. I know you are disappointed. After all, the dry, civic record of petty fines for pettier offences had merely afforded a glimpse of early-nineteenth-century municipal Malmö at its dreariest. She decided to take a calculated risk. 'Of course,' she suggested, 'there may be earlier documents. Documents of much more interest.' Unwilling to allow any lucrative opportunity to slip by, and beginning to suspect the true nature of the woman's appetite, Constance laid the bait in her trap carefully.

It was taken. The woman fished out more crumpled documents from the cricket bag, then passed them across. 'Seventeenth-century, I am given to believe.'

Constance read through the first half-page of the assembled sheets rapidly – discovering it to be no more than a treatise on the best method of fattening up geese. She felt the dark eyes studying her face keenly. She placed the top sheet down on her lap, and smoothed its wrinkled surface with the palm of her hand.

'Well?'

'I'm afraid –' Constance paused, averting her gaze coyly.

'What is it?' came the excited demand.

'I do not wish to cause offence, but I think your great-uncle acquired this particular document in error. Its contents –'

'Yes?'

'May give unnecessary offence. This was never meant for your eyes, though it is of rare antiquarian interest, if not monetary value.'

'Great-Uncle Otto bequeathed all these papers to me. I am quite prepared to be . . . shocked. Please translate.'

'I cannot do so; that is,' Constance added hastily, 'I blush to read the words aloud. I will transcribe for you.'

'Very well,' the woman replied, barely concealing her impatience.

Constance rose from her fireside chair and crossed the drawing room. Reaching a small desk, she sat down and took up a pen. Turning, she asked if the woman wanted every word. Including any indelicacies. The woman nodded vigorously. Concealing her smile, Constance gazed down at the instructions for fattening geese and let her mind wander freely. Geese. Waddling along like nuns. Nuns, whose self-denials caused sweet torments. Torments – the torments and suffering. Soon, her pen scratched busily.

Three sounds faintly filled the room as Constance wrote: the distant sound of rooks wheeling above the beech trees, the crackle of the fire and the whisper of shuffled papers. Sitting primly at the desk, perched upon the polished hardwood chair like a naughty schoolgirl recently spanked and now in detention, she laboured at her task. In order to fuel her client's suspense, Constance worked deliberately and methodically, pausing frequently in a pretence of consulting her dictionary.

'Not finished?' the woman demanded, breaking the long silence at last as she feverishly wrung her hands.

Constance noted the gesture with satisfaction.

'Can you not even hint at its contents?'

Just enough to make you damp, but not wet, Constance thought wickedly. Just enough to make that

proud bosom swell and ache. 'It is an account –
apparently, an eyewitness account – of the punishments
suffered by young nuns,' Constance replied, dropping
her voice to a conspiratorial whisper. 'As members of a
very strict order, they were made to suffer the whip –
and worse – for succumbing to the temptations of
bodily, carnal delights. Are you sure –'

'Quite sure. Please be quick.'

Constance resumed her task, pretending to translate
from the yellowing documents with a maddening
slowness calculated to provoke the waiting women into
a frenzy of expectation. A full half-hour later,
Constance placed down her pen.

'It took a little longer,' she lied, 'because the writer
chose to hide the more unseemly words in an obscure
dialect –'

'No matter,' the woman replied, her restless hands
waving aside linguistic niceties. 'Give the translation to
me.'

'If you have no objection, I will take a turn in your
beautiful garden,' Constance said, tapping the papers
with a show of unease.

Out in the garden, inspecting the late roses, Constance
could scarcely contain her delight. With three full cricket
bags of old documents to work on, she could make this a
very profitable assignment. She chuckled aloud as she
thought of her client, seated before the fire, avidly reading
– and no doubt rereading – the lubricious account she had
just conjured up with her artful pen. How did it go? Oh,
yes. Picking out a pink tea rose, she plucked it, sniffing
deeply at its fragile autumn bouquet. Closing her eyes, she
recalled the words her client would now be enjoying.

A full day's ride [Constance had begun her account]
out of Stockholm brought me at length to the gates
of the convent wherein the Daughters of Discipline

184

retreated from the busy world. I arrived in time for supper and was greeted by the Elders and welcomed to a repast of stewed carp, simple but goodly fare.

As the refectory grew dim, candles were brought to the long wooden tables. After our repast, wine was served, whereupon the Elders bid me remain to witness the discipline all of the sect observed so rigorously, so devotedly.

Three young nuns were called to confess their sins before the entire community. The first of these was a comely maiden who, when fully disrobed of her black habit, veil and white shift – her sole nether garment – revealed the tonsure, or partly shaven head, of a novice. She had been with the Daughters of Discipline for some three summers and had taken minor vows.

Utterly naked before her sisters, this wench shielded her breasts becomingly, but was forced to display the dark nest of maidenfern at the very base of her belly – that part some poets term Eve's Secret. An Elder stood beside the naked postulant, carrying a short wand of willow. With this whippy switch, the Elder tapped the pink flesh of the novice's mound of Venus – calling it wrathfully the Gate of Sinful Shame – and teased the fleshlips there with cruel strokes, forcing them to peel apart most lewdly. In the candlelight, the moisture at the flesh was plainly visible.

'Do you confess?' the Elder demanded.

'I confess,' came the tremulous response.

'To what do you confess?'

'To –'

'To what do you confess, sister? Tell us of your sinfulness.'

'When I drove the cattle down to graze upon the lush water meadows, I saw two labourers cutting wood.'

185

'And?'

'I hid from them – but kept their images in my mind. Later, when abed, I entertained them in my heated fancy.'

'Entertained them? How so, sister?'

The young novice shivered in her shameful nakedness and hugged her breasts, squeezing their softness fiercely. The Elder plied the willow switch briskly across the penitent's buttocks.

'Kneel, wretched girl, and confess all. All, mind, omitting no wicked detail.'

Stumbling clumsily down upon the hard, stone floor, the naked girl confessed, pouring out all her lascivious sins. She confessed fully to pleasuring herself, imagining the two labourers using her body for their brutal sport.

'What parts did they bespoil?' the Elder demanded, raising the whippy willow aloft.

Fearing the lash, the girl spilled out her words almost incoherently. 'Here,' she gasped, stroking her neck, breasts, belly and thighs. 'And here,' she whispered, skimming her dancing fingertips across the dark nest between her thighs.

'And in your fancy, did you permit these sons of Satan to enter you?'

The kneeling nude bowed her head and started weeping.

The Elder lashed the willow switch down across the naked buttocks of the sobbing girl. 'Well? Did you?'

The girl nodded, owning the sin.

'Show your sisters where you willed them, in your devilish fancy, to enter your sinful flesh.'

Raising her head slowly, the naked girl placed a straightened forefinger between her lips and probed her sweet mouth deeply. The willow whipped down and striped her severely.

'Where else?' hissed the Elder.

Shuffling her knees, the girl turned and presented her whipped bottom to the assembled gaze. Slowly, with every evidence of burning shame, she reached behind to insert her finger between her parted buttocks.

No more was said. They took her, a sister at each elbow, and held her firmly in a kneeling position. The Elder administered the cruel strokes – a swift and savage dozen stripes – eliciting a shrill squeal each time the whippy willow lashed the helpless cheeks.

Out in the garden, a robin bobbed upon the twig on an apple bough. Constance watched the little bird, noting its fierce, bright eyes. Dark, sparkling eyes. How dark and sparkling the eyes of the woman in the drawing room would become, she thought, smiling, as they continued to read the contrived translation.

In the drawing room, the fire settled down into neglected embers as, fingers trembling at the page, the woman in the crisp lace blouse drank in every word. After relishing the account of the young nun's bare-bottomed whipping, she continued:

That same night, in the candlelit refectory, seated among the assembled Daughters of Discipline, I witnessed a second young woman's confession and punishment. Roughly stripped of her outer habit and shift into shy nakedness, this young postulant revealed a glorious head of corn-gold hair. No more than eighteen summers old, this lithe, apple-breasted delight had been, I discovered, with the sisters for less than one whole year. The Elder did not use the cruel willow switch across her buttocks, but took the naked girl by the hand and led her to the long wooden table. Drinking cups and candlesticks were removed and the girl was forced to stretch out upon the table top, as if she were abed.

'Last night, at the hour of private prayer and contemplation, you were discovered in your bed not in prayer but in disorder and wretched sinfulness. Nor were your hands joined together as bidden. Show the sisters the state in which you were discovered, girl.'

The girl blushed deeply and slowly placed her hands, palms down, upon her naked thighs.

The Elder wound the girl's golden hair around her hand and pulled most violently. 'Do not attempt to hide your sin from our eyes. Show the sisters how you used your unholy hands.'

Squealing aloud as her hair was pulled again, the squirming nude slowly inched her fingertips into the golden hairs at her private place. Dabbling into her source of liquid sin, the young nude played lewdly with herself, toying most brazenly with her forbidden flesh.

'Enough,' barked the Elder.

The wet fingertips withdrew and the penitent writhed, rubbing the curves of her soft buttocks upon the polished table like a harlot in a bed of shame.

'Bring me a chair,' the Elder commanded.

Willing hands dragged a large, dark chair noisily across the stone flags. Sitting down in it, and arranging herself upon a crimson cushion, the Elder ordered the naked girl to kneel before her. Shyly, with vain attempts to conceal her bare bottom from her sisters' gaze, the girl obeyed. Forced to join her hands in penitence, she revealed her pretty buttocks to all assembled.

'Your sin is a childish sin, girl. And your hair,' the Elder murmured, fingering the golden tresses, 'is loose and immodest. It is time for the tonsure.'

Sobbing her protests, the nude pleaded with her Elder, but the scissors sparkled in the candlelight as they snipped away the glory of the tumbling golden mane. Shaven, naked and ashamed, the girl abased herself before her cruel superior.

'Such childish sins deserve a child's punishment,' the Elder pronounced. 'Bring me an apple. The ripest there is to be had.'

A sister brought one and placed it at the Elder's feet.

'The fruit of Eve,' the Elder murmured, stooping to pick up the apple and hold it before the naked girl's gaze. 'Red as Eve's own sin. I will punish you until your flesh is as red as this scandalous fruit.'

The girl slumped slightly and moaned softly.

'Kiss the apple – no, do not bite it, girl.'

The penitent pressed her lips against the ripe redness.

Placing the apple carefully down upon the stone floor, the Elder ordered the nude girl across her knee. Bending down across the black habit, the creamy limbs and soft buttocks of the recently shaven girl presented a not unpleasing image. The Elder pinned the penitent down firmly into the punishment position and commenced to spank the proffered cheeks.

The punisher had a broad palm – the punished, a broad bottom. Soon, squealing beneath the flurry of searing swipes, the nude's feet kicked as she thrashed in her anguish – but the spanking continued remorselessly, the sounds of flesh upon flesh echoing loudly around the stone-walled refectory. From time to time, the Elder would pause, her hand smoothing the ravaged cheeks dominantly. At such times, the Elder seemed to be in prayer, no doubt for the soul of the girl she was chastising. Then the spanking hand swept down once more, swiping the bare bottom mercilessly. All there that night watched as the punished nude squealed piteously until the discipline ceased. All there that night watched as the red apple was placed upon the hot cheeks — the redness of the fruit compared with the crimson of the punished cheeks. More spanking, and still more, until the hue of the fruit and the heat of the buttocks became one burning shade of pain.

The sun sank down behind the beech trees, and the rooks settled in their roost, just before teatime. Teatime. Constance's thoughts turned to hot buttered toast, muffins, cinnamon biscuits and cherry cake. Would she receive tea from her hostess? Surely so. Turning her back on the roses, the young translator crossed the lengthening shadows on the lawn and returned to the house. Better wait here by the low yew hedge, she thought, and give her client a little longer to enjoy the translation.

In the drawing room, the reader blinked in the gathering gloom, but was too engrossed to break off from her perusal of the text to turn on a light. Bending closer to catch the firelight, she strained to read, the fingers of her left hand fumbling blindly at the pearl buttons of her starched white blouse. Her swollen bosom felt so achingly heavy: her nipples pierced through the sheath of silk. The passage she had just completed left them peaked in pleasurable pain. Her mouth was hot, her throat tight, and she could barely see the words in the gathering gloom. There was just another page or two to complete. She read:

The Daughters of Discipline regard corporal punishment as the true path to purity. These severe sisters, dwelling not more than a day's ride out of Stockholm, live in another world entirely — a world of surrender and submission, where the flesh is purified through pain, where guilt must be confessed and where impurity must be punished.

That night, seated with the sisters in the refectory,

I witnessed a third member of their community receiving her stripes of sorrow, watched as she was forced to eat the bitter fruit of her wanton folly.

Dragged reluctantly before her brethren, this maturer, riper girl revealed a bald pate when stripped bare. The bald pate denoted her seniority – and, the Elder advised me, the necessity of a more severe punishment.

'Confess your sin, sister,' came the command.

The wretch, slowly and with unseemly lewdness of gesture, palmed her inner thighs as she tossed her beautiful face up defiantly – but remained silent, refusing to name her sin.

Clapping her hands twice, the Elder summoned three assistants, who were nimble to their feet and pressed closely around the accused, instantly dragging her to where chains dangled from a low beam. They snapped iron cuffs around her wrists and hauled her up from the floor, leaving her twisting and dangling a foot or so above stones below. Left in her bondage for a while, the nude was again prompted to confess. Punishment was promised. She remained defiant and silent. The Elder called for a whip.

'I confess –'

'Silence,' the Elder thundered. 'Too late,' she whispered, accepting the whip and cracking it aloud. 'Too late,' she repeated, presenting the whip for the penitent to see. 'These tongues of fire will loosen yours. Then, when you sorrowfully repent, we will listen attentively to your full confession – and punish you again. Stop her noise,' the Elder instructed.

Cotton cloth was forced into the whimpering nude's mouth by a nun, who climbed up upon a three-legged stool. The cloth served its purpose well, rendering all tearful pleading useless.

The whip was presented to the assembled gaze. The Elder fingered each leather tail – fourteen, in all – and

191

named them, giving each single length of hide the name of a prophet. The sisters chanted each name aloud, their chorus growing more fervent as they echoed the Elder's words. As the leather thongs were named solemnly, the nude twisted helplessly in her chains, driven to a dark ecstasy of dread at her impending – and inescapable – suffering.

The Elder plied the whip with subtle cunning, avoiding the chained nude's thighs and buttocks. Flicking the many-tailed whip upward, she lashed the belly and breasts. Only the violent rattling of the chains told of the whipped nun's torment, her moans being silenced by the thick cotton binding her mouth. It was almost painful to behold the dark nipples thickening and rising up, to be mercilessly caressed by the stinging thongs.

They took her down and released her from the chains. Then the Elder ordered her helpers to remove the cotton gag. The nude sobbed, cupping her ravaged breasts, to comfort them, all her former arrogant silence broken under the lash.

'Confess,' the Elder commanded.

Kneeling, the whipped nude plucked up the hem of her punisher's black habit and kissed it, then stretched out her hand across a nearby table and dragged a candle towards her. Snuffing out the dancing flame between licked fingertips, she placed the smoking stub of wax down upon the flagstone floor between her splayed thighs. Kneeling astride the thick candle, she lowered herself upon it, her mouth partially open, her eyes closed shut, until it entered her forbidden place.

'I abused the beeswax candle. I confess,' she sobbed, her recently whipped breasts bobbing gently as she rode the stump. 'Punish me for my transgression. Cleanse me of my dark and vile sin with the waters of sorrow.'

They took her back, arms outstretched, to her chains. The Elder forced the offending candle between the naked nun's lips – and she seemed to find some little comfort in it, biting into it to smother her cries, as her bare buttocks were kissed repeatedly by the whip. Each of the sisters present in the refectory was invited to step forward and approach the sinful wretch. Each was offered the whip, and ordered to chastise the naked buttocks twice. Soon, the rounded cheeks, jerking violently in their pain, were prettily patterned with the crimson marks of the relentless lash.

'Otto was a connoisseur,' was all the woman said, placing the written translation reverently upon the desk top.

Constance, who had rejoined her client in the drawing room, merely nodded. She noted that two of the pearl buttons at the woman's proud bosom were undone. She also noticed that the swollen leather armrest of a dimpled Chesterfield was smeared wetly – having been ridden, no doubt, between the squeezed thighs of the feverish reader.

Constance brightened up considerably after her discreet retreat into the chill of the garden. She sensed success, and the distinct possibility of money.

'Won't you stay for some tea?' her client suggested.

Constance agreed. The tea was all she had hoped it would be, the muffins leaving her fingertips slippery with melted butter. There was a substantial cheque to follow.

'Please take away some papers for translation,' the woman urged, pressing the cheque for services rendered into the translator's hand. 'I will look forward to your visit tomorrow.'

Constance slipped her hand down into the cricket bag and extracted a bundle of yellowing documents. She briefly scanned the first few lines – wincing slightly at the instructions specifying how to preserve freshwater pike and trout in barrels of brine – and pretended to gasp excitedly.

'What has dear Otto in store for me?' came the eager request.

Constance paused deliberately, both to savour her deception and whet her client's appetite. In a prim tone, she eventually relented, replying that the text appeared to deal with the struggle to preserve the virginity of a Danish princess.

To her surprise, Constance was received the following morning by her client, casually wrapped in a bathrobe.

'I thought you could read to me while I bathe.'

In the bathroom, which was already clouded with warm steam, Constance perched upon a cork-topped stool while the woman applied a face-mask.

'There,' the robed woman sighed, examining her chalk-white face in a steamed-up mirror. Satisfied with her beauty treatment, she slipped off the towelling robe and tested the foaming bathwater with the prinked toes of her right foot. Constance watched enthralled as the nude entered the bath, easing her supple nakedness beneath the shimmering bubbles.

From the moment the bathrobe had slipped silently to the tiled floor to the instant the bubbling foam had eclipsed the nude's nipples, Constance had kept her steady gaze riveted upon the bare bottom. It was a superb specimen, the creamy cheeks being fully fleshed and ripely rounded. Though heavy – swollen, indeed – the satin skin was smooth and tight. Constance felt her tongue thicken with desire: the desire to kiss, to tongue and then to bite the perfect peach cheeks. The cleft between the delicious buttocks was invitingly shadowed. As the nude climbed into the bath, parting her thighs, Constance felt her heart miss several beats, then return to hammer within her breast.

'An account of a Danish princess and the struggle to preserve her chastity, you promised.'

'That is correct.' Constance nodded, smiling secretively as she gazed down upon the supposed translation – fabricated hastily the evening before. Holding up the papers, she read aloud:

In the remote forests of Kronig stands a castle belonging to the second most powerful family in the kingdom. There, with her stepmother, the dowager queen, resides Erika, the princess, together with a household of serving women and royal guardsmen. When Erica is presented at court, she must still be a virgin, or the fortunes of her kinfolk fall.

Each night, two maids of honour are sent to spy upon the bedchamber of Erika, ensuring that the princess knows not the embrace of any man. On one such night, deep into the darkest hour, a cry woke up the dowager queen. Racing along the passage to her stepdaughter's bedchamber, she called aloud for the royal guard.

'What is amiss?' she demanded, approaching the maids of honour.

'A man, your majesty,' the two spies gasped, speaking with one troubled voice. 'A man abed with the princess.'

They had to wait for the burly guards to arrive – wiping red wine from their lips and buttoning up their hose and doublets – to batter down the locked door. Stepping through the splintered wood, they found the princess naked in the darkness. Tapers were put to torches, and soon a dancing light bathed the corners of the vast bedchamber. A torn and knotted velvet curtain trailed down from a narrow window, betraying the escape route of the midnight paramour.

'Search the room,' the captain of the guard

bellowed, stabbing at the emptiness around him with an unsheathed sword.

'Too late,' the dowager queen whispered. 'Be gone. Leave us.'

Bowing, the royal guard withdrew.

'Too late,' the dowager queen repeated, pacing across the rush-strewn floor to the large bed. Bending down over the hunched figure of her naked stepdaughter, she called aloud for tapers. The fragile lengths of sizzling wax were held aloft by the four maids of honour, each stationed at a corner of the royal bed.

'Examine the bedlinen,' the queen thundered.

The tapers quivered as they were lowered over the sheets. In their flickering light, the naked princess squirmed.

'No stains, no wetness, your majesty. All is not lost.'

'It was my scream,' the spy whose cry had raised the alarm volunteered. 'It caused the knave to leap back from the maid. See. His seed spilt upon her bosom.'

The tapers almost touched, flame to flame, as they converged above the writhing girl.

'Hold her,' the dowager queen commanded.

Firm hands pinned the nude against her linen. The stepmother stooped to inspect the shining breasts, nodding and sighing her relief as she saw the glistening breasts and wet nipples of the princess.

'She is saved,' came the pronouncement.

Erika squirmed and squealed aloud as hot wax from the spluttering tapers dribbled down upon her nakedness. The maids of honour withdrew the tapers – but the angry stepmother snatched one and held it over the girl's belly and thighs to inspect the maiden's sex. Erika squealed as the wax spilt down between her clamped thighs.

'Take her out of my sight. Bathe her and return her to me.'

Constance paused, raising her eyes from the papers to watch the woman in the bath. She noticed that, during the account of the semen-splashed breasts – and of the hot wax blistering the exposed nipples – her client had abandoned the soaped sponge and was fiercely pinching her own nipples. Pinching, punishing and painfully pulling at each thick, mulberry-dark nipple. It was as if she was experiencing for herself the torments of the shamed princess.

Licking her dry lips, Constance forced her thighs together to contain the wet heat bubbling at her panties. Already her stocking-tops were slippery. Lowering her head, she dutifully continued to read aloud:

The four maids of honour returned with Erika, having bathed and then dressed her in a white shift of lawn. The dowager queen received them in silence, her hand raised as if in warning.

The maids of honour were beckoned over into a corner, where a whispered counsel could be held privily.

'He is still within the bedchamber,' their royal mistress said.

'Your majesty?' they screamed softly in alarm.

'That window. It is but an archer's slit. It is impossible for the body of a man to pass through.'

The maids of honour saw that their mistress was wise.

'We must flush our quarry out. Bring the wretched girl to me.'

The struggling princess was dragged – protesting loudly – and forced down upon her knees before the queen.

'You threaten a noble line with disgrace, girl. I

would rather cut your tongue out by the root than hear you give voice to your wanton harlotry. Bring me a knife –'

'No,' the shrill cry of protest rang out. 'Do not harm her.' It was the naked paramour – a guardsman – emerging from a large chest. Slim, blond and sinewy of thigh, his manhood nodded proudly as he stood before the women.

'So,' the dowager queen murmured, 'my threat worked. We have captured our stag. Your gallantry was foolish, sir. Chivalrous but foolish. I would not have harmed her.'

They tied the princess to the bedposts and forced her to witness her paramour's suffering and humiliation. Threatened with the return of the captain of the royal guard – and execution – he could do nothing but submit to his captors.

A knotted rope was used to flog him, then he was forced to accept the squatting buttocks of each of the maids of honour as, in turn, they straddled and rode his upturned face. Pinning him down into the rushes, they each took turn to bury his face beneath their heavy buttocks – while the queen milked him ruthlessly, catching each liquid release in a golden goblet. Each time he emptied his loins, his groans grew deeper and more troubled. When the goblet was half-full, his punishment ceased and he was allowed to crawl away – like a whipped dog, slinking from its angry mistress.

'And as for you, my dishonourable stepdaughter, you will now feel my wrath in full measure. Bare her haunches for the lash.'

The maids of honour, now quite naked and hot between their shining thighs, snatched away the white lawn shift from Erika's body, revealing her once more in utter nakedness.

'Hold her down across the bed, the bed she almost

defiled,' the dowager queen ordered, kneeling down to gather up a handful of the thickest rushes. These she plaited deftly into a single, supple strand.

The whipping was a protracted affair, leaving the princess sobbing after thirty strokes of the biting lash across her helpless buttocks. Bending down to examine the angry weals by the flickering light of a taper, the dowager queen nodded her grim satisfaction. Handing the plaited switch to one of her attendant maids, she ordered the others to turn her naked, weeping stepdaughter on to her back and hold her firmly down, legs splayed apart.

'You,' she ordered the maid with the lash, 'punish her where she will remember it until her wedding night.' The cruel stepmother pointed down at the wet sex of the whimpering princess, jabbing her forefinger once more as she thundered her command.

'Here, your majesty?' the maid of honour gasped, unable to conceal her horror as she tapped the pubic nest with the tip of her whip.

'Give me that,' the dowager queen snarled, snatching back the plaited rushes. 'There,' she hissed, swishing it down.

The princess squealed and writhed, rasping her whipped buttocks against the sheets beneath her as she struggled to clamp her thighs to smother the burning at her sex.

'Be sure to stripe her belly and lash her breasts as well,' the dowager queen instructed, placing the cruel instrument of intimate punishment into the trembling hand of her maid. 'I will return. If she is not well whipped, you shall be.'

Constance heard the splash as her client's hands fell down into the foaming bath between her expectant thighs. Below the shimmering bubbles, the fingers worked busily at the parted flesh-lips. Above, the froth foamed furiously. Constance grinned – proud she had made the woman ravish herself, through the power of her invention – and returned to the conclusion of her lascivious narration. Raising her voice to overcome the carnal grunting of the masturbating woman in the bath, she read:

The dowager queen returned, bearing straps, a leash and a curious bridle fashioned from dark leather. Dragging the whipped princess by the hair down on to her knees, she attached a collar and leash around the naked girl's white neck, a tight band of hide around the captive breasts, and a looped girdle around the girl's hips, threading a belt between her thighs and cross-belting the leather over each striped cheek.

'This will preserve your chastity, my sweet little whore, and the family name. It is impossible to remove and will ensure that you remain a virgin until the time is ripe.'

She took the leash and handed it to a maid. 'You will each take it in turn to guard her, never letting her out of your sight. Walk with her, dine with her, sleep alongside her, but never let her loose from your keeping. If she offers promises or bribes of gold for her freedom, whip her, understand?'

The maids of honour swore their obedience. The dowager queen gave the chastity belt a final inspection, running her knuckle between the tight hide and the soft flesh it imprisoned. She adjusted the cross-belts at the buttocks, causing the whipped cheeks to bulge. Erika squealed.

'It is an idea the crusading knights conceived of when leaving their womenfolk behind. This strap here,' she added, fingering the leather that curved down from the pubis and swept up between the cleft behind, 'forbids the entry of either a maiden's curious finger or the bolder flesh of an excited man.'

Tugging at the harness, the dowager queen drew the band of hide into a taut stretch, biting into the cleft between the painfully parted cheeks and burying itself into the pink wet flesh at the weeping sex . . .

Constance paused and looked up. Unashamedly and with utter frankness, her client was feverishly masturbating – her head and neck arched back, her shoulders tensed, her fingers frantic beneath the scented foam. Lolling her head sideways, the woman gazed over the white rim of the bathtub and pleaded with Constance to repeat a certain part of the passage.

'The punishment of the princess. The gathering and the plaiting of the rushes. The whipping of her naked buttocks. Please,' the naked woman begged, 'read it to me again. Read,' she whispered hoarsely.

Constance panicked – could she remember the words? Would the woman discover the deception? All along, she had been pretending to read a translation, but had in fact been improvising – making up the account as the tale of the unhappy princess unfolded.

'Quickly,' the woman in the bath moaned, 'read to me. The punishment of the princess. I want every stripe and stroke of her suffering.'

Taking a deep breath, Constance rustled her papers and pretended to scan them earnestly. Launching back into the narrative at the point where the dowager queen plaited the rushes into a cruel whip, she took up the tale of the chastisement of the Danish princess. Each lash was lovingly described as it visited the squirming buttocks; each reddening stripe was detailed; each grunt and sob was recorded. Constance told of how Erika taloned the sheets in agony as her bottom suffered – and how the maids of honour struggled to pin her writhing nakedness down into her bed of pain and shame.

A soft scream broke into her flow. Looking up quickly, Constance glimpsed the woman's naked breasts, nipples painfully engorged, breaking the surface of the foam and heaving up as her client came, long and loud in her moaning ecstasy. Impulsively, Constance bent across and kissed the nude's parted lips at the peak of orgasm. To her delight, the wet mouth widened submissively to receive her dominant tongue.

The room was cosy, the bed was soft and warm. Ivy rustled at the window, reminding Constance of the cold, dark night. She turned over restlessly in her bed, unable to sleep.

Invited by her client to stay for the weekend, she had accepted – reasoning that the beautiful woman with the unspent inheritance would soon be parting with more of her fortune for the very special services Constance rendered.

Closing her eyes as she sank her head back into the soft pillow, Constance spread her legs wide apart. Reflecting upon the image of the naked woman's bottom glimpsed in the bathroom, her hand swept smoothly down across her breasts and belly until her fingers found her waiting slit. Constance swallowed as her fingertips brushed against the fern-fringe of her pubic nest, and her throat tightened as the image of the bare bottom intensified: the heavily fleshed, shining cheeks; the curves ripely rounded; the pronounced swell of the hips framing the superb buttocks – and the deep, inviting cleft between.

Using a technique known as the Scimitar, which she had discovered when translating a French anthropologist's study of the Al-Aqqa nomads, Constance inverted her right thumb and pressed the tip against her erect clitoris, alternately pressing hard upon it then teasing it up with her thumbnail. The effect was both immediate and electric: her belly muscles spasmed, her buttocks tightened so that her anal whorl became a fierce knot, and her juices flowed.

Helpless in her orgasm, the client had surrendered to the sudden kiss, submitting to Constance's firm mouth. As she thumbed herself expertly, the translator sensed that soon the cravings for descriptions of discipline, punishment and female suffering would become more urgent, and then her client would seek to translate mere words into deeds. Constance worked her wet thumbtip rhythmically, easing up her buttocks a fraction and clamping her thighs to contain her oozing heat.

Yes. The image of the perfect bottom loomed large in her mind. Constance decided that, by the time the weekend was over, that bottom would be hers – to palm, cup and weigh; to kiss, lick and softly bite; to spank. Then, with ownership of the submissive cheeks firmly established, cane or crop in hand, she would rule the delicious flesh with severe sovereignty. She would lash it lovingly and lingeringly, as her client, bound and bending, begged aloud for mercy – and then even louder for more.

Just as the Al-Aqqa tribeswomen commended, her thumbtip became the blur of a hornet's wing, so fast was it strumming her clitoris. Tensed and almost breathless, Constance jerked as she started to come, the first wave of delicious heat coinciding with her celebration of the cane swishing down across perfectly proffered buttocks, the second ravishing spasm coinciding with the thought of that pink line of pain deepening to an angry red across the punished cheeks.

The woman was quiet during breakfast, eating little but brimming with nervous energy. Submissive types are often like that, Constance supposed, indifferent to her client's unease as she tucked into rashers and eggs with relish. Constance took the woman's silence as subservience and her attentiveness – more toast? more coffee? – merely that of a potential slave striving to please a future mistress. Swallowing a marmaladed finger of golden toast, Constance squeezed her thighs together beneath the white tablecloth: thrilling to the prospect of having this mature, beautiful woman in her thrall soon, in her absolute thrall as a bare-bottomed submissive whining for her stripes.

After breakfast, they walked in the kitchen garden, inspecting frost-sharpened sprouts and silver-rimed cabbages. Beyond the neat rows of brassica, treading a cinder path, they reached the now withered remains of that summer's sweet peas. Constance plucked a golden cane out of the chocolate-dark soil. Brushing the earth from the bamboo, she held the cane firmly in her grip and swished it down. It thrummed, its soft whispering whistle potent with the promise of pain. Her companion shivered and hugged her breasts tightly. Constance smiled, savouring her gradual dominance, and, keeping her gaze on the woman's wide eyes, swished the cane down harshly once again. Yes. It was unmistakeable. The eyes she gazed into had widened appreciatively. She was almost ready, Constance presumed, to plead for the discipline she undoubtedly desired.

'Have you more of these?' Constance inquired. 'These are badly weathered. Too brittle, with no spring or whippiness in them.'

As if coming out of a dream, her client nodded and led Constance by the hand to a potting shed. Inside, under hessian sacking, fresh canes were brought into the daylight. They rattled eerily as Constance wrestled with them, separating them and examining them carefully, judging each specimen as she plied the bamboo wands.

'Too thin,' she announced.

'Too thin?' the woman echoed, her voice choking with enchantment.

'It would cut the buttocks, possibly splintering. And this one's too thick.

'Too thick?'

'For female discipline, administered by a female. Now

204

this specimen is absolutely perfect,' Constance purred, wielding a supple length. She was deliberately teasing and exciting her client now – forcing her to acknowledge her desires and put them into words. The possibility of punishment was now out in the open between them, no longer a dark secret but a probability – but Constance was determined to make her client beg, like all good slaves should, to be beaten.

'Female discipline,' the woman whispered, fingering the yellow bamboo reverently.

I must not rush this, Constance suddenly realised, her mind switching from the huge sums of money she could make to the sharp pleasure of whipping a bare bottom. She will ask for her pain soon, Constance decided, putting her wants into words.

'When a female disciplines a female,' the woman murmured, bending her head down to lick, then slowly kiss, the cane.

Almost there, Constance thought. The moment has come. Taking the cane and levelling it against her client's breasts, she lightly tapped the nipples straining beneath the tight blouse. Raising the bamboo up, she gently brushed it against the woman's lips.

'Discipline and dominance,' Constance said softly, 'is truly a female pleasure. Submission is so sweet,' she continued, 'and surrender so satisfying to behold.'

'Yes,' her companion whispered thickly.

The cane clattered down on to the potting-shed floor as they embraced, kissing and tonguing vigorously.

'Come down to the cellar, Constance. I have something I would like you to see.'

It was Sunday afternoon. Constance had been alone all day, lunching contentedly on succulent lamb with redcurrant jelly and a fragrant apple charlotte, in her client's absence.

'Otto's wine bin?' she inquired.

'You'll see,' came the excited, if enigmatic, reply.

At the bottom of a steep flight of steps, the door to the cellar squeaked and yawned wide. Expecting a gloomy, cobwebbed recess smelling of mice and damp, Constance was surprised to discover a recently whitewashed room which was both warm and bright. The door closed behind them. The woman locked it and placed the key upon a nail.

'I've been busy all weekend. What do you think?'

Constance gazed around the cellar in amazement, taking in the display of shackles, corded ropes, canes, whips and spanking paddles. On a low bench running along the far wall, rubber gloves, bottles of baby oil, starched white aprons, hoods and handcuffs waited impatiently for action.

'Well?' pressed the woman, anxious to hear the verdict.

'It's marvellous,' Constance conceded, instantly picturing herself as the mistress in this dungeon of discipline. 'So many instruments of correction,' she murmured approvingly, patting the dimpled surface of a table-tennis bat, 'so much to choose from for the purposes of chastisement.'

'I'm so glad you approve. I've been collecting bits and pieces, here and there, for some time. I knew that one day someone, someone just like you, would come —'

'And now that I have arrived,' Constance interrupted, unzipping her skirt briskly, 'let's not waste a single, precious moment.'

'Naked?' the woman asked.

'Naked,' Constance replied, adding, 'All punishment should be administered and received in utter nakedness.' She grunted softly as she stepped out of her panties and reached up behind to unclasp her brassière. Being completely stripped before her companion — whose trembling fingers flustered with buttons and straps — Constance assisted her. Standing directly behind her

206

client, she rasped the thatch of her pubis against the woman's quivering buttocks. Encircling her captive, she eased off the brassière's cups from the heavy bosom, then caught and weighed each naked breast in her controlling palms. The nude inched back, rising up on her toes and grinding her satin-skin cheeks into Constance. Such a submissive gesture of surrender, Constance thought, relishing the warm bottom at her belly.

'You've been waiting for this moment for so long, haven't you?' Constance whispered.

The woman nodded silently.

'What would you like to start with? Strap, crop or cane?'

'The crop.'

'An excellent choice. So supple, so severe.'

They strode, hips brushing softly, side by side towards an old hogshead barrel. The wooden staves had been decorously draped with a mantle of purple velvet. Constance bent down to stroke the plush material, rubbing it firmly with a straightened forefinger.

'Did you do all this?' she exclaimed, admiring the cunning addition of restraints at either end of the hogshead.

'Yes,' her companion replied eagerly. 'Won't you try it, test it, please?'

Better indulge her, Constance thought. I'm going to skin her twice, she thought – first for her money and then with a crop.

'I do hope it meets your satisfaction,' the woman whispered.

Constance eased herself across the barrel, shivering with pleasure as her breasts and belly kissed the velvet. Stretching out each arm, she offered her wrists up to test the bondage. The leather cuffs snapped into effect, leaving Constance perfectly poised for punishment.

'Excellent,' the translator pronounced, wriggling

furiously but finding it impossible to move. Excellent, she reflected. Soon, this beautifully buttocked nude will be across this barrel, face down and bottom up, hands pinioned helplessly for the crop. Soon, Constance grinned, with her breasts squashed and her nakedness splayed in cruel bondage, the nude would be pleading for the lash.

Constance flushed as the heat of excitement suffused her face and arched neck. At her delta, the trickle of anticipation and arousal seeped through her slightly parted labia to stain the purple velvet.

'Untie me,' she ordered, managing a stern tone. 'It is time to translate words into deeds. I will be your mistress and you will be my slave. I will punish you sweetly –'

'Mistress and slave, yes. I will pay you handsomely,' the woman whispered, her hand upon Constance's bare bottom – palming the cheeks slowly, firmly. 'Pay you as much as you demand.'

Perfect, Constance thought, grinning. The plan has worked out in every detail.

'Pay you for the pains you will take to please,' the woman continued, a cruel note entering her voice.

Constance froze, alarmed at the dominant touch of the woman's finger as it stroked down between her cheeks, exploring the warmth of her defenceless cleft – and then the sticky rosebud of her pouting sphincter.

'No,' Constance squealed, jerking at her restraints. 'Let me up. You can't –'

A gag kissed her lips fiercely, silencing all protest.

'Thank you, Constance dear, for delighting me with those naughty, wicked stories. But you were mistaken, I fear, if you thought my pleasure was that of a submissive devotee. I am a dominant,' she rasped, spanking the bare bottom harshly, 'and will fashion you into my perfect slave.'

Constance writhed, dragging her wet labia against the

smooth velvet as she squirmed her hips. But the hogshead was firmly secured to the floor – as were her tightly bound wrists in their bondage.

'You asked me what it was to be,' the woman remarked, pacing across to the array of instruments of punishment. 'I will use the crop, now. Later, you will wear the rubber hood and I will spank you mercilessly. I will oil your hot bottom and soften it for the sting of the leather strap and the splicing cut of the cane. We will explore the intimacy that only a mistress and slave can share. I will punish you, Constance, slowly and severely. Your stories, which you told with such relish, betray your dark desires. You are about to experience that which so clearly fascinates you. And, weeping, you will learn to thank me for your sweet suffering. You will come to love your mistress, Constance, and grow impatient for your pain. But enough talk. The time has come for you to taste the crop.'

The first stinging slice cracked down across her swollen cheeks – bulging up across the curved barrel – causing a crimson light to burn behind her eyes. Blinking away her agony, Constance struggled to beg for mercy – but the gag at her mouth rendered the translator silent.

11

The Actress

Inside the nightclub, the footlights flickered and the music was drowned out as, outside, a tube train rattled towards Hammersmith station. Ruby and the other girls in the chorus line kicked high as they danced off the small stage, their grins fixed against the braying from the stalls out in the darkness.

Backstage, Ruby was delicately peeling off her fishnet stockings – so difficult to replace – when she heard raised voices from the stage manager's office. Two women's voices: one stern and angry, the other a protesting whine. A brief silence followed. Ruby strained to listen, shivering in her scanties. Then she heard the harsh spanking commence, wincing as each slap of a firm hand down across bare buttocks elicited a shrill squeal.

With her pulse quickening in time with her racing heartbeat, Ruby tiptoed across the cramped dressing room to the office door. Through a chink, she saw that it was her friend getting it hot and hard across the stage manager's knee. She saw the rounded cheeks quiver and redden under each stinging smack.

'Who did the body-paint?' the spanked girl was repeatedly asked.

Before she could reply – naming Ruby as the culprit – three more harsh spanks exploded across her punished bottom. Ruby held her breath as she retreated from the door to don her coat and shoes. She had applied the flesh-coloured body-paint to her friend's thighs and shoulders. It was cheap stuff and had smeared. Ruby had made a bad job of it and knew that, in a minute, the spanked girl would confess, and then it would be Ruby's turn to bare her bottom for severe chastisement. Rolling up her fishnets, Ruby stuffed them into her coat pocket and slipped on her shoes. Raising her finger to her lips to silence the rest of the naked chorus line, she tiptoed out into the cold night.

London had celebrated VE night with so much noise and light that Ruby, only eight at the time, had thought it was another air raid. Now, ten years later, every street still had a bomb site waiting, like a rotten tooth, to be filled. Gazing out into the darkness from her seat on the last bus to Acton, Ruby wondered when the promised good times would come. When would a girl be able to buy the lipsticks, satin brassières and seamed nylons they had been promised? Spivs with battered suitcases were still supplying shoddy goods, at a price – but Ruby was impatient for a little luxury. Her young body ached for the kiss of silk at its flesh, for the tight embrace of satin, for the sheer sensation of good-quality nylon stockings – all those feminine confections she saw flaunted on the wide silver screen.

At Acton, she bought a bag of chips. Under the street lamp, she gazed down into the puddle of vinegar at the bottom of the paper bag. Then the newspaper wrapping caught her eye. Auditions would be held for ambitious girls hoping to work in the film industry. Ruby spread the crumpled sheet out flat and read the advertisement over again. Films. No more dancing in the chorus line before a house of beery louts. No more fishnets that were more darn than stocking, or chip suppers under street lamps. No more fear of a humiliating and painful hot bottom for the smallest mistake.

Turning her back on the street lamp – and her wretched job, where her bottom belonged to the fierce stage manager – she decided to attend the auditions. Already, she pictured her lips glistening with red lipstick, her legs shimmering in seamed stockings, her breasts in the delicious bondage of tight satin.

Mr Da Silva (he told all the girls to call him Tony) was of Maltese extraction. The left side of his sallow face was scarred badly. He told Ruby it was a souvenir from the war. She did not realise that he meant last summer's Soho blade-war.

'Costume and camera test,' he announced briskly to the line of hopefuls.

Ruby noticed that some of the girls had come with chaperoning mothers, and had left the drill hall almost immediately. About a dozen girls remained. Ruby waited in line for two hours.

'Next,' Tony called sharply.

She was ushered into a large room. Old blackout material had been exhumed and replaced at the windows and frosted-glass door. Tony asked several questions in a bored voice, but smiled when he learnt that Ruby was in a chorus line.

'Costume and camera test,' he repeated, nodding to an assortment of outfits hanging on a rail. 'Get busy.'

Ruby paused. There was no private changing room.

'What's up? Shy?'

Ruby blushed. Changing with the other girls in the chorus line was one thing. Naked before this man, alone with him, was quite another matter.

'Look, honey, if you want the job, I'll need to see how you look.' Again, he nodded to the costumes.

Ruby undressed slowly and shyly, missing the joggling and bumping of the naked girls in the chorus line. As she slipped off her brassière and wriggled out of her panties, she peeped across at the desk where he sat studying some papers. She relaxed a little, for Tony appeared to be engrossed, ignoring her nudity. Nevertheless, she covered her breasts and pubis with her hands and turned towards him. He continued to read, frowning occasionally. Ruby coughed softly.

'Something wrong, honey?' he asked, without looking up.

'What shall I wear?'

He glanced across the room at her. Ruby felt a flush of triumphant pleasure as his eyes narrowed then widened as they appraised the squashed flesh of her bunched breasts.

'Which outfit –'

'Milkmaid, first. Get a move on, girl. Look slippy.'

Her nipples hardened at his crisp tone. As she plucked the costume down from the rail, she felt both relieved and resentful at his resumed indifference to her nakedness.

The outfit was delicious. White cotton panties that cupped her buttocks, a white lace brassière that bound her ripe breasts tightly, white suspenders and seamed white stockings. The little white dress, matching mob cap and frilly apron felt slightly silly.

Tony fiddled with the camera – a big, black Kodak with a huge flash – as he ordered Ruby to pose with a milking stool and wooden bucket. The shots were tasteful – nothing too risqué – except the last two. Leg shots, Tony called them, but Ruby knew that her panties, suspenders and stocking tops were showing.

The next outfit was a schoolgirl's uniform. Crisp white shirt blouse, no brassière – causing her dark nipples to chafe – a blue-and-red tie which she found difficult to knot, a grey pleated uniform skirt and grey woollen full-length stockings and black patent shoes. The shoes were a tight fit. Ruby, itching from the stockings nestling at her thighs, minced across the floor to stand under the blaze of the arc light.

213

'Perfect.' Tony nodded, appreciating the wiggle. 'Getting into the part. I like that.'

'The part?' Ruby echoed, her mind more on her throbbing feet.

'Pert little minx. Saucy sixth-former. Good.'

The flash bulb popped, blinding Ruby in its dazzle. She sat on a desk, legs crossed, reading a book. She pranced, as if scoring at netball, her skirt's hem flipping up over her panties. She bent over to tie up her laces. Tony remained silent behind the Kodak – but Ruby noticed the prominent bulge in his pin-striped trousers.

'I want to see you as a Red Indian squaw next. Chop, chop.'

'Will I be in Westerns?' Ruby gasped.

Tony ignored her and loaded the camera for the next shoot.

The squaw costume troubled Ruby. It barely covered what it was meant to conceal. She felt naked, despite the buckskin fringe at her breasts and buttocks. She felt her slit growing warm and soft, and blushed with shame as her flesh-lips parted to kiss her panties. It was so naughty being nearly bare.

'It's a bit –'

'Don't forget the feathers,' he snapped rudely.

Ruby had to stretch up to reach the head-band, knowing that his gaze was on her bottom. She felt the tasselled fringe tapping against her cheeks as she struggled to adjust the feathers.

When she turned, he was already behind the Kodak, taking shots.

'That's not fair,' she blurted out. 'I wasn't ready –'

He silenced her, instructing her to kneel and pose submissively, surrendering up a rubber tommahawk. The flashbulb exploded. Four times. Tony grunted his satisfaction.

She wore a swimsuit next – so tight that the rubberised fabric spread the cheeks of her bottom painfully apart. The tight cups moulded and shaped her breasts exquisitely, giving her a deep cleavage. The bulge in Tony's trousers thickened. Ruby hoped her wetness would not stain or show. Then she squeezed into a ballerina's costume. The tutu flared up around her hips, exposing her buttocks, sheathed in the white tights. White tights so taut at her flesh they defined the contours of her cheeks severely. Undressing, Ruby plucked the moistened material away from her wet pubis. As she dressed, Tony filled out a pre-typed contract, adding her full name and date of birth.

'Have I got a part?' she asked anxiously, smoothing down her skirt with her palms.

'For you, honey,' he replied, levelling a gold-nibbed fountain pen, 'there will be work in the cinema. Just sign.'

Her eyes shone excitedly as she signed obediently on the bottom line, ignoring the closely typed paragraphs above.

'Just one more audition,' he continued suavely, pocketing the pen and locking the contract away in the desk drawer.

'Voice test?' Ruby asked, hoping to appear professional.

'Not exactly,' Tony countered. 'You're signed up to Fortune Films, now. The company likes to think we are all one big happy family. Come and meet the boss tonight. He's in town. I've got your address. Pick you up at eight.'

Tony's green Cadillac – just like the ones in the films – turned quite a few heads as it pulled out of Ruby's Acton backstreet and headed for Park Lane. As it slewed round corners, she sank back into the deep leather seat, savouring her first real taste of glamour.

'Best behaviour tonight, girl,' Tony said over his shoulder. 'Lord Chadwick likes a bit of talent, understand?'

'Should I sing for him?'

'Shouldn't bother.' He stamped down on the accelerator and swept past a couple of dark Austins and dull grey Fords. 'Best just make sure he has a good time.'

Ruby's mouth dried and her nipples tightened. A good time. She had heard several of the older girls in the chorus line talking of giving men a good time – bookies and landlords and well-heeled medical students. She knew exactly what it meant.

'Relax girl,' Tony chuckled, glancing at her in the mirror. 'He's an old boy. Won't give you a hard time.'

It was just like being in a film. The young actress being driven to the lair of the boss. Ruby placed her hand on the silver-plated door-handle and squeezed it hard until her knuckles whitened. She could get out of the Cadillac easily. The traffic was thick, the lights always red. She could jump out now, if she wanted. But she didn't. She wanted to work in films. If getting herself work in the cinema industry meant giving Lord Chadwick a good time, a good time he would get.

The penthouse was like a Hollywood set – white leather everywhere, with smoked-glass fittings. Ruby half expected to see Fred Astaire or Cary Grant saunter in, Martini in hand.

Lord Chadwick, to her dismay, was more like Charles Laughton. Fiftyish, fat and truculent as he guzzled smoked salmon and sipped champagne. He shared his supper with her. Ruby loved the sharpness as she sucked the lemon wedge after squeezing it over her pink fish.

'Mr Da Silva informs me that you auditioned very well, my girl. Hope he's not wasting my time,' he added, dabbing at his lips with a linen napkin. 'The rushes are good.'

Lord Chadwick produced a large brown folder and scattered its contents on the table – large 26-inch-square black-and-white portrait shots of Ruby sporting the array of fetching costumes. Her eyes widened as she reached out and picked up a school-uniform shot. She blushed, startled to see how revealing the pose had been. The Red Indian squaw shot was worse. The Kodak had captured her invitingly deep cleavage in close-up, with the nipples proud and thrusting through the skimpy buckskin.

'Very nice,' Lord Chadwick said softly. 'Now let's see the real thing.'

Ruby looked up at him, puzzled. He waved his fat hand over to the far side of the room, indicating the array of costumes hanging neatly from a clothes rail.

'Milkmaid first,' he decided.

Ruby knew that it was not an invitation but an instruction. Best give him a good time. Tony's words of advice came back to her. Biting her lip, she rose from her white leather chair and approached the clothes rail. He'll probably watch me undress, she thought. But where's the harm in that? It's not as if –

'We haven't got all night, girl, unfortunately,' Lord Chadwick prompted. 'Get a move on.'

She stripped quickly and inelegantly, denying her host the teasing, lingering undressing he no doubt desired. Naked, Ruby turned her back to him, hating the thought of his piggy eyes devouring her bare bottom – but hating even more the thought of their full gaze upon her breasts and pubic nest. The delicate milkmaid's outfit soothed her resentful anger, forcing her to relish the delicious silks and satins at her naked flesh. Emboldened by the pert costume, she grew more confident, turning towards him when still palming the white stockings up along the secret flesh of her thighs.

Lord Chadwick sipped from a balloon glass of brandy, eyeing her unblinkingly. She saw the glass pause at his lips, and his throat constrict tightly, as she snapped the suspenders into the white stocking-tops,

217

dragging the sheer nylon up towards her pantied pubic mound.

Silly old goat, Ruby thought. Still, if ogling a semi-naked girl dressed up as a milkmaid was all the pleasure he could manage, she was prepared to sing for her supper – and her future in films. Better give him a decent eyeful, she decided. Before buttoning up her smock, she deliberately fingered the brassière straps at her bare shoulders, causing her bosom to bulge provocatively. She heard him splutter into his brandy. Her mild contempt gave way to a warm sensation of both pleasure and power. Cupping her breasts with both hands, she squeezed and squashed them until they almost burst out of their brassièred bondage. He grunted his approval.

It would be just like this in the films, Ruby thought, closing her eyes and walking slowly towards her seated host. Dressing in delicious costumes and driving hundreds – thousands, tens of thousands – of men wild. Ruby's slit grew hot and sticky as she pictured all those men, row after row of men, sitting in the darkness with fierce hard-ons as they gazed up at her in silent adoration.

'Milkmaid,' Lord Chadwick murmured, savouring the sound of his own words. He tossed off the last of his brandy and placed the empty glass down on the deep-pile carpet, then shrugged off his silver dressing gown and eased his naked body down, kneeling over the balloon glass on all fours. 'Come over here, milkmaid,' he grunted, 'come and milk the bull.'

Ruby gasped, alarmed yet fascinated as he knelt on the carpet, the empty glass between his knees. Above, between his thighs, his long penis hung vertically. Even as she stood still, tugging nervously at the hem of her pretty costume, his length thickened and rose, nodding and twitching as it became engorged with his arousal. She watched it become fully erect, watched it wide-eyed as it tapped his belly.

'Don't just stand there, you stupid little cow. Come here and milk the bull,' he thundered.

Ruby remembered the torn fishnet stockings, the chip suppers and the catcalls from the drunken men ogling the chorus line. Shaking slightly, both with fear and excitement, she resolved to please this fat beast. She had been successful at the earlier audition – and signed a contract to prove it. This was just another sort of screen test. Acting. That was all she was doing. She had read all about the Hollywood system of method acting. Just playing a part.

Resolved, Ruby became brisk and businesslike. Kneeling down against the naked man's bulk, she pressed her breasts into him and snaked her right hand down below his belly, slowly closing her fingers around his hot length. He drew in his breath sharply as she lightly brushed the glistening glans with her thumbtip, then slid her encircling fist of fingers back and forth.

'Good girl, good girl. Milk the bull. Milk me,' he roared, almost choking in his excitement.

Ruby crimsoned with shame. She was trembling – but his hot flesh in her grasp was thrilling to touch. To have this naked man kneeling before her was powerfully erotic. She felt tipsy and sat back, sinking her buttocks into her ankles. Exhaling slowly, she composed herself and determined to complete the task in hand. Her peaked nipples probed the cups of her satin brassière and pierced his flesh as she rose slightly and pressed against him, pumping him slowly, milking him firmly and rhythmically. Her inexperience made the situation all the more wickedly exciting. Glimpsing his sweating face spasming in pleasurable anguish, she felt her panties flood with the trickle of her wet heat.

His buttocks tightened, his cleft became almost invisible as he clenched his heavy cheeks. Grunting obscenities – some of which Ruby had never heard before – he shuffled his thighs wider apart. Ruby saw his fat knuckles whiten as he gripped the deep-pile carpet.

'Faster, you little whore. Faster. Come on, bitch. Milk the bull.'

He cursed her, then blessed her aloud, as his imprisoned shaft pulsed within her controlling grip. Ruby blazed with shame and indignation at the names he called her in his ecstasy, secretly thrilling to the absolute power she exercised over the kneeling man – the film boss who held her future in his hand, just as she held him.

This excited her. She squeezed hard. He came, his release squirting out suddenly. Ruby jerked his shuddering cock down, aiming the silver stream into the brandy glass. The creamy semen turned the inside of the balloon opaque. Before she had shaken the last of the glutinous droplets from his wet cock, he collapsed with a sweet groan on to the carpet, breathing heavily, his eyes screwed up against the stinging sweat.

As he lay sprawled at her knees, she used the hem of her milkmaid's apron to wipe his cock dry. He opened his eyes and gazed up at her. She balanced the brandy glass on his hairy chest. He stared at it, suddenly comprehending its unfamiliar contents.

He laughed, delighted. 'My little milkmaid,' he whispered. He laughed again, spilling the glass so that the semen soaked his belly.

Ruby kept her head bowed as she continued to wipe his flaccid penis dry. Curious, she peeled back his loose skin and stroked the angry, purplish flesh she had exposed. He gasped and struggled up on to his elbows. Lolling his head drunkenly, he gazed down as her fingers toyed with his sensitive flesh, rolling it between the tips of her finger and thumb.

'My little milkmaid,' he repeated softly, all his rage now spent. 'Bloody perfect for the part. Bloody perfect.'

A cold wind blew litter along the length of Park Lane. Ruby shivered on the steps of Lord Chadwick's mansion block, watching an empty packet of Senior Service cartwheeling in the gutter. She drew her coat tightly round herself for warmth, missing the heat of the penthouse. Tony's Cadillac squealed to a halt at the kerb. Ruby got in. Inside the close confines of the car, she suddenly became aware that her hand smelt of dried semen. Tony drove her back to Acton, stopping on the Bayswater Road so she could dive into a corner shop to buy a quarter of Mazzawattee tea, a pink strip of Aspro and tomorrow morning's *Daily Herald*.

'Headache?'

'Champagne,' she replied, nodding.

Tony entertained her with a lurid account of black-market London. She listened as he spoke of lorries delivering crates, piled high with cabbages to hide the coffee and cigarettes beneath. Most of the drivers carried guns. Perhaps thinking he had said too much, he fell silent. Ruby read the headlines. Storm clouds gathering over the Suez Canal.

Only when the Cadillac crawled along the dimly lit Acton backstreet was her visit to Lord Chadwick mentioned directly.

'Make you wear the milkmaid's dress?'

Ruby murmured her reply, grateful for the darkness in the back of the car. Tony turned on a small interior light and studied her face in his mirror.

'Milk the bull?' he asked, grinning.

Ruby remained silent.

'I'll call for you tomorrow night. Eight sharp.'

Lord Chadwick was enjoying a scratch supper of curiously pinkish brown meat – sliced as thinly as toilet paper – and diced melon.

'Parma ham. Try some.'

He held his fork out, offering her a taste of the wafer of meat speared on the silver tines. It was not a playfully affectionate gesture, more an assertion of his

221

dominance. Ruby blushed as she dipped her head and submissively accepted the morsel. It was salty and slightly soapy to taste. She shrank back in revulsion, swallowing it down with a gulp.

'Now try the melon,' Lord Chadwick chuckled.

The proffered fork was at her lips before she could refuse. The melon proved quite pleasant. Her host eyed her keenly as she enjoyed the succulent flesh.

'Swimsuit,' he announced, tossing down the fork and jabbing a pudgy finger at the clothes rail. 'I want to see you in that swimsuit.'

Relieved that he seemed to have no desire to penetrate her, Ruby decided to play along and indulge the film mogul's whim, undressing slowly before him, then sinuously donning the rubberised costume – plucking at it to ease the taut stretch at her breasts, buttocks and pubic mound.

The rubbery sheath sculpted her bosom and bottom superbly. Ruby stole a glance in a wall mirror and preened as she saw her shapely figure in the glass. Just like a starlet. The swimsuit was a little too tight across her bottom, perhaps. She winced slightly as it forced her cheeks apart, stretching their soft curves quite painfully. It was a pleasurable pain, causing her cleft to become sticky, as sticky as her labial lips splayed apart beneath the rubbery fabric at her slit.

'Step closer,' Lord Chadwick commanded. 'I want you much closer.' He stubbed his cigar out in an onyx ashtray. In his mounting excitement, he failed to do it properly. An acrid plume curled up from the smouldering stub, causing Ruby to blink. 'Come on, girl. Come to Daddy.'

Sugar daddy. The phrase burned in her brain. She had read it in the more lurid Sunday newspapers. Young women who pleasured older, richer men. No. It was not like that. She was simply securing her career in films. Inching towards him, Ruby closed her eyes and conjured up images of bathing beauties on a beach: there would be palm trees and white-capped waves in the shot, and the swimsuited girls would be playing with a beach ball. Pretty leggy starlets, scampering on the golden sands, their lithe bodies decorously sheathed by costumes that fooled the censors – but not the stiff-cocked men packing the cinemas across the land.

'Turn around,' Lord Chadwick barked, bringing Ruby abruptly back from Rio to the penthouse in Park Lane.

She flinched slightly at the touch of his fat fingertips as they steadied then framed her hips before digging into her soft thighs to draw her buttocks towards his face. She stumbled as he impatiently yanked her bottom into his face, regaining her balance with her calves pressed into his leather chair. She squirmed as his powerful thighs pinioned her in a fierce pincer. Caught and controlled, she was helpless as he sank his face into her soft bottom, burying his nose between her cheeks and probing her cleft.

'Delicious,' he whispered, his wet tongue now licking the exposed flesh of her curved cheeks. He began to suck, then softly bite, her captive bottom. Ruby let her mind drift, ignoring the fat man nuzzling and guzzling at her buttocks through the stretchy fabric of her swimsuit. She remembered a scene in a romantic comedy in which a beautiful girl had climbed up a silver ladder out of a deep pool, pausing to sweep the diamond droplets from her glistening thighs.

Lord Chadwick turned her around until her pubic mound was level with his mouth. Inclining his head a fraction, he dug his nose into it, sniffing loudly as he had done earlier with the claret.

Ruby felt her belly's muscles tighten then spasm. She burned with shame – and excitement – at the thought of his smelling her wetness, the wetness of her arousal soaking into the rubbery swimsuit. At her buttocks, his powerful hands dragged her cheeks apart. She rose up on tiptoe, suppressing a squeal of discomfort.

'My mermaid,' he hissed, sucking hard now, his lips pressed greedily at her slit. 'My salty little mermaid.'

Oh God, he's tasting my juices, Ruby thought, buckling at the knees. No man had ever tasted her this way before. No man had ever kissed her lips, other than those at her mouth. Do I taste like the Parma ham, she wondered, recalling the savoury tang, or like the melon, sweetly succulent?

Lord Chadwick slurped, lapping her wet flesh through the rubbery fabric. Ruby came gently, crushing herself into him, smearing his face as she swept her hips from side to side. He pawed her, probing her with his brutal fingers, then licked them. Ruby closed her eyes. He's tasting me. Horrified by coming so suddenly, and surrendering to it like a back-alley bitch on heat, she shuddered at the thought of the man's fingers transferring her pussy-juice straight into his mouth. The very thought of it made her inner muscles contract – and more juices flow. She opened her eyes. He was chuckling, proud of his potency and the effect of it upon her.

He sank his mouth into her once more, using his tongue ruthlessly at her exposed flesh as his fingers prised the costume away from her sex. 'Kneel,' he mumbled, his lips making her pubic nest rustle as they spoke.

Trembling, she obeyed, conscious of her cleavage as her breasts settled upon his knees. He drew her into him, producing his erection with his right hand as he dragged down the straps of her swimsuit with his left. With a final savage jerk, he yanked the rubbery sheath down over the proud swell of her bosom. It shrivelled to a restricting curl at her belly, causing her to gasp. Her bared breasts rose and fell as she knelt before him. Just as he had used his mouth on her bottom and at her pubis, so his lips, teeth and flattened tongue ravished her exposed bosom. Greedily, with slobbering excitement, he attempted to suck in her entire left breast, but was defeated by its size and weight.

Withdrawing his face, he replaced his mouth with his fingers to pinch and pluck her nipples until they stood proud, peaking painfully. Placing his hand, fingers splayed, upon her head, he forced her down until his erection speared the cushions of her soft, bulging breasts. Ruby thrilled to the forbidden sensation of his hot shaft thrusting up at her bosom – and suddenly succumbed to the urge to capture and contain it. Palming her breasts at their outer curves, she squeezed hard, trapping his twitching cock in her cleavage.

'Good girl,' he rasped, rapidly approaching his climax.

Rocking gently, her buttocks resting on her heels, she used her bunched breasts to pleasure him, noting with both pride and perversion how his face twisted in a grimace of delight.

He came violently, much of his squirting seed splashing her face as his shaft shot upward in ejaculation and drenched her. Ruby moaned softly, disturbed yet delighted by the warm semen now dripping from her nipples. He had not finished with her. To her surprise, he plucked the swimsuit up from her belly and dragged the cups back to her breasts, carefully arranging the straps over her shoulders. She shivered as the tight rubber clung to her sticky breasts. He prodded them with his straightened forefinger, then traced their swollen curves, forcing the fabric into the wet flesh.

'Little wet mermaid,' he purred, squeezing her breasts excitedly.

Ruby glanced down. The fat, pale hands were busy at her rubber-sheathed bosom, squeezing out the semen from the spot where the taut swimsuit bit into her swollen curves.

'Little wet mermaid.'

* * *

225

A dark Humber took her home. Ruby was told by the driver, Lord Chadwick's regular chauffeur, that Tony wouldn't be around for a while.

'I'll be back for you the day after tomorrow. The boss wants to give you supper again.'

Ruby merely nodded.

'This is for you. From the boss,' he said, having nosed the Humber against the kerb.

Ruby felt the blaze of angry shame at her throat and face. Money. She was being given money – being paid off like a common little tart.

'Take it. Lord Chadwick wants you to see the new film in Leicester Square.'

It was not a folded banknote but a complimentary cinema ticket. Ruby's eyes sparkled with delight as she examined it under the street lamp after the Humber had pulled away. Of course, a cinema ticket. He wants me to perfect my acting skills. She was being groomed for stardom. These little naughty suppers were just his way of assessing her. She kissed the cinema ticket twice. Lord Chadwick clearly believed in her. The only payment she could accept had been rendered – a free ticket to London's premier cinema. It was almost like being sent to an acting coach, she thought. Being sent to the pictures by Lord Chadwick. Being groomed, the showbiz magazines called it. Groomed for a big role.

Ruby came out of the cinema in a dream. Lord Chadwick's ticket had got her in to see a deluxe musical in which white-gloved, top-hatted young men had chivalrously squired angelic girls who sang like larks ascending. All through the film, all had danced thigh-deep in billowing pink clouds.

Ruby shivered. Leicester Square seemed to be filled with grey clouds, but she sighed as she realised it was only the seasonal smog. A taxi honked at her as she drifted too close to the kerb, practising the dance routine she had seen up on the wide screen. Startled, Ruby lurched into a shop doorway.

'Business? How much?'

Still thinking of the angelic show girls, Ruby frowned. What did this rough drunk want?

'Come on, honey. Be nice to me tonight. I can pay –'

She ran, just catching the last bus home to Acton.

Delivered like his black-market cigars in Lord Chadwick's Humber to the Park Lane penthouse, Ruby was instructed to strip and don the ballerina's costume. Her host produced a small music-box and wound it up delicately. It started to tinkle out 'The Sugar Plum Fairy', the silvery notes sounding eerily in the large room.

'Dance for me,' Lord Chadwick commanded, clapping his hands twice, like a sultan in his seraglio.

Ruby, smoothing down her tutu, which sprang back up to reveal her pantied buttocks, shrugged apologetically. 'I can't,' she replied simply. 'Not properly.'

'Can't?' echoed her host with a snarl. 'Can't, or won't?'

Ruby remained silent, stubbing the toe of her white pump into the carpet.

'Come on, girl, I'm looking for versatile, accomplished performers.'

'But –'

'And I'm perfectly prepared to teach them, if need be. Train them in areas found wanting,' he said softly, extracting a length of bamboo cane from a desk drawer. 'Hands above your head, girl. No. Higher.'

Ruby obeyed, pressing her fingertips together high above her bowed head at arm's-stretched length.

'Now dance. Flex your knees. Good. Keep your toes pointing down. That's better. Twirl,' he encouraged, approaching her, the cane gripped tightly in his right hand.

She faltered. The whippy cane flickered, striping her across her rounded cheeks sheathed within the white tights. With her tutu flared up at her waist, her buttocks were totally exposed – both to his ardent gaze and his cruel cane.

'Keep dancing, my little sugar plum.'

Ruby's arms ached and her thigh muscles burned – almost as fiercely as her cane-kissed cheeks. Twice more, the bamboo sliced in against her peach cheeks, searing her bottom with lines of fire. Ruby squealed and stumbled, hating his cruel dominance but relishing being, like a true starlet, the focus of attention. Losing her concentration, she collided with a leather chair, staggered and tumbled face down across it. The cane swished down across her perfectly poised buttocks, lashing them with a crisp slice. Ruby squealed, her white pumps thrashing as she wriggled to escape.

'Up, sugar plum. Get up and dance. The music has not finished yet,' Lord Chadwick ordered, levelling the supple bamboo cane across the double-domed swell of her upturned bottom.

She danced as bravely as she could for several minutes, performing so well that his cane remained passive by his right leg. The music stopped abruptly, then stuttered for a few more seconds before fading into silence.

'Stay where you are,' he murmured, placing the yellow cane on a smoked-glass table. Bending over the music-box, he picked it up and rewound it. The music rang out. He picked up the cane and approached her, his dressing-gown wide open, his shaft showing thick and engorged.

'Dance,' he commanded, clumsily conducting the music with the cane.

Ruby's eyes dimmed with hot tears. Her protests were instantly quelled by a swish of the cane across her upper thigh. As she twirled, pirouetting coquettishly, two more strokes savagely caressed her rounded cheeks. She clamped her thighs together and clenched her buttocks, as if squeezing out the pain. He inserted the bamboo between her thighs and forced them apart, jerking the whippy wood up cruelly into her pubis.

Up on painful tiptoe, Ruby danced for her master, her tightly sheathed buttocks wobbling provocatively as she took dainty steps in time to the tinkling music.

Lord Chadwick tossed the cane down on to the carpet and grasped his swollen cock in his left hand.

'Come closer,' he whispered, beckoning her towards him.

She neared him, her arched feet teetering on the carpet as she struggled to keep up on her toes.

'Pirouette,' he instructed, thrusting his cock into the ruff of her swirling tutu.

Ruby closed her eyes and spun, shivering at the thought of the frilly layers of her tutu rasping the glistening tip of his erection. She tried to ignore the image; it was no more than using a seamed nylon stocking on him to make him spill his seed. Keeping up the spinning turns was not too difficult, once she was able to keep her balance and momentum without falling prey to giddiness. She heard his breath becoming more excited as the tutu skimmed his glans. She heard him urging her on, ordering her to spin around faster and faster. Then she felt his hot wet release splattering against her thighs and buttocks – the sudden splash made her cry out aloud and stagger, collapsing into a heap at his feet.

'Sugar plum,' he muttered, still masturbating and squeezing his hard shaft, aiming the last few drops down on to her face. 'Sugar plum.'

She rolled over, prising her thighs apart – they were stuck together by his semen. She plucked fastidiously at her wet tights, peeling the soaked fabric away from her flesh. Lord Chadwick stumbled to his knees, kneeling over her exhausted body. Raking the wet tip of his cock down her neck and over the swell of her bosom, he slumped, burying his face in the frothy tutu, drowning in the silken skeins.

She undressed alone, in front of a cheval mirror, while he slipped down a dozen chilled oysters and enjoyed a fine Chablis. He joined her, his frosted glass of white wine in his hand, as she peeled off the sticky white tights. They examined her stripes in the mirror together, Ruby looking over her shoulder and Lord Chadwick gazing into the glass. He reached down with the frosted glass and pressed it against her caned cheeks. Ruby rose up on her toes as the cold glass rolled against her punished flesh. Raising the Chablis to his lips, he drained it off and then knelt, pressing his face into her bottom, and tongue-tip-licked each red cane kiss imprinted on her buttocks.

'Now it's time to go to school,' he murmured, kissing her bottom. 'I hope you are a naughty pupil.'

Presenting her nakedness to him, Ruby allowed him to dress her in the schoolgirl's uniform. He was clumsy in his eagerness, putting the panties on back to front, then peeling them down roughly before trying again. She found his attempts to dress her in the starched shirt blouse painful; without a brassière, her breasts suffered under his frantic fingers. He knotted the striped tie perfectly and lingered a long time over the grey woollen stockings. Ruby put the pleated grey skirt and patent shoes on herself.

'Not the shoes,' he ordered.

She kicked them off, glad to be rid of their pinch.

'Stand up straight. Arms down by your side.'

Ruby stood to attention as he knelt down to inspect her closely, touching her breasts through her blouse repeatedly, then grazing his knuckles against her outer thigh through the grey pleated skirt. At length, he lifted up the hem of her skirt and peeped up at her panties. She heard him grunting with satisfaction.

'Go and wash. Use the carbolic, not the fancy soap. Wash your face and hands and then wash your bottom. I want you to smell like a freshly bathed schoolgirl. Understand?'

On her return from the bathroom, her flesh scrubbed and shining, he sniffed her, savouring the faint trace of carbolic.

'Perfect,' he pronounced, 'I love the smell of innocence.'

Belting his dressing gown tightly around his portly frame, he led her by the hand to the white leather sofa. Ruby submitted to being arranged across his lap, finding that she fitted the sofa's length exactly from nose-tip to the soles of her feet – nuzzling the white leather at one end and digging her toes into the upholstery at the other. She wriggled to ease the stab of his hard cock at her pubic nest.

He did not spank her immediately, but lingered to touch, stroke, examine and intimately peruse his schoolgirl trophy. He pawed her hair, then fingered her neck delicately, tracing the furrow of her spine through the crisp white blouse down to the waist of her grey pleated skirt. She gasped aloud and froze as he swept the hem of her uniform skirt up over the swell of her pantied buttocks – but he merely inspected the cheeks, smiling as they tightened in fearful anticipation of the impending punishment.

To Ruby's amazement, she did not feel the sting of his hot, spanking hand. He replaced the pleated skirt down over her thighs, covering her bottom modestly. The hem tickled at the backs of her knees.

'Quite a well-developed little minx, aren't you?' he teased, turning his attention to her breasts.

Ruby felt his left hand ease beneath her bosom; felt it dominantly cup, capture and squeeze her brassièreless breasts. Her nipples thickened in response to his controlling touch and kissed his upturned palm. She heard him grunt, and felt his cock twitch and spear her.

Returning to appreciate her legs, he examined their shapely length. Ruby drew in her breath silently, knowing that in a moment he would be bearing her bottom – for punishment. She aligned her legs together in strict submission as she lay face down across his lap. He smoothed his right palm down over her thighs and then followed the nubile contours of her calves. Ruby dug her toes into the soft leather at her heels.

'And has my little pupil been a good girl?' he asked silkily.

She nodded, quivering with delicious dread. Despite herself, and despite the promise of pain they heralded, Ruby had grown to relish his stern manner and strict tone.

'A very good girl?'

'Yes, sir,' she whispered, her words muffled by the soft leather pressing against her lips.

'No minor little lapses, hm? Not even the slightest naughty misdemeanour?'

Ruby remained silent.

'Just as I thought. Even minor lapses must be punished. The penalty must be paid.'

Ruby wondered at the purpose of his fingers unknotting and removing her striped school tie.

'The penalty must be paid,' he purred, dragging the tie from her collar and binding it around her wrists, leaving them helpless in the hollow of her back.

She wriggled, resenting the strict bondage, but Lord Chadwick pinned her down with his firm hand at the nape of her neck. With his right hand sliding up her thighs, beneath her grey pleated skirt, his fingertips found the elastic waistband of her panties.

'Up,' he ordered.

She inched her hips up, allowing him to drag the

panties down and leave them in a restricting band just above her knees.

'I shall spank you according to Victorian precepts, girl, after the fashion of our grandparents. With your knickers down, my dear, but through your skirt. The Victorians were sticklers for decorum, even when indulging in the pleasures – indeed, the pains – of the flesh.'

He did exactly as he promised, spanking her as she lay across his lap, her panties at her knees, her skirt covering her bare cheeks. Despite the ringing slaps and stinging pain, Ruby could not deny the delicious thrill of having her bare bottom punished through the grey pleated skirt.

After six opening slaps, Lord Chadwick paused, rubbing the serge cloth of her uniform skirt into her punished cheeks. Beneath his heavy hand, the material rasped her hot flesh. Ruby felt herself weeping freely from her hot slit, and cringed at the thought of her sticky warmth seeping through his dressing gown to moisten his supporting thigh.

Four more sharp spanks followed. The bubble at her slit popped silently, soaking her pubic fringe.

'Let us examine the results of chaste, Victorian chastisement,' he purred, flipping up the hem of her pleated skirt and exposing her pink cheeks. They dimpled as he stroked them firmly with his fingertip. 'Of course, the later Edwardians were a racier set. More enlightened, though morally lax if not loose. They preferred to punish a fully bared bottom,' he remarked, allowing his fingertip to follow her grey woollen stockings down to the tight band of her panties. 'Fully bared.'

With her upturned cheeks now naked and helpless, Ruby bit her lower lip and clenched her buttocks. The spasm attracted his attention. He thumbed her cleft deeply, then repeated the gesture, prising her clenched cheeks apart. He ordered her to relax, to slacken her buttocks. Meekly, she obeyed. He dabbled his fingertips on the crowns of her freshly spanked rump, satisfying himself with their softness.

The ensuing flurry of spanks rang out, echoing much more sharply than those administered across her skirt. Lord Chadwick curved his right hand expertly – actually pausing between the blistering blows to mould it perfectly to the contours of her wobbling cheeks – and then cracked it down fourteen more times.

'No –' Ruby wailed aloud after the seventh. 'Please –' she squealed at the tenth. Then she started to jerk across his lap, rocking forward over his thighs, despite the limited space allowed by the confining sofa. Ruby rasped her pubic fuzz at the silk of his dressing gown, then rubbed her labia along its smooth sheen.

Lord Chadwick was so engrossed in spanking her bottom – and watching keenly as the cheeks turned from scarlet to an angrier shade of crimson – that he did not notice her furtive action. When he did, he taloned her hair cruelly in his left hand and quelled her into submissive passivity. She flinched as he took a finger-and-thumbful of her left cheek and twisted it.

'Stop that at once, you little whore,' he thundered, thoroughly enjoying her wickedness. He released the flesh-fold and dragged his thumbtip down her cleft's hot length, continuing until it probed her wetness beneath.

'Sorry, sir,' Ruby whispered, clamping her thighs together and squeezing the juice out of her slit.

'Naughty,' he roared, cracking his palm down fiercely.

Ruby, pinned down and immobile, cried out as he blistered her buttocks. She squirmed as she felt his excited erection jabbing up into her. He's going to explode any minute, she thought, shuddering. He's going to drench my belly.

At the last moment, Lord Chadwick pushed her from

his lap and forced her down on to the carpet. Ruby crouched, her hot cheeks raised. He slumped down from the sofa, straddling her spanked bottom just in time to squirt his cream all over her buttocks. Ruby moaned as the throbbing cock jerked up stiffly as he ejaculated, raking her cleft with his wet cock.

The soft leather kissed her bottom as she eased herself down into the back seat of the Humber. Ruby squirmed as her panties stuck to her cheeks, still wet with Lord Chadwick's seed.

'Cinema or theatre, miss?' the chauffeur asked, making small talk at the Paddington lights.

Ruby did not reply, busying herself with her sticky lingerie.

'Actress, aren't you, miss?'

'Oh, yes,' she replied. 'Cinema. Does Lord Chadwick own theatres as well?'

The chauffeur smiled and sucked his tooth before telling her that his boss ran a couple of live shows up West. The traffic lights turned to green. The Humber pulled away. The brief conversation was over, but Ruby was left wondering if she would ever get to perform on stage. There were so many openings for a young actress now. The classics and Shakespeare, Travers and Coward. All the new writers, too. Osborne and Rattigan. Why had Lord Chadwick not mentioned his live shows? Live shows, indeed. What a quaint term. Ruby suppressed her giggle at the chauffeur's ignorance.

'It'll be Tony tomorrow night, miss. He's back in circulation.'

There's only the squaw costume left, then I'll be free of Lord Chadwick. Probably be at rehearsals next week. Maybe out on location. Would she be taken in the Humber or in the racier Cadillac?

'Where have you been?' she asked Tony.

Hunched behind the wheel, his sallow face eerily pale in the dashlight, Tony tapped a sinister bulge in his left inside blazer pocket. 'Delivering cabbages, honey.'

Ruby swallowed silently and consoled herself that the Maltese with the scarred face was just having a little joke at her expense. She said no more as the Cadillac bore her towards Park Lane.

'I'm going to scalp you.'

Ruby was standing with her back to the end of the huge bed – the swell of her buttocks just skimming the deep mattress – spreadeagled and bound at the wrists and ankles to the tall end-posts. She felt naked, despite the scanty squaw costume. Her feathers were awry; she had struggled while being bound to the four-poster.

'I'm going to scalp you,' Lord Chadwick repeated, turning from the hand-basin in the corner of the bedroom with a foaming mug and shaving brush in one hand and a silver razor in the other. 'You'll have to keep perfectly still. No wriggling at the stake.'

Ruby immediately writhed in her bondage, but the knots he had tied remained secure, biting into her soft flesh until it burned.

'Keep still,' he warned, kneeling down and placing the mug, bristled brush and razor on the carpet beside him.

Gagged, Ruby could not plead or protest. Her eyes widened in fear. Reaching up, he unfastened the bottom of her Red Indian costume – no more than a mere tasselled fringe – and tossed it aside. Ruby stiffened as she felt his fat fingers tracing the outline of her exposed pubic mound, and shuddered as she suddenly understood the meaning of his words. He was going to shave her.

'Scalp my little squaw,' he murmured, thumbing her pubic curls away from her labial lips, then stroking the wisps firmly to the right and to the left of her slit.

He's going to shave me. Ruby's left leg trembled as a

thrilling frisson coursed down its sleek length. The bastard is going to shave my poor little pussy. Stung by both fear and humiliation, Ruby began to sob.

'Want to look the part, don't you?' he reasoned, his affable tone barely concealing the icy threat. 'Can't have you looking bad in a great role.'

He foamed up the lather in the mug with the bristled brush and applied it to her pubic nest, flattening the dark curls. The bristles tickled as they tackled her fuzz. Ruby ached to free her hand and soothe her tingling bush. The razor approached, glinting. He plied it expertly; she barely felt the blade's cold burn. She did not look down: there was a mirror on the opposite wall. In the glass, she watched as the razor erased the curl of foam, revealing a broad, pink band at her delta. It felt curious to be hairless down there. Strange – and deliciously wanton. All the movie starlets were shaven, Ruby supposed.

Lord Chadwick rinsed her, then towelled her dry, patting her pubis firmly with the soft cotton. Ruby trembled as he cupped – and palmed – cool talc into her shaven pubis. The talc brought relief to her sore flesh. Ruby swayed slightly in her spreadeagled bondage. He's done with me. It's all over. I'm through all the auditions – and I'm going to work in the cinema.

He knelt on the bed and nestled up close behind her nakedness. He found her anal whorl to be tight, the flesh within dry and resisting. He probed it with the shaft of her rubber tommahawk, pumping it between her bunched cheeks for eight long minutes until it emerged wet and shining. Her rosebud was now softer, more pliant. He fingered it, nodding with satisfaction as the relaxed sphincter puckered and opened. He thrust his hips; his cock glanced off her curved cheek. He speared again, entering her ruthlessly. Ruby squealed, her shrill alarm audible despite the tight gag. He heard her squeal and started to come at once. His wet stream dribbled back and soaked his cock, then dripped down her hot cleft. He remained within her, thrusting deeper, his seed lubricating her virginal anal muscles, affording maximum penetration.

Ruby spat the gag out of her mouth with a supreme effort and screamed softly, cursing him with words and names she didn't even know the meaning of.

Kneeling into her, his hairy thighs pressed at her smooth flanks, his hands gripping the bedposts just below the bound wrists, he hammered into her bottom.

Ruby sobbed, her head lolling in shame. She groaned as she sensed him – still inside her – thicken. Her belly tightened and her hot juices spilled down to scald her inner thighs. She hated his fierce length inside her, but hated even more the idea of its absence. She knew she was about to come. He would discover her secret and gaze down into her shame.

The thrusting became more rhythmical, more assured, more dominant. Ruby squealed as his large fat hands dropped down from the end-posts and squeezed her breasts, punishing their swollen flesh viciously. She shuddered as he grunted, coming once more deep inside her bottom.

Tony picked her up a little after two-thirty the following day.

'Where are we going?' she asked. Her voice was dull, the tone flat and weary. Lord Chadwick had played Red Indians until well after midnight.

'Fortune Films,' Tony replied. 'One of the cinemas the boss has just opened in Soho.'

'To a cinema? But –'

'Shut up, honey. Don't play games with me. You're under contract, remember? You work for us, now.'

The Fortune was already open and the stalls were full. A queue of men loitered impatiently in the cramped foyer. It was a dingy little establishment, reeking of disinfectant and stale tobacco smoke.

'I want to go home,' Ruby announced, turning away abruptly from the small screen, upon which two naked women were thrashing a handcuffed man's bottom with riding crops. His screams sounded uncannily real. 'Just let me go, now.'

Tony gripped her arm and shook her roughly. 'You are under contract, understand? You want a job in films. You've got one. You're our new cigarette girl. Go and get into your costume and get back up here.'

She returned, twelve minutes later, shivering in her tiny silver skirt, frilled blouse and red bow tie. Her black fishnet stockings were seamed. The seam ran right up over the cheeks of her exposed buttocks. They had already been darned in several places.

'It'll be over in a few minutes,' Tony said, glancing at his watch. 'That's when you get out there and do your stuff. You're on commission. Fourpence a packet, OK?'

Ruby looked at him in disgust. 'If you think I'm going to –'

He captured her face in his left hand and squeezed it hard before twisting it up to the flickering screen. 'See that?' he whispered.

Ruby screwed her eyes up tightly, refusing to look. He shook her till she opened them and gazed up obediently at the screen.

'They're not actors, honey. See that bloke getting it with the belt?'

A howling man, naked and bound across a desk, was being lashed by a belt-wielding blonde. The blonde's bare breasts bounced as the leather whistled down across his whipped cheeks.

'Let's just say he lost a crate or two of Lord Chadwick's cabbages. Get my meaning?' Tony whispered. 'And see the bitch giving it to him?'

Ruby, her face still in his grip, managed to nod. Up on the screen, the robust blonde had peeled down her black panties and was threading the hot leather belt

239

between her thighs – the belt she had just plied across her victim's buttocks – and was rubbing her pussy furiously. The audience growled their approval.

'She's under contract. Just like you. Wanted to work in the cinema. Worked as a cigarette girl for a few months. Look at her now. Done well, hasn't she, honey?'

12

The Nanny

The purple smudge of distant hills slowly became more distinct as the old but serviceable Bentley roared towards them. Soon Edwina, sinking her bottom into the vintage upholstery, could discern the dark patches of dense pines covering the steep slopes. The Bentley rounded a sweeping bend. As she slid across her seat, her nylon-stockinged thighs rustled as they rasped against the hide.

'Arnaig House up ahead, miss,' the uniformed chauffeur announced through the speaking-tube. He dropped gear as the heavy car tackled the ascent.

Edwina automatically preened herself, straightening the skirt of her nanny's uniform and patting her soft dark curls. Stealing a glance in her vanity case, she inspected her lipstick-free mouth, brown, serious eyes and stern expression. Excellent. Edwina knew from experience that a pretty, frivolous nanny at interview rarely got the post.

Arnaig House was a granite pile perched on a windswept hill. Edwina shivered in her nanny's uniform as she left the warmth of the Bentley and stepped out into the bracing highland air.

The door was opened by an impeccable butler. Edwina was ushered into the library, where two middle-aged spinsters sat before a blazing fire. The butler returned. Tea was served. The two women watched, catlike, as Edwina managed her scones, honey and teacup adroitly.

'You come highly recommended. Your references indicate that you do not shirk from a challenge. You take a disciplined approach to your duties.'

Edwina accepted the compliment modestly and sipped her hot tea.

'We do hope you are a firm believer in punishment, my dear.'

'A strict disciplinarian,' the other chimed in.

'Spare the rod,' Edwina murmured, 'and spoil the child.'

'Precisely so. Our young nephew, Tom, has, I'm afraid, been thoroughly spoilt. He's practically running wild. Do you think that you can take him in hand?'

Edwina nodded, studying the grim faces of the two aunts. More questions followed, then details of her post were discussed, and matters settled. The interview came to a mutually satisfactory conclusion.

'We are away to Edinburgh tomorrow. I trust we can leave Tom with you for the week?'

'Certainly.'

'The young rascal is completely out of hand. You will be firm, my dear?'

Edwina promised that she would.

Up in her room, Edwina undressed slowly, wondering about Tom, her new charge. She smiled as she imagined the imp, probably an unruly twelve-year-old – the aunts hadn't said – running amok all over the estate, to the despair of all the household. Fishing in the loch, romping in the heather, disappearing in the surrounding hills in driving rain or swirling fog.

She unbuttoned her crisp blouse and shrugged it off, then unzipped her tight skirt. Her room was chilly, despite the log fire crackling in the hearth. In her white brassière, suspender belt, panties and dark-bronze stockings, she felt a chill draught keenly. It was coming from the sash window which overlooked the loch down at the foot of the hill. Striding over to close the window, Edwina noticed that there was a shallow balcony outside. She paused, her brassièred breasts pressed against the cold glass, to appreciate the hardy specimens in a window box, surprised that the night-scented stock could flourish in the bleak climate.

Back at the fire, she unclasped her brassière and loosened the deep cups from her soft breasts. After the cold glass, her darkened nipples were peaked. She thumbed them absently, pleasuring the stubs gently, and decided that what she needed was a hot bath after her long journey.

As she shed her suspender belt and stepped out of her panties, she had a sudden sensation of being spied on. Impossible. She was quite alone. The door was firmly shut. Looking over her shoulder, she thought she saw a slight movement at the window. Probably a bird.

Naked except for her dark-bronze nylon stockings, she strode into the adjacent bathroom and bent over to turn on the hot tap. To her horror, the water was almost brown, discoloured with a peaty hue. Edwina relaxed as she remembered the butler's polite warning. All the water at Arnaig ran brown.

Rising from the edge of the bathtub, she inspected her face in the mirror above. She had to wipe the steam-clouded glass. Her fingers froze. There – a face. It was unmistakeable. The face of a young man perched on her balcony next door. Peeping in at her as she shivered, bare-bottomed, in her nylon stockings.

Edwina's first flush of anger melted into a sensual pleasure. She would punish him for peeping at her. She was safe inside her room, she reasoned. She was naked and in control; he was still peeping, unaware that she had discovered his presence. Edwina raised her right leg, slowly, and positioned her foot on the edge of the bathtub. Knowing full well that her bulging buttocks were now perfectly displayed, she fingered her nylon stocking down over her thigh, and then palmed its sheen into a shrivel at her ankle. Pausing to cup and spread her cheeks apart – deliberately giving him an eyeful of her dark cleft – she thumbed the stocking over her toes and planted her foot down on the cork tiling.

Hands on her hips, thighs slightly parted, she gazed down into the bath. The hot tap spluttered as the ancient boiler drained empty. She bent down to turn it off, then squirted gel into the water, swirling her right hand to whip up the foam. She knew that his eyes would be burning into her as her hips and proffered bottom swayed.

She peeled off her other stocking and threaded it carefully between her parted thighs, taking the darker bronze top between her teeth and gripping the toe in the fist of her straightened arm. Nodding her head slowly, she dragged the glistening nylon against her slit. She grinned as she heard the muffled cry out on the balcony. Glancing up into the mirror, she saw that her hidden admirer had fallen from his perch. Giggling, she tossed the stocking aside, palmed gel into her breasts and eased her naked body into the bath.

Dinner was served at seven forty-five. The butler hesitated at the sideboard, hovering uncertainly at a silver tureen of aromatic lobster bisque.

'Seven fifty-four. Tom is late. This is intolerable,' one aunt muttered, angrily fussing with her napkin.

'We hope you will make it a priority to teach the young scoundrel the importance of punctuality,' the second aunt remarked, ominously tapping the face of her watch.

Edwina thumbed her bread roll open and buttered it carefully. The tension at the dining table was tangible.

Any moment now, she thought, the heavy double doors would burst open and the unruly schoolboy would charge in – late and breathless.

'Ah, here he is.'

The doors opened gently and a young man, handsome as he was elegantly carefree, sauntered in unapologetically. Edwina's heart thumped. It was the peeping face at her window as she had undressed for her bath that now smiled across the dining table. It was the young man to whom – from the safety of the bathroom – she had flaunted and displayed her nakedness in a pretence of unawareness of his presence.

'Tom, you young hound, where have you been?'

Tom. The butter knife slipped noisily from Edwina's fingers, clattering on her plate. The butler's head turned from the sideboard, a censorious frown at his eyebrows.

'Bird-watching, Auntie,' Tom replied.

Edwina flushed. The butler came to her rescue, placing a plate of delicious bisque before her.

'Never mind your damn bird-watching. Let me introduce you to Edwina. Your nanny.'

The butler appeared at Edwina's elbow. 'Hock, miss?'

Edwina nodded, grateful for the distraction. Surely there had been some misunderstanding? Tom, the young man sitting opposite, was at least twenty-three. Older, possibly. Was he to be her charge for the week? Was she being appointed by the testy aunts to nanny and firmly discipline this Adonis?

The butler cleared the soup plates in silence. Tom had wolfed his quickly, catching up with the rest.

'Hold the next course for the moment. We will ring when we are ready.'

'Very good, ma'am.' The black-suited butler withdrew.

'Now, Edwina. What do you think of young Tom's lateness?' an aunt demanded.

'It was very rude of him,' Edwina replied primly, in her strict nanny tone.

245

'Very rude,' echoed the second aunt. 'Tell me, nanny. What happens to rude little boys?'

'They are punished.'

'Then do your duty, nanny. Tom,' she barked, 'across the chair with you this instant. Bare-bottomed, please.'

Tom reddened, his handsome face beneath the tousled hair growing surly.

'At once, boy.'

To Edwina's amazement, he stood up, dropped his trousers and pants, and bent down across his dining chair, his thick cock squashed into the leather seat.

'Nanny –' the two aunts spoke in unison '– please do your duty.'

Edwina rose unsteadily, her tongue thickening in her dry mouth. As she rounded the dining table and approached the bare-buttocked man, her labia pouted and kissed the cotton of her panties. Kneeling down alongside her charge, she placed the palm of her right hand across his upturned cheeks.

'Bird-watching, indeed,' snorted an aunt, raising her Hock to her lips. 'Spank the rascal good and hard.'

To Edwina's surprise, Tom eased his hips up gently, offering his cheeks submissively to her controlling hand. She spanked him harshly five times – each measured spank echoing loudly as it reddened the bare bottom.

'Harder, nanny –'

'Faster, nanny,' the second aunt urged. 'You have our full authority to punish him as you please.'

Edwina paused to finger the young man's cleft dominantly. 'Why were you late this evening?' she demanded sternly.

'I was bird-watching,' he mumbled, rolling slightly from hip to hip, pressing his shaft into the warm leather.

'Come across anything interesting?' Edwina said softly.

Tom squeezed his buttocks anxiously but remained silent.

'In future,' Edwina continued crisply, 'nanny expects you to be punctual for all your meals. Understand?'

'Yes,' Tom muttered sulkily.

'Yes, what?'

'Yes, nanny.'

The aunts raised their glasses of Hock to salute this display of strict nanny-dominance and encouraged Edwina as she pinned the young man down by his neck across the leather chair and spanked his bare bottom savagely. Several minutes later, Edwina paused, thumbing his blistered cheeks and inspecting them intimately.

Rebuttoning the starched cuff at the wrist of her punishing arm, she rose and gazed down at the ravished buttocks.

'Get dressed,' she ordered.

Tom slumped down from the chair on to his knees, his red cheeks supported by his heels. Edwina's eyes widened as she saw the tip of his glistening cock – and widened even more as she saw the dark, wet stain on the leather seat where he had come.

An aunt tinkled a little glass bell. The butler appeared, skilfully bearing eight roast grouse. As Tom pulled up his trousers, the butler intervened.

'Allow me, sir,' he whispered.

Taking a linen napkin, the butler dried the wet knout of the young man's erection, then wiped up the smear of sticky semen from the dining chair. 'Claret or Beaune with the grouse, ma'am?'

'Are the grouse high?'

'Hung for six days, ma'am, so cook assures me.'

'The claret,' the aunts decided.

Edwina resumed her seat at the table. Arnaig House had returned to decorous normality. Had she imagined it all? Her right hand felt hot after the discipline it had dispensed. Despite the delicious aroma of roast grouse, she could just detect the rank smell of the spanked man's orgasm.

'No grouse for Tom,' Edwina heard herself saying. 'He's to go straight to bed, supperless.'

The butler bowed, clearly approving of her decision. Tom left the table with a scowl.

'I believe we are leaving Tom in very capable hands,' an aunt remarked, helping herself to chestnut stuffing. 'Very capable.'

Edwina wasn't listening to their praise. She was thinking of the young man's eyes – eyes brimming with servile devotion. She closed her teeth over a forkful of well-hung game.

'Be sure to call into his bedroom before you retire, won't you, nanny?'

Edwina, taking coffee in the drawing room with the two aunts, replied, saying that she considered it the duty of every conscientious nanny to visit their charge before lights-out.

'Tom, as we told you, is thoroughly spoilt. Never went to school. Joined a rock band –'

'Lived in a tree-house commune in Java. The worry –'

'Went to New York to be a poet. The bills –'

Edwina listened as the two aunts poured out their past concerns and future hopes for their wayward nephew.

'The last of the line. We need you to train and discipline him. A suitable fiancée has been found. Sensible girl, with very stern views. There is an opening for Tom in her family's business. But he must be licked into shape, and quickly.'

Edwina nodded, promising to do what she could.

'We have every confidence in you, nanny,' the other aunt replied. 'We want you to civilise Tom. Train him rigorously in matters of etiquette, and instil in him certain of the social graces.'

'His bottom is entirely yours, nanny. Tom can be wilful, most wilful. He is used to freedom and irresponsibility. Bring him to heel, nanny. Whip him in.'

* * *

Later, entering his bedroom without knocking, Edwina turned on the light. Tom rose from his pillow, rubbing his eyes.

'Just look at the state of this room,' she exclaimed angrily, picking her steps carefully through the litter of paperbacks, discarded clothing and fishing tackle. 'Get out of bed this instant and tidy it up.'

He was naked. She folded her arms and stood dominantly over him as he bent down to pick up and fold his clothes, then restore the books and fishing tackle to their proper place. As he moved about the bedroom, she saw his semi-erect shaft nodding. Edwina thrilled to his lean body, his athletic grace, his balls swinging between his thighs. He was all hers, she suddenly realised, to dominate and discipline.

Working for an exclusive agency who supplied nannies for very special – and unusual – posts, Edwina had owned the soft bottoms of sixth-formers who had been suspended from private boarding schools and had caned the buttocks of an Arab princess entrusted to her stern care. Tom was her first grown male, and she was determined to enjoy every well-paid minute of her duties.

He stood, a fishing rod in his hand, yawning as he scratched his left buttock.

'Can't I do this in the morning, nanny?'

A burning wave of contempt surged through her. She seethed at this moneyed, overindulged young waster. *His bottom is yours, nanny. Discipline and train him.* The words of the young man's stern aunts revisited her. Edwina needed little prompting.

'You may put that away and then go back to your bed, but I want you across it, not in it.'

His shaft pulsed and rose up to salute her strict instruction.

'Quickly. Bend over and give me your bottom.'

He responded to her command with the reluctant

alacrity of a true submissive – fearful, yet resentful, of her absolute sovereignty. Kneeling at the bed, he bent his face down into the rumpled duvet.

'Up. Now get right across the bed, you wicked little boy. Nanny wants your bare bottom right up for punishment.'

As he squirmed, easing his belly across the bed, she opened a wardrobe and searched for a leather belt. To her annoyance – supple leather stung so satisfyingly across naked cheeks – there wasn't one to hand. The pairs of braces, though decorative, did not suit her present purpose. Noting them for possible use in future punishments, Edwina closed the wardrobe door.

'Stay still. Nanny is watching you,' she announced. Such was her sense of control, she did not even bother to glance over her shoulder, knowing instinctively that her stern command would leave him quivering in an agony of delicious dread. 'Nanny is always watching you.'

Tom whimpered and clamped his upper thighs together.

'Ah, perfect,' Edwina pronounced, taking an end-cane from a fly rod she had discovered in the tackle box. She flexed it, then thrummed the whippy wood, testing it for suppleness. 'Perfect.'

The pale length of bamboo weighed lightly in her firm grip, but she was certain of its capacity to deliver a venomous bite. Pacing softly over to the naked man across the bed, she tested the cane, swishing the wood across his buttocks. He grunted, jerking his hips and buttocks in response as a thin red line appeared across his cheeks.

'Stay still, young man. Nanny is going to cane your bottom.'

She smiled as she saw his toes whiten as he scrunched them into the carpet, straining obediently to submit his bottom up for the kiss of nanny's cane.

Edwina tapped his cheeks dominantly with the quivering tip of the rod. 'In future,' she announced, 'nanny will expect to find this room – and, indeed, every other room you use – to be left in a neat and tidy state. Understand?'

'Yes, nanny,' he whispered into the duvet at his lips.

Planting her feet slightly apart, Edwina commenced the caning, swishing the whippy bamboo eight times across his bare buttocks, pausing between each slicing stroke to tap and quell his jerking cheeks. She relished the authority invested in her, and tried to deny the excitement at her tightened throat and nipples. Try as she did, Edwina could not deny the wetness at her slit.

Digging his fingers into the duvet as the cane cracked down, Tom gasped aloud at the fifth stroke, and was moaning by the seventh. After administering the eighth cut across his cheeks, Edwina ordered him to leave the bed and face her, kneeling. His twitching shaft, painfully erect, tapped his belly as he turned towards her, shuffling awkwardly on his knees. She saw his fingers inching furtively down towards his engorged cock. She swept them aside with her cane.

'Keep away from that,' she commanded, raking the tip of the bamboo lightly up the length of his erection, causing him to almost buckle and collapse in a spasm of exquisite torment. 'Get into bed and go to sleep. You have a very demanding day – week – ahead of you, young man. So no touching or playing with yourself. When nanny inspects your sheets in the morning, nanny will be very cross with you if she finds any sticky stains, understand?'

'Yes, nanny,' he whispered huskily.

'Wait.'

He froze, his eyes never leaving her glinting cane.

'Lie down, face down, on the bed. Nanny must inspect your caned bottom.'

'No, please –' he begged, writhing at this additional humiliation.

She did not speak, just flicked her cane. He obeyed promptly, presenting his buttocks as prescribed, stretching full length on the duvet. Edwina sat on the bed, her nanny's uniform skirt pressed at his naked thigh. She shuddered as he inched into her, snuggling into her warmth, surrendering to her intimate authority.

'Lie still,' she whispered. She dimpled the crowns of his caned cheeks with her fingertips and finger-traced the horizontal ravages of her cane.

'Before I tuck you in, I shall kiss you good night, young man. Nanny is not cruel. She is firm but fair.'

He twisted his face up from the duvet, eager for her lips.

'No. Face down. Nanny does not kiss naughty boys on the mouth. Not when they have been wicked.'

He buried his face in the pillow and arched his bottom up from the duvet.

'In fact,' Edwina whispered softly, 'nanny does not kiss her little men with her mouth. Keep still.'

Unbuttoning her starched blouse, she eased her breasts out from their brassièred bondage. Tom jerked his hips impatiently, yearning for her nipples against his caned cheeks. Guiding her heavy breasts down over the striped buttocks, she fleetingly brushed them with her thickened nipples.

'Please, nanny, please –' he begged, burning for the kiss of her breasts upon his bottom.

'No,' she said sternly. 'You have been a bad boy. Get into bed. Nanny is cross with you. No goodnight kiss for naughty Tom.'

He scrambled under the duvet, his huge cock raking the sheets. He gazed up at her imploringly as Edwina slowly forced her breasts, one swollen mound of quivering satin at a time, back into her white brassière's cups.

Thumbing her nipples, she gazed at him sternly. 'Remember. Any sticky stains on your sheets and nanny will be most severe with you in the morning.'

Under the duvet, his erection jerked disobediently. Their eyes met, certain in the knowledge of a caning after breakfast.

She returned to the bedroom an hour before breakfast. Out in the chill mist, capercaillies clucked their haunting cries. Edwina knew that Tom would have masturbated furiously last night – several times, probably – and that she would have to punish him, as promised. Pulling away the duvet briskly, her suspicions were confirmed. The dry but unmistakeable stain attested to his disobedience.

'Out of that bed, you wicked boy,' she barked.

He struggled to obey, shivering in the cold air of the highland dawn.

'What did nanny say about this?' she demanded, jabbing a straightened forefinger down directly at the dried semen on his sheet.

'I couldn't help –'

'Silence. Come here.'

He clambered off the side of the bed, head bowed, his eyes avoiding her stern, searching gaze.

'Bend over, across the bed.'

He sank to his knees and positioned himself for the impending punishment. Edwina selected one of a pair of substantial, flat-backed hairbrushes from his dressing table and returned to the bed. Taloning his tousled hair with her left hand, she forced his face down at the spot where he had ejaculated. He struggled, but nanny was very firm. Sweeping the polished wood of the hairbrush across his upturned cheeks, she spoke sternly, reminding the naked young man in her thrall that, when nanny gave an instruction, nanny expected to be obeyed.

The hairbrush spoke, more harshly, more severely, than Edwina's stern eloquence. The faint pink stripes across his bottom – a legacy from last night's caning – soon disappeared under the angry red blotches of pain

253

bequeathed by the swiping brush. Tom wriggled and squealed under the furious flurry of strokes, but soon slumped in abject surrender as the hairbrush crushed his rebellion. Administering a final blistering four strokes across his scarlet cheeks, nanny noted with satisfaction that his flattened tongue was pressed into the soiled sheet.

Returning the hairbrush to its proper place alongside its partner on the dressing table, Edwina paused at the sound of an engine. At the bedroom window, she looked down and saw the venerable Bentley departing. The aunts had departed for Edinburgh. Turning to the bed, she gazed down at the reddened bottom she had just beaten. It was hers – entirely hers – to control, own and punish throughout the coming week.

A respectful tap at the bedroom door broke the silence. The butler entered, bearing an armful of equipment.

'Breakfast will be served in the blue room, miss, in seventeen minutes. I thought you may find these of some use.'

Edwina's tongue thickened as she examined the riding crop, table-tennis bat, leather tawse and curled leather belt.

'A selection of instruments suitable for the chastisement of the young master's bottom, miss.'

The butler withdrew. Edwina fingered the little loop of leather at the tip of the riding crop, then glanced at the bare bottom still bending across the bed.

Her task was simple enough. She had to civilise and train this weak, wayward young wastrel. Her methods were certain – discipline and domination. Her reward? The aunts had hinted at a generous bonus over and above the substantial salary, if Edwina proved successful. But for Edwina, as she stood gazing down at the beautiful young man she had just thrashed, the pleasures of punishment were reward enough.

Pleasure. The word reminded Edwina that, beneath her crisp nanny's uniform, her nipples ached and her slit was sticky with a delicious wet heat. Tom was hers, now. Utterly hers. The aunts were gone. He had no hiding place. Could she? Dare she?

'Nanny wants her little soldier to perform a simple task for her before we go down for breakfast,' she announced, her cool tone just managing to disguise her racing heartbeat.

He rose from the bed and stood before her, his throbbing cock angry and proud.

'Kneel down, Tom.'

He knelt.

'Good boy,' she whispered, patting the side of his upturned face gently as he gazed at her devotedly. 'You were spying on me yesterday, weren't you, Tom? Spying on nanny preparing for her bath.'

He tried to shy away from her serious brown eyes. She held his face firmly in her gripping hand.

'Weren't you? Don't lie. I warned you, nanny sees everything.'

'Sorry, nanny.'

'You certainly will be, young man. But more of that matter later. Plenty of time for nanny to demonstrate the severity of the strap and the cruelty of the crop. For the moment, nanny has a little task for you to perform. Nanny wants you to lick her. Here,' she murmured, thumbing her pubis firmly beneath the stretch of her uniform skirt.

Despite her controlling grip, Tom jerked his head up. His eyes were sparkling. Releasing his face, Edwina used both hands to inch her skirt up over her hips, exposing her suspender belt, dark stocking tops and white-pantied pubic mound. Tucking in her skirt, she eased down her panties, revealing her dark pubic nest. The black matted coils rasped under her thumbnail.

Tom closed his eyes, swallowed noisily and swayed on his knees.

255

'Look at nanny,' she instructed.

He opened his eyes and moaned softly.

'Now put your lips to mine.'

Her thumbtip had been worrying her sticky labia with firm downward strokes. She used it to prise the flesh-lips wide apart. Her fragrance was released. Tom bent closer, sniffing deeply. His cock strained, the pale-blue veins prominent.

'Kiss nanny properly. Suck her gently and then use your tongue. No biting, though –'

Tom came. Edwina shuddered and then snarled angrily, fishing out a tissue from her breast pocket to wipe away the dripping semen as it soaked her stockinged inner thighs.

'What a very rude, bad mannered little boy you are. My word,' she whispered venomously, 'your aunts were right when they said you needed training and discipline. I ordered you to kiss nanny like a perfect little gentleman, and what did you do?'

Trembling, Tom shrank back from her sudden fury.

'Come back here,' she thundered, grabbing his hair and pulling his face into her. Quickly slipping off her soiled nylons, she used them to bind his ankles tightly and tie his wrists together behind his back. Returning to stand, thighs parted, in front of his face, she drew his face into her open sex.

'Lick.'

Tom's tongue worked feverishly to please his stern nanny.

'Harder, deeper,' she commanded, inching up on her toes and lowering her open flesh on to his mouth.

Smothered by her wet heat, he served her devotedly. As her taut belly's muscles melted and the first rippling spasms of her climax approached, Edwina hauled his bound body back to the bed. Tossing him face down across it, she straddled his bottom and wiped her slit down savagely, repeatedly, on his punished cheeks.

Gripping his muscular shoulders, she rode him, crying out long and loud as she came several times in a collision of multiple orgasms.

Moments later, as she staggered drunkenly from her naked mount, Edwina froze as she saw the butler hovering in the doorway.

'Breakfast, miss, has been waiting for the past six minutes. The devilled kidneys will spoil.'

The week passed all too quickly for both the nanny-mistress and her helpless slave. Edwina ensured that Tom arrived punctually for every meal. She monitored his dress code, forbidding his customary casual wear and insisting – quite painfully – that formal attire was worn at all times. Manicured, scrubbed and intimately talcumed, Tom became quite presentable. He was taught – severely – to be attentive, courteous and charmingly considerate: all those qualities a potential fiancée would seek and hope to find.

Every morning, Edwina visited the bedroom, to wash, punish and dress her little man. She shadowed him throughout the day, lunching, dining and dispensing discipline regularly at the appointed hour. Edwina had the young master of Arnaig House eating out of her hand – as well as submissively eating her out. He became utterly enslaved, and she became accustomed to his squirt of hot seed drenching her belly and nylon stocking-tops as she chastised his bare bottom across her lap.

On Thursday afternoon, Edwina returned to her bedroom after a particularly punishing schedule, to attend to the frenzied heat at her slit. Dealing with Tom had kindled an arousal within her that her slave could not – dare not – satisfy. Happy to spill his seed over her when being whipped or caned, he had not the temerity to penetrate her and fully extinguish the delicious flames that licked her remorselessly.

In her room, she drew the curtains together and stripped naked. She had not packed either of her dildos and had taken the precaution of stealing a thick, beeswax candle from the butler's pantry. A private half-hour on her bed, with the candle probing her pussy, was exactly what her aching void needed. The beeswax shaft slid in with delicious ease.

A tap at the door startled her. Tom must not discover her like this – it would shatter the mystique within which he was enslaved. Before she could reply, the door opened, admitting the butler. Edwina curled up on the bed, hastily covering her breasts and pubic nest. The white candle, wet with her excitement, slipped out as she drew her knees up to her bosom.

'Tea, miss. I thought perhaps you would take it in your room. Arnaig House has a fine tradition of hospitality. Indeed, the clan motto – in peacetime, you understand – is "To each, all they desire". You've done a fine job on master Tom. The family line will continue.'

Edwina snatched up a sheet and dragged it over her nakedness as the butler placed a large tray on the bedside table.

'Your candle, miss,' he said softly, bending to retrieve the wax length. 'His aunts are going to be so pleased when they return with master Tom's fiancée.'

Edwina, who had shared a dram every evening with the loyal retainer, wriggled under the sheet.

'No need to be shy, miss. I know what the candle is for,' he purred, tapping his open palm with the improvised dildo. 'Let me be of service to you.'

Edwina blushed and avoided his knowing eyes. She pretended to examine the contents of the tea tray. The butler swept it away and placed it down upon a distant occasional table.

'The tea can wait, can it not, miss? Unlike other appetites. And if you will allow me to say so, miss,' he continued suavely, 'you will enjoy it with more relish once your more pressing needs have been attended to. Turn over on your tummy, if you please, miss.'

As if mesmerised by the butler's unctuous tones, Edwina rolled over on to her belly, squashing her breasts beneath her.

The butler removed the sheet, exposing her naked body. 'May I suggest the legs a little wider, perhaps?'

As she obeyed, inching her thighs apart obediently, she felt the wet bubble at her slit burst and drench her pubic fringe.

'Although this service does not strictly come under the butler's office, miss,' he purred, nuzzling her wet labia with the tip of the candle, 'let me assure you that I am quite adept. Arnaig House has two maids and a cook. We're a remote little community. I have an understanding with the maids and an arrangement with the cook. Cook,' he observed, grunting slightly as he drove the candle home, wetting his knuckles at her slit, 'is particularly demanding. Bottom up a little, if you please, miss.'

Edwina brought her hands to her breasts, cupping their warmth and squeezing rhythmically in time to the thrusting length of candle. Inching her buttocks up as he had directed, she suddenly moaned into the pillow as the shaft probed her at a sharper angle, raking her inner muscles ruthlessly.

'Faster, please,' she heard herself pleading.

'Trust me, miss. I know my business well. Dip your tummy a fraction more.'

Just as Edwina rolled her face across her pillow to blot up the perspiration stinging her eyes, the butler slowed down the penetrating thrusts, easing the pumping until each insertion took several seconds to complete. Her flesh-lips adhered to the sliding wax just like shower curtains cling to a soaped bottom – a delicious, heavy, dragging sensation. The butler's slower thrusts ensured that the smooth thickness caressed each ribbed muscle inside her, maddening and delighting the spreadeagled nude.

'Please –' she choked, shedding every vestige of dignity and jerking her bottom up. 'Harder, faster, finish me, please –'

He soothed her, urging her to surrender herself up into his care. 'Trust me,' he murmured, bending his face down closer to her parted thighs and sniffing the perfume of her wet excitement.

'Yes,' Edwina muttered abjectly, 'yes.' Suddenly, her task of being the dominant nanny – and the heavy burden of responsibility – melted away and flowed out of both her body and her mind. Forced to be in control for every moment of the last week, she luxuriated in the sensation of surrendering her body up to the candle. No longer the dominant nanny-bitch, Edwina was a wet woman with a wanton desire. 'Yes,' she whispered, 'just do what you want with me.'

The butler's cufflink grazed her sensitive flesh as he twisted the candle slowly, rotating it as he probed her deeply. Like a hypnotist, he seemed to sense when his subject was completely, helplessly, under his spell. Easing the candle out of her – it emerged with a soft plop – he smiled indulgently as Edwina threshed in her nakedness, writhing her hips and buttocks up in his face and squealing for the candle.

'One moment, miss. Cook has done some excellent muffins for your tea. Allow me.'

Sensing his departure from the bed, Edwina groaned and begged him to return. He did so immediately, nursing a hot muffin in a napkin. Sitting down on the bed, he split the muffin open – the steam rose from the exposed crumb – and crushed it directly against her slit. Edwina squealed her delight.

'Hold it there; no, spread your fingers. That's it. Now, miss, hold it tightly, if you please.'

He picked up the candle from where it had fallen

down beneath her parted thighs and inserted it in her anus, holding her sphincter wide apart with a finger-and-thumb pincer. Burying her sobs of delight into the pillow, Edwina knuckled the hot muffin into her hotter sex. He gripped the candle like a dagger, stabbing it into her rosebud hole with savage tenderness. Seconds later, Edwina cried out in the first of four orgasms. At her final climax, she bit the pillow in her violent ecstasy, releasing a snowstorm of swirling feathery down.

Wiping the sticky candlestick in a handkerchief – which he pocketed for closer attention, afterwards – the butler rose from the bed. 'The walnut and date slice is particularly good, miss. Deliciously moist. Cook is a marvel with his spoon. And do not overlook the anchovy toast. May I take the liberty of thanking you once again for the way you have improved young master Tom? You certainly seem to have taken him in hand.'

'Your aunts are due back for lunch,' Edwina remarked, rinsing the soaped flannel under the hot tap and squeezing it in her fist. 'I understand that your fiancée will be accompanying them.'

Tom, bending over the hand-basin as nanny washed his bottom, remained silent.

'Victoria, isn't it?'

'Yes, nanny.'

'Pretty girl?'

'Mm.'

'Then we'd better make sure that we look smart when we get dressed, hadn't we? I think a kilt is called for.'

'Yes, nanny.'

Edwina spread the hot flannel over her fingertips, then applied it roughly between his cheeks. He grunted as it ravished his sensitive cleft.

'Take extra care when dressing, Tom. I want you turned out perfectly when Victoria arrives. Understand?'

'Yes, nanny.'

She tossed the flannel aside, dried his bottom with a towel and spanked it sharply. 'Off you go,' she admonished. 'No mistakes, or you'll pay dearly.'

Two hours later, Tom presented himself for inspection. Edwina perused him carefully, noting with approval the combed sporran and polished dirk. Then her eyes narrowed as she saw his muddy brogues.

'Come here, young man,' she ordered, snapping her fingers.

Tom, crestfallen, slouched towards her.

'Turn around and look at yourself in the mirror. Now, can you see anything amiss?'

'No, nanny.'

'Look carefully. You'll see what I mean if you try.'

Tom stared into his own puzzled reflection.

'Kilt up,' she barked.

His fingers fumbled at the hem of the green and white tartan as he raised the kilt over his bare bottom. Edwina picked up a long-handled clothes-brush and tapped the smooth side against Tom's cheeks.

'No, please don't, nanny –'

'Silence. Now look carefully in the mirror. Name each item you are wearing and tell me if it is in perfect order.'

He sulked, and remained silent. She swiped his bottom with the clothes-brush to prompt him. Wincing, Tom stared into the mirror and blurted out each item he was wearing – his catalogue punctuated by severe strokes of the polished wood across his exposed buttocks.

'Socks,' he whispered thickly, dreading the clothes-brush hovering at his cheeks. Swish, swipe. The brutal stroke flattened them as it bit.

'Shoes.'

Edwina paused, slowly reversing the clothes-brush so that the bristles tormented his scalded buttocks. 'Are they clean and polished, as nanny instructed?' she demanded, prickling his hot cheeks with the bristles.

'No, nanny,' he confessed.

'And why not?'

'I forgot –'

Crack. The clothes-brush, polished wood once more turned inwards, whipped down across his bottom. 'Clean them at once.'

Tom crossed over to the cupboard and took out the brushes. Kneeling down, he started to polish the dull brogues.

'Keep your kilt up, young man. Nanny wants to see your red bottom.'

Tom obeyed, tucking up his kilt and revealing his punished cheeks.

'That's much better,' Edwina murmured, inspecting her charge as he stood once more before the mirror. She inverted the clothes-brush and guided it, bristles uppermost, to his balls. He moaned softly as she tapped and tormented them, shuddering as her hand brought the brush up the length of his erection. She tapped the tip of his cock with the bristles, then brought the brush firmly down upon it, rubbing hard.

'Nanny has to be firm, Tom. I must punish you for neglecting to polish your shoes.'

Holding the brush down on his shaft with her left hand, she spanked his bare bottom with her right palm. Tom screamed softly and buckled at the knees, staggering tipsily as he approached his climax.

'No, not yet,' she warned, sensing his imminent ejaculation. 'You know the rules, young man. Not until nanny –'

He came, pumping fiercely. Edwina was prepared, trapping his shaft beneath the clothes-brush and forcing the hot length down.

'That was very naughty of you,' Edwina murmured, gazing down at the semen-splashed brogues. 'Now

you're going to have to clean them all over again, and –'
she sighed, as if resigning herself to the task '– nanny is
going to have to punish you with her horrid little crop.'

Edwina did not lunch with the aunts, Tom and Victoria,
but tactfully withdrew below stairs, to join cook, the
maids and the butler in their cold game pie and
Chardonnay. With Victoria's arrival to meet her
betrothed, it was deemed unsuitbale for Tom's nanny to
be present. After lunch, a polite note penned by the
elder of the two aunts instructed Edwina to remain in
her room until the following morning, when she was due
to depart.

The visitation by both aunts at cockcrow caught
Edwina completely by surprise. They sat down on her
bed, one at either side.

'Victoria is eager for the match –'

'But a problem has arisen –'

'Tom will not submit to her –'

'He is still enslaved to you –'

'She will only have him if she can exercise supreme
authority over him, mind and body –'

'But you've done such a thorough job on him, that
you still own and control him –'

'We want you to release Tom from his servitude –'

'And allow Victoria full sovereignty over him.'

Edwina considered the justice of this. 'Yes,' she
agreed. 'It shall be done.'

Victoria was a cold, stern beauty with flame-bright hair
and ice-blue eyes. She will have no problems in the
dominance and disciplining of Tom, Edwina thought on
their first meeting. Matters were quickly settled between
them and they mounted the staircase together hand in
hand, heading towards Tom's bedroom.

Tom sat up in bed, startled and amazed, as they
entered briskly and snapped on the light.

'Nanny has been telling me all about you, Tom. How naughty you have been and how she has had to punish you.'

Tom scowled.

'Don't sulk, Tom,' Edwina chided. 'I'm leaving Arnaig House shortly, but Victoria is going to continue with your training and discipline.'

'Can't you stay, nanny? Please?'

'No,' Victoria snapped. 'I'm taking control from now on. Now get out of bed and get your bottom across that chair.'

Tom appealed to Edwina. 'Nanny?'

'Do exactly as Victoria says, Tom. Across the chair.'

To Victoria's clear annoyance, Tom obeyed at once.

'We are going to spank you, Tom,' Edwina said softly. 'I shall commence, then hand over control of your bottom to Victoria. She is taking you in hand from now on. After tonight, your bottom belongs to her.'

The two women knelt facing each other across his bare buttocks. Fingering Tom's bottom gently, Edwina relished the memories she had of nannying the soft cheeks, disciplining and reddening their curved flesh. Tom thrust his bottom up, eager for chastisement. Edwina responded, spanking him painfully for three and a half minutes. The staccato of firm flesh across helpless cheeks rang out in the silent bedroom.

'Thank you, nanny,' Victoria murmured. 'We will now take turns to chastise him.'

Sharing the discipline, they spanked him between them, Edwina reddening his left cheek then pausing as Victoria spanked his right cheek harshly. Tom grunted and stiffened, jerking his hips into the seat of the chair. Victoria's eyes widened as she noticed – and understood – the movements.

Edwina ceased the spanking and watched as Tom's fiancée took control.

'You may come only when I say so,' Victoria rasped warningly. 'Do you understand?'

'Yes,' Tom hissed.

'From now on,' she continued, 'your bottom belongs to me. All your pleasure and all your pain is mine, and mine alone, to dispense as I see fit.'

'Spank me,' he whispered, offering his hot buttocks up to her hovering palm. 'Spank me hard, please.'

Savouring her moment of absolute control, Victoria hesitated then launched into a searing attack upon his upturned cheeks. Tom moaned and came massively into the seat of the chair. His fiancée gathered up a handful of his tousled hair and forced him up and away from his seat of punishment. Kneeling in her dominant control, his cock still twitching, he revealed a wet belly and chest.

Edwina rose and left the bedroom in silence, carrying with her the perfect picture of submission and dominance, of devotion and discipline.

With her two bags neatly packed and brought down to the hall by the efficient butler – who had slipped four candles into her luggage, as a souvenir of Arnaig – Edwina was preparing to depart. It had been a thrilling assignment, she reflected, and quite lucrative. She had a few moments before the Bentley was due to take her to the station. Just time to say farewell to Tom's aunts and receive their thanks, together with the promised payment.

The butler appeared at the library door, bearing a tray of morning coffee. Edwina was too preoccupied to notice the three cups. He emerged and beckoned Edwina into the library, guiding her to a seat. Coffee was poured and served in silence. Edwina smiled but declined.

'My train,' she explained.

'Serve nanny with her coffee and then take her bags back up to her room,' an aunt said, selecting a gingernut and snapping it neatly in half.

'But –'

'Have a biscuit, my dear. Cook's speciality.'

The butler retired. Edwina looked inquiringly from one aunt to the other.

'There will be no train today, nanny. There is, I fear, a little unfinished business for you to perform.'

'It's Tom, you see. Grown so attached to you –'

'And, though he's transferred his devotion to Victoria –'

'Who rules him with a rod of iron –'

'He cannot quite get rid of your presence –'

'You haunt him, dear girl –'

'Your shadow falls between them. So far, there has not been a complete union –'

Edwina blinked, her head almost dizzy from turning from one aunt to the other as they jointly unravelled the dilemma of Tom's continuing fixation.

'There is only one solution,' the gingernut-eating aunt mumbled through her crumbs. 'Tom must expunge you from his mind –'

'Exert himself masterfully over you –' the other aunt chimed.

'Bed you, my dear –'

'But –' Edwina began, protesting.

'Don't you see? If you let him master you, he would purge himself of this slavish devotion to your memory.'

A silence fell upon them for a few moments, then the aunt with the cheque in her hand held it up. 'And, of course, we'd make it worth your while. You've done so much for him: indeed, for all of us, here at Arnaig. Won't you now release him from his bondage?'

He came to her that night, after eleven. Tentative at first, he stroked Edwina's hair but hesitated to kiss her upturned face.

'Nanny,' he whispered hoarsely, tracing her soft throat and softer breasts with a quivering forefinger. He was naked and erect but timid – inhibited by his reverence for her domination and nanny-discipline.

Edwina sensed his mounting frustration, sensed his desire to dominate what he adored, to defile that to which he was devoted. She remained passive, her thighs demurely parted, doing nothing to assist his conquest of her. It must be his and his alone.

She felt his fingertips at her sticky labia, prising them apart with increasing excitement. Suddenly, he shrank back and huddled at the end of the bed, kissing and licking her feet slavishly.

Edwina knew that she must break the spell she had cast over him and free him from this thraldom. Slowly, unhurriedly, she rolled over on to her belly, dragging both pillows down the bed and sliding them under her hips. Her bottom rose up to entice him.

Tom whimpered with tormented desire, clearly yearning to penetrate and possess the nanny who had pleasured him with punishments – but unable to do so, because of the shadow of her dominance in which he still cowered.

Edwina shivered as she felt a draught. The door had opened. Somene had entered the room. Victoria? The aunts?

'Allow me, sir.' The reassuring tones of the butler caused Edwina to freeze. 'Perhaps if we were to arrange the young lady thus,' the butler continued suavely, taking Edwina's wrists and positioning them up at the bedposts. 'Look, sir. I'm tying nanny to the bed with her own nylon stockings. See how tightly she is bound, sir. She cannot move.'

Edwina struggled, but the butler had been as efficient as ever in applying the impromptu bondage. Her arms ached and her wrists burned in their restrictions.

Edwina felt Tom's weight as he crawled up along her legs and thighs. He paused, his knees pressed down upon her buttocks. He straddled her; she felt his stiff cock rake up between her thighs. He was mounting her.

'This is not nanny, sir, who whipped your bare bottom without mercy. This young lady is a whore, sir. Yours, master Tom, for the usage and the pleasure. Mount her, sir, and ride her hard. Good night, sir.'

The butler withdrew.

'Nanny,' Tom murmured into her bottom. He licked her cleft. He remained, his face forced down between her cheeks. Edwina's throat tightened as his tongue grew bolder, now lapping down at the wet heat of her crease. Twisting in her bondage, she gasped as his fingers replaced his tongue, first in her cleft and then at her labia.

'Nanny punished Tom,' he whispered. 'Now Tom will punish nanny.'

He spanked her harshly, then entered her confidently – crying out loud as he came almost immediately. Edwina felt his excitement spilling into her muscled warmth, but refused to contract her vaginal muscles. He must work for the delicious bliss he craved.

'Bitch,' he hissed, tormenting her nipples with cruel fingers. But Edwina remained passive and relaxed. Tom must do all the work. His frustration grew into anger. He resented her and spanked her hard, biting the buttocks he had just beaten. Soon, he was stiff again.

She cried out as he prised her cheeks apart, forbidding him to enter her there. He grunted dismissively and drove his shaft mercilessly in between her buttocks.

Edwina closed her eyes, hating his dominance and his brutal contempt. After delicious hours as his ruthless dominatrix, she was now bound and helpless as he relished his revenge. As if repaying her for every fierce stroke she had administered across his bare bottom, he thrust into her, remaining inside her even after he had climaxed, squeezing her cheeks between his thighs.

Neither spoke, but Edwina knew that the spell had been broken. Tom clambered down from the bed, dried his penis in her silk panties, then forced the wet silk into her mouth. Gagged and bound, she dreaded what he might choose to do with her next. There was a riding crop – an old hunting souvenir – hanging from the back of her bedroom door. She shivered as she imagined the burning lashes across her soft cheeks. She knew his dominance over her naked helplessness was absolute and that she could expect no mercy. He could do anything he desired.

Tom simply walked across to the dressing table, picked up nanny's hairbrush and, palming the stiff bristles meditatively, stared into the mirror. Edwina clenched her buttocks, dreading the moment when the spanking wood exploded across her upturned bottom. She closed her eyes, opening them moments later to discover her former slave taming his tousled locks with the brush. Her belly muscles loosened and her taut body slumped as he tossed the hairbrush down and strode out of the bedroom.

With his hot semen still trickling out of her rosebud sphincter, down to soak her pubic fringe beneath, Edwina sighed in her bondage.

She dozed, stirring and waking when the cold draught from the opening door caused her to shiver in alarm. It was Victoria. Edwina relaxed. She's come to thank me.

But the woman's tone was venomous.

'They didn't tell me. The aunts didn't tell me everything.'

Gagged, Edwina was unable to explain.

'He's been in here tonight, hasn't he? He's been to see you.'

Edwina strained to soothe the fiancée's tortured mind.

'Wedding present, was it, bitch?'

Edwina choked on her panties as she tried to expel them with her tongue. If only she could explain.

'You were employed, I understand, to train him. To civilise him and correct his erring ways. Perhaps you did. I will make a better job of it. But it was, I am quite certain, never in your contract to debauch him. As his betrothed, it is my duty and my pleasure to punish you.'

Edwina felt the cold sweat of terror prickling her face. An accomplished disciplinarian herself, she had good cause to both fear and respect Victoria's proven prowess. She had witnessed Tom being punished – and had pitied his poor bottom under Victoria's lash.

'Tied and gagged. How very convenient,' Victoria murmured, palming Edwina's bare bottom. 'And still wet from your wicked seduction. Very well, nanny, let's see how you respond to a taste of your own bitter medicine.'

She didn't use the hairbrush – or a wire coat-hanger from the wardrobe – to whip Edwina's bare buttocks. Gazing down at the nanny, Victoria unfastened her brown leather belt from her slender waist (it already bore Tom's teeth marks, where he had bitten it in an anguish of ecstasy) and doubled it up in her fist.

NEXUS NEW BOOKS

To be published in April

THE PALACE OF PLEASURES
Christobel Coleridge

The city-state of Estra is a thriving port and trading centre, ruled over by a Sultan who finds relief from the pressures of power amidst a selected bevy of intimate Companions. Carria, a mysterious and striking young woman arrives one night aboard a trading ship and rapidly finds herself offered the opportunity of joining the Companions. However, before she can she has to pass the schooling and selection, run by the Sultan's mistress J'nie. The training is, of course, very rigorous, and discipline is maintained with a firm hand. There are many different uniforms and articles to wear, and there are many strange and elaborate punishments for failure, including both humiliation and pain. Carria, however, has her own agenda. When it comes to fruition, nothing in Estra will be quite the same again.

£6.99   ISBN 0 352 33801 6

PEACH
Penny Birch

Penny Birch is currently the filthiest little minx on the Nexus list, with 15 titles already published by Nexus. All are equally full of messy, kinky fun and, frankly, no other erotic writer has ever captured the internal thrills afforded by the perverse shamings and humiliations her characters undergo! In *Peach*, Penny's friend Natasha comes unstuck – stickily. The peach in question is of course Natasha's bottom, as ripe as ever for a spanking, and everyone want a piece. The pert but mischievous Natasha is bound to get her just desserts.

£6.99   ISBN 0 352 33790 7

MISS RATTAN'S LESSON
Yolanda Celbridge

Thomas Peake joins an Oxford set of female devotees of discipline: dominant Edwina Cheshunt; voluptuous mulatto dancer Lucinda Lalage; and Miss Mann, whose disciplinary academy painfully recreates a Lady's schooldays. Thomas's London delights with his group of enthusiastic submissives are interrupted by a summons to claim his Caribbean inheritance. Ransomed after enslavement by the fierce Queen Orchid, he makes his plantation a ladies' holiday resort with a difference – always governed by Miss Rattan's rules.

£6.99   ISBN 0 352 33791 5

To be published in May

CHALLENGED TO SERVE
Jacqueline Bellevois

Known simply as 'The Club', a group of the rich and influential meet every month in a Cotswold mansion to slake their perverted sexual appetites. Within its walls, social norms are forgotten and fantasy becomes reality. The Club's members are known to each other by the names of pagan gods and goddesses, or those of characters from the darker side of history. Two of them – Astra and Kali – undertake to resolve a feud once and for all by each training a novice member. After one month, the one who's deemed by the other members to have done the best job will be allowed to enslave the other, finally and totally, for the duration of the Club's activities and beyond.

£6.99   ISBN 0 352 33748 6

BENCH-MARKS
Tara Black

Continues the stories of Judith Wilson, Kate Carpenter and their boss at the Nemesis Archive, the imperious Samantha James. The Archive is a discreet but global concern dedicated to cataloguing the perverse excesses of errrant female desire throughout history. Tara Black is a sophisticated writer of up-to-date erotica who manages to combine a thoughtful look at the conflicts that face intelligent, self-possessed young women who like to spank and be spanked, with taught, horny flagellatory prose.

£6.99   ISBN 0 352 33797 4

THE TRAINING GROUNDS
Sarah Veitch

Charlotte was looking forward to her holiday in the sun. Two months on a remote tropical island with her rich, handsome boyfriend: who could ask for more? She is more than a little surprised, then, when she arrives to find that the island is in fact a vast correction centre – the Training Grounds – presided over by a swarthy and handsome figure known only as the Master. But greater shocks are in store, not least Charlotte's discovery that she is there not as a guest, but as a slave.

£6.99   ISBN 0 352 33526 2

If you would like more information about Nexus titles, please visit our website at www.nexus-books.co.uk, or send a stamped addressed envelope to:
Nexus, Thames Wharf Studios,
Rainville Road, London W6 9HA

NEXUS BACKLIST

This information is correct at time of printing. For up-to-date information, please visit our website at www.nexus-books.co.uk

All books are priced at £5.99 unless another price is given.

Nexus books with a contemporary setting

ACCIDENTS WILL HAPPEN	Lucy Golden ISBN 0 352 33596 3	☐
ANGEL	Lindsay Gordon ISBN 0 352 33590 4	☐
BARE BEHIND £6.99	Penny Birch ISBN 0 352 33721 4	☐
BEAST	Wendy Swanscombe ISBN 0 352 33649 8	☐
THE BLACK FLAME	Lisette Ashton ISBN 0 352 33668 4	☐
BROUGHT TO HEEL	Arabella Knight ISBN 0 352 33508 4	☐
CAGED!	Yolanda Celbridge ISBN 0 352 33650 1	☐
CANDY IN CAPTIVITY	Arabella Knight ISBN 0 352 33495 9	☐
CAPTIVES OF THE PRIVATE HOUSE	Esme Ombreux ISBN 0 352 33619 6	☐
CHERI CHASTISED £6.99	Yolanda Celbridge ISBN 0 352 33707 9	☐
DANCE OF SUBMISSION	Lisette Ashton ISBN 0 352 33450 9	☐
DIRTY LAUNDRY £6.99	Penny Birch ISBN 0 352 33680 3	☐
DISCIPLINED SKIN	Wendy Swanscombe ISBN 0 352 33541 6	☐

DISPLAYS OF EXPERIENCE	Lucy Golden ISBN 0 352 33505 X	☐
DISPLAYS OF PENITENTS £6.99	Lucy Golden ISBN 0 352 33646 3	☐
DRAWN TO DISCIPLINE	Tara Black ISBN 0 352 33626 9	☐
EDEN UNVEILED	Maria del Rey ISBN 0 352 32542 4	☐
AN EDUCATION IN THE PRIVATE HOUSE	Esme Ombreux ISBN 0 352 33525 4	☐
EMMA'S SECRET DOMINATION	Hilary James ISBN 0 352 33226 3	☐
GISELLE	Jean Aveline ISBN 0 352 33440 1	☐
GROOMING LUCY	Yvonne Marshall ISBN 0 352 33529 7	☐
HEART OF DESIRE	Maria del Rey ISBN 0 352 32900 9	☐
HIS MISTRESS'S VOICE	G. C. Scott ISBN 0 352 33425 8	☐
IN FOR A PENNY	Penny Birch ISBN 0 352 33449 5	☐
INTIMATE INSTRUCTION	Arabella Knight ISBN 0 352 33618 8	☐
THE LAST STRAW	Christina Shelly ISBN 0 352 33643 9	☐
NURSES ENSLAVED	Yolanda Celbridge ISBN 0 352 33601 3	☐
THE ORDER	Nadine Somers ISBN 0 352 33460 6	☐
THE PALACE OF EROS £4.99	Delver Maddingley ISBN 0 352 32921 1	☐
PALE PLEASURES £6.99	Wendy Swanscombe ISBN 0 352 33702 8	☐
PEACHES AND CREAM £6.99	Aishling Morgan ISBN 0 352 33672 2	☐

PEEPING AT PAMELA	Yolanda Celbridge ISBN 0 352 33538 6	☐
PENNY PIECES	Penny Birch ISBN 0 352 33631 5	☐
PET TRAINING IN THE PRIVATE HOUSE	Esme Ombreux ISBN 0 352 33655 2	☐
REGIME £6.99	Penny Birch ISBN 0 352 33666 8	☐
RITUAL STRIPES £6.99	Tara Black ISBN 0 352 33701 X	☐
SEE-THROUGH	Lindsay Gordon ISBN 0 352 33656 0	☐
SILKEN SLAVERY	Christina Shelly ISBN 0 352 33708 7	☐
SKIN SLAVE	Yolanda Celbridge ISBN 0 352 33507 6	☐
SLAVE ACTS £6.99	Jennifer Jane Pope ISBN 0 352 33665 X	☐
THE SLAVE AUCTION	Lisette Ashton ISBN 0 352 33481 9	☐
SLAVE GENESIS	Jennifer Jane Pope ISBN 0 352 33503 3	☐
SLAVE REVELATIONS	Jennifer Jane Pope ISBN 0 352 33627 7	☐
SLAVE SENTENCE	Lisette Ashton ISBN 0 352 33494 0	☐
SOLDIER GIRLS	Yolanda Celbridge ISBN 0 352 33586 6	☐
THE SUBMISSION GALLERY	Lindsay Gordon ISBN 0 352 33370 7	☐
SURRENDER	Laura Bowen ISBN 0 352 33524 6	☐
THE TAMING OF TRUDI £6.99	Yolanda Celbridge ISBN 0 352 33673 0	☐
TEASING CHARLOTTE £6.99	Yvonne Marshall ISBN 0 352 33681 1	☐
TEMPER TANTRUMS	Penny Birch ISBN 0 352 33647 1	☐

THE TORTURE CHAMBER	Lisette Ashton ISBN 0 352 33530 0	☐
UNIFORM DOLL £6.99	Penny Birch ISBN 0 352 33698 6	☐
WHIP HAND £6.99	G. C. Scott ISBN 0 352 33694 3	☐
THE YOUNG WIFE	Stephanie Calvin ISBN 0 352 33502 5	☐

Nexus books with Ancient and Fantasy settings

CAPTIVE	Aishling Morgan ISBN 0 352 33585 8	☐
DEEP BLUE	Aishling Morgan ISBN 0 352 33600 5	☐
DUNGEONS OF LIDIR	Aran Ashe ISBN 0 352 33506 8	☐
INNOCENT £6.99	Aishling Morgan ISBN 0 352 33699 4	☐
MAIDEN	Aishling Morgan ISBN 0 352 33466 5	☐
NYMPHS OF DIONYSUS £4.99	Susan Tinoff ISBN 0 352 33150 X	☐
PLEASURE TOY	Aishling Morgan ISBN 0 352 33634 X	☐
SLAVE MINES OF TORMUNIL £6.99	Aran Ashe ISBN 0 352 33695 1	☐
THE SLAVE OF LIDIR	Aran Ashe ISBN 0 352 33504 1	☐
TIGER, TIGER	Aishling Morgan ISBN 0 352 33455 X	☐

Period

CONFESSION OF AN ENGLISH SLAVE	Yolanda Celbridge ISBN 0 352 33433 9	☐
THE MASTER OF CASTLELEIGH	Jacqueline Bellevois ISBN 0 352 32644 7	☐
PURITY	Aishling Morgan ISBN 0 352 33510 6	☐
VELVET SKIN	Aishling Morgan ISBN 0 352 33660 9	☐

Samplers and collections

NEW EROTICA 5	Various ISBN 0 352 33540 8	☐
EROTICON 1	Various ISBN 0 352 33593 9	☐
EROTICON 2	Various ISBN 0 352 33594 7	☐
EROTICON 3	Various ISBN 0 352 33597 1	☐
EROTICON 4	Various ISBN 0 352 33602 1	☐
THE NEXUS LETTERS	Various ISBN 0 352 33621 8	☐
SATURNALIA £7.99	ed. Paul Scott ISBN 0 352 33717 6	☐
MY SECRET GARDEN SHED £7.99	ed. Paul Scott ISBN 0 352 33725 7	☐

Nexus Classics

A new imprint dedicated to putting the finest works of erotic fiction back in print.

AMANDA IN THE PRIVATE HOUSE £6.99	Esme Ombreux ISBN 0 352 33705 2	☐
BAD PENNY	Penny Birch ISBN 0 352 33661 7	☐
BRAT £6.99	Penny Birch ISBN 0 352 33674 9	☐
DARK DELIGHTS £6.99	Maria del Rey ISBN 0 352 33667 6	☐
DARK DESIRES	Maria del Rey ISBN 0 352 33648 X	☐
DISPLAYS OF INNOCENTS £6.99	Lucy Golden ISBN 0 352 33679 X	☐
DISCIPLINE OF THE PRIVATE HOUSE £6.99	Esme Ombreux ISBN 0 352 33459 2	☐
EDEN UNVEILED	Maria del Rey ISBN 0 352 33542 4	☐

HIS MISTRESS'S VOICE	G. C. Scott ISBN 0 352 33425 8	☐
THE INDIGNITIES OF ISABELLE £6.99	Penny Birch writing as Cruella ISBN 0 352 33696 X	☐
LETTERS TO CHLOE	Stefan Gerrard ISBN 0 352 33632 3	☐
MEMOIRS OF A CORNISH GOVERNESS £6.99	Yolanda Celbridge ISBN 0 352 33722 2	☐
ONE WEEK IN THE PRIVATE HOUSE £6.99	Esme Ombreux ISBN 0 352 33706 0	☐
PARADISE BAY	Maria del Rey ISBN 0 352 33645 5	☐
PENNY IN HARNESS	Penny Birch ISBN 0 352 33651 X	☐
THE PLEASURE PRINCIPLE	Maria del Rey ISBN 0 352 33482 7	☐
PLEASURE ISLAND	Aran Ashe ISBN 0 352 33628 5	☐
SISTERS OF SEVERCY	Jean Aveline ISBN 0 352 33620 X	☐
A TASTE OF AMBER	Penny Birch ISBN 0 352 33654 4	☐

------ ✂ --------------------------

Please send me the books I have ticked above.

Name   ....

Address   ....

            ....

            ....

            .... Post code....................

Send to: Cash Sales, Nexus Books, Thames Wharf Studios, Rainville Road, London W6 9HA

US customers: for prices and details of how to order books for delivery by mail, call 1-800-343-4499.

Please enclose a cheque or postal order, made payable to **Nexus Books Ltd**, to the value of the books you have ordered plus postage and packing costs as follows:

UK and BFPO – £1.00 for the first book, 50p for each subsequent book.

Overseas (including Republic of Ireland) – £2.00 for the first book, £1.00 for each subsequent book.

If you would prefer to pay by VISA, ACCESS/MASTERCARD, AMEX, DINERS CLUB or SWITCH, please write your card number and expiry date here:

....

Please allow up to 28 days for delivery.

Signature ....

Our privacy policy.

We will not disclose information you supply us to any other parties. We will not disclose any information which identifies you personally to any person without your express consent.

From time to time we may send out information about Nexus books and special offers. Please tick here if you do *not* wish to receive Nexus information.   ☐

------ ✂ --------------------------